Murder at the Castle

M.B. Shaw is the pen name of *New York Times* bestselling writer Tilly Bagshawe. A teenage single mother at seventeen, Tilly won a place at Cambridge University and took her baby daughter with her. She went on to enjoy a successful career in the City before becoming a writer. As a journalist, Tilly contributed regularly to the *Sunday Times*, *Daily Mail* and *Evening Standard*, before turning her hand to novels.

Tilly's first book, *Adored*, was a smash hit on both sides of the Atlantic, becoming an instant *New York Times* and *Sunday Times* bestseller. She now divides her time between the UK and America, writing her own books and the new series of Sidney Sheldon novels. *Murder at the Castle* is the second mystery in the Iris Grey series. For more information, please visit www.tillybagshawe.com

Murder at the Castle

An Iris Grey Mystery

M.B. Shaw

First published in Great Britain in 2020 by Trapeze
an imprint of The Orion Publishing Group Ltd
Carmelite House, 50 Victoria Embankment
London EC4Y 0DZ

An Hachette UK Company

1 3 5 7 9 10 8 6 4 2

A CIP catalogue record for this book is available from the British Library.

ISBN (Mass Market Paperback) 978 1 4091 8939 8
ISBN (eBook) 978 1 4091 8940 4

Typeset by Born Group
Printed and bound in Great Britain by Clays Ltd, Elcograf S.p.A.

www.orionbooks.co.uk

For Sarah Glynn, with love

Prologue

The girl knelt before the altar, alone. Dawn had barely broken over Venice and the stone floors of the church of San Cassiano were cold to the touch. Directly in front of her, faint chinks of light filtered through the stained glass and danced across Tintoretto's masterpiece, *The Resurrection of Christ*. This morning, she alone was the master's audience. The glow of the rich red cloth, draped around Jesus' loins; the chubby folds of skin on the angels' thighs; the upturned faces of the adoring women, so exquisitely rendered, so alive – all were for her, a lowly hotel chambermaid's daughter from Fusina. A nobody.

This was the wonderful thing about Venice. She, the poorest of the poor, could walk in off the street into almost any church and be transformed into a queen, surrounded by gold and magnificence, her senses overwhelmed with beauty and brilliance, with art unparalleled anywhere in the world. Her heart broke to say goodbye to it. But what choice did she have, after what she'd done? She must go to him now. Even though she knew what that would mean. Even though she knew how her mother would suffer.

Poor Mamma! That was the worst part. Tears welled in the girl's eyes and spilled down her dirty cheeks, leaving salty streaks through the grime. For seventeen years it had been just the two of them, struggling but happy, or so she had thought. How had it come to this? The thought of leaving was unbearable; of slipping away like a criminal before the sun was even up, of disappearing, like a shadow. And yet she must bear it. She must do it.

Stubby fingers, rubbed raw, caressed the old wooden rosary beads her godmother had given her for her First Holy

Communion. Where had that little girl gone, the one in the white dress with the gap-toothed smile? The girl who had grown up believing she was a lady, a princess, someone special, and that one day her life would be different? One day there would be no more mouldy apartments, cheap pasta suppers and late nights helping Mamma scrub rich men's floors. Instead, there would be palazzos and ballgowns and their own floors being scrubbed. When, exactly, had that dream been snuffed out? She couldn't remember now.

She could remember only what happened afterwards. What she'd done.

Help me, she pleaded, gazing into the eyes of Tintoretto's Jesus. *Give me strength*. It wasn't a prayer. She no longer believed in God, not after everything that had happened. But she still believed in art; in the transcendence of beauty; in the spirit of Venice, her city, her beloved home.

Perhaps, one day, she would return. Perhaps, then, the God she didn't believe in might forgive her.

She knew her mother never would.

From the shadows of the sacristy, the young priest watched her turn, wiping her eyes on her sleeve. Later, Father Antonio would remember every detail of this moment. He would remember her stooping to pick up her rucksack, green and white and with filthy hanging straps and a fake Adidas logo sewn onto the canvas. The way her hair trailed behind her like the dark tail of a comet, tangled and wild. The *slap, slap* of her flip-flops on the stone. Her last, longing glance back at the altar, to the face of the risen Lord, judging her. Judging them both.

But now, in the moment, all he felt was the dreadful wrench of her leaving, like an organ being ripped from his body. He had loved her for so long, wanted her for so long, in ways he knew he could never have her, clinging stubbornly to a wretched, angry longing that had made his life torture, yet had been the breath in his body and the beat in his heart. And now she was going and he was dying because he knew he couldn't stop her, couldn't save her, any more than he could save himself.

Only the Lord can save, he reminded himself. *Only he can redeem.*

Forgive me, Father, for I have sinned.

How inadequate those words were. How futile and worthless, a coward's mantra.

In his anguish, the young priest waited patiently for his tears to come. But they never did. Slipping into his robes, he found his mind drifting back to a line from an English poem he'd learned at school – Yeats, wasn't it? – *Too long a sacrifice can make a stone of the heart*. Was that what was happening to him? Was that what God wanted? For him to feel nothing? For his heart, or at least the part of it that belonged to her, to turn to stone? And was it really sacrifice that did that – or hatred?

Across the city, the pealing of the matins bells called him back to reality, to the rhythms of the city and the life he had chosen. Soon, worshippers would be arriving for the first Mass of the day. Slowly, methodically, he began lighting the candles.

He knew he wouldn't see her again.

PART ONE

Chapter One

Iris Grey scanned the faces of the crowds milling around Aberdeen railway station, hunting for her driver. Scotland was not what she expected. For one thing, it was boiling hot. The intercity train from London had been air-conditioned and stepping off it onto the platform was like stepping into an oven. The red-faced Scots sweating uncomfortably beneath the station's modern glass roof seemed as surprised as Iris by the blazing sunshine. Many of them wore jeans and long-sleeved shirts, which must be very uncomfortable. According to the headline in the *Aberdeen Citizen*, currently Scotland was experiencing the hottest August bank holiday weekend on record. Evidently, the locals hadn't had time to update their wardrobes.

Amid the clammy, irritated throng, Iris searched in vain for a sign with her name on it. Jock MacKinnon, Baron of Pitfeldy Castle and Iris's latest patron, had assured her that her train would be met in his latest, terse-but-efficient email:

> Newcomers find the coast roads treacherous. A driver will bring you to the castle. Mrs Gregory will show you to your room.

Iris was in Scotland to paint Jock's new, young fiancée, an American socialite by the name of Kathy Miller. The portrait was to be a wedding present, which meant that it needed to be finished by Christmas as the wedding (both Baron Pitfeldy's and Ms Miller's third, apparently) was being planned for New Year's Eve.

To her initial delight, Iris had been invited to stay at the castle for the long weekend, to meet her subject and to get to know her latest patron's family better before moving into her own rental house in the village. Pitfeldy had been the MacKinnon family seat for over four hundred years and was (according to Google) steeped in romantic Scottish history that fascinated Iris. As the time for her arrival grew nearer, however, she'd begun to get jittery about the idea of staying at the castle rather than going straight to her own place. Jock's missives hadn't exactly been warm and welcoming. If his family turned out to be awful, or boring, or served haggis for breakfast and insisted on sword dancing every night, there'd be no escape for three long days. Since separating from Ian, her husband of more than twenty years, Iris had grown used to having her own space again. Perhaps agreeing to be the house guest of a set of complete strangers had been a mistake.

'Miss Grey?'

A tap on her shoulder made Iris spin round and find herself face to face with a grinning giant.

'Yes,' she said, nodding warily.

'Ah'm here to tek ye to Pitfeldy,' said the giant, his smile spreading even more widely across his enormous face. 'Is this wee bag the only one ye've got? I'm William, by the way.'

'Iris.'

Six foot four in his socks, completely bald, heavyset and with bare arms that were more tattoo than skin, 'William' was not the uniformed chauffeur Iris had expected. Picking up her heavy suitcase as if it were a child's toy, he swung it happily back and forth as he led her to the car park.

'Pretty nice weather we're having,' he observed convivially, tossing Iris's case into the back of a sleek-looking navy-blue Range Rover with *Moray Cars* embossed on the side. Iris was surprised. In her mind Jock MacKinnon's message about sending a driver had implied an employee, not a local taxi driver. Not that it mattered. 'Have ye been to this part o' Scotland before?'

'No, actually,' said Iris, who decided she liked William and hoped his friendliness would turn out to be a local trait. 'My husband – ex-husband – was from Edinburgh. I went there once years ago, for Christmas, but that's it.'

'Edinburgh's not Scotland,' William announced bluntly.

'Is it not?' Iris laughed.

'Nah. Full of southerners and tourists.'

'I'll have to let Ian know,' said Iris, warming to William even more.

'This is the real Scotland, up here,' he continued, pulling out onto Guild Street and cutting right in front of a rubbish truck that came within a whisker of hitting them. 'You're in for a treat, believe me,' he told a flinching Iris, simultaneously giving two fingers to the truck driver who was leaning on his horn furiously and mouthing obscenities out of his window. 'Pitfeldy's the prettiest wee village in Banffshire, and that's sayin' something.'

He wasn't wrong. From the moment they left Aberdeen, the landscape was breathtaking. Hugging the coast road, they passed rugged cliffs, sheering off dramatically to reveal a string of pretty stone fishing villages, rings of simple grey houses huddled around sandy bays that couldn't have changed much in the last three hundred years. Then, turning inland towards Fyvie Castle and the famous Glenglassaugh distillery, the seaside quaintness gave way to magnificent open vistas, broken here and there by swathes of pine forest, with the peaks of Bennachie looming in the distance like a benign gathering of giants. Most striking of all was the sky; it seemed wider and lower to Iris than any she could remember, almost like a radiantly painted ceiling pressing down on this beautiful corner of the earth. Long, thin clouds like stretched candyfloss streaked across the horizon, and as they drove, Iris watched in awe as the palette above her changed from a pale grey to a dusty blue. By the time they turned back to the Moray coast, taking the long, narrow road down from the A96 towards Pitfeldy, it was almost white, the sunlight bouncing in dazzling reflection off the North Sea in a wild dance that had the artist in Iris transfixed. The contrast with Hampshire, where she'd spent most of the last six months, could not have been more striking. Not that Hazelford wasn't idyllic in its own way; it certainly was. But here prettiness had been swept aside for something altogether grander, wilder and more awe-inspiring. And *empty*.

'We haven't passed a single car since we left the main road,' Iris said to William. 'Is it always this quiet?'

'Aye, for the most part, it is. It's the Highlands that see most of the tourists. Places like Pitfeldy are still working communities. Fishing and farming, that's us. O' course there's the castle. But that's no open to the public, not like Drum or Castle Fraser. Not yet anyway,' he added darkly. 'There she is, look.'

They rounded a bend and the narrow road opened up dramatically on both sides. To Iris's right, the town of Pitfeldy came into view for the first time, or at least its rooftops and the squat, square tower of its thirteenth-century church, overlooking the harbour. To the left, perched high on a craggy hillside dotted with pines, was Pitfeldy Castle, complete with turrets and crenellated battlements, looking for all the world like an illustration from *Grimm's Fairy Tales*.

'She's a beauty, all right,' said William, with admirable understatement, as Iris's jaw dropped. She'd seen pictures, of course, online, but none of them did justice to the romance of the place, especially on such a glorious evening.

'You're here to paint the baron's latest, are you?' William probed, shifting down to first gear as they swung left over a cattle grid and began the sharp ascent to the castle, past the first of a series of 'Private' signs.

'That's right,' said Iris. 'His fiancée, Kathy Miller.'

'*Fiancée*,' William scoffed. 'Those two'll never marry, you mark my words.'

'Oh?' Iris's ears pricked up. 'Why do you say that?'

'Because,' said William, 'it's a joke, isn't it? I mean, for one thing, he's three times her age. And for another, they've nothing in common. And that's leaving aside the young lady's character,' he added cryptically.

'Do you know Kathy?' asked Iris.

'I know as much as I care to,' said William, oddly prim all of a sudden.

'You don't like her?'

He shrugged his vast shoulders in a failed attempt to seem neutral. 'She's no popular locally.'

'Because she's American? An outsider?' Iris offered innocently.

'O' course not. Nothing like that.' William sounded hurt. 'Around here we take people as we find them. Newcomers are welcome. But have some respect for the community, you know? For the way of life you're marrying into.'

'What do you mean?' asked Iris, fascinated.

'Well, take the baron,' said William, by way of explanation. 'He's never been the most likeable man in the world, OK? Jock MacKinnon can be rude. Snobby. You'd no want to sit down for a pint with him, if you know what I'm saying. But he understands his role in Pitfeldy. He supports the local fishing fleet. He treats his tenant farmers fairly. He pays to stop the church from crumbling into the sea, and he always hosts the St Kenelm's fair up at the castle on the August bank holiday. Or at least he did until this year, when *she* put paid to it.'

'I don't understand. Why would Jock's fiancée refuse to host the church fair?' Iris was suitably astonished.

'Oh, well, I'll tell ye why,' said William, warming to his theme. 'Because the vicar, Reverend Michaela . . .'

'Pitfeldy has a woman vicar?' Iris couldn't help interrupting.

'Aye, and she's bloody fantastic,' William said firmly. 'The nicest lady you'll ever meet. In any case, Reverend Michaela refused to let Jock's girlfriend hold her crystal-munching, chanting, barefoot, bullshit Californian wedding ceremony in the local church. There was no malice in it, mind. She agreed to officiate and all that, up at the castle. But St Kenelm's is Church of Scotland and there're rules, you know. Anyway, Miss Miller decided to hold a grudge. And of course the baron, wrapped around her little finger, supported her – "I'm afraid Kathy doesn't feel comfortable hosting the fair this year, reverend".' William did a passable upper-class English accent, halfway between Dom Wetherby, the subject of Iris's last portrait, and Jacob Rees-Mogg, which made Iris grin. 'I mean, I'm sorry, but who the hell does she think she is? First, she wants to turn the castle – *our* castle – into some sort of Disneyland; paying guests and visitors' centres and God knows what. And then she goes and refuses to host the fair on a whim, and then wonders why nobody'll give her the time of day! Life may be all yoga mats and transgender mindfulness retreats where she comes from, but this is Pitfeldy. This is bloody Scotland, if you'll excuse my French.'

A screech of brakes and spray of gravel announced that they had arrived. Distracted by the driver's gossip, Iris had barely registered the approach to the castle. Now here it was, towering over her in the early evening light like a great stone monster.

'I'm all paid up, don't you worry,' said William cheerfully, unloading Iris's case as she fumbled in her handbag. 'You take care now. And good luck painting the Wicked Witch of the West,' he added cheekily, under his breath.

Before Iris could say anything further he was gone, heaving his vast frame back into the driver's seat and hurtling off down the drive.

For a moment Iris stood completely alone outside the castle, with only two imposing stone lions for company. What on earth had she let herself in for? Was Kathy Miller really as bad as all that, or was the taxi driver exaggerating? Iris fervently hoped it was the latter. People had probably taken against her because she was new, and young, and perhaps had fresh ideas. Iris had also heard that she'd been Jock's mistress before her promotion to fiancée number three. So perhaps there was some loyalty to the last Lady Pitfeldy being thrown into the mix? She must try to reserve judgment and not to assume, on the basis of a conversation with one taxi driver, that she was about to spend the next few months cooped up in a studio with a moronic, grudge-bearing, gold-digging airhead whom the entire local community loathed.

Give her a chance, Iris told herself, reaching for the sturdy brass knocker on the castle's vast front door. *Give all of them a chance.*

Chapter Two

The door swung open and a plump middle-aged woman stood in front of Iris, radiating efficiency like a boarding-school house mistress in her sensible tweed skirt and crisp white blouse. Not Kathy Miller, surely?

'You must be Ms Grey,' she stated. 'Welcome to Pitfeldy. I'm Eileen Gregory, the housekeeper here. I'll show you to your room so you can catch your breath before dinner.'

Her handshake was as firm and businesslike as she was.

'Dinner is at eight. No need to dress formally, in case you were wondering.'

As she followed the housekeeper up a spectacular wide stone staircase and along a straight, slightly gloomy corridor to her room, it struck Iris that should she ever get the heave-ho from the MacKinnons, Mrs Gregory would be welcomed with open arms by the Swiss Railway Service. She was already getting the strong sense that life at Pitfeldy Castle ran like clockwork and with military precision. The hallway was lined with equally gloomy art, most of it Victorian and in need of a good clean, in Iris's opinion. One or two wall-mounted pieces of armour completed the dour, baronial look. Pushed back against the walls every ten feet or so were the sort of overly delicate, spindly antique chairs that Iris hated, on whose cushioned seats someone had helpfully placed thistles, in the unlikely event that anyone should be tempted to try and sit down on them. A grand house, then, but not a warm one. On reflection, Iris decided the vibe was less Downton Abbey and more Scooby Doo: a huge, empty, spooky house with, on the face of it, no people, no voices, no life at all.

'Here we are.' The housekeeper opened the door to a simple but pretty bedroom, made up in crisp white linens and with a vase of fresh peonies on the dressing table. Walking straight to the mullioned window, Iris found herself looking out over a spectacular view of rolling parkland that seemed to stretch right to the sea. She knew from her drive up here that there was a village between the two, but the gradient was too sharp to be able to see any of Pitfeldy from here. 'I hope you have everything you need, but if not, don't hesitate to ring.' She pointed to an antiquated bell on a pulley next to the door. 'Eliza will be looking after you during your stay and she'll be more than happy to help. She'll also show you to the dining room later.'

Mrs Gregory left her and Iris took a quick shower – the water was a lukewarm, rust-brown trickle, much more the Scotland she remembered. She changed into what she hoped was an appropriate outfit for dinner. The long, floaty, Indian-style dress had a muted paisley print and just enough embellishment to keep it on the right side of 'hippie'. In the past, Iris had frequently been singled out for her eclectic, colourful dress sense, and not always in a good way. Her ex, Ian, once described her look as 'jackdaw-meets-lunatic'. It was tough to put a positive spin on that. Since her divorce, Iris had made a conscious effort to rein in her wilder sartorial urges.

Spritzing gardenia scent into her short, towel-dried hair, she applied her usual minimal make-up (primer, mascara, gloss) and cast an appraising look at the result in the antique bathroom mirror. Although others disagreed, Iris had never thought of herself as especially pretty, and that wasn't about to change as she approached her mid-forties. But she didn't dislike her face either. Elfin and birdlike, with cartoonishly large eyes, it was at least striking – and relatively wrinkle-free. This evening, however, she was tired after her journey and was still slathering on under-eye concealer when the maid arrived to escort her down to dinner.

Pitfeldy Castle seemed to consist of a large, central section containing all the reception rooms, adjoined on either side by two conical wings consisting mainly of bedrooms and bathrooms. Iris followed Eliza past an impressive-looking library, study and drawing room, all empty, as they made their way to the dining room. (Not to be confused with the much larger dining *hall*, the maid explained, which was only for big, formal occasions.) There was even a ballroom, vast, empty and covered in dust sheets, adding to the general air of chilly grandeur.

'When it's just the family here, they mostly stick to the parlour in the evenings and the morning room during the day,' Eliza told Iris, who'd wondered aloud where everybody was. 'But they should all be in the dining room by now, ready to meet you.'

All? thought Iris, wondering who was going to be there, besides Jock MacKinnon and his fiancée. But before she had a chance to ask Eliza, they'd arrived.

'Here we are.' Pulling open a set of heavy double doors, the maid ushered Iris into a more modest room, hung on all four sides with rich tapestries of hunting and feasting scenes. In the centre was a long refectory table, sumptuously laid and ringed with wine-red velvet chairs, five of which were already taken. The low hum of conversation stopped abruptly when Iris entered, and five faces turned simultaneously to look at her.

Iris took a quick mental picture. There was a man of about seventy at the head of the table, rigid-backed and tense, flanked by two young women. One was strikingly pretty, the other not. Next to the attractive woman was a younger man, also attractive in a skinny, dark, vulpine sort of way, but his good looks were marred by a sour, miserable expression. Opposite him sat a third man, middle-aged, balding and with the sort of pale, translucent ginger colouring peculiar to the Scots, which might look Lady-of-Shalott ethereal on a woman, but always looked terrible on a man. Older and uglier than the other younger man at the table, he did at least have the advantage of not looking as if he were choking to death on a wasp.

The old man stood up stiffly.

'Miss Grey.' He extended his arm robotically and without a trace of warmth, like a retired general meeting a tiresome new recruit. 'Jock MacKinnon.'

My God, thought Iris, *he looks about a hundred and ten.*

'Please call me Iris,' she said nervously, shaking the leathery hand. 'Miss Grey makes me sound like a schoolteacher.'

A look of irritation flashed across the baron's face. First names were clearly not his thing. But it passed quickly as the breathtakingly beautiful young woman sitting to his left stood up and laid a proprietorial hand on his bony shoulder, simultaneously beaming at Iris like a lighthouse.

'Iiiiiiiii-ris,' she sighed, her drawly American accent stretching the first syllable out into what felt like twenty. 'What a perfect name for a painter! I'm Kathy.'

'I thought you might be,' said Iris.

In a tight, red T-shirt dress that showcased her slender figure and toffee tan, and with her tousled, honey-blonde hair framing a face so perfectly featured it almost made you want to laugh, Kathy Miller looked as if she'd just walked off a modelling shoot on Malibu beach.

Iris's first thought was the same as everybody else's: *How on earth did this goddess of a woman end up with a crumbling, crusty old ruin like Jock MacKinnon?* 'Lovely to meet you,' she said, exchanging Jock's age-spotted hand for Kathy's manicured perfection.

Quickly pulling her hand away, Kathy pressed both palms together, bowing deeply and with more than a hint of drama. 'Namaste, Iris,' she breathed heavily. 'Welcome to our home.'

'This is my daughter Emma Twomey and her husband Fergus,' Jock announced before Iris had a chance to react to Kathy's greeting, nodding brusquely and without obvious affection towards the other woman at the table and the middle-aged man beside her.

Iris smiled at Emma, who struggled to return the compliment, her entire face having begun to curdle at Kathy's 'namaste', as if she'd just ingested dog shit.

'Twomey Castle's north of here, in the Highlands,' added Jock, injecting a note of withering disdain into the word 'Highlands', as if he were boasting to Iris that his daughter had married another baron with a castle of his own, while simultaneously declaring his son-in-law's estate as inferior to his.

'And this is my son, Rory.'

'Charmed,' drawled the vulpine man, shooting Iris a look that made it quite plain he was nothing of the sort. 'So you're the famous painter?' He stifled a yawn as she sat down.

'Artist. She's an *artist*,' Kathy corrected him, earning herself a look that would have turned a lesser mortal to stone.

'Painter's fine,' said Iris. Not because she wanted to stick up for the horrible Rory, but because it was fine. 'It's a pleasure to meet you all.'

A horrible silence fell. Everyone except Kathy returned their attention to their food, while she cocked her head like a curious dog and gazed at Iris, staring quite unashamedly, as if Iris were a puzzle she were trying to decipher.

'My boxes should have arrived at my rental house in the village this morning,' said Iris, hating herself for filling the silence with inane babble but doing it anyway. 'But it's a luxury not to have to start unpacking right away, especially after such a long journey.'

'I never travel with more than an overnight case, do I, baby?' said Kathy, looking lovingly at Jock. 'Our modern obsession with material things has become such a *burden*. The lighter our loads, the lighter our hearts, that's my motto.'

'And the lighter Pa's wallet, since he met you,' Rory muttered in a deliberately audible sotto voce.

'Sorry, Rory, what was that?' Kathy asked guilelessly. 'You really must speak up.' Turning to Iris, she said, 'The British upper classes are terrible mumblers, don't you find? I can never understand half of what they're saying.'

'It's an acquired skill,' Iris agreed, tactfully.

'I *said* . . .' Rory began.

'Never mind what you said,' growled Jock. 'Either you keep a civil tongue in your head, or you can find your own dinner.

That goes for both of you.' He glared at Emma, who looked suitably affronted, her pendulous bosoms rising and falling like barrage balloons beneath her prim, high-necked blouse.

'What did I do?'

'For one thing, you let that bloody woman in here earlier, pleading about the fair,' Jock said. 'You knew how distressing that would be to Kathy.'

'For heaven's sake, Pa, "that bloody woman" is the vicar,' Emma protested. 'What would you have me do, slam the door in her face?'

'She slammed the door in *our* faces, about the wedding,' said Kathy, reaching out for Jock's hand and squeezing it, her eyes welling with tears.

Iris watched the drama, gripped, remembering her taxi driver's commentary earlier about the 'lovely' Reverend Michaela, and the spat over the local fair.

'She did nothing of the sort,' snapped Rory, turning on Kathy like a roused viper. 'You do realise just how petulant and spiteful it makes you look, refusing to let her host the fair here? Oh, wait a minute, I forgot. You *are* petulant and spiteful.'

'I'm the one refusing,' Jock boomed, banging his fist down on the table so hard it made the cutlery jump. 'Not Kathy. Me. It's my bloody house, and I'm damned if I'm going to have my fiancée upset. Besides, why shouldn't they hold the damn thing in the village for once?'

Dinner dragged on – beef Wellington and dauphinoise potatoes with a side of tension – and although Iris enjoyed playing the observer (clearly both of Jock's adult children hated his girlfriend with a passion) she was also tired and ready for her bed. Trying not to get drawn into the embarrassing familial sniping about the impending wedding, Iris spent most of the evening talking to Emma's husband Fergus, whose sole interest in life appeared to be hunting, and the injustice of the 'bloody socialists' all but banning it with their 'damned Hunting Act'. 'They don't understand country life, you see,' he opined pompously to Iris. Like Jock, he spoke with a cut-glass English accent with no hint of Scots. 'These oiks from London or Birmingham or wherever it is they crawl out from – I mean, what does a shop girl from Leeds know about farming or tradition or the life of a wild animal? They think of foxes as fluffy bloody teddy bears.'

'Perhaps they just think it's cruel to watch living creatures being torn to shreds by dogs?' Iris suggested mildly. 'I mean, there are more humane methods of control.' But Fergus was having none of it. As far as he was concerned, the urban lower classes had no business expressing an opinion on the matter and, in a decent world, would not have been allowed the vote but instead would have to defer to those such as himself.

How worrying, Iris thought, listening to Rory MacKinnon and his father take shots at one another, to think that Fergus was actually the least objectionable person at the table. (Apart from Kathy, who appeared to exist in a weird world of her own, smiling at everybody and exuding an odd serenity as the insults flew around her like bullets.)

After dinner, coffee was served in the parlour. Emma and Fergus immediately excused themselves, pleading exhaustion, and Rory followed suit soon afterwards, mumbling something about 'work'. Iris had gleaned over dinner that he was a lawyer, based in London, but that he was up at Pitfeldy working on something for his father – a little odd, given the naked hostility between the two men.

'I am so looking forward to sitting for the portrait,' Kathy told Iris, as Jock draped a soft cashmere throw lovingly around his fiancée's bare shoulders. Now that the couple were alone together, the affection between them was obvious. 'The painting was Jock's idea, as you know. He is sooo romantic. I mean, what a perfect wedding present, right?'

'Hmmm.' Iris nodded but privately thought that a picture of oneself might not be what every new bride was hoping for.

'*I* was the one who insisted on you,' Kathy said proudly.

'Oh,' said Iris, genuinely surprised. 'Do you know my work?'

'Sure.' Kathy's eyes lit up. 'I was glued to the Dom Wetherby murder case. *Glued*.'

'Ah,' said Iris, disappointed but not entirely surprised. Dom Wetherby, Iris's last sitter, was a famous book and television writer whose death by drowning last Christmas had gripped the nation. For some reason the media had picked up on Iris's personal role in bringing Dom's killer to justice, and she'd found herself a minor celebrity ever since, a sort of artistic Miss Marple.

'After I saw you on TV, I looked up all your stuff, and I was, like, 'Yes! She's the one,' Kathy gushed. 'Wasn't I, honey?'

Jock smiled at her indulgently, a different man from the brittle patriarch Iris had just witnessed with his children at dinner.

'I know it probably sounds weird to you, but I just felt this strong connection to you right from the start,' Kathy went on, looking at Iris again with that disconcertingly penetrating stare. 'Having the chance to work with you will be a beauuutiful experience. I know it.'

'I hope so,' said Iris awkwardly. 'I should warn you that sittings can be long and, frankly, boring sometimes. You might not love every minute.'

Leaning forward on the deep chintz sofa, Kathy clasped Iris's hands in hers. 'As long as I *grow* every minute,' she rasped huskily. 'That's what I care about.'

'My girlfriend's a very spiritual person,' said Jock, reverting to his earlier clipped tones, as if daring Iris to deny it. She noticed his gnarled hands caressing the back of Kathy's neck in what struck her as a distinctly non-spiritual manner, and was thinking again how strange the dynamic was between the two of them when a knock at the door disturbed them.

'Sorry to disturb you so late.' The man in the doorway was young, about thirty, and spoke with a soft Scots accent, his voice altogether gentler than the rough-edged speech of Iris's taxi driver. He wore workman's clothes, overalls and heavy boots, but his pale, freckled face and everything about his manner suggested a more refined, educated background than his appearance suggested. 'I wondered if I could have a quick word?'

'Angus!' To Iris's surprise, Jock's face lit up like a street lamp. 'Of course. Come in, my boy, come in.'

The young man hesitated, glancing at the sofa and apparently noticing Iris's presence for the first time. He was attractive in a diffident, boyish way, she decided.

'Best not,' he said to Jock, holding up oil-stained hands.

'Ah, all right,' said Jock, still smiling. 'I'll come out in that case. But you two must meet. Angus, this is Iris Grey, the portrait painter. She'll be staying in the village for a few months, working on a painting of Kathy.'

'Hello.' Angus nodded shyly.

'Hello,' said Iris.

'Angus is our gillie,' Jock explained to Iris. 'He grew up on the estate, just like his old man, so he's part of the furniture here. You're bound to run into each other.'

Angus glanced anxiously at his watch. Taking the cue, Jock kissed Kathy on the top of her head and followed him outside, presumably to talk estate business.

'What's a "gillie"?' Iris asked Kathy once they'd gone and the two women were alone.

Kathy rolled her eyes conspiratorially. 'I know, right? Like you're automatically supposed to know all these crazy, feudal job titles they have up here? A gillie is a guide who takes people fishing or stalking, or any of that other stuff that these rich Scots seem to want to do. It sounded so demeaning to me when I first heard the term, but Angus doesn't seem to see it that way. In any case his actual job is way more than just a gillie, even though that's what Jock calls him. He's basically the estate manager. He's organising everything for our wedding, for example. Jock couldn't run the place without him.'

'They seem close,' Iris observed.

'They are,' Kathy agreed, making space on the sofa for two ridiculously small, ridiculously fluffy dogs that had suddenly trotted in, hurling themselves towards their mistress like jet-propelled pom-poms. 'Angus is a breath of fresh air compared to Emma and Rory, that's for sure. Talk about two stiffs, right?'

Iris raised an eyebrow but said nothing. What a strange young woman she was, spouting Californian mumbo jumbo one minute, all namaste and spiritual growth, and the next cutting to the chase with searing honesty. Emma and Rory were indeed a pair of stiffs. But it hardly seemed tactful for Kathy to say so.

'Sometimes I think Angus is the only person in the world Jock really loves,' Kathy went on. 'Except me, of course.' She grinned. 'Angus's father was Jock's best friend when they were kids,' she explained, in between showering her dogs with kisses. 'I guess it's kind of a loyalty thing.'

'Is his father still around?' asked Iris, intrigued by this snippet, even as she felt her own tiredness creeping up on her like a shadow.

'Edwin,' Kathy answered. 'He's alive but he's in a home. Isn't he, my babies?' she added in a sing-song voice to the dogs. 'Yes, he is. He's in a home because he's lost – his – mind. Oh yes he has. So saaad.'

She pouted, pushing her pretty lips forward into a faux sympathetic expression as she ruffled the dogs' hair. In that instant, Iris could see why so many people seemed to dislike Kathy Miller. Envy might explain a part of it – her looks, her wealth, her position – but the future Lady Pitfeldy didn't help matters, unaware of how insincere she sounded with outbursts like these.

'This is Milo, by the way,' she told Iris, patting the smaller dog, which was not much bigger than a guinea pig. 'And this is his brother, Sam Sam. At least we think they're brothers. They were rescues and they are literally the LOVES of my LIFE. Aren't you, boys? Do you like dogs?'

While Iris searched for the right answer ('no' would be truthful but alienating, 'yes' an outright lie and 'sometimes, but not ones that look like mohair cushions' didn't feel like a viable option), Kathy ploughed on regardless.

'I adore them. Jock does too. His kids claim to, but I can't tell you how cold they've been to my boys, Rory especially. It's almost like he sees them as an extension of me.'

Iris smiled to herself. *I can't imagine why.*

'They hate me for replacing their mother, of course,' Kathy continued glibly, pressing her face into the dogs' snuffling snouts again. 'But you know what? We don't care. Do we, Milo, hmmm? Do we, Sam Sam? No, we don't. We don't care because we won, and they lost, and we're not going *anywhere*.'

It was an astonishingly steely display, all the more so for being delivered in such soft, husky, Californian tones.

Iris yawned, rubbing her eyes. 'I really must get to bed.'

'Before you do,' said Kathy, walking over to one of the walnut bookcases, 'there's something I need to show you. But you have to swear to keep it between us. Nobody else knows.'

'OK,' Iris said warily, not sure where this was going.

Pulling out a dusty leather-bound copy of something dull enough not to have been read for at least fifty years, Kathy rifled through its pages and pulled out a crisp white envelope. Unlike the book, the envelope was obviously new, with the word 'Kathy' handwritten in bright blue ink on the front.

'This was the first one,' said Kathy, lowering her voice and handing it to Iris. 'I found it slipped into my purse just a day or two after I arrived at the castle.'

The envelope had been torn open crudely at the top. There was a note inside, on a single folded sheet of writing paper. Expensive, watermarked paper, although the note had been typed.

You don't know who you're marrying, it read. *Get out, now.*

'What do you think?' Kathy asked breathlessly.

'Well, I . . . I don't know.' Iris frowned. 'You said this was "the first one". Have there been more?'

'Two more,' said Kathy, sounding, Iris decided, more excited than troubled as she scanned the shelves for two other, nondescript books. For some reason she'd chosen a different hiding place for each. 'One was left in my underwear drawer. Which is kind of creepy, obviously. And the third one I found in my car. Someone had slid it underneath the sun visor. I was driving home from Buckie when it fell into my lap.'

Both the other messages followed the same pattern, from the handwritten envelope to the typed missive inside, the fancy paper, all of it.

The second note read: *Once you know the truth, it will be too late. Leave now.*

The third, more ominously, said: *Jock MacKinnon is a dangerous man. This is your last warning.*

'Have you shown these to Jock?' Iris asked. 'Or the police?'

'No. I told you. No one knows. But that was part of why I wanted Jock to commission *you*. I need your advice. You know, to solve the mystery?'

'Kathy . . .' said Iris, not sure where to begin. 'I'm really not sure I can help you. It's true I ended up getting dragged into what happened to Dom –'

'Dragged in?' said Kathy. 'You found the killer, Iris! You totally solved that crime.'

Iris smiled weakly, handing back the notes. 'I'm not a detective.'

'OK, fine.' Kathy pouted, replacing the notes carefully in their respective hiding places before sitting back down on the couch and summoning the dogs to her lap. 'You're not a detective. You're just someone – a friend – I've asked for advice.'

'Right,' said Iris.

'So what's your advice? Am I in danger?' She injected this last word with such pantomime suspense, it was clear that she viewed the whole thing as more of a diverting prank than anything serious.

'Hopefully not,' said Iris. 'I mean clearly, someone wants you to leave Jock. And Pitfeldy.'

'Everyone around here wants that,' said Kathy breezily. 'Except Jock, obviously. But it's not gonna happen. I'm gonna drag this place into the twenty-first century whether they like or not.'

'Well,' said Iris, getting to her feet, 'my advice would be to show these notes to your fiancé.'

'Nuh-uh, no way.' Kathy shook her head vehemently. 'I don't want to upset him.'

'And then I'd take them to the police,' Iris continued, undaunted. 'These are threats, Kathy. Threats left in personal, private places, places close to you. Are they dangerous? I really don't know and nor do you. It depends who sent them.'

'Exactly!' said Kathy, smiling broadly up at Iris again as she left the room. 'It depends who sent them. *That*'s what I need you to help me find out.'

Later, tucked tightly beneath crisp linen sheets in her guest bedroom, the sleep Iris so desperately needed eluded her as she found herself thinking about Kathy Miller. What a fascinating young woman she was, and what a mess of contradictions. Soft, yet steely. Loving, to Jock and her dogs, yet ruthless and unforgiving to her perceived enemies.

Clearly, she had a great many of the latter – beside the mysterious writer of the threatening notes – and it wasn't hard to see why. In many ways, from first impressions at least, Kathy Miller was not an easy young woman to like. Entitled. Arrogant. Immature. And yet Iris found that she *did* like her. She could imagine how isolating it must be, stuck out here in the middle of nowhere in this magnificent but alien place, wedded to its traditions and fearful of change, knowing that everybody except your future husband and your dogs loathed you. All the way down to the local taxi driver.

Iris found herself wondering whether the much talked-about wedding would actually take place. And, if it did, how long the latest MacKinnon marriage would last. So far, at least, the relationship between Kathy and Jock was the most inexplicable and baffling part of all. On paper it might seem to be a simple case of a beautiful young gold digger setting her sights on a rich old fool. But in reality none of that rang true.

It was well after midnight by the time Iris finally fell into a fractured, dream-tossed sleep.

Chapter Three

On the morning of the bank holiday, as tactfully as he could, Jock tried over breakfast to persuade Kathy not to come to the fair.

'I have to go. Someone's got to judge the sodding marrows. But you've a choice, my darling. Why put yourself through it?' he said.

But Kathy was having none of it. 'Fiona always went, didn't she?'

'Well, yes,' admitted Jock.

'My mother was Lady Pitfeldy,' Rory observed pithily from behind his newspaper. 'You're not.'

'Not yet,' Kathy shot back, wounded.

Iris looked away awkwardly. Understandably, Kathy's comparing herself to Jock's ex-wife, and Emma and Rory's mother, had gone down like a turd in a swimming pool. But Kathy herself seemed oblivious to the fact that Emma looked as if she might choke on her eggs Benedict at any moment, or that her husband Fergus's cheeks had flushed from their usual pink, through red and scarlet to a sort of nuclear vermilion that Iris would have loved to paint, if only she'd had her brushes handy.

'Mummy didn't *go* to the fair,' Emma observed waspishly. 'She *hosted* it. St Kenelm's fair has always been held at the castle. It's part of our duty as the baron's family.'

'That's enough,' said Jock firmly.

'You all know our reasons – *my* reasons – for not hosting the fair this year. I appreciate that the Reverend Michaela may feel differently, and that's her prerogative.' Turning back to Kathy, he added, 'But I don't want you going down there, my love, only to get yelled at.'

'I'm a tough cookie. I can stand a little yelling.' Kathy smiled back at him, an odd mixture of vulnerability and defiance. 'No, I'm sorry, honey, I'm holding my ground. If those bullies in the village think they've shamed me out of coming to the fair, then they're in for a surprise. You have to meet negative energy with positive. Right, Iris?'

'Hmm? Oh, err – well, yes, I suppose so,' Iris stammered, blushing, horribly aware of Rory's eyes boring into her, and embarrassed to have been dragged into a family quarrel. It was bad enough to have to witness it. The sooner she moved into her own place the better.

'Rory's been telling his father for years that the estate won't survive unless we open it to the public. But of course when *I* say it, I'm the devil incarnate,' Kathy said to Iris as they drove down to the fair together in Jock's new Tesla. (Yet another sign of Kathy's influence: *I'm encouraging him to think more environmentally. We're all global citizens, after all.*)

Kathy certainly didn't look like a devil. In fact, she was utterly radiant this afternoon in a white lace cut-out dress and with her hair sexily piled up into a messy bun. Iris felt positively frumpy sitting next to her in cut-off jeans shorts and an old Labatt's T-shirt she'd stolen from Ian decades ago that had worn so thin she felt as if she were naked.

She spent most of the short drive down to the village trying to talk to Kathy about the threatening notes. The more Iris thought about them, the more they worried her. If Kathy really *was* in danger, and she'd done nothing to stop it, she would not be able to forgive herself. But Kathy's own focus was elsewhere, namely on proving to all the local 'haters', as she called them, that she was here to stay.

'I mean, who do they think they are? Do they think I'm intimidated?'

Once they'd arrived at the fair, Iris watched, part horrified and part awestruck, by Kathy's chutzpah as she sauntered like a supermodel into the judge's tent in search of Jock, ignoring the death stares and muttered asides as she passed. 'You go enjoy yourself,' she insisted blithely to Iris. 'I don't need a wing man.'

You don't need anything, as far as I can see, thought Iris, impressed. At least Kathy's supreme self-confidence meant that Iris was free to explore the fair on her own, a prospect that filled her with childish excitement. It all looked such fun.

Iris felt the heat rising up from the turf as she stepped through the lichened gate onto the school playing field, as if the ground itself were sweating. Pitfeldy's annual church fair had fallen on the hottest Bank Holiday Monday in anybody's memory. Throngs of locals milled around, marvelling at the weather and the turnout, even while they muttered complaints about having been banished from the castle.

'I doubt we've half as many stalls this year as last,' Iris heard the old biddy who was manning a bric-a-brac stall grumbling to her friend on the tombola. Iris had been delighted to find an entire set of vintage dolls' house furniture stuffed into an old shoebox, for sale at the bargain price of five pounds, and was standing waiting for her change. Dolls' houses were a passion of Iris's, her secret, guilty pleasure.

'Aye, well, how could we?' the biddy's friend replied. 'The field's half the size of the castle grounds. Takings'll be down, that's for sure. Thanks to Lady Muck.'

As Iris took in the scene in front of her, she could only imagine the church would be raking it in. She didn't think she'd ever seen a busier fair in her life. Children tore around in sticky-fingered posses, clutching melting ice creams from the Mr Whippy van and enjoying the rare taste of total freedom, while their parents gossiped and drank in the beer tent or sunned themselves outside at the stalls. In the background, a genuinely fabulous brass band provided a live sound track of classics from Elgar to Percy Fletcher to John McCabe, and as well as the usual bric-a-brac, toy and book stalls, Iris spotted traditional games, from coconut shies to splat-the-rat and wellie tossing. Some local teens had organised a 'fun' dog show, while the pony club was running considerably more serious horse competitions, from dressage to jumping and everything in between. A decent-sized, tartan marquee housed various farming exhibits from home-grown vegetables to 'prettiest sheep'. Finally, up in the far left-hand corner of the field, a beautiful array of painted fishing boats had been lined up in a spectacular rainbow of blues and reds and gold, all vying for this year's coveted 'Best Decorated Boat' trophy from the Pitfeldy RNLI.

'They're bonny, aren't they? Better this year than last, I'd say.' The landlady from the Fisherman's Arms noticed Iris gazing at a glossy dark blue boat inscribed with what looked like black tribal markings. It was simpler than the others, but for Iris at least it stood out from the crowd.

'They're all amazing,' Iris replied truthfully, wracking her brains for the woman's name. They'd met only yesterday, when Iris had popped into the pub for lunch, but she'd forgotten her name already. Some symptoms of middle age were more irksome than others.

'Of course, they'd have looked better up at the castle, you know, where they should have been,' said the landlady. 'But what can ye do? Until that dreadful American slings her hook, we'll all have to grin and bear it, I suppose.' She shook her platinum bobbed hair in disappointed resignation. 'Anyway, nice tae see you again, Iris.'

'And you.' *Beryl? Brenda?*

It was no use. Luckily the landlady didn't seem to notice that Iris had blanked on her name, and was as friendly today as she had been yesterday, when Iris had ventured down into Pitfeldy to pick up the keys to her rental house and explore the village for the first time. Some of it had been as she'd expected. The grey stone architecture and steep cobbled streets. The sense of community: kids playing in the street, mums chatting to each other on the high street and in the Asda car park, dads tinkering with their cars, revelling in the long-weekend freedom.

But other things were a surprise. The poverty, for one, was pronounced in ways that weren't familiar to Iris. Poundlands and pawn shops and Ladbrokes betting parlours seemed to have usurped half Pitfeldy's available retail space, and the Job Centre, although closed over the weekend, was evidently much frequented. Also much frequented were the village's two fish-and-chip vans, unsurprising, perhaps, in a fishing town, although judging by the size of some of the denizens of Pitfeldy, Iris suspected that the chips were outselling the fish six to one. And there was a video rental shop still going, something Iris hadn't seen in the south for years.

But if Pitfeldy was poor, it still retained its charm and character, and almost all of that was due to the fishing fleet. Every morning the trawlers and line-fishing boats continued to head out in search of their respective catches: monkfish and flatfish for the twin-rig trawlers, haddock, sole and skate for the line boats and almost exclusively herring from the single-boat pelagic trawlers, designed to plunder only the North Sea's upper waters. Once upon a time every boy in the village would have gone to sea when he reached adulthood as a matter of course. These days the fishermen were a dwindling group. But they were much respected in Pitfeldy and the signs of their trade were everywhere, from the pervasive smell of fish as much as half a mile from the harbour, to the fishing names and references in every pub, shop, park and civic building, to the 'fishermen's sweaters' for sale in Millie's, the expensive woollen shop next to the town hall, where the few tourists to the town were enticed to spend their money.

'You'll faind some lovely knitwear at Millie's for a fraction of what ye'd be charged in London,' Iris's landlady, Mrs Rivers, had explained helpfully when Iris had popped into Murray House to pick up the keys. A primly dressed woman, originally from Edinburgh's posh Morningside (famously described by one Scottish stand-up as the 'Cultural kairnel of the known wairld'), Mrs Rivers was from the outset keen to establish Pitfeldy's more genteel credentials in Iris's mind. 'Murray House might not be Pitfeldy Castle,' she'd admitted, 'but I think you'll faind the home to be very tastefully appointed.'

'I'm sure it's lovely,' Iris had said. She'd seen nothing so far except a living room piled high with her packing crates from Hampshire and London.

'The Fisherman's Arms does a much-admaired cheese-and-haddock pie, should you be peckish after unpacking all your boxes,' Mrs Rivers had continued, pressing the keys into Iris's palm. 'And then, of course, once you're settled in, we do now have Harriet's on the high street for all your hair and beauty needs. Including gel manicures,' she'd added excitedly, perhaps having glimpsed Iris's stubby, bitten-down painter's nails.

Back at the fair, Iris strolled down the hill towards the coconut shy.

'Singles or doubles, miss?' the bloke manning the coconut shy asked her. He wore a shiny pair of football shorts and no shirt, allowing his vast, sunburned beer belly to jut forward freely like an enormous, hairy egg.

Iris, who'd never heard of 'doubles' coconut throwing before, now noticed couples lining up to compete in pairs against one another. One of the pairs were Angus, the gillie from the castle, and a kind-looking girl, probably in her twenties, who was wearing a yellow sundress and a wide-brimmed hat to protect her fair skin. Angus's girlfriend, presumably, although from the look of them they could almost have been brother and sister.

'Doubles looks brilliant,' she told beer-gut man wistfully, 'but I'm here on my own, so I'd better go for singles, please.'

'Story o' my life, love. That'll be a pound.'

'Nah, don't do that,' came a voice from behind Iris. 'I'll pair up with you. We can take on the vicar and Mr Donnelly here.'

Iris spun round to find herself face to face with an odd-looking trio. The man who'd spoken to her was young, solidly built and handsome, with a mop of dark brown hair in constant danger of flopping into his sea-grey eyes. To his left was a woman around Iris's age, in full vicar's attire despite the heat, dog collar and all. *The famous Reverend Michaela, presumably.* Next to her was a thin, wiry man whom Iris judged to be in his sixties, in smart-casual khaki trousers and an open-necked shirt that revealed a small tuft of greying chest hair. He exuded an air of friendly authority and looked as if he might have been a bit of a looker in his youth.

'Oh, OK. I suppose I could,' Iris said awkwardly, feeling slightly thrown by both the young man's directness and his attractiveness.

'You won't beat us,' the vicar told Iris playfully. 'The headmaster and I are a winning team, and Jamie here knows it. That's why he's been reduced to accosting strangers to try and help him.'

'On the contrary.' The young man stepped forward, grinning. 'The Reverend Michaela is clearly running scared of an imminent, coconut-related drubbing. Unfortunately my prior partner's been unavoidably detained . . .'

'Plastered in the booze tent,' translated beer-gut man, who probably knew what he was talking about.

'So I'm in need of a replacement. I'm Jamie Ingall, by the way.'

'Iris Grey,' said Iris, shaking his hand.

Leaning in closer, Jamie whispered in her ear, 'So are you any good at this, Iris Grey? Please tell me you are, because this pair need taking down a peg or two.'

'I'll see what I can do,' said Iris, who was starting to enjoy herself. Ian always used to get embarrassed about her competitiveness at games, but evidently in Banffshire it was all the rage. As the little wooden balls started flying, and the coconuts started toppling from their precarious perches, Iris quickly forgot that she didn't know any of these people from Adam and found herself focusing with wild intensity on knocking more off than her opponents. A quick glance to her right confirmed that Reverend Michaela and Headmaster Donnelly were taking things every bit as seriously, splitting their targets into high and low just as Iris and Jamie were doing. In the end, to Iris's utter delight, her team were the winners by two points, putting them at the top of the leader board.

'And you said I'd never come to anything, headmaster,' Jamie teased John Donnelly good-naturedly, as the latter patted him on the back.

'Nor would you have, Ingall, had it not been for this young lady.'

'Wait,' said Iris, confused. 'You mean *you* were *his* headmaster?'

'I don't seem old enough, do I?' The older man looked at Iris with a twinkle in his eye. 'To have taught a world-weary trawlerman like this one?'

'Don't you believe it. Mr Donnelly's as old as the hills,' Jamie quipped back. 'He's been head at Pitfeldy School since – when was it now, John, 1886?'

After a bit more banter, the headmaster and vicar retired to the beer tent for a consoling pint of Ossian Ale. Jamie turned happily to Iris. 'I definitely owe you a drink after that performance. What a throwing arm! I doubt St Kenelm's fair runs to champagne, but I could maybe rustle us up a glass of Pimm's?'

'Or a cup of tea and a slice of cake?' countered Iris, who inexplicably felt nervous at the idea of having a 'drink' drink with a handsome fisherman she'd only just met. Not that he was flirting with her, exactly. But still. 'It's a bit early for me.'

'Even better,' said Jamie, apparently unfazed by the change of plan. 'I love cake. Follow me.'

They walked past the pony ring, where Jock MacKinnon was awarding a rosette to a pretty dappled grey, ridden by an immaculately turned-out child with pigtails. Kathy was nowhere to be seen, but Iris noticed the way the little girl bowed her head to the baron as he approached her pony, as if she were meeting Prince Charles. Clearly, whatever ill feeling there was about the fair being banished from the castle, it was directed exclusively at Kathy rather than Jock. *Sexism?* wondered Iris. Or was it simply that folks in Pitfeldy looked out for their own?

Inside the produce tent, Emma Twomey was judging the

home-made jams, gliding regally up and down the trestle tables in her eighties polka-dotted dress like a self-important ship in full sail.

'It's all a bit feudal, isn't it?' Iris observed to Jamie, as he brought them over a pot of Earl Grey and two doorstep slices of coconut cake. 'The Lord of the manor and his family judging all the competitions, with the villagers bowing and scraping?'

Jamie laughed. 'Only if you take it seriously, which nobody here does. It's just Pitfeldy. Tradition and all o' that. So what brings you all the way up here?'

Iris explained about her work and her latest commission up at the castle.

'What do you think about Kathy Miller?' she couldn't resist asking him.

Jamie shrugged. 'I don't think anything, really. I don't know the woman.'

'A lot of the locals seem to disapprove,' Iris ventured.

'Yeah, well, not the fishermen,' said Jamie. 'We've got more important things to worry about than where the church fair's gonna be held, or who old Jock MacKinnon's banging from one week to the next. Some folk around here get far too involved in other people's business, if you ask me. I've got nae time for gossip.'

A bagpiper started up just outside the tent, and for the second time that day Iris found herself thinking of Ian, her ex. He'd always hated the bagpipes. Once, at a Scots Guards' event in London where they'd both been drunk, a misty-eyed officer had made the mistake of accosting Ian while the pipers were playing.

'So evocative, isn't it? The sound of home.'

'Evocative? It's bloody appalling,' Ian had snapped. 'As far as I'm concerned, every single one of those kilted, caterwauling cunts should be lined up against a wall and shot.'

Needless to say, they weren't invited back.

'Dreadful, aren't they?' said Jamie, smiling ruefully as he polished off the last of his cake. He seemed to have inhaled his vast slice in the time it took Iris to pour the tea. 'Ach, dammit,' he said, looking at his watch. 'I'm afraid I have to go. They're judging the boats in a few minutes, and I ought to be there. Lovely to meet you.' Thrusting out a warm, calloused palm, he shook Iris's hand in a distinctly non-flirtatious way. 'I daresay I'll see you around in the village. Enjoy the cake!'

And just like that he was gone, like a Labrador after its next squirrel.

Iris wasn't sure whether to feel disappointed or relieved. In the end she decided to plump for neither.

What seemed most important right at this very minute was to enjoy every delicious bite of her coconut cake. After all, she'd earned it.

Half an hour later, Kathy caught up with Iris at the second-hand book stall and announced that she could not stomach any more of the villagers' 'aggressive energy' and was heading back to the castle soon, if Iris wanted a lift. Suddenly tired, Iris decided that she did. Kathy told her she would meet her at the car in a few minutes, and Iris began to make her way back to the car park along with a number of happy but weary families.

She was approaching the path that led to the gate when raised male voices in the coppice to her left caught her attention. Peering through the trees she could make out the unexpected figures of Angus Brae, the castle gillie, and the sweet old headmaster she'd beaten at the coconut shy earlier, John Donnelly.

'Don't threaten me, boy,' Donnelly was saying, although both his tone and his aggressive body language suggested he might be the one doing the threatening. This was a completely different man to the one Iris had just seen joking around with his old pupil.

'Or what?' Angus snarled back. He, too, was utterly unrecognisable as the polite, shy young man Iris had met briefly up at the castle. Putting a flat hand on the older man's chest he physically pushed him, raising the stakes. 'You're not untouchable, you know.'

After a bit more pushing and shoving on both sides, and

some insults carried off by the wind, both men walked away red-faced and fuming, Donnelly towards the village and Angus back to the fair.

Iris waited at the car for Kathy, and was still thinking about what she'd witnessed when Kathy arrived and they got into the Tesla. What had they been arguing about? Something serious, obviously. Both had acted so jarringly differently from their usual, 'public' selves.

'Are you OK?' Kathy asked, concerned by Iris's puzzled look.

'I'm fine,' said Iris. 'How about you? Did people give you a hard time?'

'No harder than usual,' said Kathy, starting the engine. 'But look, I found this under my windscreen wipers just now.'

It was another note, but this one was different, a much more off-the-cuff affair. Handwritten in felt-tip pen, and with no envelope, it simply said: *Hands off our history, you stupid bitch. If you want Disneyland, go back to California.*

'As if Pitfeldy Castle could ever be Disneyland!' Kathy scoffed. 'All I'm talking about is converting the old ruined bothy into a visitors' centre and maybe a gift store. You know, sell some shortbread or, I don't know, bagpipe CDs.'

'Do that and I'll write you some hate mail myself,' joked Iris, handing her back the note. This one, at least, didn't seem that serious. Apart from the 'bitch' thing.

'You'd think I was planning to tear the castle down and put up a shopping centre, the way these people are overreacting.'

'Who are "these people"?' asked Iris. 'Who's objected, I mean?'

'There was a letter, a petition – "Save the bothy". Quite a few locals signed it but it was John Donnelly's baby.'

'The headmaster?' Iris sounded surprised. From her brief encounter with Donnelly, he didn't seem like the NIMBY-ish type.

'He's not the only one. But he was kind of the ringleader in the village, I guess. And of course Rory and Emma are against everything I suggest. But Jock agreed with them on this one.

Even Angus. It just makes me so frustrated, you know? Can't they see we *need* to adapt in order to survive? I love Pitfeldy as much as they do.'

I doubt that, thought Iris. Or rather, if Kathy did love the castle, it was in a different way to the villagers. To her, no doubt, it was a grand and beautiful house and a part, one assumed, of her attraction to Jock MacKinnon. But to people here the Pitfeldy estate was a piece of their birthright. It was in their blood, in a way that Iris suspected Kathy neither respected nor really understood. That would have to change if she were going to find a way out of her present troubles.

There was clearly plenty of trouble brewing in picture-perfect Pitfeldy. And it wasn't just confined to the MacKinnon clan.

Chapter Four

Kathy Miller sat at the breakfast table, pushing the remnants of her avocado toast around her plate with a fork and sighing heavily.

'What's the matter, darling?' Jock asked, forking a dollop of marmalade onto his venison sausage. The question was put lovingly, but there was a hint of fear to it, as there always was when he suspected she might be unhappy. Jock may have played the heartless lothario in his youth, but deep down women's sadness had always frightened him. He didn't understand it and that made him feel weak.

'Oh, nothing, my love.' Kathy sighed again. In a faded, buttercup-yellow slip dress and no make-up, she looked even younger than usual this morning and could have passed for a schoolgirl. 'I think the long weekend took it out of me a little bit. All the tension, you know? I'm glad it's just the two of us again.'

'As am I,' said Jock with feeling. He preferred this softer, more vulnerable version of his fiancée, although he knew full well that without the other, steelier side they would never have ended up together. 'Rory's about as much fun as a wet weekend. Always on at me about the damned prenup.'

'Then sign it,' Kathy replied breezily. 'You know Rory won't rest easy till you do.'

'None of his bloody business,' muttered Jock.

'He's your lawyer, honey, as well as your son,' Kathy said gently. 'That makes it his business. Besides, I couldn't care less about your money. You know that.'

'I do know it.' He squeezed her hand gratefully. 'But you still need to be provided for.'

'And I am,' she reminded him. 'In your will.'

'Yes, yes, in that sense you are. But if we ever *did* divorce . . .'

'We won't,' Kathy said firmly.

'Well,' said Jock, changing the subject, 'I'm glad to see the back of him – and his sister too.'

'*Jock!*' Kathy grinned.

'Oh, come on, you know I'm right. Emma may be less trouble than her brother, but she can moan for Scotland. And as for that bloody bore she married . . . *Fergus*' – he spat out the name like a rotten grape – 'even his name sounds like a germ.'

Kathy laughed out loud.

'At least this time they didn't bring their ghastly children,' Jock went on, pleased to have pleased her.

'Jessica and Wilfred are your grandkids, honey,' Kathy reminded him.

'I daresay. They're still ghastly.' Jock grunted. 'The girl's a pudding like her mother, and the boy's a whinger. I really can't abide a whingeing child. Anyway, I must be off.'

He pronounced it 'orf', much to Kathy's amusement. When she'd first contemplated marrying a British aristocrat she'd wondered whether the accent would end up grating on her, but somehow with Jock it had always been endearing.

'Angus wants to show me some problems with the herd over at Yeoman's farm.'

Kathy did her best to feign interest.

'Vet's out there today testing for Johne's disease' said Jock. 'Old man Finlay's twitchy, apparently. Said I'd show my face. Just to keep the tenants happy.'

'Well, good luck.' Getting up, Kathy kissed him softly on the mouth. 'I'm going to be spending my day talking to designers about my wedding dress. And I have my first sitting with Iris Grey.'

'Already?' Jock sounded displeased, pulling on his jacket.

'Sure,' said Kathy. 'Why wait?'

'No reason, I suppose.'

'I really liked her, when she was staying here. Didn't you?'

He shrugged. 'What matters is that *you* like her. And that she produces a damned decent portrait at the end of all this. The money she's charging me!' He rolled his eyes indulgently. 'See you tonight.'

After he'd gone, Kathy moved over to the window seat, curling her lithe legs up beneath her like a cat. The late summer heatwave continued, but the sky was greyer today, heavy and muggy and oppressive. The weather reminded Kathy of the East Coast summers of her childhood in America and, for a moment, she felt a stab of homesickness, so sharp it made her clutch at her chest. Just then she saw the odd, diminutive figure of Iris Grey bouncing up the drive with a spring in her step.

Kathy had meant it when she'd told Jock she liked Iris. She'd chosen her because she loved the idea of having her very own Miss Marple in residence to help her figure out who was sending those horrid notes. Despite playing it off as a joke to Iris, and somewhat to herself, there was a part of her that *did* feel threatened and would like to know what was going on. But over the weekend she'd decided that Iris could become more than just a partner in crime. She could end up being a real friend. She found her refreshingly direct and open-minded. Iris was fun, not like the rest of the stiffs Angus invited to the castle; a dreary array of chinless porridge eaters. Kathy hadn't realised till Iris came along just how much she'd missed having fun, having someone besides Jock to talk to and pal around with. The portrait would give her something else to do with her days besides planning the wedding. With so much local opposition, Kathy had agreed grudgingly to put her ideas for opening up the castle to the public on hold until after the wedding. But there were only so many fabric swatches and flower arrangements one could look at in a single day. Apart from walking Milo and Sam Sam, the wedding had become her life, and that wasn't healthy.

'Iris!' Flinging open the kitchen window, Kathy leaned out and waved cheerfully. 'I'll be right out.'

Ten minutes later, the two women were walking through the castle searching for a suitable room to paint in. There were certainly enough to choose from. Kathy led the way with her little toy dogs trailing excitedly at her heels, while Iris followed behind, taking in all the corners of this remarkable building that she'd managed to miss during her stay.

'It's a labyrinth, isn't it?' she observed to Kathy, following her through the ballroom to a little wooden door that looked like a cupboard, but actually led to yet another narrow spiral staircase. 'It just goes on and on.'

'Tell me about it,' said Kathy. 'When Jock first brought me here, I got lost every day. It's like a maze. But, you know, that's all by design.'

'Really?' Iris asked. 'How so?'

'It was to protect the occupants from invaders,' Kathy explained. 'To give them the best chance of fighting back. You have to remember this place was built as a fortress, not a home. That's one of the things I love about it, actually.'

'That it's a fortress?' Iris raised an eyebrow.

'Sure,' said Kathy. 'No one can hurt you in a fortress, right? You're safe.'

While Iris digested this revealing comment, Kathy ran on ahead, eventually flinging open the door to a room at the very top of the stairs.

'How about in here?'

'Oh my.' Iris gasped.

In front of her was an oval room, ringed with arched windows. It wasn't large, perhaps only sixteen feet across, but it was as rich and warm and alive as the rest of the castle was cold, silent and forbidding. There was a low couch under one of the windows, strewn casually with furs and pieces of silk brocade. The floor was covered with a patchwork of antique Persian rugs, and all around beautifully bound, gilt-edged books seemed to tumble out of bookshelves stuffed to bursting. An eclectic collection of knick-knacks and treasures was dotted here and there, everything from ethnic tribal masks to a group of Royal Doulton china milkmaids in gorgeous shades of grey and blue. All sorts of paintings hung on the walls, from simple watercolours, to darker, more elaborate oils, to charcoal sketches, including one dazzlingly good reclining nude. And in pride of place beneath the central window was a desk, prettily made of turned oak, but at the same time scratched and battle-scarred with age. It was the sort of desk that greeted you as an old friend, inviting you to sit and create, and not to worry if you spilled a cup of tea.

'This is lovely,' said Iris. 'So full of life.'

'Isn't it?' said Kathy.

'The light is perfect. And that couch . . .'

Skipping across the room, Kathy sprawled out on the furs in reclining-goddess pose.

'Amazing,' said Iris truthfully. 'Oh yes, this is definitely going to work. Is it your room?'

'It is now,' said Kathy archly. 'Fiona, Jock's ex, put it together.'

'Ah,' said Iris, her face falling.

'She used to practically live up here, apparently,' said Kathy, 'locked away like the mad old woman in the attic. And she wonders why her husband ran off and found someone else.'

The comment was said more wistfully than spitefully, Iris thought, but even so, it was a remarkably insensitive thing to say.

'If it has those associations, then perhaps it's *not* the right setting for your portrait?' Iris ventured. 'I do think it's vital that this painting represents you.'

'So do I,' said Kathy brightly, brushing aside Iris's concerns. 'And it will, trust me. This is definitely the room I want. Come on, I'll help you bring up your things.'

Iris couldn't quite determine whether Kathy was actually blind to the message she was sending by using her predecessor's sanctuary, or whether her choice of room was a deliberate act of territorialism. On the whole, she suspected the latter. Either way she was left with an unpleasant taste in her mouth, and a small knot of anxiety in her chest where before there'd been only joy.

You're a professional, she reminded herself twenty minutes later as she set up her easel and sketchbook. *Draw what you see and keep an open mind.*

'I'm only doing preliminary drawings today,' Iris explained. 'We'll try out different poses, see what feels most natural, and I'll take some photographs to assess the light. Later, if you decide you want to change your clothes or wear your hair in a different style, we can do that. But once you decide, you must stick with it.'

'That's OK,' said Kathy. 'Once I make a decision I always stick to it. I'm not a big one for doubts, or for changing my mind once I'm set on something.'

No, thought Iris, *I bet you aren't.*

'Can my babies be in it?' Kathy gazed adoringly at the two white pom-poms asleep at her feet. 'I'm sure they'll be good,' she added in the high-pitched baby voice she often used around her dogs, which made Iris want to pull out her own teeth. 'Won't you, my boo-boos?'

'Of course, if you'd like,' Iris replied with a sinking heart. She hated painting animals. They never sat still, or listened. Then again, that probably applied to a good half of Iris's human subjects. 'But today I'd like to focus on you, if that's all right.'

'Sure,' said Kathy.

'So tell me a little more about yourself. How did you and Jock meet?' asked Iris. Usually when subjects started talking about themselves they relaxed and began to look more natural. Necks and arms softened, faces became more animated and more 'true' to the person inside. Kathy Miller was no exception.

'At a party in London.' Her face lit up. 'The Orangery in Holland Park, to be precise. I was there with my last husband, Warren, and Jock was with some old friends from Cambridge.'

'Your "last" husband?' said Iris. 'How many have you had?'

'Only two,' replied Kathy, without a hint of irony. 'Jock'll be my third.

'I met my first husband, Brandon, at eighteen, and we married a year later. That lasted three years. Then I left him for Warren, and we were together nine years, mostly in New York. And then I met Jock.'

'What happened with Brandon and Warren, if you don't mind my asking?' said Iris, who couldn't help but be a tiny bit impressed by the way Kathy ticked off her ex-husbands like mere footnotes to her life story. It had taken Iris three miserable years to summon the courage to divorce Ian, but this woman spoke about her former marriages like buses that one could get on or off at will without any problem at all.

'Nothing dramatic,' said Kathy, bending double and grabbing her bare feet for a moment in an impressively limber yoga stretch. 'With Brandon, we were too young. Also his dad was a billionaire and he took too much coke.'

'Which was the problem?' Iris laughed. 'The billions or the drugs?'

'Both, in the end,' said Kathy, deadpan. 'Plus we were living in Tennessee, which is where his dad's gas stations were. I was nineteen. I was so bored.

'Warren was different.' She smiled fondly at the memory. 'He wasn't as rich as Brandon but he was still rich, and ten years older, and he had a Wall Street job and was, like, super-smart. We moved to Manhattan and of course I loved that after being stuck in the south – can you even imagine?'

Iris could. Sort of. 'So what happened?'

'Nothing, really,' said Kathy. 'I mean, he kind of wanted children and I definitely did not. So that was maybe brewing for the future. But I did love Warren. I probably would have stayed with him if I hadn't met Jock.'

Iris tried and failed to imagine how a gruff, moody, elderly Scots landowner like Jock MacKinnon had wooed a young woman like Kathy away from a handsome banker husband she purported to love.

'I actually thought I'd have to stay in that marriage another year,' Kathy confided happily. 'Because, you know, ten years used to be the threshold for a fifty-fifty split of marital assets. It still is in LA, where I grew up, but in New York it's seven, so' – she shrugged – 'I had nothing holding me back.'

Except your marriage vows, thought Iris.

'Don't look so horrified,' Kathy teased her. 'Life is all about phases. New chapters. People think I fell for Jock for the money, but that's baloney. I already had money. Besides, his son is drawing up a prenup.'

'Rory's doing his own father's prenup?' Iris's eyes widened.

'Yup,' said Kathy. 'And it's gonna be tighter than a virgin's ass, not that I care.'

Iris couldn't help but laugh at her turn of phrase.

'Jock offered me love and safety. That's what I fell for. And, you know, adoration. I mean, he *literally* carried me off to his castle. How romantic is that?'

Iris looked at her intently as she sketched away. What a total enigma this woman was. Money-driven, yet romantic. Hard-headed, but childlike, too, in need of adoration and a fortress and a man to 'carry her off'. Fascinating.

'The point is, I choose not to see either of my divorces as failures,' said Kathy. 'To me they were beautiful, loving chapters that came to an end.'

'And you and Jock – is that a chapter too?' asked Iris, making an effort to keep her face neutral.

'A long one, I hope. But sure. Everything's a chapter.' Kathy smiled beatifically as she bestowed these words of wisdom.

She was like a cross between the Dalai Lama and the *Runaway Bride*, Iris thought.

'You don't believe in "happy ever after", then?' she mused, unconsciously biting her tongue as she struggled to capture the curve of Kathy's left shoulder.

'I believe in living for the moment,' said Kathy, her body stiffening. 'And in relying on yourself. And in looking forward, never back. I learned those lessons the hard way as a kid.'

Sensing she was on the brink of confiding something more, Iris paused and leaned back, waiting silently for her to continue.

Patting her legs and summoning her dogs into her lap, Kathy bent low over them, breathing in their comforting scent before going on, keeping her eyes fixed on the dogs and averted from Iris.

'My dad died when I was twelve.' Kathy's voice was calm, emotionless. 'He jumped from the roof of his office building in LA, right onto Santa Monica Boulevard. June twelfth, the same day he filed for bankruptcy.'

'I'm so sorry,' breathed Iris.

'Yeah. So was I. I thought he was happy. I thought we were all happy – him, me and my mom. But it turns out I was wrong. We lived in a big house in Brentwood Park. That was the life I knew. Dad drove Ferraris, Mom shopped in Paris. We had a boat.'

Her eyes had glazed over. Iris realised she was back there, a child, seeing it all again.

'Dad made his money in real estate but then he over-leveraged and it all came crashing down. He knew we'd have to sell the house, knew we'd be poor – or at least not rich. So he checked out. But *I* didn't know. My *mom* didn't know. He never warned us, never prepared us, never made any kind of plan. He just left us to deal with all of it: the funeral, the grief, the creditors. It was awful.'

'You're angry,' Iris observed, treading carefully.

'No,' said Kathy, not sounding offended. 'I was at the time, but not anymore. Like I say, chapters. That was a difficult chapter, but it made me who I am. I just feel sad for my dad now. And my mom.'

'How did she cope with it all?' asked Iris.

Kathy laughed bitterly. 'She didn't. I mean, really, she just didn't. She was so depressed. She drank a lot. Self-medicated, the whole bit. It was as if she had died, too. She was so *dependent* on him.' Bewildered, she looked at Iris. 'How could that happen? It was like he was her oxygen or something, like she couldn't breathe once he'd gone. Watching what happened to her, I decided that I would never be like that. I would live for the present. Rely on myself.'

And make sure you got rich and stayed that way, thought Iris, *because people who lost all their money wound up dead.*

It seemed to Iris that Kathy Miller had been building herself a fortress long before she ever met Jock MacKinnon. And that whoever was sending her those notes was determined to breach that fortress.

'I've been thinking more about those notes you showed me,' she said, putting down her pencils.

'Oh?' Kathy brightened.

'I still think you should show them to the police,' said Iris, earning herself a scowl and a headshake from her sitter. '*But*, as I can see you aren't going to, I wondered if you could let me borrow the envelopes.'

'Just the envelopes?' asked Kathy. 'Not the letters themselves?'

She was delighted that Iris had decided to play ball and help her unravel the mystery of the poison-pen letters, but she was baffled by her methods.

'Just the envelopes,' said Iris. 'For now.'

'Sure,' said Kathy, shooing the dogs off her lap and opening a drawer in what must once have been Fiona MacKinnon's writing desk. 'The others are downstairs in the library, but I can give you this right now. I found it in my laptop case this morning.'

She passed Iris another note, exactly like the others.

Iris read it aloud: '"Ask Jock what happened to Mary".'

She looked up at Kathy. 'That's it?'

'That's it.'

'Who's Mary?'

Kathy looked at her blankly. 'No idea.' Then, with a smile, she added, 'but you will help me find out, Iris, won't you?'

Iris spent the afternoon back at her Airbnb in the village, unpacking. Murray House was a sturdily built town house a few streets from Pitfeldy harbour. It was to be Iris's home until Kathy's portrait was finished. Yesterday, when she'd returned from the fair, she'd started opening boxes, but there was still a long way to go. Crucially, she'd only just begun unpacking her beloved dolls' house and its occupants, a labour of love that wouldn't be completely finished for weeks.

Iris had collected miniature furniture for over three decades – her shoebox from the Pitfeldy fair had turned out to be a rare hoard – and had always found a quiet pleasure in arranging and rearranging the tiny rooms of her treasured 1920s dolls' house. Yes, it was a bit weird. Potentially a bit 'mad cat lady'. But it made her happy and, especially since her divorce, happiness had become a bigger priority on Iris's agenda.

She'd made good headway with the boxes yesterday – Iris had never believed in travelling light, and certainly never went anywhere for more than a week without her precious dolls' house collection – but, dear Lord, it was exhausting. As she bent down now, her mind wandering back to Kathy and the notes and the mysterious 'Mary', her lower back throbbed with pain, like that of an arthritic eighty-year-old after a particularly nasty car accident. She decided to run a hot bath later and sink into it with a large glass of wine.

Iris's landlady, Mrs Rivers, was right. Iris did 'faind' Murray House to be extremely well appointed. Not least among its charms was the plentiful supply of hot water that gushed out of the taps and showerheads in a powerful, clear stream that put Pitfeldy Castle's rickety plumbing to shame. The kitchen was also a thing of beauty, spanking new and full of appliances so white and sparkling and modern and brilliant that Iris had no idea how most of them worked.

As for the rest of the house it was a pleasant but twee mixture of antique features and an aesthetic that *Homes & Gardens* magazine would probably have described as 'Highland Chic'. This translated as lots of heavy-weave woollen carpets and taupe sofas, offset by tasteful hints of tartan: a cushion here, a bedspread there. Mrs Rivers had clearly thrown caution to the wind in certain rooms and gone wild with a stag motif wallpaper, or curtains in a tongue-in-cheek Highland Games fabric, depicting pipers and kilted figures tossing the caber.

But overall the house was welcoming, spotlessly clean and quiet. The bed in Iris's room was also ridiculously comfortable, so while Murray House might lack the charm of Mill Cottage back in Hazelford, Iris was still definitely filing the rental as a win.

Popping two ibuprofen for her back, Iris spent a solid two hours carefully unwrapping more of her dolls' house things, before the call of a plate of Hobnobs and a cup of tea became too strong to resist. Sinking down into the overstuffed embrace of the living room sofa, she laid Kathy Miller's envelopes carefully out on the cushion beside her, before lifting and inspecting each one.

Iris was no expert, but even to the untrained eye it was clear that the single handwritten word '*Kathy*' was identical on each of the three envelopes. Not only was there a distinctive, squashed look at the top of the initial 'K', but the slight purplish tint to the ink made it plain that they had been addressed by the same person.

An easier clue to follow would be the envelopes themselves. They too were identical, small and very stiff, like formal invitations. And on the back, below the line where Kathy had torn each one open, Iris had noticed a small round imprint. Very faint, halfway between a watermark and an old-fashioned seal, you could barely make it out without a magnifying glass. But after much squinting, Iris decided that the design was of a thistle flower.

Idly, she opened Google on her phone and searched for 'stationery, thistle logo' but nothing useful came of it. Still, the envelopes were distinctive, which was a start. Given that each one had been delivered by hand, and inside the castle, the first obvious step would be for Kathy to see if there was a packet of them in a drawer somewhere – if not in Jock's office, then perhaps in one of the guest rooms or in the staff quarters.

Iris would suggest it at their next sitting, she decided, laughing inwardly at herself as she walked back into the kitchen with her empty mug. Poison-pen letters? Threats and clues and mysterious Marys? She'd only been here a few days. How *did* she keep getting dragged into these things?

She was standing at the sink, staring blankly out of the kitchen window, when suddenly she started.

'Hey there! Iris? Helloooo?'

It was Jamie, the distractingly attractive trawlerman from the fair, waving at her animatedly from across the street and miming 'open-the-window' gestures with his hands.

'I thought it was you,' he shouted, loud enough for passers-by to stop and stare. 'Is this where you're living, then?'

'Yes,' Iris shouted back. 'I've just moved in.'

'Very nice.' Jamie whistled approvingly, before crossing the road to approach the house. Leaning out of the open kitchen window, Iris was only a few feet away from him.

'I'm still unpacking,' said Iris, conscious of the mess of boxes behind her, not to mention her sweaty, make-up-free face as she pushed her hair back out of her eyes. 'It's going to be a long job, I'm afraid.'

'I'd offer to help but I'm off to play football just now,' he said, regretfully. 'The lads are expecting me.'

'Oh, I wasn't fishing,' said Iris, mortified, feeling more like a tragic cougar than ever.

'We should go for a drink some time,' said Jamie, either oblivious to her embarrassment or ignoring it. 'Now that I know where you live, I'll give you a knock.'

And with a friendly wave, he was gone, before Iris even had a chance to answer the question.

Come to think of it, *was* it a question? Or yet another assertion? Those seemed to be Jamie Ingall's speciality: 'We *should* have a drink', 'I *will* give you a knock'.

Smiling to herself like an idiot, Iris returned to her boxes, not sure exactly what had just happened.

Chapter Five

'Jock?' Reaching over in bed, laying a slim brown arm across his chest, Kathy Miller looked into her fiancé's eyes beseechingly. 'Can I ask you something?'

Propping himself up on his elbow, Jock MacKinnon gazed down at the miracle that was Kathy, wondering for the hundredth time how on earth he had got this lucky so late in his life. How this goddess, this sweet, stunning woman, had come to choose him. He was going to Edinburgh later after breakfast to attend to some business, only for one night, but the thought of being away from her already hurt him like a physical pain, like a pin jabbed into the flesh and twisted cruelly.

'Of course.' Clasping her hand, he pressed it to his lips. 'Anything.'

Kathy cleared her throat nervously. 'Who's Mary?'

'I'm sorry?' Other than a slight narrowing of the eyes, Jock gave no hint of his shifting emotions.

'Mary,' Katy repeated. 'Was there ever an important "Mary" in your life? I mean . . .' She blushed, realising belatedly how odd and paranoid the question must make her seem. 'Does the name Mary have any special significance for you?'

'Why are you asking me this?' His voice was gentle, and he even tried to smile, but it was clear she'd hit a nerve. Tension tightened all the muscles in his face like pulled strings on a puppet.

'You'll laugh,' said Kathy, thinking on her feet. She couldn't tell him about the note, but she realised she was going to have to say something, provide some explanation of how she knew that name – how it had come up.

'I won't,' said Jock, with more emphasis than he'd intended. 'Tell me where you heard the name Mary?'

'In a dream,' said Kathy.

'A *dream*?'

'I told you you'd laugh. But it's been a few dreams, actually. I don't know, I just . . . I keep hearing that name. Forget I said anything.'

'No, no,' he said, pulling her close, his face suddenly a study in profound emotion. 'That's all right. You really heard Mary's name in a dream?'

'Mmm-hmm,' said Kathy, burrowing her face into his chest to conceal her guilt.

'That's . . .' He choked up. 'I don't know what to say. Mary was my daughter.'

Kathy sat up. 'You have another daughter?'

'Had,' Jock spoke quietly. 'A long time ago.'

'What happened?' asked Kathy, her heart swelling with tenderness and feeling more guilty than ever for bringing this up, especially in such a duplicitous way.

'My first wife, Alice, had Mary the year after we got married. She died in her sleep one night. We never knew why. She was eight months old.'

'Oh, Jock!' Kathy flung her arms around his neck. 'I'm so sorry.'

'Oh, now, now, it's all right,' he said gruffly, his usual British reserve reasserting itself in the face of her tears and emotion. 'It was dreadful at the time, of course. It broke Alice and me completely. But that was many years ago.'

'That doesn't matter,' said Kathy, with feeling. 'It's obvious that you're still grieving.'

He looked at her lovingly. 'No, dearest. Not really. All that "time heals" guff turns out to be true in the end. I was just surprised to hear you mention her name, that's all, after all these years. A *dream*.' He shook his head in astonishment. 'Remarkable.'

⋆

Later that day, Kathy and Iris took a walk together through the castle grounds.

'Don't you find it amazing how quickly the weather can change here?' Kathy asked Iris, pulling her waxed Barbour jacket more tightly around her skimpy cotton dress and shivering as she peered into the misty woods. Bending down, she let Sam Sam and Milo off their leashes. 'I swear to God it is twenty degrees colder than it was a week ago.'

'I'm used to it,' said Iris, who was well insulated in a pair of corduroy trousers, boots and an oversized mohair sweater with appliquéd felt hearts sewn onto the sleeves. 'But I agree, autumn does seem to be upon us all of a sudden.'

The two women were taking a break from their sitting together. Although still early days, Iris was modestly pleased with the progress she was making on the portrait, but for whatever reason, this morning's session had felt like an effort. After more than two hours holding the same pose, Kathy was getting antsy, and Iris was struggling to think of further responses to questions about wedding flowers, winter menus, the pros and cons of fake snow, and whether or not it would be 'too much' for Kathy to have her dogs as bridesmaids: 'I saw it at a wedding in Ojai once and it was soooo darling!'

So when Kathy suggested a walking tour of the estate, Iris jumped at the chance. Other than the castle itself and its surrounding gardens, she'd seen next to nothing of the vast swathes of land owned by the barons of Pitfeldy for countless generations. She was curious to explore more of this wild, untamed kingdom for which a young American socialite had traded in her glamorous Manhattan life, not to mention a perfectly serviceable husband.

But the more they walked, the more Iris began to understand the trade. The MacKinnon estate truly was a kingdom. They'd only been going twenty minutes and already they'd passed an impressive, sprawling stable block, complete with a menagerie and acres of well-kept paddocks. Past the stables was a walled kitchen garden that looked like something out of a Victorian children's book, all climbing roses and wisteria-covered gates, through which rows of sweet peas and artichokes and raspberries beckoned invitingly. A lone, stooped old gardener was tending the beds. Kathy pointed out his cottage as they approached the entrance to 'the woods', in reality more than a hundred acres of ancient pine forest.

'Jock told me old Mr Bertram's lived there since before Rory and Emma were born,' Kathy told Iris. 'It's pretty basic, apparently, but Bertram likes it. Waaay down the end of that track, more than a mile away, is Angus's place.'

'Sounds remote,' said Iris.

'Oh God, it is. Kathy frowned. 'They call that a cottage too – Keeper's Cottage – but I'd say it's more of a lodge. It has, like, four bedrooms and a good-sized yard. It's quite cute, actually, as long as you don't mind being out in the sticks. But what I really wanted to show you is the bothy.'

'The bothy,' Iris mused. 'Isn't that the ruin you wanted to turn into a visitors' centre for the castle?'

'Exactly,' said Kathy, as they ventured deeper into the woods. 'You're going to die when you see it – this priceless piece of "heritage" that I'm *ruining* with my evil plans for keeping this estate afloat. It's a pile of stones, I swear to God. Even Jock doesn't want me to convert it. Oh, I forgot to tell you!' She grasped Iris's hand. 'I asked him about Mary.'

'When?' Iris asked, surprised.

'This morning. In bed.'

'So you told him about the notes? That's great, Kathy, I'm so pleased.'

'No, no, no.' Kathy shook her head. 'I didn't tell him anything. I feel kinda bad, but I actually said the name Mary came to me in a dream.'

Iris laughed loudly. 'And he bought that?'

'I think he did,' Kathy said, looking away. 'Anyway, it turns out Mary was the name of his baby daughter who died. Like, years ago. Isn't that *crazy*?'

'Wow,' said Iris, digesting this information while Kathy's

little dogs raced off happily in front of them, sniffing and exploring, chasing after birds and the occasional rabbit or red squirrel that dared to cross their path. 'So, you never knew about this baby before today?'

'No idea,' said Kathy. 'I knew he'd been married before, prior to Fiona, and that they'd divorced when Jock was still young. But he never mentioned a daughter.'

'Don't you find that strange?' Iris probed, slowing her own pace, taking in the soft sensation of dropped pine needles like an eiderdown under her feet, and the rich, resinous smell of the trees. The combination of the dark, towering trunks and the cold tendrils of mist snaking around them gave the whole place a distinctly Tolkien-like, fantasy feel. But the thing she noticed most was the quiet. There was something deep and peaceful and transcendent about it, like an ancient church in the early morning.

'Not really.' Kathy shrugged. 'It was so long ago.'

True, Iris thought. But having a child who'd died was the sort of thing most people would expect to know about the person they were about to marry. Wasn't it? Long ago or not, it was the sort of tragic life event that defined a person. Too big *not* to mention, Iris would have thought. Unless one had a specific reason to hide it.

'Why do you think the note writer mentioned Mary to you?'

Kathy shrugged again. 'No idea,' said Kathy, shivering. 'I mean, whoever it is, they're trying to drive a wedge between me and Jock. Or to get me to leave. Or both. Maybe they figured I'd be mad he hadn't told me? Or maybe they're trying to insinuate he had something to do with his own baby's death? Which is gross, obviously, and bullshit, and exactly why I'm choosing *not* to show him these stupid-ass letters.' A distinct note of anger had crept into her tone. 'Frankly, I don't give a shit what their twisted motive is. I just want to know who they are.'

Right at that moment a magnificent stag leaped out from the trees in front of them, less than ten yards from where she and Iris were standing.

'Jesus!' Kathy gasped, instinctively gripping Iris's arm. The animal stopped, turning his head and displaying an impressive but dangerous-looking set of antlers as he picked up scents on the breeze.

'Stand still,' whispered Iris. While the two women watched, entranced, three young does approached behind him, elegant and ethereal with their prancing gait and sleek brown heads, flecked with white at the sides of their noses, waiting like handmaids for their master's signal. Just then the two dogs, who'd been sniffing around a badger's sett a few yards back, suddenly caught on to the presence of the deer and a deafening cacophony of barking ensued. With a pounding of hooves, the skittish animals scattered, melting back into the forest as swiftly and mysteriously as they'd emerged from it. Meanwhile, Sam Sam and Milo ran around for a bit in futile circles of excitement, two delusional, testosterone-fuelled balls of fluff. One kick from the stag's hindquarters, and they'd have been dispatched to the next world in an instant, yet they clearly viewed themselves as the predators in the situation.

'Good boys!' Kathy praised them lavishly as they returned, tails wagging, to her side. 'Did you protect Mommy from that big ole deer, hmm? Were you very brave?'

'You really love them, don't you?' said Iris, who was getting used to the dreadful baby voice Kathy always used around her pets and now found it approximately 3 per cent less annoying.

'I do,' said Kathy. Reaching up to undo her bun, she shook her head and released a cascade of golden-blonde hair. With her flushed cheeks and glowing, make-up-free complexion, she could have stepped straight out of a Pre-Raphaelite painting. *She can be calculating*, thought Iris, *but when she forgets herself, it's as if she doesn't really realise just how beautiful she is. She knows she's attractive. But she doesn't get the magnitude*. She tried to imagine how Jock must have felt when he first saw her. Jolted back to life, to youth, to happiness. Drawn inexorably to Kathy's wild radiance like a moth to the light. Poor Fiona MacKinnon couldn't have stood a chance.

'Here we are,' Kathy panted, scrambling up to the crest of the hill, where the tree-line ended and the moors began. '*This* . . . is the bothy.'

Iris cast her artist's eye over what was, indeed, a complete ruin: four crumbling walls and a collapsed roof, little more than a giant pile of ancient, grey, weathered stone. It was idyllic, though, in an overgrown, Rapunzel's tower sort of way: a tangled confluence of man-made beauty and the abundant loveliness of nature. Briar roses and honeysuckle forced their way through cracks in the centuries-old structure, reclaiming it for themselves, and several generations of rabbits appeared to have dug their burrows in what must once have been the building's ground floor.

'What do you think?' asked Kathy.

'Gorgeous,' said Iris. 'Unexpected. A little spooky, I suppose.'

'A little? It's a wreck. A wasted, rat-infested wreck.'

'I bet it's spectacular at night,' said Iris. 'Under the stars.'

'The stars are spectacular,' Kathy allowed. 'But this place? With a little *vision* it could be amazing. You could have a visitor's centre here, maybe a little gift shop at that end.' She gestured around her. 'And it wouldn't cost much to smarten up the path we just took, let people walk down through the woods to access the castle from this side, rather than use the main gates and inconvenience the village. But, of course, heaven forbid that anyone would actually try to make any improvements around here.'

Stepping through the rubble to what once would have been a window, Kathy looked out over the moor. 'Most of the estate, well over a thousand acres, is moorland,' she told Iris. 'We can't touch that; it's all protected.'

'Stunning,' Iris sighed. 'Desolate, but stunning.'

'I call it "the killing fields" because Jock still hosts shoots up there,' said Kathy, screwing up her pretty face in disapproval. 'It's so barbaric.'

'You're not a fan of blood sports, I take it?' asked Iris, who was starting to wonder if there was anything at all about rural

Scottish life that would meet with the future Lady Pitfeldy's approval.

'Of course not!' said Kathy, appalled. 'What civilised person is?'

'Well, I think in rural communities . . .'

'Jock promised me he'd stop the stalking parties,' Kathy interrupted her. Clearly, she wasn't interested in hearing the other side of the argument. 'And hunting's no longer allowed on our land, thank God. But Angus threw a fit about not being able to "control" the rabbits, and Jock caved.'

'Hmmm,' said Iris, non-committally. She was firmly with Angus on this one. Rabbits were a menace. She dreaded to think of the havoc they might wreak on Mr Bertram's perfect rows of radishes.

'I hear the shots sometimes when I'm out walking,' said Kathy, pouting as she turned and began picking her way back out across the fallen stones. 'I think about those poor little innocent bunnies and it just makes me so *sad*.'

'OW!' With a shriek of pain, she suddenly dropped to the ground like a sack of potatoes, clutching her foot. 'My ankle,' she hissed, through gritted teeth. 'God damn it.'

'What happened?' said Iris, squatting beside her.

'I don't know. I tripped, I guess. Fuck.'

'Let me see. Is it broken?'

'It might be.' Kathy frowned. 'It hurts like crap.'

Gently Iris examined the joint, feeling gingerly around the bone with her fingers. 'I suspect it's a sprain,' she said at last, watching the swelling grow before her eyes. 'But you can't walk on it, can you?'

'No way.' Kathy shook her head.

'And I'm not sure I can carry you all the way back to the castle. Not if we want to get back there before nightfall, anyway. We'd better call for help.'

'Jock's gone to Edinburgh for the night,' said Kathy. 'But Mrs Gregory and the cook should both be back at the house.'

Pulling her mobile out of her trouser pocket, Iris rang the castle landline. After about a hundred rings, Mrs Gregory picked up. When Iris explained that she and Kathy were up at the bothy, she could feel the housekeeper's disapproval vibrate down the line. But grudgingly she promised to dispatch Angus to come and rescue them in the Land Rover.

'Angus is on his way,' said Iris, taking off her sweater and draping it over Kathy's bare legs, despite the latter's protests. 'Try to keep the leg still till he gets here.'

A frenzied yelping from Milo and Sam Sam distracted both of them. About twenty feet away, on the far side of the bothy, both dogs were scrabbling away frantically at the bare earth.

'What's wrong with them?' Kathy sounded concerned.

'Nothing,' said Iris. 'They're probably hunting a rat.'

'Don't say that!' Kathy sounded scandalised. 'My babies don't "hunt" innocent creatures.'

'Of course they do,' Iris laughed. 'They're dogs. What do you think they were chasing those squirrels for earlier, on the castle lawn? So they can invite them back for tea and biscuits?'

'Would you mind putting them back on their leashes?' Kathy asked Iris plaintively. 'I'd feel better if they stayed with me until Angus arrives.'

'Sure,' said Iris. Taking the matching baby-pink dog leads from Kathy's coat pocket, she picked her way back across the rubble to where the dogs were alternately digging and barking, their excitement growing. *It must be quite some rat.*

As she came up behind them, she saw to her horror that one of them – Milo, the bigger one – already had something clenched between its jaws. So much for their pacifist nature. *Oh God, please don't let it be still alive*, she thought. She wasn't sure she had the stomach for finishing off a half-dead rodent.

'Milo!' she called, clapping her hands reluctantly against her thighs as she fumbled for the clasp on the end of the lead. To her surprise, the little dog immediately turned and trotted obediently in her direction, followed by his even smaller brother. Both dogs had something in their mouths, Iris could see now.

'Drop,' she commanded firmly, clipping on the leads. Sam Sam duly released the surprisingly long bone he'd been carrying.

But Milo was more resistant, turning his head away from Iris as she grabbed hold of his collar.

'Milo. Drop!' she said again.

With a resentful look, the little dog opened his mouth.

'Oh good God,' Iris gasped.

There on the ground, glistening wet on a bed of pine needles, moss and broken stone, was a perfectly preserved jawbone, complete with a full set of teeth.

Human teeth.

Chapter Six

Angus laid Kathy down in the back seat of the Land Rover, elevating her ankle to make it as comfortable as possible.

'I'll get you some ice back at the castle,' he said, his face still the same shade of ashen white it had been since Iris first showed him the jawbone.

'It's definitely human,' she'd said grimly, turning the gleaming white object gently over in her hands as she squatted next to Kathy. 'My guess is that the other bone is too. What do you think?'

She held them out for Angus to examine, but he stepped back, visibly repulsed by the remains and managing only a muttered, 'Jesus.'

'Milo and Sam Sam found them,' added Kathy, temporarily distracted from her pain by the gruesome but fascinating discovery. 'I suppose we ought to call the police.'

'Aye.' Angus nodded, shooing the dogs into the back of the car.

'Do you have a bag or something I can put these in?' asked Iris.

Wordlessly, Angus handed her an old Lidl shopping bag. Iris couldn't quite decide whether he was just being the strong and silent type, or whether it was squeamishness at the sight of human remains that had rendered him tongue-tied. Either way he said almost nothing on the drive back to the castle.

'That's Rory's car,' Kathy said indignantly as they pulled up next to a gleaming, midnight-blue Aston Martin. 'What's he doing here? We weren't expecting him. Jock's not even at home tonight.'

Angus shrugged. 'I know.'

'Well, how long has he been here?'

'An hour or two. Mrs Gregory was unloading his things when I left to get you.'

Once inside, with Kathy safely resting and Angus dispatched for ice, Iris buttonholed the housekeeper.

'Mrs Gregory, I wonder if I might use the house phone,' she explained. 'I can't get mobile reception in the castle and I need to call the police.'

Holding up the Lidl bag, she explained briefly about the bones. True to form, Mrs Gregory was neither shaken nor stirred, but instead handled the situation with her usual calm efficiency.

'How dreadful,' she said, matter-of-factly. 'If you'd like to follow me, you can use the telephone in my office. You won't be disturbed there. The number for the local police will be in the book in the top desk drawer.'

By the time Iris returned to Jock's study, Kathy and Angus had been joined by Rory MacKinnon. Still in his office attire of dark suit and tie, he wore the same expression of sneering superiority that Iris remembered from dinner on her first night. Perhaps it was how he always looked – a masculine version of resting bitch face – or perhaps it was being at Pitfeldy, or, more specifically, being around his father's fiancée, that brought it on.

'The police are on their way,' Iris announced to the room in general, setting the bag of bones down on Jock's antique card table. She turned to Rory. 'Hello again.'

'Hello,' he said coldly. Pulling an old 1930s silver cigarette case out of his jacket pocket, he flipped it open, removed a cigarette and lit it, blowing smoke in Iris's general direction like a louche dragon. 'So, I gather you and my wicked stepmother-to-be have been snooping around the bothy? Showing you her plans for world domination, was she?'

'For God's sake, grow up,' Kathy hissed through gritted teeth. 'You do *know* what we found up there?'

'A few old bones, as I understand it,' drawled Rory. 'I highly doubt that will be of much interest to the police, even in a backwater like Pitfeldy.'

'Really?' Iris matched his offhand tone. Rory was even more obnoxious than she remembered him. What sort of pretentious twat carried a cigarette case in this day and age, for God's sake? 'In my experience, dead bodies buried in abandoned buildings are just the sort of thing the police *are* interested in. They certainly sounded keen on the phone.'

'That's because they're mostly morons with barely a Higher between them who've overdosed on *CSI* and think they're dealing with a murder,' said Rory dismissively. 'Chances are those bones are centuries old. They could be Iron Age, for all we know. Ancient tribes have lived in the forests up here for ever, and there's been a structure of some kind on that site since before the conquest. That's one of the reasons people have been so opposed to Kathy's plan for concreting it over.'

'It's certainly possible the bones are old,' agreed Iris, who actually hadn't thought of this at all but was damned if she was going to let this supercilious wanker get her on the back foot. 'Important to know for sure, though, don't you agree?'

'Hmmm,' grunted Rory. 'What do you make of all this, Angus? You're unusually quiet this evening, even by your own standards.'

'Perhaps Angus has given up on trying to get a word in around your ego?' said Kathy sarcastically, leaping to the mute gillie's defence. Lying back on Jock's favourite Harris tweed sofa with her injured leg propped up on a cushion and her two dogs curled loyally on the floor next to her, she looked every inch the lady of the house. Iris noticed that she was less inhibited with Jock being away. More confident in her own status. 'Besides, why would you need to hear other voices when you're so in love with the sound of your own?'

The two glared at each other in open enmity.

Might Rory be the mysterious note writer? Iris wondered. He certainly hated Kathy, and, no doubt, would be delighted to see her romance with his father come to an end.

Angus's quiet, measured voice interrupted her musings.

'I do think the bones could be old,' he observed meekly.

Rory's eyes narrowed. 'Well, well. So the gillie finally agrees with me on something. Wonders will never cease.' Turning to Kathy, he added, 'You realise Dad's going to go ballistic that you dragged Iris up to the bothy? After you promised to let this appalling "visitors' centre" idea drop.'

'It's not an appalling idea,' said Kathy.

'Nobody "dragged" me anywhere,' Iris added. 'We were going for a walk, that's all. I was curious to see the building, after hearing so much about its history.'

'Hmmm,' grunted Rory.

Iris found it hard to cut through the toxic soup of negativity that seemed to swirl around Rory's every word, expression and movement; not just towards Kathy, but also towards Angus and herself. *He's like bitterness personified*, she thought, although she had to admit that he brought a handsome face to that ugly characteristic. Notwithstanding his heavy, hooded eyebrows and lean, sunken cheeks, Rory MacKinnon was unquestionably an attractive man. With his moss-green eyes and olive skin, his long limbs and elegant, languid movements, he was as close to the complete opposite of his sister Emma as one could conceive. Iris could detect traces of his father in both his features and bearing, but Rory was a physically superior version of Jock, and not only by virtue of his youth. Iris found herself wondering what his mother looked like.

'Speaking of Dad, where is he?' Rory asked Kathy.

'He's in Edinburgh.'

Rory's eyes danced mischievously. 'Is he now?'

'On business,' said Kathy, through gritted teeth.

'Monkey business, more like,' Rory chuckled. 'Up to his old tricks. Oh dear, oh dear. Is he getting bored of you already? Poor Kathy. Did you think he was a changed man? That *you*'d changed him?'

'The only thing I want to change about your father is his will,' Kathy replied, flushing with pleasure as she watched the smile die on Rory's lips. 'I'd say I'm making pretty good progress on that score, despite your best legal efforts.'

Iris caught Angus's eye. He looked pained. It truly was the most unedifying display of loathing on both sides. It was a relief when Mrs Gregory knocked on the door and announced the arrival of the local police.

A slight man about Iris's age with thinning, once-blond hair and wearing a cheap grey suit that did him no favours, introduced himself in a broad Glaswegian accent as Detective Inspector Stuart Haley. 'And this is my sergeant, Danny Spencer,' he added, nodding towards a spotty young man with a shock of red hair and a faintly anxious expression.

'Who found the bones?' Haley got straight to business.

'I did,' said Iris. 'Well, technically, it was the dogs. Miss Miller's dogs unearthed them up at the old bothy.' She gestured towards Kathy.

'And you have them here?'

'Yes.' Iris retrieved the plastic bag from the card table. 'I did touch them, I'm afraid. When the dogs first dropped them, I didn't realise . . .'

But Haley wasn't listening. Peering into the bag, he looked at the jaw, making his own assessment.

'OK,' he said, closing the bag with a grimace and handing it to his sergeant. 'Well, I'm no pathologist, but I agree those teeth look human. What's your name again, ma'am?'

Iris told him.

'And who else was there when the wee doggies – you know.'

'I was,' said Kathy. 'I'd tripped and fallen on one of the loose stones – that's how I twisted my ankle – and I heard Milo barking like crazy. Iris went over to put the dogs back on their leashes and –'

'OK, OK,' said Haley, hurrying her on. 'Was anybody else at the scene?'

'Angus came later to pick us up in the Land Rover,' said Kathy, looking across at Angus. 'He manages the estate.'

'Right.' Haley made a note of the above. 'And do you have

anything to add, Mr . . .?'

'Brae. Angus Brae,' said Angus. 'No, sir. Not really. I just drove Miss Miller and Miss Grey back home.'

'We were just observing before you arrived, inspector,' Rory's cut-glass, entitled voice rang out around the room like a ricocheting bullet, 'that in all likelihood the remains are ancient. Tribes have roamed these moors and forests for centuries. And that bothy's as old as the hills.'

'And you are?' Haley asked, an unmistakable note of disdain in his voice.

'Rory MacKinnon,' came the clipped reply. 'My father is the baron here.'

'Right. OK. Well, thank you, Mr MacKinnon. When I'm in need of your theories I'll be sure to ask for them.'

Iris hardly dared glance at Rory, who had flushed bright red and looked as if he might be about to explode.

'I'll need brief statements from all of you tonight,' Haley continued brusquely. 'Sergeant Spencer will take those down in a moment. And then, Mr Brae, if you would be so kind as to drive me and two of my officers back out to the bothy, we'll tape that off tonight and leave a man here, just in case. It'll be dark soon so I won't bring forensics in until the morning. And then, depending on their findings, I may need to talk to you all again.' Turning to Iris he added, 'Thank you for calling us, Ms Grey. Let's hope we can get to the bottom of it all quickly.'

At seven o'clock the next morning, Stuart Haley climbed into his car wishing he felt a bit more alert and a bit less like a man who hadn't had an unbroken night's sleep in seven months. It was nearly three years since Jean had died, so he couldn't blame grief anymore. Or 'play the widower card', as she had memorably put it, instructing him on her deathbed not to 'whinge like a girl' but to 'get out there and grab life by the bollocks'.

He had tried. Most days, he even felt like he'd done a

pretty good job of it, fighting for his promotion at work, making time to see old friends, to go out and have fun. But the last seven months had been – well, shite. First, he'd got sick. Shingles, brought on by stress and a low immune system, apparently; a deeply unpleasant experience. Apart from the pain, fever and vomiting, for six straight weeks the entire left side of his face collapsed, making him look like he'd had a stroke, or had melted himself by accidentally falling asleep on a radiator. Then when he finally recovered, his dad had had a heart attack and had dropped dead. They weren't close, but still. Dead was dead, and horribly final, as Stuart was only just beginning to learn. And then, a month after the funeral, came the cherry on the cake: some lying toerag of a recruit from years ago filed a sexual harassment suit against him, every single syllable of which was a steaming pile of horse ordure, but which had still gone to tribunal. It had taken twelve weeks for Stuart to be exonerated on all counts. 'That's as good as it gets, Haley,' the chief inspector had assured him. 'You're in the clear.' Which was great, of course. But three straight months of waking up in a cold sweat, wondering if you were going to lose your job and be branded a groper for the rest of your life, was proving to be a hard habit to break. As was the perennial 'brace for impact' mental attitude he'd developed ever since Jean's diagnosis. Fucking cancer.

The drive to Pitfeldy Castle from Haley's bungalow near Fochabers was about twenty minutes. It took him through some of the most beautiful scenery in Banffshire, and he made an effort to try and appreciate it. But his trip to the castle yesterday, and the human mandible still sitting in the Lidl bag on his passenger seat right now, kept pulling his attention away from the majesty of the landscape and back to the case at hand.

Were the bones old? Chances were, Rory MacKinnon was correct about that, but Haley hoped not. For one thing, he enjoyed the challenge of a murder inquiry. It sounded morbid – it *was* morbid – but it was his job and he was good at it. But, beyond that, if the bones were ancient, it would mean that that posh bastard Rory MacKinnon was right, and Haley would be denied the privilege of making him look like the know-it-all, chinless, Etonian chump he undoubtedly was.

SNP to the very core of his being, Stuart Haley's natural prejudices against the likes of the MacKinnons ran deep and strong. The entitlement of these 'lairds' of the manor, with their English public school educations and ruling-class accents, stuck in Haley's craw almost as much as the obsequiousness of the ordinary locals that allowed them to get away with it.

Almost before he knew it, Haley found himself snaking back up the long, stately drive to Pitfeldy Castle. This time, however, he continued straight past the house, following the track through the forest that led to the deserted bothy, almost at the edge of the moor. The crime scene was already a hive of activity, with the ruined building surrounded by cones and orange crime-scene tape. Inside the crumbling walls, three white-suited technicians were busy excavating. Outside the tape, three uniformed officers sipped coffee from plastic cups and chatted among themselves, although they did their best to look busy when their boss arrived.

'Any updates?' asked Haley, climbing out of his Ford Fiesta and cracking his neck extravagantly.

'Yes, sir.' Sergeant Spencer, the perennially surprised-looking redhead stepped forward eagerly. 'Quite a big one, actually.'

'Well, don't keep me in suspense, man,' Haley snapped. 'What have they found?'

Sergeant Spencer cleared his throat. 'According to the techs, sir, there's more than one body in there.'

Chapter Seven

Drawing in a sharp breath, Stuart Haley ducked under the orange crime-scene tape. As he stepped into the ruined building, one of the white-suited men walked over to meet him.

'Tell me it isn't true, Dave,' said Haley.

'Sorry, Stuart.' David Gaffney was one of the top forensic CSIs in all of Scotland, renowned for being both thorough and profoundly cautious.

'So it's a mass grave?' Haley sighed.

'No, no,' Gaffney shook his head, 'not a mass grave. Only two bodies. At least, that's all we've found so far.'

'"So far" – meaning there could be more?'

Gaffney shrugged. 'There *could* be. But judging by the scatter pattern of the remains, I doubt it.'

This was as close as Dave Gaffney was likely to get to a 'no'.

'OK, well, what can you tell me about them?' asked Haley.

'Not much, I'm afraid,' the CSI admitted. 'They're both female. Both adult. That's about it.'

'Cause of death?'

'Can't say.'

'How old are the remains?' asked Haley.

'Can't say that, either.'

'Well, are they ancient or modern?' Haley pressed. 'You must know that at least? Ballpark.'

'Sorry,' said Gaffney. 'A forensic pathologist might be able to tell you more. But even then it's far from an exact science, especially once animals have had a go at the bones. These are reasonably well preserved. That's the most I can say at this stage.'

'Which means what? That I'm not looking at cavewomen?' said Haley, casting around desperately for anything he could use.

'You're not looking at cavewomen, no.'

'And that's the best you can do, is it?'

Dave Gaffney grinned. 'I found you two bodies before nine in the morning. What more do you want?'

DI Haley took a look around him. The bothy had been built in a remote spot, that was for sure; about as far off the beaten track as one could get on a private estate. Not a bad spot to bury a body or two.

But there was something else that struck him about this precise location, this lonely clearing in the woods in which the ruined building stood. Something more than just its isolation. Perhaps his imagination was running away with him, but Haley couldn't shake the feeling that there was something ritualistic about this particular site, a spiritual resonance that ran old and deep. Whether or not the skeletons Iris Grey had found turned out to be ancient, he strongly suspected that the place they were buried in held secrets older than the hills.

Rory MacKinnon had mentioned that the bothy itself was an ancient building. Haley found himself wondering who had built it, originally, and why they had built it here.

On the other side of the tape, standing a few feet back from the action, Haley spotted the young gillie he'd met last night, Angus Brae, watching the technicians at work. There was a young woman with him clasping a thermos. His girlfriend, presumably. Every now and then she would reach out and rest a comforting hand on Angus's arm as the bones emerged, one by one, from the rubble.

Raising a hand in greeting, Haley walked over. 'Morning.'

'Good morning,' said Angus.

'Is it true they've found a second body?' the young woman asked, introducing herself as Hannah Drummond.

'Aye,' Haley admitted. He'd likely release a statement by the end of the day anyway, so there didn't seem any point in being secretive about it. 'At the moment we think we're looking at two sets of remains. Two women.'

'How terrible,' said Hannah with feeling. 'I suppose you've no idea who they are? Or how they ended up buried here?'

'Not yet.' DI Haley smiled, then turned to Angus. 'As I mentioned last night, I'm going to need more detailed statements from yourself, Ms Grey and Ms Miller. I'll also need to speak to the baron when he gets back from Edinburgh. Do you have any idea when he's expected?'

'Oh, Jock's back already,' said Hannah, blithely jumping in before Angus had a chance to speak. 'I saw his car earlier. Angus called last night to let him know what had happened and I think he must have raced back first thing this morning to be with Kathy. She was quite upset by the whole thing, Angus said. And of course Rory being here doesn't help.'

'Hannah!' gasped Angus.

Haley clocked the look of displeasure that the mortified gillie shot his girlfriend.

'Sorry, inspector. We don't mean to gossip. But Baron Pitfeldy is back at the castle, if you need him.'

'In that case, I think I'll head back down to the house,' said Haley. 'Will you join me?'

'I've some things I need to attend to on the estate this morning,' said Angus, his eye still half drawn to the technicians as they eased yet another fragment of bone from its resting place. 'Is it OK if I give you a statement a bit later?'

'That's fine,' said Haley. 'I'm in no rush. I'll talk to the baron first.'

'It's more than an inconvenience, detective inspector,' Jock snapped, his extravagantly bushy grey eyebrows knitting above his beetroot-red complexion. 'It's a bloody outrage. Littering my estate with Christ knows how many cars and men and hideous orange tape, closing down my *shoot*, for God's sake, and all because of a few old bones that, for all we know, have been buried up there for hundreds of years? Preposterous.'

DI Haley shot him a withering look. The two men were in the castle's formal drawing room, a space so extravagantly outsized that Haley could hear the echo of his own voice when he spoke.

'When were you personally last up at the bothy, sir?'

'What's the matter with you, man?' snapped Jock. 'Did you not hear a word I just said?'

'Oh, I haird it,' said Haley. 'I just don't have time for it. Human remains were discovered yesterday, Lord MacKinnon. On your land. Not "a few old bones". Two human beings, two women, buried in one of your outbuildings. I'm not sure you appreciate quite how serious that is.'

'For God's sake,' Jock muttered. 'You haven't the faintest idea how old those bones are. They've probably been there since long before this was my land.'

'That may be,' said Haley. 'But we don't know that for sure. What we do know is that whoever they were, they didn'ae bury themselves. So until we know otherwise, at a minimum, we're looking at an illegal interment, and quite possibly at murder. You wouldn't want to be seen to be obstructing a murder inquiry now, would you, baron?'

The two men glared at each other, but Jock said nothing further.

'So I'll ask you again. When were you last up at the bothy?' Haley repeated.

'Last week,' said Jock, turning his back on him to pour himself two fingers of whisky, without offering any to his 'guest'. 'The structure itself is condemned, so I don't go inside very often. But the woodland around it makes up part of my shoot, as I told you. I walk there regularly, as do my guests.'

'Who else has access, other than you and your friends?'

'No one, officially,' said Jock. 'Although I daresay village boys are up there from time to time, poaching or playing silly buggers.'

'Has poaching been a problem at Pitfeldy?' Haley asked.

'No more than anywhere else,' grunted Jock. 'My old gillie, Edwin, used to take a tougher line on it.'

'But you don't?'

'Not really.' Jock sipped his Laphroaig, supremely bored. 'As long as they're not significantly depleting the shoot, I don't have the energy or resources to bother with them. It's not cheap, you know, running an estate of this size. One has to prioritise.'

Just then, Rory MacKinnon stuck his handsome head around the door. At first glance it was hard to tell whom he was less pleased to see – his father or DI Haley. In the end, though, Jock got the worst of it.

'I'm leaving,' he announced bluntly to his father.

'Don't let me stop you,' drawled Jock.

'You're heading back to London already, Mr MacKinnon?' Haley raised an eyebrow. 'That was an awfully long drive for a one-night stay.'

'I fly,' Rory said, pityingly. 'Although if you must know, I'm going to Edinburgh first to visit my mother. I'd rather she hear about all this bodies business from me. She'll only worry if she hears gossip or reads about it in the papers. She still feels an incredibly close connection to the castle, you see. It was her home for thirty years, after all. Until my father decided to transfer the dregs of his remaining blood flow from his brain to his cock and install that American scrubber in Mummy's place.'

'*Out!*' Jock sprang to his feet and half lunged, half staggered towards his son. 'Get out of my house!'

For a moment, Haley thought he was going to have to step between the two of them, but, somewhat to his surprise, Rory backed down immediately, leaving the room with no more than a muttered 'my pleasure' as a passing shot.

'I understand Ms Miller had been considering converting the bothy into some sort of visitors' centre,' said Haley, after Rory had gone. 'As part of her plans for opening up the castle as a commercial enterprise. But that you opposed the idea. Is that true?'

Jock put his head in his hands, struggling to control his temper. 'Kathy's going to be mistress here once we marry. She has every right to make suggestions. But developing ancient buildings is a sensitive issue. A lot of local people were unhappy with the visitors' centre idea. So yes, I asked her to drop it, at least until after the wedding.'

'Hmmm,' Haley mused. 'Strange that she was up at the bothy yesterday, then, with Ms Grey. D'you have any idea why she went?'

'No.'

'Not to worry,' Haley made a note, 'I'll ask her myself.'

'I warn you, detective inspector,' Jock hissed, 'I won't be harassed, and I won't have my family harassed either. So I suggest you have your lackeys dig up whatever it is they're digging up, take our statements and then piss off out of our lives. If you don't, I can make things very unpleasant for you, I assure you. The chief constable happens to be a close friend.'

Haley stood up slowly. 'I would nae threaten me, if I were you, baron. That's no a good look for a man with two dead bodies in his back garden. I'll see myself out.'

Stepping from the cold street into the warm fug of the Fisherman's Arms, Iris quickly removed her coat, scarf and beanie and hunted around for a place to sit. The pub was unusually busy tonight, partly because the abrupt drop in temperature had driven people back indoors, but also, Iris suspected, partly fuelled by a collective desire to indulge in a spot of gossip. After all, it wasn't every day that a dead body was found buried up at the local estate. Never mind two.

She was curious to hear what the locals were saying about yesterday's gruesome discovery. She'd been thinking about the bones all night herself, and the human story that must lie behind them, but that nobody yet knew.

She'd also been thinking about Kathy's poison-pen letters, and whether there might be any link between them and the bodies. Probably not, given that the notes all seemed to be focused on Jock – *you don't know who you're marrying, ask him about Mary*, etc. But there had also been the warning pinned to her windscreen – *Hands off our history* – which Kathy had assumed was a reference to her plans to convert the old bothy. Was it really a coincidence that the very building which certain people were determined should be left alone at all costs should turn out to have two women buried beneath it?

So who *had* opposed Kathy's plan to develop the bothy? The writer of the windscreen note, presumably. The local headmaster, John Donnelly. Jock *and* Rory; it was a rare point of agreement between them. Angus Brae . . .

'Hello again.'

A heavy hand on her shoulder made Iris jump. Jamie Ingall, looking as handsome as ever in a thick Shetland sweater and baggy jeans, took the seat next to her at the bar.

'Given up on your boxes, then?'

'Boxes?'

'Unpacking. You were up to your eyeballs the other day, remember?'

'Oh. Yes,' Iris stammered. Suddenly their encounter at the kitchen window felt like weeks ago.

'Can I buy you a beer?' he asked, raising his own half-full glass, while simultaneously pushing his dark curls out of his eyes.

'Sure,' said Iris. 'Thanks.'

Only when the frothing pint of amber liquid arrived did she remember that she hated beer, which she'd always thought both looked and tasted like dirty dishwater, but it was too late now.

'Is it true you were there?' Jamie asked. 'When the dogs dug up the bones?'

Iris nodded, sipping her revolting drink with forced enthusiasm.

'Kathy and I were taking a break from her portrait and she offered to walk me around the estate.'

'It was the bothy, wasn't it? Where they found the skull?'

'Jawbone,' Iris corrected. 'But yes. In the bothy.'

'And it was definitely human?'

Iris nodded with a shiver. 'It had human teeth.'

'Cool,' said Jamie, impressed.

'It wasn't "cool",' Iris admonished him, feeling her age

suddenly. 'It was horrible. To think that someone's lain buried up there for years.'

'Well, yeah,' he acknowledged. 'Horrible, but kind of cool too. I mean, how often do you find dead bodies just lyin' about under an old outhouse, you know what I mean?'

Iris reflected that *she* had seemed to find them considerably more frequently than other people, particularly over the course of the last year, but she kept the thought to herself. Despite his bluntness, or perhaps because of it, she found herself enjoying Jamie's company. Maybe it was a function of his youth, but nothing seemed to be taboo for him. She admired the way he ploughed through moral nuances without overthinking everything the way she did. He reminded her of a boat bouncing cheerfully through the waves, buoyant and determined.

'You know they're saying there were two of them?' Jamie went on.

'So I heard,' said Iris.

'Two women.' He sipped his beer contemplatively, watching Iris's expression, and the way her compelling, wide-set eyes gave little away.

Leaning forward, he lowered his voice to a stage whisper. 'D'you reckon they might have been old mistresses of Jock's?'

Iris frowned. 'That seems highly unlikely. Why, is that what people are saying?'

Jamie nodded knowingly. 'Aye. That, or maybe one of 'em's his first wife, Alice. The one who ran off and was *never seen again*.'

Alice, Iris thought. She must have been Mary's mother.

'What do you mean, "never seen again"?' she asked. 'That's not really true, is it?'

Jamie shrugged. 'Who knows. Whatever went down happened before I was born. All I do know is, it's shrouded in mystery. *Woooooo*,' he added melodramatically, doing a little 'spooky' movement with his hands.

Iris laughed despite herself. 'You do realise this isn't an episode of *Scooby Doo*?'

Jamie drained the rest of his pint cheerfully. 'It's as close as

Pitfeldy's gonna get, though, so you have to let us have our fun. Have dinner with me.'

The last part was such a non sequitur, it took Iris a few seconds to register what he'd said.

'You may as well,' he pressed her, sensing hesitation. 'There's no much else to do in Pitfeldy of an evening, other than hang around in here and talk about herring quotas.'

'Not wildly appealing,' Iris agreed.

'And you're obviously no enjoying that beer.'

'Sorry,' Iris admitted guiltily.

'It's a date, then?' said Jamie.

Iris looked at him curiously, matching his bluntness with her own. 'Don't you think I'm a bit old for you?'

He leaned back, his eyes locking playfully with hers.

'No.'

Grabbing a pen from behind the bar, he scrawled down his number on a napkin and handed it to her. 'Look, it's only dinner. But I'll leave it up to you. I'd like to get to know you a wee bit better, that's all.'

'I'll think about it,' said Iris, slipping the napkin into her handbag as he returned to his friends.

Later, tucked up in bed, Iris reflected on what a strange few days it had been. Kathy's latest note. Learning about Mary, and now about her mother, Alice. Discovering the bodies. Being asked out for dinner by a fisher— boy. Iris's instincts told her that dinner with Jamie Ingall would probably be harmless fun. Then again, the last time Iris had trusted her romantic instincts things had not gone well. In fact, it would be fair to say they'd gone catastrophically, apocalyptically badly. Time to exercise a little caution, perhaps? To steer clear of boys, and bodies, and focus on her work? Then again, she reflected, she'd only got the commission to paint Kathy Miller's portrait in the first place because of her involvement in the Wetherby murder case. And because Kathy needed her help with these threatening notes. She'd been so distracted today, she'd completely forgotten to do any more research into the watermarked envelopes.

Each new subject was a mystery. As a portrait artist, Iris had learned that long ago. Perhaps unravelling the mystery of Kathy Miller would help some of the other pieces fall into place? Perhaps.

She fell asleep dreaming of envelopes and bones and handsome trawlermen.

Chapter Eight

Professor Martha Lane walked between the two tables, each with their carefully arranged collection of bones, pointing out the salient points of her examination to DI Haley.

'So. What we have here are two partial skeletons,' she began in her soft, southern American accent, making sure to go slowly so that the policeman could keep up and ask questions if he needed. 'Both are female.'

'That's definite, is it?' asked Haley.

'Yes. With the first skeleton, you can determine the sex from the recovered pelvic bones *here*.'

Haley watched closely as Edinburgh University's top forensic pathologist gently prodded the bright, white bones with a gloved finger. He only knew of Professor Lane by reputation, and had been pleasantly surprised by her helpful, non-patronising demeanour, both in person now and yesterday, when they'd spoken on the phone and he'd begged her to squeeze him into her schedule. In DI Haley's experience, academics tended to have a low opinion of the average policeman's intelligence. But Professor Lane had welcomed him into her lab on Nightingale Way, near the University Library, with an open mind and what appeared to be a genuine eagerness to help him identify the Pitfeldy remains.

'With the second set of remains, the pelvis is missing,' Professor Lane continued. 'However, we can still infer gender from the skull. This smoothness and gracility here?' Again her finger gently traced a line across the relevant bone fragment. 'You wouldn't find that in a male.'

'Any idea how old they were when they died?' Haley asked, making a mental note to look up 'gracility' on his phone later.

'I can give you a range,' the professor replied cautiously. 'But no more than that. We look for factors such as changes in pubic symphysis or medial clavicular epiphysis.'

'Course you do,' muttered Haley.

Martha Lane grinned. 'What I mean is, I can't be exact about it. But both were grown women, no younger than twenty, say. And neither made old bones. Twenty to forty, if I had to guess.'

'OK,' said Haley. It wasn't the smallest of windows, but he'd take what he could get. 'Cause of death?' he asked nervously, more in hope than expectation. Dave Gaffney had as good as told him that it would be practically impossible to determine how the women died, given the degree of 'animal interference', as he put it, that had occurred since they'd been in the ground. But again, Professor Lane surprised him.

'With the second set of remains, I can't say, I'm afraid. From the bones alone it could have been disease, or accident, although obviously given where they were found . . .'

'Yeah,' Haley said grimly. 'I think we can safely rule out disease. Unless they buried themselves.'

'Well, quite,' agreed Martha. 'But there's nothing conclusive, or even strongly suggestive, in the remains. But this young lady,' she pointed to the second table, 'died from a blunt-force trauma to the head.'

Haley grinned. 'You're sure about that?'

'Absolutely. That indent to the skull there? That's what killed her. No question.'

'Fantastic,' said Haley.

'Not for her,' quipped Professor Lane.

'Well, no,' he agreed. 'So now for the million-dollar question. When do you think they were buried? Am I looking at a murder inquiry or a case for the history books?'

Martha Lane sighed. 'That's where it gets really tricky, I'm afraid,' she said. Taking off her gloves, she placed them on a table at the far side of the room before turning back to face him. 'I'll need to see soil samples from the burial site.'

'I'll get you those.'

'This bothy was partially exposed, you say?'

'Mostly exposed,' said Haley. 'No roof to speak of.'

'Then weather data would also be helpful.'

'Sure. No problem.'

'There are so many things that can affect skeletal age determinations, you see,' she explained. 'Even with all the data in the world, it's a grey area. Not like carbon dating a tree. I can give you a balance of probabilities, based on what you've given me. But at the end of the day that's all it would be. An educated guess.'

'I understand,' said Haley. 'And I hate to push, but if I got you those samples and the other information this afternoon, do you think you might have a wee guess for me by tonight?'

Encouraged, Stuart Haley left Professor Lane's lab and headed down the hill towards New Town and his old haunt, the Red Lion just off Charlotte Square. A dark, cosy pub with a big open fire in the bar and no pretensions to be 'gastro' anything, it was a perfect spot to while away the afternoon, pondering the case while he waited for the American pathologist's verdict.

He ordered a fortifying plate of smoked sausage and mash, and a lemonade to wash it down with. Gone were the days when he could think clearly after a lunchtime pint. Now the mere whiff of booze in the middle of the day was likely to send him straight to sleep, yet another depressing symptom of middle age. After calling back to the station to make sure the soil samples were on their way to Dr Lane's lab, he pulled out his tablet, and began searching idly through articles on Pitfeldy Castle and the MacKinnon family while he ate. As ever, the web yielded a variety of results, some more interesting than others. There were turgid academic papers about the history of the castle and the ancient Celtic tribes that lived along the Moray coast. Then there were newspaper snippets about 'Baron'

Jock MacKinnon's various divorces, some dutifully factual, others more salacious and gossipy. A search of public records revealed that Jock had been married twice – first to Alice Ponsonby, then to Fiona Harris for three decades starting in the eighties. In a few months' time, he was to tie the knot for a third time with Kathy Miller, the pretty American socialite whom Haley had only just met, but whose name had been mud in and around Pitfeldy for some time now.

Kathy's name produced hundreds of search results of its own, all of them considerably more lurid and fascinating than anything relating to her soon-to-be husband. Like Jock, it appeared, Ms Miller had been married twice before. DI Haley hadn't warmed to her particularly when they had met, although he had to admit she was a strikingly attractive young woman, prettier than all of the other glamorous young things whose pictures had popped up online as rumoured former mistresses of Jock MacKinnon. The artist Jock had commissioned to paint Kathy's portrait – Iris Grey – would have a job on her hands doing the young lady justice without making her look like a cartoon character or some sort of cheesy Disney princess.

Haley *had* liked Iris Grey during their brief encounter. He'd also been impressed by Angus Brae, the gillie. It was funny how instinct kicked in when it came to first impressions. Over the years, Stuart Haley had learned to trust his instincts, but not blindly. It was important to keep an open mind.

After about an hour, the thought struck him that, if nothing else, there appeared to be an awful lot of young or middle-aged women – women who fit Professor Lane's 'twenty to forty' window – with connections of one sort or another to Pitfeldy Castle's ageing baron. A lifetime of flagrant womanising on Jock MacKinnon's part had seen to that.

Slipping a contemplative forkful of mash and gravy into his mouth, Haley turned his attentions to the other members of the MacKinnon family. Apart from the dreadful son, Rory, whom he'd met, Jock had had two other children, both daughters. Emma, who appeared to have joined herself in matrimony to some other inbred member of the Scottish aristocracy, and another girl by his first wife, Mary, who'd died in infancy over three decades ago.

Now *that* was interesting. Was it that tragedy that had ended Jock MacKinnon's first marriage? Or had Jock's philandering been to blame, as it had been with his second marriage to Fiona, Rory and Emma's mother? Not that either scenario was likely to have any bearing on the bodies in the bothy, specifically. But Stuart Haley was interested in what made a domineering cold fish like Jock MacKinnon tick, not to mention what caused him to defend his privacy so stridently. He'd made it very clear yesterday that he wanted Haley's investigation closed, and the sooner the better.

By the time he left the pub, darkness was already falling, shrouding the cobbled streets of the old town in a mellow orange-red glow. Haley hadn't spent much time in Edinburgh since the days of Jean's illness and the endless trips back and forth to see her oncologist at Western General. Dreadful times, and yet they'd also shared some of their deepest laughs on those trips to the city, bound together by a black humour and a determination not to let cancer defeat their spirits, as well as Jean's body. Perhaps for that reason Haley still felt a fondness for Edinburgh, and he took his time walking to his car to begin the long drive back to Fochabers.

His phone rang just as he got back to the NCP car park on Edinburgh Castle Terrace.

'OK. So I ran the samples.' Martha Lane's distinctive southern drawl had him holding his breath. 'Like I said this morning, I can't be one hundred per cent definitive. But from the evidence available, I believe it's highly likely that these remains are modern and relatively recent.'

DI Haley exhaled. A surge of adrenaline coursed through him.

'How recent?'

'I would estimate the bodies went into the ground between ten and fifteen years ago. I can't get it any narrower than that, because the first skeleton had slightly more signs of deterioration than the second.'

'Hmmm,' mused Haley. 'OK. Any ideas why that should be?'

'Not really. Full decomposition in that particular soil would have taken at least eight years, but beyond that there are different microbial factors at play, as well as variations in the degree of animal disturbance. Ten to fifteen is my best guess.'

'Right,' said Haley. 'Thank you, Professor Lane. Thank you very much.'

'My pleasure.' She was about to hang up, but something made her hesitate. 'I won't presume to tell you how to do your job, DI Haley,' she said suddenly. 'But from a scientific perspective, I'd say the best evidence you have is those teeth from the first skeleton. There were no fillings or crowns, so nothing to positively confirm modernity. But they're in excellent shape. Very well preserved, in life and post-mortem. Perhaps, if they were to match somebody's records . . .?'

'Absolutely,' said Haley. 'We'll run them through missing persons first thing tomorrow. Thank you again, professor. Goodnight.'

He started the car, his heartbeat and mind both racing.

Ten to fifteen years.

Blunt-force trauma to the back of the skull.

Two women, buried deep in private woods on the Pitfeldy Castle estate.

And a near-perfect set of teeth, to get the ball rolling.

Guiltily, Stuart Haley realised that he was feeling more excited, more energised, than he had in years.

He had a murder inquiry on his hands.

Chapter Nine

Iris dipped her brush into the pale, buttermilk oil paint she'd mixed earlier with various shades of yellow and white, and tried again to capture the light as it played through Kathy's hair. Bloody hair. For something so incidental to the soul of a portrait it always seemed to take up an inordinate amount of time, at least for Iris. There were too many colours and textures and layers of movement. In Kathy Miller's case there was also just too much of the damn stuff. Iris must remember to ask her next subject to wear a hat.

Two weeks had gone by since an official murder inquiry was launched into the 'Girls in the Wood', as the bothy skeletons were now being called. During that time, Iris had been up at the castle most days for sittings with Kathy. There had been no more threatening notes. Perhaps having so many police sniffing around had frightened the letter writer off. In any event, with no more attempts to scare her into leaving, Kathy had resumed her laser-like focus on arrangements for her wedding. Most of the talk during her sessions with Iris revolved around make-up artists and the pros and cons of antique veils. But the murders were also a source of endless fascination, with Kathy offering various half-baked theories as to who the mysterious victims might have been. Today, in particular, the Girls in the Wood were on Kathy's mind, thanks to last night's televised press conference. It was the second DI Haley had held in as many weeks, earning himself the proverbial *nul points* from Jock MacKinnon.

'You can't really blame poor Jock for getting mad,' Kathy said loyally, running a frustrated hand through her hair and immediately ruining all of Iris's work of the last half-hour. 'I mean, Haley as good as implied he was involved.'

'I don't think that's true,' said Iris, who had also watched the press conference and found herself warming more and more to DI Haley. In her view, the man was down to earth, hard-working, bright and, most unexpected of all in Iris's own limited experience of police detectives, open-minded.

A few days after news of the bodies' discovery was made public, Iris's own name leaked into the press, and the online 'true crime' community immediately went into conspiracy theory overdrive. Most people simply remarked on the coincidence of Iris having a connection to both the Girls in the Wood case *and* the Dom Wetherby murder. But a few of the postings on Iris's public Facebook page had been less benign, accusing her of involvement in the killings to 'raise her profile'. A few days ago things reached the point where Iris's agent, Greta, insisted she call the police.

'It's one thing to make you out to be Carole Baskin,' said Greta. 'It's another actually to threaten you.'

Iris agreed, and dutifully forwarded the worst of her online abuse to DI Haley, without expecting much of a response. But, to her surprise, he'd called her back the same afternoon.

'Most of these nutters are all talk,' he reassured her. 'But that doesn't mean they should be allowed to get away wi' it.'

The following day, one of the trolls had been arrested. So Iris was very much a fan of DI Haley.

Not so Kathy Miller.

'Didn't you hear his answer to that question about "access" to the castle grounds?' she protested, still fixated on the press conference. 'He made a point of stressing that whoever buried the bodies in our bothy must have had "intimate knowledge" of the estate.'

'Well, they must have,' said Iris. 'I don't think he meant to accuse Jock, specifically.'

'Sure he did,' Kathy insisted. 'The man's an out-and-out socialist, did you know that? He hates the landed gentry and everything we stand for.'

Iris noticed the 'we'. How disappointed the author of the poison-pen letters would be to know that, in Kathy's mind, she was already Lady Pitfeldy.

'What were the police like during the Wetherby case?' Kathy asked her, eager to hear Iris's 'inside track' experience. 'I mean, is this kind of harassment normal?'

Iris frowned. 'What kind of harassment?'

It was one thing for Kathy to stick up for her fiancé, but another to parrot Jock's patent nonsense about being harassed.

'This Haley guy was up here again yesterday, asking Jock questions about his first wife. And about Mary, their baby who died. I'd call that harassment. Like, what the fuck does that have to do with anything?'

'I don't know,' Iris admitted, her mind drifting back to what Jamie Ingall had said in the pub about Jock's first wife, Alice, 'never being seen again'. She'd dismissed it as a joke at the time. Empty local gossip. But perhaps the police – or whoever wrote Kathy the note about Mary – knew something that she and Kathy didn't?

'I know it must feel like you're under siege at times,' said Iris, adopting a more conciliatory tone. 'But actually I don't think Haley's hounding anyone. Until he knows who those women were, the only lead he has is the place they were buried. It's his job to talk to Jock, and anybody else who had a connection to the estate ten or twenty years ago.'

'OK, but bringing up a dead child?' said Kathy. 'I know Jock can come across as kind of brittle. And that a lot of people find him aloof.'

And downright rude, thought Iris. *And snobbish, and self-centred and entitled.*

'But he does have feelings,' Kathy insisted. 'He could barely bring himself to talk to *me* about what happened to Mary. And he tells me everything.'

Iris smiled. For all her outer toughness, there was a naivety to Kathy Miller that reminded Iris how young she still was. No one ever told anybody 'everything'. Least of all one's lover.

'Well,' she said brightly, gesturing for Kathy to resume her former reclining pose as she picked up her brush again. 'I daresay it'll all be over soon. I can't imagine *two* women could disappear without a trace up here without somebody reporting them missing.'

'You'd think so, wouldn't you?' Patting her legs, Kathy summoned her dogs back up onto her lap, gazing wistfully out of the window. 'All I wanted when I moved in here was some peace,' she sighed.

Really? thought Iris, thinking of all Kathy's battles with Rory and Emma, and the combative, feisty tone she took with any villagers who disliked her or dared to challenge her plans for the estate.

If peace was what Kathy Miller wanted, she had a funny way of showing it.

Angus Brae was finishing the washing-up and listening to the cricket round-up on Radio 4 when he spotted the slight figure of DI Haley lifting the latch on his front garden gate. Drying the plate in his hands methodically with a tea towel, he set it down on the sideboard and walked over to open the door, trying to shake the automatic feeling of nervousness that seemed to overtake him whenever he saw a policeman, whether or not he'd done anything wrong.

'Afternoon, detective inspector.'

'Good afternoon, Mr Brae.' DI Haley was all smiles, which helped put Angus at ease. It hadn't escaped his notice that Haley seemed to like him, as instinctively and wholeheartedly as he seemed to dislike the baron. 'Do you have a moment for a wee chat?'

'Of course.' Angus returned the smile. 'Come in.'

Haley took a seat on the small, red-checked sofa opposite the fireplace.

'Can I get you anything? A cup of tea?'

'No, thanks.' Haley shook his head. 'I shan't be staying long.'

This was true, although DI Haley wished it weren't. With Jock MacKinnon being so relentlessly obstructive and difficult, he'd had high hopes for extracting some more useful information about the estate and its workings from the young gillie. But thanks to the call he'd just had from his boss, Detective Superintendent Kirkwood, he'd have to scurry back to his desk by two to turn up the pressure on the missing persons team.

'It's been two weeks, and we still don't know who the victims are,' Kirkwood bellowed, stating the obvious. 'Have you run the dental records yet?'

'Yes, sir,' Haley explained. 'No matches yet. But not all of the missing women who fit our age profile had records on file. We've been chasing down the missing information –'

'Well, chase it down faster, man!' boomed Kirkwood. 'And stop fannying about up at the castle. Am I clear?'

'Sir.'

Clarity wasn't the superintendent's problem. Patience, on the other hand, was sorely lacking. An ability to listen would also have been a refreshing change. No one was more frustrated than DI Haley that they hadn't found a match to the dental records. But in the absence of that easy win, he'd been working day and night to build up a picture of the tight-knit Pitfeldy community at the time of the killings, in the hopes of unearthing a concrete lead. In two short weeks, besides 'harassing' the MacKinnon family, he'd exhaustingly interviewed everyone from the local publican to the vicar, schoolteachers, fishermen and even the drug dealers known to have been working the area back then. One was in prison at HMP Barlinnie in Glasgow, an exhausting four-hour drive from Pitfeldy. The other had found God and had become a social worker in Elgin. Haley had spent over an hour with them both, as a result of which he was only just beginning his research into female migrant workers in this part of rural Scotland. Migrants, and in particular prostitutes, were the most common 'Jane Does' in cases like these, where no one seemed to have reported the victims missing. But all of this took time. And while it was true that Haley hadn't cracked it yet, nobody could have worked harder, or more thoroughly, to turn over every possible stone.

'How can I help you?'

Settling into his father's old armchair, Angus's voice was as gentle and inviting as Kirkwood's had been loud and angry.

'I'd like to ask you about your father.' Haley cut right to the chase. 'He was gillie here before you, is that right?'

'Aye. That's right,' said Angus, stiffening slightly.

'So he pretty much managed the estate overall, like you do?'

Angus nodded. 'The job's not changed much. Fewer staff these days, and more of the estate's sublet than in Dad's day. But otherwise the same.'

Haley looked around him at the bright, comfortable cottage, considerably better furnished than his own bungalow. 'Did he live here, too?'

'He did.'

'So you grew up in this house?'

'I was born here,' Angus confirmed, relaxing again slightly.

'Your parents divorced when you were young.' Haley looked down at his notes, then up at Angus, whose pale face was impassive. 'And your mother, Linda Brae, moved away from the area. That must have been hard.'

A muscle next to Angus's left eye twitched slightly.

'I suppose.'

'So it was just you and your father here?'

'Aye.'

'He never married again?'

'No.' The faintest of smiles suggested that this idea amused Angus.

'Where is your mother now, do you know?'

Angus cleared his throat. 'She lives on Shetland,' he replied, apparently without emotion. 'Last I heard, anyway. We're not in touch.'

'OK.' Haley nodded understandingly. 'I gather your father's living in a care home now, near Buckie?'

'He is,' said Angus. 'Dad has Alzheimer's. It's pretty advanced at this point, I'm sorry to say.'

Haley had heard the same story from a number of sources in Pitfeldy. How Edwin Brae had gone from being a sharp, laconic, capable man – albeit a bitter one after his divorce – to a dribbling wreck who couldn't tell you what day of the week it was, or recognise friends he'd grown up with. It was a shame from Haley's point of view, as it was really Edwin Brae he would have liked to have quizzed on the comings and goings up at the castle at the time the Girls in the Wood were buried beneath the bothy.

'He was diagnosed young, at fifty,' said Angus. 'Early-onset, they call it. That was why he had to give up the job here.'

'And you took over.'

'That's right.'

'How well do you remember life on the estate ten or fifteen years ago, Angus?' asked Haley, leaning forward with his hands on his knees. 'The bothy was a ruin back then too, I assume.'

'Oh aye. It's been in a state for years.'

'Were there any young or middle-aged women who used to frequent the estate during your childhood? Friends or girlfriends of any of the farm workers, maybe. Or even friends of the baron that you remember?'

'No,' said Angus firmly.

Haley frowned. 'Really? None at all?'

'The baron and Lady Pitfeldy had house guests, obviously. Men and women. But I never knew them. There were labourers that came through sometimes, pickers mostly,' said Angus, rubbing his brow, as if trying to coax the memories back. 'Bulgarians and a few Romanians. My dad didn't trust them, but some of the tenant farmers took advantage of the cheap labour. On the side, you know.'

Haley nodded. He knew. Up until a few years ago, when the Government finally cracked down on it, there'd been a scandalous use of virtual slave labour in parts of rural Scotland, exploiting illegal immigrants and refugees.

'They were mostly men, though,' said Angus. 'I suppose I did see the occasional lass looking for work.'

'Prostitutes?' Haley asked bluntly.

'Maybe, some of them, I suppose.' Angus blushed and looked away awkwardly. 'I don't know.'

'And did Jock MacKinnon?'

'The baron knew nothing about it,' Angus leaped to Jock's defence before Haley could even finish his question. 'He was never hands-on with the estate workers, not then and not now. My dad oversaw all that.'

It wasn't what Haley had been about to ask. He was more interested in Jock MacKinnon's womanising fifteen years ago than he was in dodgy hiring practices at Pitfeldy Castle. But he let it drop. Angus Brae's unexpectedly fierce and defensive loyalty towards Jock suddenly seemed more relevant.

'You're close to the baron?' he probed gently.

'He's a good man.' Angus shifted his gaze uncomfortably.

'Is he? Not everybody seems to think so.'

'Look, I'm no' pretending he's a saint,' Angus admitted. 'The way he treated Fiona was . . . let's just say he's not an easy man to be married to. But he's always been very kind to me. And to my father, who also wasn't an easy man.'

'He and your father were boyhood friends?' Haley asked.

'Aye,' Angus nodded, 'they were like brothers.'

'Does Jock visit him, in the home?'

Perhaps he imagined it, but Haley could have sworn he saw Angus wince at this question, as if it caused him physical pain.

'No.' He cleared his throat.

'Why's that?'

'There's no point. Dad wouldn't know who he was.'

'But you visit?'

Another wince. 'Sometimes. Not often anymore, to be honest with you.' He looked up at the clock above the kitchen dresser. 'I really ought to be getting back to work.'

'Yes. So should I,' said Haley, getting to his feet. He would have preferred a longer interview with Angus, but at least today's initial chat had borne some fruit.

The prostitute angle might well become more important,

especially if they failed to score a dental records match. It had always saddened Haley that the public tended to lose interest in murder cases once it emerged that the victims were sex workers. Or perhaps it wasn't interest they lost so much as sympathy. It was the same story with addicts. As if falling prey to heroin or being driven to sell one's body for a living made someone less of a person. Stuart Haley certainly didn't share this view. But plenty of his colleagues did. If the Girls in the Wood did turn out to have been prostitutes, he knew he would have to fight even harder for resources and access than he was doing now.

Haley liked Angus Brae, but it rankled that what Stuart considered to be forelock-tugging, self-abasing feudal allegiance to one's 'laird' was still alive and well, even among the younger generation. Was Angus's affection for Jock MacKinnon based on his view of the baron as 'a good man'? Or did Angus leap to his defence simply because Jock was his master, and the boy had been raised since birth to think of working on the estate as a kindness he'd been given, rather than a job of work that he was paid to do because he'd earned it?

It was enough to make DI Haley despair for the future.

Fiona MacKinnon sat at the desk in her Edinburgh flat, carefully smoothing down her Viyella skirt before flipping open her pristine-clean laptop computer. All of Fiona's movements were measured and thoughtful, as carefully curated as the objects that surrounded her. Never beautiful in the classical sense of that word, she had long taken pride in being considered elegant; a word she felt implied a certain orderliness, not only of mind and body, but also of one's environment. Thanks to her husband's cruelty, she'd been forced to exchange a fairy-tale castle for a relatively modest Victorian conversion on Belgrave Crescent. Jettisoned in her late fifties like a piece of rotten fruit, by a man she'd supported and forgiven and, if not loved, then at least loyally tolerated for most of her adult life, she'd had no choice but to swallow this bitter pill.

Even so, within her new, limited environs, Fiona had created something lovely, something 'elegant' that reflected her eye for both beauty and restraint. The flat was neither cluttered nor bare, neither a museum piece nor a dissonantly modern attempt at 'new beginnings'. Instead, it was a warm, feminine, classically designed space. She felt at peace here, amid her Victorian furniture and Osborne & Little fabrics, with her bespoke Danish standard lamp lighting the lonely evenings and her vintage typewriter adding a discreet touch of nostalgic glamour to her Renaissance-style escritoire – a smaller desk reserved purely for letter writing. Above her main work desk, a small sixteenth-century Venetian oil painting of an Italian noblewoman was one of the few treasures Fiona had brought with her from Pitfeldy. Ironically, Jock had bought it for her as a gift on one of their early anniversaries, but she'd kept it for its beauty and the skill of its execution, rather than for any sentimental reasons. The time for sentiment had long passed.

Clicking onto her newsfeed, she opened the latest breathless article on the Girls in the Wood, reading each word carefully, several times. No longer having a grand house to run left one with a vast amount of time to indulge in reading. Now that initial shock had faded (when first Rory had told her that two women's bodies had been exhumed from underneath the old bothy, she'd had to grab onto the kitchen counter to stop her knees from giving way), she was beginning to enjoy following the ins and outs of the investigation.

Well, perhaps 'enjoy' was the wrong word. An inelegant word, at any rate, given that two poor souls had lost their lives and their corpses hidden away up there to rot. Fiona MacKinnon might be physically alive, but she knew what it was like to lose the life you'd built for yourself and then be stuffed away out of sight. Hidden. Denied. Forgotten.

Only she hadn't forgotten. She, Fiona, knew a lot of things that had happened at Pitfeldy Castle. Fifteen years ago. Ten years ago. And much more recently. She'd already had a call from the police, asking her to contact them if she had any pertinent information or felt she could contribute to their inquiries.

She could. And she would, eventually. But for the moment she was still weighing up exactly what her contribution would be. How could she exact the maximum revenge and destruction on those who had conspired to destroy her, without at the same time hurting her children? Rory still stood to inherit the castle in Jock's will, and Emma had been left some significant MacKinnon family heirlooms, despite the new slut's best efforts to grab as much for herself as possible. At the moment, despite their estrangement, Rory was still in charge of drawing up the prenup for his father's impending marriage. But things could change. Fiona MacKinnon knew that better than anybody.

She'd half expected Jock to call her once the news about the bodies broke and leave some bullying message, warning her to keep her mouth shut about her years as Pitfeldy's chatelaine. But he hadn't. Too besotted, no doubt, with the American she-wolf he'd installed in her place, even to realise that the wife he no longer loved might be a threat to him. To *them*.

Scrolling down, Fiona clicked on a photograph of Iris Grey, the renowned portrait painter who'd apparently discovered the remains. Evidently, Jock had commissioned Iris to paint a portrait of the she-wolf for a six-figure sum, an extravagance he would never have countenanced back in the old days. The picture showed a small, fragile woman with dark hair and wide-set eyes, who seemed to be inordinately fond of beads. Odd that Jock should go for a hippyish type – he'd always loathed them. Perhaps Iris Grey was pretty enough for him to have made an exception?

There was a lot of nonsense flying around online about Iris's connection with another murder. Somehow Fiona had managed to miss all the media hype about the Dom Wetherby case. Reeling from her divorce at the time, she'd had little appetite for tabloid scandals. But she was interested now. Interested in Iris, and the Wetherby murder, and the Girls in the Wood. It was surreal to see people openly discussing Jock's affairs on the Internet. Bloggers had even brought up Alice, his first wife who'd run off after Mary had died, muckraking through Jock's 'colourful' past in a way Fiona knew would enrage him like a stuck bull. Hopefully, to a point where he might do something stupid and lash out.

Deep down, the person Fiona MacKinnon really wanted to see convicted was that scheming bitch Kathy Miller. If anyone deserved to be buried in Pitfeldy woods, preferably with a stake through the heart, it was her.

Closing her laptop, she walked slowly over to her escritoire.

She felt a letter coming on.

Kathy was in her dressing room when she found it, carefully lodged behind her yoga mat.

Pushing down the sense of dread that momentarily assailed her – she wouldn't be afraid; she *mustn't* be afraid – she picked up the envelope, feeling the familiar texture of the stiff paper as she held it between her thumb and forefinger. She'd only finished her yoga session just before teatime and put the mat back right afterwards. So whoever had left the note had done so in the last few hours.

Angrily, and more carelessly than usual, she ripped it open and read the note inside.

Then, closing the door, she rang Iris.

'You're right,' she said, unable to keep the tremble out of her voice. 'We need to go to the police.'

Chapter Ten

Retired GP Dr Gerald Bowman was a fit, upright old man with twinkling blue eyes set deep into a face as brown and wrinkled as a pickled walnut.

'I'm sorry to bother you unannounced,' DI Haley apologised as Pitfeldy's former doctor showed him into his handsome Georgian town house. 'But I happened to be passing, and hoped you might be able to answer a few questions.'

'Of course.' The old man seemed delighted. He seemed delighted by the unexpected company. 'I can't imagine what I might know that would be useful to you, but do please fire away.'

Walking into the Bowman house was like stepping onto the set of a Richard Curtis film. Everything here was picture-perfect, full of warmth and happiness, steeped in solid but not ostentatious wealth mixed with a certain all-pervasive nostalgia, like a ripe strawberry dipped in chocolate. A fire crackled away merrily in the beautifully appointed drawing room, old-fashioned but lovely in its way with its antique Knowle sofas and battered-leather club fender. Copies of *Fly Fishing Today* and *Horse & Hound* littered every side table and bookshelf, and an arthritic Labrador that looked as old as his master lay farting contentedly in a rattan basket by the door. From the kitchen came the sweet smell of freshly baked biscuits, as well as the unmistakable sound of the cricket commentary on Radio 5 Live, which the old man immediately offered to turn down.

'So we can hear ourselves think. We're playing dreadfully badly anyway, I'm afraid.'

The 'we', along with the resonant RP accent, belied the fact that the old man was not a Scot. But despite this, and despite his self-evident poshness, DI Haley found himself immediately drawn to Doc Bowman. Unlike Jock MacKinnon, he wasn't a snob. And the elements of the past that he clung to and chose to surround himself with at home struck Haley as endearingly sentimental. *Perhaps I'm getting old*, he mused. Or maybe it was just a nice change to be spending time with somebody who appeared to be unambiguously happy.

After a few minutes the two men were ensconced on one of the sofas, drinking tea and helping themselves from a generous plate of shortbread biscuits.

'These are delicious,' said Haley truthfully, through a mouthful of crumbs.

'They're home-made,' said Bowman, 'not by me, I hasten to add. That'd be your fastest way to an early grave, detective inspector, eating my cooking. No, these were baked by my daughter Cassie. She's quite the Delia Smith of the family, I can assure you. Anyway, I'm rambling. You didn't come here simply to eat biscuits. How can I help?'

'I'm wondering if you can tell me anything about Alice MacKinnon,' Haley asked. 'She was a patient of yours, I believe? Before she and the baron divorced?'

'She was.'

'You remember her, then?'

'Oh Lord, yes.' The lines in the old man's face deepened into crevices as he frowned in concentration. 'I remember her very well. I saw Alice throughout her pregnancy. And afterwards, of course, when her baby died. Dreadful thing.'

'How *did* she die?' Haley asked. 'The baby, I mean.'

'It was a cot death,' said Dr Bowman. 'Which is really just shorthand for "we don't know". Of course this was going back to the early eighties. Much of the advice given to new parents then we now know to be wrong. Putting infants to sleep on their stomach, and so forth.'

Haley nodded thoughtfully. 'Alice MacKinnon left Pitfeldy shortly after the child's death.'

'That's right. Mary, that was the baby's name,' he remembered suddenly. 'The marriage collapsed completely, I'm afraid.'

'Were you surprised by that?'

The old man's frown deepened. 'No.'

He paused for a moment to gather his thoughts, then continued. 'Jock was a patient of mine, too. The little girl's death hit him very hard, perhaps harder even than it did his wife. Looking back, one can see he was in shock. But at the time, there was just this tremendous well of anger. He was raging at the heavens, really, but it came out in these dreadful flashes of temper towards poor Alice.'

'He hit her?' Haley asked bluntly.

'I've no proof of that but it wouldn't surprise me,' said Bowman cautiously.

'She never came in with a black eye or broken bones?'

'No. But she was frightened of him, that much I do know. Jock MacKinnon changed after that child died, detective inspector, beyond all recognition. He went from being a happy, loving young man to a – well, to a bully, I suppose. Angry at everything. Poor Alice was grieving, she needed him, but he couldn't support her. He was tearing her to shreds. So no, I was not surprised when she left him.'

Haley took all of this in. Jock the bully required no particular stretch of the imagination. The hard part was picturing him before baby Mary's death, as a 'happy, loving' husband. But he had no reason to believe Bowman was misremembering.

'Did you ever see or hear from Alice again, after she left Pitfeldy?' Haley asked.

'I used to get Christmas cards for a while.' The doctor said. 'But at some stage they stopped. The later ones came from Shetland,' he added wistfully. 'Beautiful place, Shetland. I lost track of her after that.'

Shetland. Haley's mind raced. Who'd been talking to him about Shetland recently? And losing touch?

It came to him suddenly. Angus Brae. *His* mother had left Pitfeldy too, ran out on her marriage to his father Edwin, the old gillie and Jock MacKinnon's boyhood pal. Linda Brae's departure would have been a few years after Alice MacKinnon took off. But she'd also fled to Shetland. Was that a coincidence? Or was there a link between these two women, something that had drawn them both to each other and to these faraway islands?

'I don't suppose you remember when Alice's cards stopped arriving, Dr Bowman?' Haley asked.

The old man shook his head. 'Not exactly, no. But a good while ago now. If I had to guess, I'd say about – fifteen years?'

Fifteen years. Haley felt a dryness in his throat.

'Thank you. One last question,' he said, looking the old man in the eye. 'You don't happen to know the name of Alice's dentist?'

Back at the station, Haley was immediately ambushed by his sergeant, Danny Spencer. The young man was so excited, and speaking so rapidly, that it took Haley a few moments to understand what he was saying.

'Hold on, Danny, You're telling me that Kathy Miller called you . . .'

'Yes, sir. She called first, and then later she drove down to the station and dropped off a wee baggie.'

'A bag containing glass beads?'

'That's right, sir.'

'Beads that one of Ms Miller's dogs had *swallowed* at the crime scene and subsequently –'

'Excreted, sir. Yes.'

Haley rubbed his eyes. Was this what this case was coming to? A little plastic bag of pooed-out beads?

'She does realise that no one's supposed to be going near that bothy?' he said angrily. 'What was the dog *doing* up there? And is she certain that's where these damn beads came from? Couldn't he have picked them up somewhere else?'

'I don't know, sir. According to Ms Miller, the animal ran off while she was out for a walk yesterday and made straight for the bothy before she could stop him.'

'Hmm,' Haley grunted, unconvinced.

'She said the dog ran under the tape, and when it came out again she could see it had something in its mouth. Something *dangling*, she said. But by the time she got hold of it again, it had swallowed whatever it was. So then today, when the doggie did his business, she saw the beads, all blue and shining, and she thought maybe they belonged to one of the victims.'

'Right,' Haley sighed. 'Anything else?'

'Yes, sir,' said the sergeant, a little disappointed that the DI wasn't as excited by the beads development as he'd expected. 'The artist lady is here to see you – Iris Grey. She's in the waiting room.'

'Did she say what it was about?' asked Haley, perking up slightly. He'd liked Iris Grey during their first, brief meeting.

'No, sir. She said she preferred to wait for you. Should I show her in?'

Iris sat nervously while DI Haley read Kathy's notes, a look of deepening consternation on his face.

'Why didn't she come to us earlier?' Placing the first five envelopes to one side, he picked up the last note and read it aloud: '"Do you believe me now? You're not the first whore he's taken up with and got tired of. Leave, or you'll be next." That's pretty clearly a reference to the bodies.'

'I agree,' said Iris. 'Whoever's been writing these notes wants her to believe that Jock killed whoever was buried up there.'

'And that he's going to kill *her*,' said Haley. 'That's a threat.'

'Or a warning,' suggested Iris. 'But the tone of the other notes isn't exactly friendly. So I agree, it's probably meant as a threat. I did try to persuade Kathy to come to you sooner, but she preferred to try and handle it herself.'

'Why?' asked Haley.

Iris shrugged. 'She didn't want to upset Jock. And I don't think she took them terribly seriously. As the notes were addressed to her, I felt it was her decision to make.'

'Hmmm. But this latest one changed her mind?'

Iris nodded. 'That and the fact that two bodies have turned up on the estate. I think she's scared.'

Haley frowned, thinking about Jock's 'missing' first wife and the Christmas cards to Dr Bowman that stopped fifteen years ago.

'Maybe she should be. I'm curious. Why didn't she bring me these letters herself? She was down here earlier, dropping off these, so it would have been easy enough for her.' He held up a small plastic bag of pretty, blueglass beads.

'What are they?'

'Apparently, they came from the crime scene.' He told Iris about poo-gate, which she seemed to find in equal parts fascinating and hilarious. 'It all sounds like a bit of a shaggy dog story to me, but we'll see what forensics have to say about it. In any case, I'm wondering why she sent you with the letters?'

Iris shifted uncomfortably in her seat. 'I think she felt awkward. She still hasn't told Jock about them yet, although I imagine she will now. Anyway, I already had the earlier notes at my place, so when she brought the last one over this morning, I said I'd do it. I've been unofficially helping her for the last couple of weeks, you see. Trying to find out who was sending them.'

'Ah.' Haley grinned broadly. 'You've had your Miss Marple hat on again, have you, Ms Grey?'

Iris blushed. 'Like I said, I did try to convince her to go to the police.'

'Ach, it's all right, I'm only teasing,' he said kindly. 'Have you made any progress?'

'Not to speak of,' said Iris. 'The envelopes are interesting. Handmade, and there's a little watermark on the seal, if you look closely. But I haven't been able to track down the source yet.'

'OK,' said Haley, interested, turning the letters over.

'Given the times and places each one was left, it has to be someone who either lives up at the castle or has regular access and knows Kathy's routines,' Iris continued.

'A fairly small group, I'd imagine,' said Haley.

'Very. But it's possible that one person writes them and another hides them for Kathy to find. That would widen the net considerably.'

'So it would.' Haley nodded. 'Well, I'll have these finger-printed and we'll see what our labs can come up with on those envelopes. It may be that the ink or the paper are unusual, too. Thank you for bringing them in.'

Standing, he offered her his hand.

'Of course.' Iris shook it. 'Good luck. And with the beads.'

After she'd gone, Stuart Haley sat back down and looked at the items on his desk, wondering if they would turn out to be leads or red herrings. He knew he didn't like Jock MacKinnon. But he also knew that he mustn't allow that to cloud his judgment. As much as he might like to come across a photo of Alice MacKinnon wearing a string of those blueglass beads around her neck, he didn't expect it to happen. More likely than not, Alice was alive and well somewhere in the Outer Hebrides and the skeletons under the bothy belonged to a couple of hapless Romanian prostitutes that some migrant farm worker had done away with over a decade ago.

Most likely.

Still, he thought, reading Kathy Miller's letters again, *someone wants us to believe it was Jock.*

And that someone, it seemed, also wanted Kathy Miller out of the picture. At all costs.

Chapter Eleven

Iris blew on the tips of her fingers as she turned out of the castle driveway and back onto the Pitfeldy road. Up until last week she'd walked to and from her painting sessions with Kathy, but autumnal weather had arrived with astonishing speed to Banffshire and it was so cold now that she'd started to drive instead. After about five minutes, the heating on her rental car, a cheerful royal-blue Mini Cooper, would be toasty warm. But until it kicked in, getting into the car was like climbing into an ice box. She found herself praying that she would finish the portrait before winter kicked in in earnest, although at her current rate of progress this seemed unlikely.

In recent weeks, Kathy had taken to postponing sittings due to various wedding-related appointments. 'It's less than three months away, you know,' she kept informing Iris, as if three months weren't more than enough time to buy a cake and a dress and order in a few flowers. When they did have sessions together, Kathy was forever moving, usually when talking animatedly about her latest theory on the Girls in the Wood, or her mysterious letter writer. Even once Iris finally persuaded her to sit still, her hair remained a sticking point. And then, finally, there were the constantly wriggling dogs.

Though she wouldn't admit it to their besotted mistress, Iris had secretly grown fond of Milo and Sam Sam. She loved that they were so naughty and out of control that they'd managed not only to contaminate a crime scene, but also to ingest and then shit out potentially vital evidence. But there was no doubt that having two fluffy tyrants involved in every sitting had slowed down her work to a frustrating degree, and no amount of begging on Iris's part could get Kathy to change her mind about including them in the picture.

Today's session had gone slightly better than usual. Both dogs had helpfully fallen asleep, allowing Iris to concentrate on them for once, while Kathy talked non-stop as usual, this time about Jock.

'He handled the whole letters thing better than I thought he would,' she told Iris, shivering beneath her cashmere cardigan and dabbing a blob of rose balm on her sore lips. Even cold and sniffly, and with zero make-up on, she looked more beautiful than any woman had a right to. 'He just said he wished I'd told him sooner, and that I mustn't let whoever was sending them get to me.'

'Did he have any thoughts on who it might be?' asked Iris.

'Not really. "A local" was all he said. Some idiot with a grudge. I asked if he thought it might be Rory or Emma, but he just laughed and said they wouldn't dare. Which I guess is probably true.'

'What about the whole "you'll be next" thing?' Iris pressed. 'Didn't that worry him?'

'It honestly didn't seem to,' said Kathy, pensively. 'I mean, obviously *he* knows he had nothing to do with whatever happened to those women. So I guess he has no reason to be worried. The only thing that did bother him –' She hesitated.

'What?' said Iris.

'Don't take this the wrong way,' Kathy said awkwardly. 'But I think it upset him that I'd confided in you about the notes, rather than him.'

'I see,' said Iris.

'He can be quite possessive when it comes to my affections,' Kathy explained. 'Plus, he wasn't thrilled that I'd let you show the notes to the police. He's not a fan of that Haley guy. But anyway, all in all, I'd say he was pretty chill.'

Turning right just as the road crested over the hill and began its sharp descent towards Pitfeldy harbour, Iris pulled into the

Lidl car park. She needed bread and milk and a ready meal for tonight's supper, ideally something warming like a curry or a cheesy fish pie. Stepping out of the Mini, she pulled her coat more tightly around her before grabbing a trolley. This morning's frost had melted in the weak midday sun, and the leaves in the hedgerows glistened slick and dark in the fading afternoon light. A light drizzle had begun to fall. Dashing into the store, Iris was wondering if it would turn to sleet by nightfall, or even snow, when she ran slap bang into 'that Haley guy'.

'Ms Grey.' He smiled a little awkwardly. 'We really must stop meeting like this.'

He looked tired, Iris thought, hovering with his shopping basket beside a giant display of cereal boxes and with a paper list clutched in his hand. *There's something so faint about him, with his pale skin and thinning hair and that awful grey suit, that makes him almost invisible.* She wondered if the attempt to fade away was deliberate, and if so whether it was professional – a detective's need to observe and stay in the shadows – or personal, a more profound wish to disappear, to withdraw from a world that had hurt him.

Or maybe he's just pasty and Scottish with crap taste in suits, thought Iris, laughing out loud as this pithy counterpoint popped, unbidden, into her head.

'Something funny?' Haley looked confused.

'Oh, not really.' Iris blushed, getting a grip on herself. She liked Haley and the last thing she wanted was to be rude. 'Any progress on the letters? Or those beads?'

'Not much,' he sighed. 'The beads did come from the bothy site, and were probably once part of a bracelet or a necklace. *Possibly* belonging to one of the victims, but we've found almost no other traces of clothing up there. Just a few fragments of cloth that could have been anything. So we're not sure.'

'I see,' said Iris. She was pleased, and not a little surprised that he would choose to share so much information with her. Evidently, the admiration and trust between them was mutual. 'Well, that's good news, I suppose.'

'Not good enough,' said Haley wearily. 'To be frank with you, Ms Grey, although I'd appreciate it if you kept this between us, I'm under increasing pressure to shit or get off the pot, if you'll pardon the expression.'

'You still don't have leads on who the women were?' Iris asked.

'I've got some open lines of inquiry,' Haley answered cautiously. 'But nothing I can hang my hat on, no. The bottom line is, if I cannae get an ID on at least one of the bodies soon, the investigation's likely to be shelved.'

'Shelved?' Iris sounded shocked. 'As in, the police just walk away?'

He nodded.

'But it's a murder!'

'I don't want to drop the case, believe me,' said Haley with feeling. 'But no one's come forward to claim our girls, and they don't match any known missing persons on the Scottish register.'

'What about the English register?' asked Iris.

'That's a bigger list and we've got men still running through it, but so far nothing,' said Haley. 'Dental records were our big hope, but that's been a "no" too, unfortunately, at least so far. I've got one more door I'm still knocking on. We'll see.'

He didn't want to tell Iris his suspicions about Alice MacKinnon until he had something concrete. But already he'd had calls in to Lerwick police in Shetland, and to Dr Jillian Vaisey, Alice MacKinnon's old NHS dentist in Buckie, and was tentatively crossing his fingers.

'People in the village have been talking about migrant workers,' said Iris. 'Is there a possibility the girls came from abroad?'

'Every possibility,' admitted Haley. 'The problem is, especially if they entered illegally, as most transient workers do, we have no way to find them in any records or to cross-reference databases. Migrants are as good as invisible. It's one of the things that makes them so vulnerable. Plus, when we're looking at women, you've got to think about the sex trade.'

'You mean you think they might have been prostitutes?' asked Iris.

'What I mean is, we still don't know who they were. And that's the problem. If they *were* sex workers from abroad, it'll only make it harder for me to argue for more time and resources.'

'That's terrible,' said Iris, appalled. 'After all, murder's murder, isn't it? Surely one life's just as valuable as another.'

Reaching out, he put a sympathetic hand on her shoulder.

'It should be, Ms Grey,' he said wistfully. 'It absolutely should be.'

Haley woke early the next morning, sitting bolt upright in bed like Frankenstein's monster, startled by some dreamed shock he'd already forgotten. Knowing he wouldn't be able to fall back asleep, he got up and stumbled groggily into the shower, allowing the pounding hot jets to coax both his body and brain into some sort of life.

By six he was in the kitchen, dressed and on his second cup of coffee. He'd had emails overnight from Lerwick. According to the station there, Alice MacKinnon had never actually lived on Shetland.

'She may have rented a croft or a cottage for her holidays one year,' Sergeant Thane had emailed Haley. 'But she never owned property here, or registered to vote. We've no NHS records for any Alice MacKinnon.'

Out of curiosity, Haley had also inquired about Linda Brae, Angus's mother and the old gillie's wife, as Angus had mentioned that she'd moved to Shetland after she'd left his father. The news there was more positive.

'Linda Brae was definitely resident and registered to vote here until 2009. As far as we can tell, she left Shetland that year and hasn't been back. She registered a new address in Glasgow.' Haley made a mental note to check that out later. 'She's still listed as the owner of Tithe Cottage over at Braehoulland, but the place is completely derelict. It's actually due to be demolished next month – health and safety. All attempts by the council to trace the owner failed, so they got a court order to tear it down.'

Gulping down the last of his coffee and taking a second Lidl cinnamon bun for the road, Haley grabbed his car keys from the hook by the door. Doolally or not, it was time he paid Edwin Brae a visit. He wanted to ask Pitfeldy Castle's old gillie to his face about the bodies in the bothy, and about migrants and prostitutes hanging around the estate during his years in charge.

He'd also like to know exactly when Edwin Brae had last laid eyes on his wife. And what had happened to make Linda run off, abandoning her son, friends and life, never to return.

Passages Care Home was an ugly, modern brick building with hideous double glazing, crouched at the end of a nondescript no-through lane on the outskirts of the fishing town of Buckie. In front of it was a tarmacked circle for visiting cars and a single flower bed that was mostly just mud, interspersed with a few desultory grasses and 'hardy' flowers, all bowed and battered by the recent storms.

Making a mental note to kill himself rather than ever allow anyone to pack him off to a place like this, Haley parked and went inside.

In the foyer, some attempt had been made at cheer. The building was at least warm, with tartan armchairs scattered throughout the common areas and vases of plastic flowers plonked in the windowsills and on the edge of the reception desk. Inoffensive, piped classical music drifted out of speakers recessed somewhere in the ceiling. There was art on the walls too, most of it kitsch photography: kittens playing with balls of string, or naked babies in aprons flashing their peachy bottoms. It was all pretty awful, in Haley's opinion, but it did at least provide some distraction from the stench of disinfectant and overboiled vegetables, and the pervasive sense of death hovering in the air, an awkward but familiar visitor.

'Can I help you, love?'

The fat, bottle-blonde receptionist looked up at Haley kindly. He showed her his badge.

'I've come to talk to a Mr Brae. Mr Edwin Brae? I understand he's one of your residents.'

The receptionist looked at him quizzically. 'He is, yes. Been here longer than I have, has Edwin. You do realise he has advanced Alzheimer's?'

'Yes,' said Haley. 'So I've been told.'

'What I mean is,' the woman tried again, 'he won't know who you are. Most of what he says, if you're not familiar with the condition – he doesn't make a lot of sense.'

'I understand,' said Haley, though it was obvious to the receptionist that he didn't. 'I do need to talk to him all the same. Just in case he remembers something. It's important.'

With a 'suit yourself' shrug, she directed him to the old gillie's room. Number 206, right at the very end of the hallway.

Through the half-open door, Haley could see a frail, bent figure sitting in an upright leather chair with a tray across his lap, gazing out of the window at Passages' scrubby rear garden. A nurse or carer of some sort was in the room with him, bustling about stripping sheets and propping the old man's back with cushions. As he drew nearer, Haley could see that the room was mostly bare: just a chair, bed and side table with a narrow fitted wardrobe crammed into one corner. The only exception were a few rather well-executed watercolours hanging on the walls, including an eerie painting of what looked like a Venetian canal at dawn that particularly caught his eye.

'Hello.' Haley walked in and introduced himself, first to Edwin Brae, who looked through him as if he wasn't there, and then to the nurse. 'Nice painting, that.' He pointed to the canal picture above the bed.

'Isn't it?' said the nurse. 'His son did it. He did all of these, believe it or not.' She pointed towards the other paintings, mostly of local landscapes. 'How can we help you, detective inspector?'

'Detective? Is it police?' the old man blurted, visibly distressed all of a sudden. They were the first words he'd spoken, and they sounded simultaneously frightened and angry.

'It's all right, Edwin,' the nurse reassured him. 'Nothing for you to worry about.'

Haley squatted down on his haunches, so that he and Brae were at eye level. 'I'm investigating a possible double murder, Mr Brae,' he explained. 'Two bodies were found buried under the bothy, up at Pitfeldy Castle.'

'You mean the Girls in the Wood?' the nurse piped up. 'We read about that, didn't we, Edwin?' She smiled benignly down at her charge, but his rheumy eyes gave nothing away. In fact, he seemed to be completely absent.

'I manage the Pitfeldy estate,' Edwin announced suddenly, with more than a little pride.

'You used to manage it, Edwin,' the nurse corrected him gently. 'That's right.'

The old man stared at Haley. 'You're police, you say?'

'That's right.'

Brae's eyes narrowed. 'Is it Angus?' he demanded. 'Is he in trouble again?'

'No, no,' said Haley. 'Nothing like that.'

'Because if he is, I swear to God I'll skin the wee beggar. I will! And I don't care what the baron says aboot it. Ten years old, he should know better. Jock's too soft on him.'

'It's not Angus,' Haley assured him. 'I wanted to ask *you* a couple of questions, Mr Brae.'

'Questions? What about?'

'A few different things. But let's start with Angus's mother, Linda.'

Edwin startled, then turned away. Haley watched as the veil came down again: a shroud, falling over the old man's memory, turning everything to grey.

'You've lost him, I'm afraid,' the nurse whispered. 'Try again in a few minutes.'

She was right. As Haley looked on, Edwin visibly retreated back into his own inner world, a muffled chaos where no one could reach him. The change was so pronounced, it almost looked deliberate.

Perhaps it is? Haley found himself wondering. *Perhaps he only remembers what he wants to remember.*

'Mr Brae,' he tried again, 'when did you last see or hear from Linda?'

'What?' The old man looked up, pained. 'Who are you, now?'

'Edwin, do you know what happened to your wife after she left Pitfeldy?' Haley pressed him. 'Do you know where Linda is now?'

'GET OUT!' The eruption came out of nowhere, and was quite spectacular. Tea and biscuits flew everywhere as the wizened old man jumped out of his seat like a jack-in-the-box, his liver-spotted arms flailing around wildly and balls of spittle like tiny silver drops of mercury spraying from his shrivelled lips. 'You get out of here, you bastard. Go!'

'Edwin!' The nurse stepped forward in horror. 'Edwin, you stop this at once. Calm down, please. Calm down, and sit in your chair.'

Still shaking with rage, the old gillie did as he was told.

'I'm so sorry,' the nurse said to Haley. 'I don't know what's got into him. But I think you'd better go. Maybe try another time,' she whispered under her breath as Haley stood up. 'In an hour or two he'll have forgotten this ever happened.'

Outside in the car park, Haley reflected on his brief encounter with Edwin Brae. A number of things were bothering him about it, but right at this moment those things were tangled together in a giant, swirling, unhelpful mess.

Clearly, the mention of his wife had brought on a state of profound agitation. Haley didn't doubt the reaction was genuine. He just wasn't sure how to interpret it. One thing he knew for sure was that Edwin's outburst had very effectively brought their interaction to a close, and he found himself wondering if that had been the old man's intention. Something made him suspect that Angus's father and Jock MacKinnon's childhood friend was a lot smarter than he looked. Haley had had a string of questions, not only about Edwin's missing wife but also about the illegal foreign workers, nameless men and women to whom Edwin had turned a blind eye while he ran the estate. Now, thanks to the old man's tantrum, he was leaving without an answer to any of them.

That was irritating. But it wasn't the only thing bothering him. There were also Angus's paintings. By his own account, Angus rarely visited his father at the home, and yet his presence was everywhere in Edwin's tiny room. The old man had brought up his son's name almost immediately, too, albeit referring to Angus as a ten-year-old boy, one who was often in trouble. Was that true? Haley wondered. He'd also said something about 'the baron' being soft on Angus, implying that Jock had played some part in the boy's upbringing. Which might explain their present-day closeness, and the rivalry between Angus and Jock's own son, Rory. But it also begged questions of its own. Not least *why* would Edwin Brae defer to Jock MacKinnon on how to raise his own son, or even involve him in those decisions.

According to Angus, Jock never visited his old friend at Passages because Edwin wouldn't have known who he was. But that wasn't the impression Haley got at all. Edwin Brae might be confused about many things, but that confusion came and went. Both his son and Jock MacKinnon still appeared to be very much to the forefront of his consciousness.

They were with him in that poky little room, always. Not as their present selves, perhaps. But they were there all right.

A loud ringing from his mobile shattered Haley's reverie.

'DI Haley? It's Jill Vaisey.'

'I'm sorry, who?'

'Jill Vaisey. We spoke earlier? I'm Alice MacKinnon's dentist.'

'Oh, yes. Yes, of course,' stammered Haley.

'I found the records you were after.'

For a glorious moment Haley's spirits soared. But only for a moment.

'I'm afraid the teeth you found definitely weren't Alice's.'

Shit.

Shit, shit, shit.

'Your victim's teeth were in wonderful condition. But Alice MacKinnon had had several fillings, a crown and one full implant by the time she left our practice. Good dental habits don't appear to have been a priority in her youth, I'm afraid to say. Sorry I couldn't be more help.'

Haley could feel the exhaustion creeping into his bones as he got back in his car and made the short drive home to his bungalow. So much had happened today, and yet at the end of it all, he was no further forward identifying the Girls in the Wood than he had been when he woke up.

Things that *felt* important – the relationship between Angus Brae and his father; Jock MacKinnon's closeness to the family; the bizarre, mirror-image vanishing of the two ex-wives, Alice and Linda; the link to Shetland – turned out *not* to have been important in the end. It was looking definitively as if neither body belonged to Alice MacKinnon or Linda Brae. Nor were they listed on any missing persons databases, or at least not the ones that DI Haley had ready access to.

Which left, what? Not much. The migrant angle; a bag full of blueglass beads; and the threatening notes to Jock MacKinnon's fiancée that Iris Grey had brought him, crude attempts to implicate Jock in the killings. What had the notes made reference to? To the long-dead daughter, Mary. To Jock's 'whores' from the past.

Haley's thoughts drifted back to Iris Grey. He'd been impressed with her logic in trying to track down the letter writer, and he already knew her to be persistent. He'd read up on Iris's close involvement with the Dom Wetherby murder case down in Hampshire, and her dogged determination to bring Dom's killer to justice. It was all rather fascinating. *Iris* was fascinating.

By all accounts she hadn't known the famous author for long before he died, in what was initially ruled a suicide. She'd been commissioned to paint his portrait, just as she had with Kathy Miller, and Wetherby had been found dead when she was halfway through, drowned in the pond in his own back garden on Christmas Day. Any normal person would have taken their cheque and gone home at that point. But Iris Grey had stayed on in Hampshire, convinced Dom had been murdered and refusing to let the thing go, hammering away at the useless local police and following leads on her own until she'd tied all the threads together and had got a conviction.

Two convictions, in fact. In the end.

In some ways, Haley reflected, Iris would have made a great detective. But in other ways he wasn't so sure. You needed a tough hide to survive in this job, emotionally, and he definitely had Iris pegged as sensitive, like most artists. Then again, by those criteria, maybe he wasn't such a good detective himself anymore. Since Jean's death, he'd found himself caring more. Noticing more. Feeling more. He might not be an artist, but he could cry for Scotland.

Wearily, Stuart Haley stumbled into his bungalow, alone as always, and headed straight for his bed.

Chapter Twelve

The next morning, Kathy was still at her dressing table, blending the minimal make-up she always wore for her sittings with Iris, when Jock burst in.

'That's it,' he muttered furiously. 'That is *it*! I want that man fired. I mean it. I'm going to speak to Will Roebuck this morning and put a God-damned stop to this farce.'

'Who's Will Roebuck?' Kathy walked over to him, loosely tying the belt on her peach silk Agent Provocateur dressing gown so that a hint of cleavage was still visible.

'He's the chief constable, that's who. DI Haley won't know what's hit him.'

'Ah. Haley.' She sighed softly. Over the course of their year together, Kathy had learned to remain calm in the face of Jock's rages. The storm usually passed more quickly that way. 'What's he done now?'

'I'll tell you what he's done,' seethed Jock, unable at that moment to be distracted, even by his young fiancée's killer body. 'The jumped-up little oik has been harassing Edwin Brae. Grilling the poor fellow about his ex-wife, and God knows what. As if he hasn't been through enough.'

'How do you know he saw Edwin?' Kathy asked gently, pressing herself into his back as she snaked her arms around his chest.

'Angus told me,' said Jock, taking a single, deep breath and allowing himself to be embraced. 'The Johnnies at the home rang him last night. Told him Edwin was in a terrible way.'

'Well, I'm sorry to hear that,' murmured Kathy, 'but I'm sure DI Haley must have had his reasons.'

Kathy herself was torn about Haley. She knew that Iris liked him, and on the whole she trusted Iris's judgment. But at the same time, she suspected Iris shared some of the policeman's prejudices, particularly when it came to Jock, and that as a result she was blind to the way that Haley picked on him. All of which made her feel doubly protective of the man she was soon to make her husband.

Tightening her grip around him, she closed her eyes. Despite his age there was a solidity to Jock's body that had always comforted Kathy, and brought back cherished memories of her father, long-dead recollections that stirred back to life deep under her skin. Jock was yin to Kathy's yang in so many ways, hard to her soft, cold to her warm. He gave her something that her last husband never had, something that was hard to put into words, but that he expressed perfectly with his body, and the lean, unyielding physical strength that always felt protective, never threatening.

'You know, honey,' she said now, entwining her slender fingers with his, 'from what you've told me, Edwin probably won't even remember it happened. I bet he's fine this morning.'

'Maybe,' Jock grumbled. 'But that's not the point. This bastard Haley's up to something.'

'What if he is?' said Kathy, releasing him. 'He can't hurt you. Can't hurt *us*.'

Turning around, Jock took her in his arms, gazing down into her loving eyes with deep gratitude. It was a source of unending wonder to him that this heaven-sent woman, this girl who could have had anyone, had chosen him. And not just chosen him – *rescued* him – from Fiona and the brittle, loveless marriage that he'd come to accept as normal, an inevitable consequence of growing old and becoming set in one's ways.

Of course, intellectually he recognised that he hadn't behaved well with Fiona. He'd been a damaged man when he'd met her, having never fully recovered from the twin tragedies of Mary's death and Alice's abandonment. Fiona had tried her best to put him back together. But he'd repaid her kindness with cruelty, selfishness and relentless infidelity. The resulting resentment on Fiona's part became a poison that ran to the very roots of their union and ultimately made a split inevitable. But it was Jock who had caused it. Jock who was to blame, as his children never ceased to remind him. Especially Rory.

With his head, he knew it. But emotionally, he couldn't face what he'd done, couldn't cast himself as the villain. Now, thanks to Kathy, he didn't have to. It was all about 'chapters' and 'growth' and 'moving forward in love'. She saw only good in him, and he loved her for that more than he had ever loved anyone.

'I adore you,' he told her, sincerely. 'You're wonderful in every way.'

'How about my babies?' she replied teasingly, looking across at Milo and Sam Sam curled up adorably together in their basket. Jock's intolerance for Kathy's dogs had become something of a joke between them. 'Are they wonderful too?'

'No they are not.' Jock grinned. 'Look at them, sprawled all over each other, like some ghastly Hallmark greetings card.'

'You love them really,' Kathy cooed.

'I bloody well don't. Let's not forget, if it hadn't been for those mutts sniffing around my bothy, none of this would be happening.'

Kathy gave him a curious look. 'You don't mean that.'

'I *do*,' said Jock with feeling.

'But honey, two innocent women were killed up there,' Kathy chided him.

'How do you know they were innocent?' Jock clapped back. 'We don't know the faintest thing about them.'

'We know they existed,' said Kathy, who was beginning to find the conversation less amusing. 'And that someone murdered them. If Milo and Sam Sam hadn't found those bones, no one would ever have discovered them. Their killer would never be brought to justice. Doesn't that bother you?'

'Only because it bothers you, my love,' said Jock, adopting a slightly more conciliatory tone. 'What bothers me is that bastard Haley. You assume he's looking for justice for those women because that's what *you*'d be looking for. Because you're a good person, Kathy. But this has nothing to do with justice, my darling, and everything to do with envy. Class envy, and the politics of hatred,' he fumed, his dark mood returning. 'It's a witch hunt, and yours truly is the sodding witch.'

Kathy looked troubled, but Jock was on a roll.

'Angry, insignificant little men like Haley don't care who they trample over, just as long as they get the likes of me locked up, and justice be damned. But he picked the wrong enemy this time.'

Taking Kathy's face in both his hands, he kissed her tenderly on the mouth. 'You watch this space, my angel. I'm going to shut that man down.'

Iris was still in her painting overalls when the doorbell rang. Deep in concentration, she was rearranging the first floor of her dolls' house, adding some new bedroom furniture and, in pride of place, an exquisitely carved set of library steps that she'd ordered from a specialist dealer in Holland and that, finally, had arrived this morning. Since she'd got to Pitfeldy she'd been so busy, between working on the portrait and Kathy's letters and settling into Murray House, she'd barely had any time to indulge her hobby. But this evening at last, after a long and gruelling session up at the castle with Kathy, she'd opened an expensive bottle of Brunello, and a less expensive but equally delicious bar of Cadbury's fruit and nut chocolate, and settled down to focus on her beloved dolls. Nothing, absolutely nothing, relaxed her like creating these tiny rooms, imagining and staging an endlessly varied litany of domestic scenes in which she, Iris, was both writer and director. Or, as her ex, Ian, used to say, 'God'.

'You just like playing God,' he would tell her, only half jokingly. 'You can dress it up as artistry all you like, my dear, but I see through you.'

Occasionally, Iris admitted, Ian could be quite insightful. Just not about himself, unfortunately.

Please be a delivery, she thought, getting up as the door buzzed a second time. *Or anyone else I can get rid of quickly.* All she asked for was one solitary evening with her dolls. *And please don't be Mrs Rivers*, she added, with rising panic. Her landlady's impromptu visits were well intentioned but they'd been known to take over an hour. Now that Iris came to think of it, she wasn't sure that anyone else had ever rung the doorbell at Murray House in the time she'd been there.

Putting on her best, 'this had better not take long' expression, she pulled open the door.

'Have I come at a bad time?' Jamie Ingall hovered nervously on the doorstep. He'd debated the wisdom of showing up at Iris's place, especially dressed as he was in oilskins, having come straight from the boat. But if they were ever going to have a proper date, he needed to do something. Much to his disappointment, Iris hadn't called since he'd given her his number at the Fisherman's Arms, all those weeks ago – which put the ball firmly back in his court.

'No, no,' she stammered. 'Not at all.' But everything about Iris's face and body language suggested otherwise.

God, he was good-looking, standing there on her doorstep, smelling of herring and seawater (which, oddly, wasn't nearly as bad as it sounded). 'Well, I mean actually, yes, sort of,' she corrected herself hurriedly, remembering the dolls' house paraphernalia scattered around the room behind her. She told herself she was no longer ashamed of her hobby, but at the same time she absolutely did *not* want Jamie to see it.

She'd almost rung him a few times since their meeting in the pub, but on each occasion her nerve had failed her. Or perhaps common sense had got the better of her, depending on how you looked at it. The boy was half her age after all, and apart from an undeniable urge to jump each other's bones, it was hard to imagine what they might have in common.

'Right. OK.' He looked crestfallen. 'I should have called first. Then again, you never called *me*, about dinner.'

Iris's stomach churned so violently she felt sure it must be audible.

'I'm sorry. I meant to. I've just been really busy.'

'Me too, as it happens,' said Jamie. 'I've been out a lot, on the boat.'

'Right.'

A painful silence ensued. *Oh God*, thought Iris. Why was this so difficult? Why couldn't she just talk to him naturally and go out for dinner like a normal person?

'How are the fish?' she blurted.

Jamie's worried face suddenly cracked into a huge grin. 'They're well, thanks.'

How are the fish? Iris cringed inside. What on earth was wrong with her?

'How are your paints?' he teased her.

'Good.' Iris cleared her throat and blushed scarlet. 'Thank you. Yes. The paints are, erm – excellent.'

'So can I buy you dinner tomorrow night?' Jamie asked, still smiling.

'Tomorrow?'

'Aye. As you're busy tonight. How does eight o'clock at Maria's sound? It's the wee Italian opposite the Fisherman's.'

Iris made a noise that could have been anything, but Jamie chose to take it as an affirmative.

'Grand. I'll pick you up here at seven-thirty. And I promise to take a shower first.' He looked down apologetically at his smelly oilskins one last time, before quitting while he was ahead and disappearing into the twilight.

Closing the door behind her, Iris let out a wail of embarrassment, before walking back over to her dolls' house, picking up her glass of wine and downing what was left of it in one gulp. Stuffing her mouth completely full of chocolate, looking and feeling increasingly like a nutcase, she poured herself a second glass and sat down to steady her nerves.

Dinner. That was all it was, she told herself firmly. Just a simple dinner. Now why was that so terrifying?

For the millionth time, Iris wished that her real life was as calm and under control as the world of her dolls' house.

Chapter Thirteen

'Ms Grey? Iris? Do you have a minute?'

Iris had just stepped out of the post office and was heading back to her car when an animated Stuart Haley flagged her down.

'Are you off somewhere?' he asked, looking at the Mini Cooper keys in her hand.

'Just to the castle. Another portrait session,' said Iris, blowing on her fingers against the cold. It was only the first week of October, but this morning's frost had been as thick as snow. Even in her puffa coat, gloves and fur-lined boots, Iris felt underdressed. She glanced towards her warm car longingly.

'We can talk in the car, if you like,' said Haley, following her line of sight. 'It won't take long.'

Ensconced in Iris's tiny car, with the ignition on and the hot air blasting, he got straight to the point.

'I need your help.'

'Of course,' said Iris. 'With what?'

'With the case.' Haley looked at her seriously 'Off the record, obviously. If anybody asks, I never asked you to get involved, and we never had this conversation. But the truth is, I'm getting nowhere fast identifying these bodies. I was impressed by your thinking on those threatening letters.'

'Well, thank you,' said Iris. 'But I'm really not . . .'

'And I know how instrumental you were in bringing Dom Wetherby's killer to justice,' Haley interrupted her.

Iris held up a hand. 'Hold on. That was different.'

'Was it?' asked Haley. 'How?'

'Well, because it was a one-off,' said Iris, feeling increasingly flustered. 'I happened to be there when it all kicked off, you see. So I sort of found myself drawn in. It wasn't a conscious decision.'

'You happen to be here, too, don't you?' Haley pointed out.

'Yes,' admitted Iris.

'And you've already been "drawn in" with these threatening letters to Kathy Miller.'

'Well, yes, I suppose so,' said Iris. Was it just her, or had it suddenly become uncomfortably hot in here? 'But it's still different. I knew Dom. I was painting his portrait and living in his guest cottage. I saw him every day, so when he drowned, it was personal.'

Haley nodded understandingly. 'I get it. You don't know these victims, these women,' he said. 'But that's the problem, isn't it? Nobody knows them. Nobody cares. Whoever they were they've been forgotten. Their lives, and deaths, don't matter to anyone at all. Except the bastard who killed them, of course, and who thinks he's got away wi' it. At this rate, unfortunately, he's probably right.' He let his words hang in the air for a few moments, watching Iris squirm as she wrestled with her conscience, and with the deep sense of empathy that Haley had noticed in her from the start and was now attempting to manipulate, with consummate skill. 'I don't mean to pressure you,' he said softly.

Iris laughed. 'Oh yes you do.'

'OK, well, mebbe I do a little bit,' he admitted, smiling. 'But only because I know you care. And that you don't like letting things lie. Also, you know, you're actually pretty good at this stuff.'

'Don't try and flatter me.' Iris's eyes narrowed.

'OK, OK,' Haley said. 'I won't. Take a look at these.' Reaching into his jacket pocket, he pulled out a clear plastic evidence bag containing the blue-green glass beads that Milo had so helpfully 'removed' from the bothy. 'They're blown glass, and we now think they probably came from a necklace belonging to one of the victims,' he told Iris. 'I've posted pictures on our public appeal website, in case anyone recognises them. But as about two and half people log onto that per week, I'm no holding my breath.'

'May I?' said Iris, opening the bag.

Haley nodded and she reached inside thoughtfully, rubbing her fingers over the smooth glass balls.

'Remind me,' Haley said casually. 'How many people visited your Facebook page during the Wetherby case? Just . . . ballpark.'

Iris scowled at him. 'That was *different*!'

'So you keep saying.'

'That case was national news.'

'So might this be, if you got involved. Ach, come on, Iris, I've seen those online trolls of yours, and they're only a fraction of the people logging on. If you were to set up a Facebook page, specifically for the Girls in the Wood, I bet you we'd have thousands of hits. You've got a far better chance of finding someone who recognises that necklace than I do.'

If this was DI Haley not pressuring someone, Iris dreaded to think what he was like when he decided to turn the screws.

It was working, though. Holding the pretty orbs of glass in her hand, she couldn't help but imagine the necklace hanging around a young woman's neck, each bead iridescent against her skin like a miniature glass earth. She pictured the necklace breaking, snapping, perhaps at the moment of the woman's death; the beads scattering into the earth, just like her bones. Broken. Destroyed. Buried, deep beneath the rubble and the Scottish peat, never to be discovered. Or so the killer must have thought.

'All right,' she said, resealing the bag.

'You'll do it?' Haley couldn't hide his elation.

'I'll set up a Facebook page and post some pictures of the beads.'

'That's fantastic!' Without thinking, he leaned over and hugged her.

'Just the beads, though. And maybe a general press release about the bodies. Not the letters. I promised Kathy I'd keep them secret, and they're probably not related anyway.'

'Understood,' said Haley.

'Don't get your hopes up,' Iris pleaded. 'I can't make any promises, and for what it's worth, I think you've greatly overestimated my powers.'

'No promises,' said Haley, reaching for the door. He knew how to quit while he was ahead. 'And like I said, should anyone ask, you and I never had this conversation. Enjoy your painting.'

Just like that, he was gone. And for the second time since she'd got to Pitfeldy, Iris found herself sucked into helping solve a mystery.

Is it that I'm crap at saying no? she wondered. *Or that I'm crap at admitting that I actually want to say yes?*

She was still pondering the question ten minutes later, when she pulled into the drive at the castle.

The sitting went better than usual. Deciding it was probably safer to steer clear of the topic of Haley and the Girls in the Wood, at least for the time being, Iris happened to let slip that she'd been asked out to dinner by a local fisherman. Kathy's gossip radar went into instant overdrive. She insisted Iris tell her every last detail about Jamie Ingall – how they had met, what he looked like, where he was taking her tonight. Usually, Iris would have bristled at being asked to reveal so much about herself, but on this occasion it was a relief to have Kathy distracted. And sitting still for once, happy to listen instead of talk. By the time Iris left, she'd almost finished the dreaded hair, which was looking a *lot* better. Both women felt that progress had been made.

'You look happy, darling,' Jock observed, walking up behind Kathy at the front door as she waved Iris off. The rain had just begun to set in, and a grey sheet had soon swallowed Iris's little car completely. 'Good sitting?'

'It was,' Kathy sighed, filling him in on the exciting developments in Iris's social life. 'Do you know this place, Maria's? Maybe we should go out for dinner some time. I can't remember the last time we didn't eat at home.'

'I'll take you to Edinburgh or to London, if you want to go out.' Jock smiled indulgently. 'But I'm not about to sit in some dreary café in Pitfeldy frequented by trawlermen. We'll both be poisoned.'

'Don't be such a snob,' Kathy teased him, punching him affectionately on the shoulder. 'Iris said it looked really cute when she drove by. She's playing it down, but I think she's kind of excited.'

Jock pulled her to him, taking a stray strand of honey-blonde hair between his fingers and stroking it lovingly. 'You're fond of Iris, aren't you?'

Kathy nodded. 'She's becoming a good friend.'

'What is it you like about her?' he asked, cocking his head curiously to one side.

'I don't know, exactly,' admitted Kathy. 'I suppose I like that she's smart. And honest. And she doesn't judge.'

'Doesn't she?' Jock asked, still fiddling with the strand of hair. 'I wouldn't be so sure about that. I'd say she's already judged *me* pretty harshly.'

'Well, you haven't exactly been very warm towards her either,' said Kathy, standing up on tiptoes so as to be able to reach her arms around his neck.

'What do you mean?'

'Just that you could make a bit more of an effort,' said Kathy.

'I don't see why I should.' Jock bristled.

Kathy pulled away abruptly. 'For me. You should for me, Jock. Iris is the only friend I have here. The only one. Don't you *see* that?'

'That's not true,' he mumbled half-heartedly, because he knew it was. 'It takes time to settle in when you move somewhere new, that's all.'

'Bullshit,' Kathy retorted passionately. The last thing she'd intended was to get into an argument, but some lock inside her seemed to have slid open suddenly, and a torrent of suppressed emotions came gushing out. 'This has nothing to do with *time*, Jock. Your children hate me because I'm not their mother.

The locals hate me because I'm American, and a woman, and young, and because I have ideas of my own, good ideas, and I refuse to shut up about them. I mean, why shouldn't I write my own vows, hmm? Why shouldn't I?'

Jock opened his mouth to speak but Kathy wasn't done yet.

'*Someone* hates me enough to have spent the last three months writing me spiteful letters, designed to intimidate me and to get me to leave *you*.' She jabbed a finger in Jock's direction, her eyes welling up with angry, exhausted tears. 'You have no idea what that's been like, Jock. I turned to Iris because she understood. From the beginning, she was the only one willing even to give me a chance, the only one willing to listen.'

'*I* listen,' Jock objected, finally forcing a word in edgeways. 'Be fair, darling. You didn't even tell me about the letters till the other day.'

'I know you were annoyed that I took Iris up to the bothy,' Kathy went on, too caught up in her own emotions to be able to listen to reason. 'But I wanted to show her what I was planning for the visitors' centre. I wanted the opinion of the one person – *one* – who hadn't already written me off.'

'My darling, I never wrote you off . . .'

'But of course, I never got Iris's approval because we found those poor girls and – and –' She broke off, exploding suddenly and spectacularly into sobs.

Shocked, Jock wrapped his arms around her. There didn't seem much else to be done, at least not until she calmed down.

After a few minutes, once the worst of the storm had passed, he cleared his throat and risked a speech of his own.

'Listen, my angel. I know this isn't what you want to hear, but I think, with hindsight, we made a mistake picking a fight with the vicar and refusing to hold the fair up at the castle. I know, I know, it was my decision as well. And you have every right to write your own vows,' he said quickly, holding up a hand to stop the torrent of objections he suspected were imminent. 'But life isn't always simply about one's rights, is it? It's also about feelings, and emotions and *traditions*. Tradition is very important in a place like Pitfeldy. I'm not saying it should be. Only that it *is*, and you must try not to take that so personally.'

Kathy looked up at him, astonished by this speech. It wasn't like Jock to talk about 'feelings' and 'emotions'.

'When did you get so wise?' she sniffed. Even red-eyed and with a shiny nose from crying, she looked heartbreakingly ravishing.

'I've always been wise,' Jock grinned, 'you were just too stroppy to notice.'

'Stroppy,' said Kathy. 'That's a great word. Do you think people here will ever accept me?' she added in a rare flash of vulnerability.

'Of course they will. They were miffed about the fair, and perhaps a bit about all the visitors' centre stuff as well. But that's all, and it's easily fixed. We just need to do something to make it up to them. Host some sort of – event.'

'A party!' Kathy brightened. 'That's a great idea.'

'Well, not necessarily a party, per se,' said Jock. But it was too late for notes of caution.

'A Halloween party,' Kathy gasped, struck by sudden inspiration. 'I mean, it's October, and this place would be perfect for that. Spooky fun up at the castle. Oh my God, how awesome would that be?'

'Hmm. Possibly.' Jock sounded doubtful. 'Halloween's not really as big a thing here as it is in the States.'

'Oh, sure it is, honey,' said Kathy. 'Or at least, it will be once we throw the party of the century, right here. Oh Jock!' She kissed him passionately. 'Thank you for suggesting it. And thank you for letting me moan. I'll organise everything. Maybe Iris can help me –'

'About Iris,' said Jock, treading carefully. He didn't want to risk upsetting her again. 'I'm happy that you've found a friend.'

'Are you sure about that?' Kathy asked archly.

'Yes,' Jock insisted. 'But I would also ask you to be careful. Iris seems to make a bit of a habit of poking her nose into other people's lives. There was that business in Hampshire, as you know, with that chap Wetherby –'

'You mean the "business" where she solved the guy's murder?' Kathy challenged him. 'Isn't that a good thing? I mean, wouldn't it be a good thing if Iris helped find out who killed the women in our woods?'

'Of course it would,' said Jock placatingly. 'Although seeing as no one even knows who those women *were*, it seems unlikely. But that's not my point, dearest. All I'm trying to say is you haven't known Iris very long.'

'I've known her long enough to know I like her.'

'Liking someone is one thing,' said Jock. 'Trusting them with your deepest secrets, or even sharing personal, private family matters? That's something else. Like I say, I don't doubt that Iris likes you too. But her feelings for *me* may be more complicated. Especially with that blasted Haley whispering in her ear.'

'OK, honey,' Kathy said kindly. She felt more willing to meet him halfway now that he'd been so sweet to her. Plus, now she had the distraction of a party to plan, as well as the wedding. She felt sure she was up to the challenge and that, this time, she'd win the prickly locals over and get them to like her, or at least to accept her before she became Lady Pitfeldy. 'I'll be careful with Iris. I promise.'

Maria's turned out to be exactly as Iris had described it to Kathy – charming, friendly and intimate. A small room with white-washed walls and scrubbed wooden floors housed a minuscule bar, an open pizza oven and ten modest tables set with cheerful red gingham cloths and mismatched china. There were paper menus, plus a long list of daily specials handwritten on the chalk board behind the bar, most of them simple pastas and salads. The place was full, which made for a good atmosphere, if a little more noisy than Iris would have liked. All the bodies also served to raise the temperature, especially combined with the heat blasting from the pizza oven. Jamie peeled off his sweater the instant they arrived, revealing toned but pasty-white arms beneath his grey T-shirt. Meanwhile, Iris slipped out of her raincoat, feeling relieved that she'd chosen a more summery cotton dress to wear underneath and not the slinky cashmere number she'd almost gone for, but had rejected for being too sexy. In fact, it would have made her look like a boiled lobster, so that was one bullet dodged at least.

'Am I talking too much?' she asked suddenly, putting down her wine and taking a slow and deliberate bite of prosciutto pizza, being careful not to let any straggly bits of melted mozzarella attach themselves wantonly to her chin.

'No. Not at all,' Jamie assured her, refilling her glass.

But she knew she was. Jamie had started asking her questions the moment they sat down, and a lethal combination of nerves and wine seemed to have acted like some sort of Tourette's-inducing serum on Iris's brain. They were only halfway through the main course, and she was already borderline drunk and spewing out anecdotes about which of her past portrait subjects had been the worst lungers, like a teenage girl gossiping to her gay best friend.

'Tell me about your work.' She attempted to change the subject.

'Like what? There's nothing to tell.'

'I don't know,' said Iris. 'You must have some stories.'

Jamie pulled a face. 'Herring aren't really known for their wild and crazy antics.'

'So you're not like George Clooney in *A Perfect Storm*?' Iris teased him.

'Sadly not.' Jamie laughed, finishing the last forkful of his vast plate of spaghetti carbonara. 'So what's the latest with the bodies in the bothy?' he asked casually. 'Or what is it the papers calling them now? The Girls in the Wood? Do they know who they were yet?'

'I don't know why you're asking me,' said Iris.

'Ach, come on, sure you do. You're my woman on the inside,' said Jamie, perusing the dessert menu before beckoning the waitress over and giving his order. 'So what's new?'

Impulsively, she decided to confide in him about Haley's request for her help. 'It's all very off the record,' she explained as the waitress came to clear their plates. 'I think the main thing he wants is for me to use my social media platform, such as it is, to get the word out there.'

She told him about the glass beads found at the scene, for some reason omitting the part about exactly how the police had stumbled upon that evidence.

'I didn't know they'd found any jewellery up there,' said Jamie.

'Well, exactly. Nobody does – or did,' said Iris. 'I posted the images on my Facebook page this afternoon. You never know, maybe someone will recognise the beads as part of a necklace they once made, or bought, or saw somebody wearing.'

'Your Facebook page, eh?' Jamie mused, looking at Iris in a way that made her stomach flip over. 'I'll have to give that a wee look.'

Raised voices near the door made both of them turn and look.

'There's no need to make a scene, Simon,' a young woman was saying plaintively, as her boyfriend stood up suddenly, demanding their bill. 'Let's just go.'

'We are just going,' the boyfriend snarled. 'D'you think I'd stay here now? D'you think I could eat another bloody bite?'

Tossing notes down on the table, he pushed his way towards the door, where an older customer had just walked in. Only now, when he turned, did Iris recognise him as the headmaster from the church fair. The man she and Jamie had beaten at the coconut shy the day they first met.

'Isn't that . . .?' she whispered, the name escaping her.

'John Donnelly. Aye. You've a good memory.'

The angry young man seemed to make a point of glaring at Donnelly, even banging into him deliberately with his shoulder as he stormed out, trailed by his unfortunate-looking girlfriend. Iris watched the interaction closely and with interest. Was John Donnelly's arrival the reason that the young man had left? Moments later, the headmaster picked up his own lonely bag of takeout and also left, and the normal hum of conversation resumed.

'How well do you know him?' Iris asked Jamie, a connection beginning to form in the back of her mind.

Jamie shrugged. 'He was my headmaster. I see him around. I like him. Why?'

'It's probably nothing,' said Iris. 'It's just that he seems to rub a lot of people up the wrong way.'

'Does he?' Jamie frowned.

'Well, there was obviously something going on just now, between him and that fellow,' said Iris.

'Was there?' Jamie's frown deepened. He wasn't angry, just surprised.

'Definitely,' Iris insisted. 'And the last time I saw him, as I was leaving the fair, I remember he was arguing heatedly then too, with Angus Brae. I'd forgotten all about it till now.'

'John and Angus?' repeated Jamie. 'Are you sure about that?'

'Quite sure,' said Iris. 'Donnelly was accusing Angus of threatening him about something. And Angus did *seem* threatening at the time, I remember it distinctly. Which is odd, because every other time I've seen Angus, he's always been so gentle and calm, not aggressive at all.'

'Well,' said Jamie, beaming with childish delight as a large, steaming bowl of treacle tart was set down in front of him, and apparently forgetting all about John Donnelly. 'Angus has always been a bit of an odd bod, if you ask me.'

'I didn't know you knew him,' said Iris.

'Everyone knows everyone in Pitfeldy,' observed Jamie, digging into his pudding with glee.

'Do you know him well?'

'Well enough. We were at school together, all the way through our Nationals.'

'What happened after that?' asked Iris.

'Angus stayed on for his Highers,' said Jamie. 'He's always been really bright.'

'And you didn't?'

'Me?' He looked at her, astonished. 'No way. That was never on the cards for me. I left to go on the boats.'

Iris paused for a moment to take this in. Was it weird that she, an Oxford graduate in her forties, was being taken out to dinner by a thirty-something fisherman who'd left school after his Nationals?

Yes, surely, was the answer to that. And yet it didn't feel weird. In fact, it felt weirdly normal.

'What was Angus like at school?' she asked, curious suddenly about this previously unknown connection.

Jamie thought about it. 'Quiet. He was quiet.'

'Unpopular?' Iris tried to read between the lines.

'Not exactly. He wasn't disliked, but he was a loner. "Gentle and calm", like you said, I suppose. Arty. We all thought he was gay.'

'Really?' Iris looked up. 'But isn't he with that girl?'

'Hannah, aye. He is now, so who knows,' admitted Jamie. 'Maybe we were wrong.'

Iris digested this. 'And John Donnelly – is he gay?'

'As a maypole,' Jamie confirmed cheerfully. 'But he's also a really good guy, whatever you've heard to the contrary. Kind, upstanding, super-moral. I'll eat my hat if anything ever went on between him and Angus sexually, if that's what you're driving at.'

Iris wasn't sure what she was driving at. Other than the fact that there *was* bad blood between Angus Brae and his old headmaster. She knew she hadn't misremembered what had happened at the fair. And that it must have come from somewhere.

'John Donnelly could no more shag one of his pupils than fly to the moon,' said Jamie, reading her mind. 'He's like the Sam Eagle of Pitfeldy.'

'I'm amazed you know who Sam Eagle is,' observed Iris, watching Jamie dispatch the last spoonful of tart in record time. He might be laid-back in all other ways, but he certainly ate like a man in a hurry.

'I'm not a total philistine, you know,' he said, reaching across the table and grabbing both Iris's hands in his without even a flicker of hesitation. Whatever else he lacked, it wasn't confidence. 'I might not know about Shakespeare or classical music, but I've heard of the bloody Muppets.'

Jamie walked Iris home, slipping one long arm easily around her shoulders as they strolled through Pitfeldy's dark streets, still slick with rain from the afternoon's downpour. Iris leaned into him, happy, saying little as her mind whirred, flitting between thoughts of Angus Brae and John Donnelly, and a mental image of those blueglass beads, hanging around the neck of a smiling young woman. A young woman Iris was starting to feel increasingly close to, but whose face she still couldn't see.

Who are you?

'What was that now?' Jamie looked down at her with a puzzled look, removing his arm. They'd arrived at Murray House, and Iris realised she must have spoken aloud.

'Nothing. Sorry,' she blabbered. 'I was miles away.'

'I noticed.'

He said it kindly. Unusually for a young person, Jamie seemed to be perfectly comfortable with silence. Yet another sign of his self-confidence, Iris reflected, his happiness in his own skin.

'Thank you for a lovely dinner.'

She stood on the doorstep, her raincoat belted tightly around her, swaying slightly.

'My pleasure.'

He took a step towards her, stopping with his face just inches from hers. With Iris standing up on the step, and Jamie in the street, their eyes and lips were level. Instinctively, Iris closed her eyes, waiting for the kiss. But when it came it was chaste and brief, little more than a brush against her cheek.

'Goodnight.'

'Goodnight.'

Iris's eyes snapped open. Hiding her blushes in the darkness, she watched him turn and walk away.

Chapter Fourteen

Iris felt a small thrill as she crunched her way across the gravel towards the castle. Tonight's Halloween party had been hotly awaited in the village for the past three weeks, with even the most ardent Kathy-haters excited by the prospect of a night of dancing, costumes and, most importantly, a free bar, all at Baron Pitfeldy's expense. God knew there was usually precious little to do in rural Scotland in late October, and the added excitement of a double murder provided an additional frisson to the general spookiness.

Iris saw at once that Kathy had made a titanic effort. Even before you got inside the castle, you walked down a driveway lined with grinning, candlelit pumpkins – Jack-o'-lanterns as the Americans called them – some elaborately carved to look like bats or ghouls or witches' cats. The weather had been kind, offering up a rain- and cloud-free night where you could see the stars, as well as your own breath in the crisp, cold air. On either side of the castle doors, thrown open to welcome revellers, two enormous flame torches had been lit and chained to the walls, and all sorts of delicious smells wafted out on a warm cloud from the kitchens. Savoury scents of onion and garlic and fresh-baked bread battled it out with sweeter rivals like cinnamon, apple and sugary clove, heavy-baked treats to help soak up the (free-flowing) whisky. Iris could feel her mouth start to water, and her body start to sway to the fiddle music coming from somewhere deep in the recesses of the house, only partially audible over the low, humming throb of conversation. A lot of people were obviously here already, and it was only eight o'clock.

Good, Iris thought. Kathy needed a win, and she deserved one. After the whole debacle with the church fair back in August, refusing to hold it in the castle grounds, she'd lost what small modicum of support she'd ever had in the village. And for all her protestations that she didn't care what Pitfeldy folk thought of her, Iris knew full well that she did. Once she married Jock and became Lady Pitfeldy, Kathy would need the locals' acceptance. Especially if, one day, she wanted to make good on her plans to open the castle to the public and run it as some sort of going concern. The fact that so many villagers had turned up tonight was definitely a good sign, and in costume, too, really getting into the spirit of things. Iris saw Frankenstein's monsters, Disney princesses, latex-masked politicians and a solid smattering of kilted Bravehearts all rubbing shoulders happily. For all the mutterings she'd heard locally, about Halloween being an American affectation and Kathy having 'turned Jock's head', it seemed to Iris that an effort had been made on both sides.

She herself felt slightly self-conscious in her home-made Dorothy from *The Wizard of Oz* outfit, complete with short gingham dress, ruby slippers, cape and wicker basket, with a little toy dog inside. Her hair wasn't long enough for pigtails so she'd gone for drawn-on freckles and a bow, all of which she'd been thoroughly pleased with yesterday, but which she now worried looked a bit Schoolgirl Porn and over the top.

'My goodness, Iris. Don't you look marvellous.'

A Regency fop in silk breeches, tights, a brocade jacket and elaborate wig greeted her somewhat leeringly at the door, his eyes roving appreciatively over Iris's mostly bare legs.

'Do I?' Iris blushed. It took her a moment to recognise the fop as Fergus Twomey, Emma MacKinnon's huntbore husband. She hadn't seen Fergus since the weekend she'd arrived at Pitfeldy, and she had to admit she hadn't missed him. 'Well, thank you. You look pretty natty yourself.'

Fergus did his best theatrical bow as Emma bustled up beside him. Crinolined up in an ugly pink blancmange of a dress, the bodice of which thrust her huge breasts vertically upwards like two giant softballs beneath her chin, she looked as plump and ruddy-cheeked as Iris remembered.

'Hello, Iris.' Emma smiled thinly, eyeing Iris's bare legs with matronly disapproval. Iris suspected that she had been filed by both the MacKinnon children as 'Kathy's friend' and therefore not to be trusted. 'You look – cold.'

'I am a bit,' Iris admitted cheerfully. 'Still, I expect it's warmer inside. Which way to the bar?'

'The closest one's in the library,' said Fergus. 'But you'll have a job battling your way through. It's wall-to-wall grockles, I'm afraid,' he added in a stage whisper. 'My future stepmother-in-law's idea of noblesse oblige.'

'Noblesse? Please,' Emma sneered, sounding more like her brother Rory than Iris remembered. She wondered whether the siblings had been spending more time together recently. 'Kathy's more of a pleb than any of them. You should see her in there, swanning around like she owns the place in that ridiculous dress, pressing the flesh.'

In a couple of months, she will own the place, thought Iris, wondering what Kathy had chosen to wear for tonight's event and whether it was, in fact, ridiculous, or whether Emma was just being bitchy.

'Poor Daddy,' Emma sighed. 'He's smiling away next to her, but you can tell inside he's mortified. This entire party's an abomination.'

Unable to stand the meanness a minute longer, Iris made her excuses and pushed through to the bar, suddenly feeling more in need of a drink than ever. She didn't blame Emma for disliking the woman who'd bewitched her father and put the final nail in the coffin of her parents' marriage. That was understandable. It was the ingrained snobbery that she found so horridly depressing, especially among the younger generation.

She quickly forgot about Emma and Fergus, however, distracted by the throng of guests packing the library and the drawing room and ballroom beyond. There were at least three hundred people here, not counting the waiting staff, whom Kathy had brilliantly dressed as skeletons in black jumpsuits with painted-on, glow-in-the-dark bones. Iris only knew a smattering of the guests: Jock's family and one or two locals, although even they were hard to pick out beneath the various masks and disguises.

Emma's and Fergus's children were running around, both dressed as Power Rangers and having a whale of a time playing chase with village kids whom their parents would no doubt deem 'unsuitable', stuffing their faces with crisps and peanuts from the skull bowls Kathy had put out everywhere.

Rory stood out like a sore thumb in a suit and tie, a plain, Zorro-style mask his only concession to fancy dress or the Halloween theme. Was it vanity that made him reluctant to dress up, Iris wondered? Or snobbery, his usual, above-it-all aloofness? He certainly had plenty of both, and was fully aware of how handsome he looked, and the attention women paid him. Iris wondered if the sexy brunette standing next to him was his date, or just a colleague or friend from London. Dressed as Catwoman, the girl leaned in towards him when he spoke, visibly hanging on his every word. But Rory as good as ignored her, continuing to regale a small group of Jock's aristo cronies without paying her any particular attention.

Moving into the drawing room, Iris spotted the vicar, Michaela, dressed rather splendidly as Joan of Arc complete with a stake up her back. John Donnelly was there too as a paunchy Batman, chatting up some of the Pitfeldy School parents. Iris hadn't seen Donnelly since that night at Maria's with Jamie. Their dinner date had only been just over three weeks ago, but it felt far longer, probably because Iris hadn't seen Jamie since, and had heard nothing from him beyond a few friendly texts. She tried not to mind. After all, they were both busy, and she was by no means sure she wanted things to go any further with Jamie anyway. *She* hadn't called *him* either, so she could hardly complain. But on some subconscious level it rankled, enough to make her turn away from Donnelly and the unwanted memory.

Walking into the ballroom, the first person Iris saw was Brenda, the landlady from the Fisherman's Arms, knocking back the whisky chasers with a group of girlfriends. She was dressed as Bet Lynch from *Coronation Street*, a tower of hair-sprayed blonde curls teetering precariously over her shiny round face, and she looked spectacular. Smiling, Iris moved past her and immediately found herself confronted by a gaggle of local trawlermen. Wearing their oilskins and rubber boots, presumably playing themselves – one or two even carried nets – they were laughing loudly at one another's jokes and availing themselves frequently of the glowing skeletons' trays of goodies.

To Iris's simultaneous disappointment and relief, Jamie didn't appear to be among them. She was wondering where he was tonight when the trawlermen turned as one, like a school of fish, gawping at something at the far end of the room.

Following their gaze, Iris's own mouth fell open, like the proverbial stunned mullet. Kathy, holding Jock's hand, had appeared in the wide, double doorway like a vision. She looked exquisite, more beautiful than even Iris had ever seen her. In a clinging white chiffon gown that seemed glued to her spectacular body, with matching gold and diamond bracelets at her wrists, and something similar encircling her head – a wreath of some sort, from which flowed a long, gossamer-fine lace veil – she lit up the room like a firework. A red, jagged line of fake blood painted across her neck and down towards the top of her breasts was weirdly erotic; more so, although in a rather disturbing way, when Jock, dressed all in black as a horribly convincing Dracula, leaned down and pretended to plunge his fangs into the smooth white skin above her collarbone.

The monster and his bride, thought Iris.

If Jock was 'mortified' by his fiancée's outfit, as Emma Twomey claimed, then he was doing a bloody good job of hiding it. Standing there in his cape like a vile, predatory black crow, grinning and preening himself, he seemed to Iris to be practically throbbing with pride that Kathy was at his side. As well he might be. She looked amazing.

'Hello.'

Iris jumped. Rory MacKinnon had materialised beside her, minus Catwoman, with two flutes of champagne in his hands.

'On your own tonight?'

He handed one of the glasses to Iris, who accepted it warily.

'Yes. You?'

He gave a tight smile. 'I came with a friend. I thought you might have brought your policeman chum along. Haley.'

Iris frowned.

'Why would you think that?'

'Oh, I don't know.' Rory shrugged. 'Just village talk, I suppose. I heard the two of you were thick as thieves.'

Iris found it hard to believe that anyone in the village would be talking about her and DI Haley. Although, coincidentally, she had been wondering where Stuart was this evening, before Rory had brought it up.

What's he fishing for? she wondered.

'No one in Pitfeldy seems to have anything better to do than gossip about these bodies of yours,' Rory drawled, apparently determined to needle her into a response.

'The bodies aren't *mine*,' she replied coolly. 'I just happened to find them.'

'Indeed. You and your *muse*.' He layered the last word with sarcasm, looking over to where Kathy had freed herself from Jock and was now chatting happily to the wife of one of the tenant farmers.

'You could give her a break, you know,' Iris found herself saying. 'She's trying.'

'Oh, she's trying all right,' said Rory wryly, sipping his champagne. 'Trying to get her hands on every last penny of Dad's money.'

'I thought you were drawing up the prenup?' Iris observed, sipping her own drink.

Rory's eyes narrowed. 'Did she tell you that?'

'Why? Was it supposed to be a secret?' Iris asked guilelessly.

'Not a secret,' he sounded irritated. 'But a private family

matter, yes. Although God knows why I'd expect *her* to respect something like that,' he added bitterly.

'Surely the important thing is that if you're drawing up the prenup, then Kathy's no threat to you,' said Iris. 'You can protect your and your sister's inheritance, if that's really what you're worried about.'

'Oh, I'm worried about a lot of things, Miss Grey,' Rory said sourly. 'If your friend Kathy Miller had a modicum of sense, she'd be worried too.'

'Oh?' Iris eyed him suspiciously. 'About what?'

Rory grunted and looked away, aware perhaps that he'd said more than he'd meant to. 'Never mind.'

Raised voices from the other side of the room distracted both of them momentarily. It appeared that Mrs Gregory, the castle housekeeper, was having a heated exchange with Hannah Drummond, Angus's girlfriend.

'I'd better go and sort that out,' said Rory, draining his drink. Then, looking Iris squarely in the eye, he added, 'I hope you and I can at least be civil to one another while you're in Pitfeldy, Miss Grey.'

'Of course,' said Iris, surprised. 'Why wouldn't we be?'

'I just meant – I've no quarrel with you, personally.'

'Nor I with you,' said Iris, more confused than ever.

Why was he so awkward all of a sudden? Was he trying to tell her something? Or was he playing some sort of double game?

If so, Iris had no idea what it was, or why he was playing it. She felt very much on the back foot all of a sudden.

'Good,' he said, apparently satisfied, 'that's settled then. Oh, and do give your detective friend my regards when you see him again, won't you?'

And with that, he was gone, slipping into the throng of guests and making his way towards his father's housekeeper like a slimy black eel.

Chapter Fifteen

'You're a lucky man, MacKinnon. A damned lucky man.'

Sir William Roebuck, Chief Constable of Banffshire Police and an old poker friend of Jock's, gazed admiringly at Kathy's back view. Specifically, at her shrink-wrapped bottom, Pilates-pert and as tempting as a ripe peach in its chiffon casing.

'So what is she supposed to be? A virgin bride?' he asked, a fine spray of pastry crumbs falling from his full lips as he bit into a slice of warm apple pie, his third. 'Is that what the veil's all about?'

'*Dracula*'s virgin bride,' Jock corrected smugly, gesturing to his own outfit. 'Only two months to go now till the wedding.'

'Ah yes, that's right. New Year's Eve, isn't it?' said Sir William, his fat jowls quivering. 'Will her real wedding dress be as sexy as that one?'

'I hope so,' said Jock. 'Of course, all that's assuming this nonsense with the bodies and your lot running around the estate is over by then. I'm not getting married in a sea of yellow crime-scene tape, I can tell you that.'

Sir William looked uncomfortable, his beady eyes darting around as if seeking some way out of the conversation.

'It *will* be over soon, won't it, Bill?' Jock pressed.

'I'll do what I can, Jock,' the chief constable said, dropping his voice to a whisper. 'You know that. But at the end of the day it *is* a murder inquiry. Stuart Haley's usually pretty efficient.'

'Dear God, don't mention that loathsome oik's name to me, Bill, I beg you,' Jock snapped. 'I mean it. I won't have that man in this house.'

'I understand.' Sir William tried to put a placating hand on his friend's arm, but Jock shrugged him off.

'Do you really think he's all that good?' he asked curtly. 'Your "efficient" DI Haley's been harassing me and my family. He's even been upsetting my old gillie, Edwin Brae, and Edwin's not a well man, as you know. I've told you all this, Bill. But as far as I can see, nothing's been done.'

'That's not true, Jock,' the chief constable defended himself. 'I made it clear to Haley that I didn't want him coming tonight, for example. He wasn't happy about it, I can tell you. There were a number of people, witnesses or perhaps even suspects, he'd hoped to talk to. But I put my foot down.'

'Well. Thank you for that,' said Jock grudgingly.

'But I can't simply call the whole investigation off just because it's an inconvenience to you,' Sir William clarified, nervously, loosening the collar of his priest's outfit with a clammy finger.

'Can't you?' Jock raised an eyebrow knowingly. 'I thought you were in charge.'

'Two women are *dead*,' Sir William hissed, his voice so low it was barely audible.

'Two women nobody seems to have missed,' Jock hissed back. 'Migrants, probably. Or prostitutes. No one's looking for them. No one cares, Bill.'

'Maybe,' the chief constable admitted. 'But even so . . .'

'I'm asking for a favour,' said Jock, bringing his face menacingly close to his friend's. 'Like the favour I did for you last year, when the papers came sniffing around my door. You do remember that, don't you?'

The fat man flushed scarlet. 'For God's sake. You know I do. And I'm very grateful.'

'I appreciate that,' Jock said silkily. 'But it's not gratitude I need right now, Bill. It's something just a bit more concrete.' There was no mistaking the latent threat in his voice. 'You *are* the chief constable, after all. Have a think about it.'

He walked away, leaving Sir William staring after him, anxiety etched into every fold of his round, doughy face.

*

'Do you have a second?'

Kathy grabbed Iris by the elbow, dragging her away from Reverend Michaela, by now a distinctly worse-for-wear St Joan.

'Of course,' said Iris, feeling a little tipsy herself and still struggling to process her odd encounter with Rory earlier.

'How was she, by the way?' asked Kathy. 'The vicar? Do you think she likes me again? I mean, do you think she's forgiven me over the whole fair thing?'

'Definitely,' said Iris, smiling. 'Forgiving's part of her job. You look stunning, by the way.'

'Oh – thanks,' said Kathy, touched.

'And so does the house. It's a great party.'

'Do you really think so? Are people enjoying it?' Kathy asked nervously. For one so blessed and beautiful she could be touchingly insecure at times. 'I put a lot of thought into it. I really wanted to make Jock proud.'

'Well, I'm sure you've done that,' Iris reassured her. 'But what did you want to talk to me about?'

Kathy made a face. 'I've had another one,' she said, lowering her voice.

'Another note?'

She nodded. 'Come with me.'

Iris followed her upstairs and into one of the guest bedrooms.

'Here,' said Kathy, once the door was closed. The letter was in the same stiff, watermarked envelope as all the others, with the name handwritten, clearly from the same sender.

'When did you get it?' Iris asked, pulling out the neatly folded, expensive writing paper.

'I found it at around five-thirty p.m., inside the zipped-up dry cleaner's bag that contained my dress. You can take it with you when you go. Give it to the police.'

Iris read the note aloud. '"Leave him, before *you*'re sliced open like a pumpkin. Go home now".'

'What do you think?' Kathy asked anxiously.

'I think they're getting worse,' said Iris. 'Have you told Jock?'

'Not yet. I don't want to spoil tonight.'

'Maybe it's time to think about protection,' Iris suggested. 'At least until the police have a lead on who it might be.'

'No. I don't want protection.' Kathy bit her lower lip. 'I guess I kind of read that one differently to you.'

'How did you read it?' asked Iris, surprised.

'As this person getting frustrated. You know, because I haven't left Jock yet? Because the other notes didn't work? So now they're, like, changing their strategy.'

'I agree,' said Iris, exasperated. 'The problem is that their new strategy appears to be outright threatening to kill you. I don't think "slicing you open like a pumpkin" is open to that much interpretation, do you?'

'I think they're implying that Jock would be doing the slicing,' said Kathy. 'They're trying to make me afraid of him.'

'Does it matter who's doing the slicing?' asked Iris.

'Yes,' said Kathy, defiantly. 'And anyway, no one's doing any slicing. No one's hurt me, or even tried to hurt me. It's only words. A coward's words.'

'That's true,' said Iris. She detected a trace of fear beneath Kathy's bravado. But she also detected courage, and a fierce loyalty towards Jock, both of which she needed to navigate with caution. 'But don't forget, two women *have* been killed here, by somebody. Two women whom we found.'

Despite herself, Kathy's eyes welled up. 'I know.' She paused, gathering her thoughts. 'The thing is, I know this is serious. That's why I let you show the notes to Haley, even though he hates Jock, and the feeling's mutual.'

Iris didn't correct her.

'I don't want to be cavalier. But I also don't want to be frightened off by some spiteful, shitty coward, who hides behind lies and empty threats. I don't want to let *this*,' she pointed to the note, 'ruin my party, or my wedding, or my relationship with Jock, or anything else.'

'I understand,' said Iris.

'But they are,' Kathy went on, passionately. 'They *are* ruining those things! I mean, this person, whoever they are, already has me questioning so many things. That's why I invited you up here in the first place, Iris. Because ever since this started, I've looked at Jock differently, suspiciously. Which is exactly what this bastard wanted, isn't it?'

'Probably,' Iris countered. 'But don't *you* want to be sure, before you marry him? Whatever the letter writer's motives. Don't *you* want to know who those dead women were, and how they got here, and whether or not Jock was involved? Don't *you* wonder why he's so hostile to Haley, and so keen to have this investigation shut down? Or why he never told you about Mary? Or why he's so obsessively protective of Edwin Brae? Or why his first wife left him and then seemed to disappear off the face of the earth?'

'No,' said Kathy hotly. 'I mean, yes, I do want to find out who the bodies belonged to. Of course I do. And yes, I want answers to lots of those questions. But I *was* sure about Jock, before I started getting these damn notes. Sure about us. And whenever I'm with him, I still am. But when we're apart . . .'

'When you're apart, you're not sure. Not totally,' said Iris.

'No,' Kathy admitted bleakly. 'Shit, Iris, I don't know. I just don't know anymore.'

A sharp rap on the door made both of them jump. Mrs Gregory, wearing a witch's hat and clutching a broomstick, burst in disapprovingly.

'There you are.' She bustled over to Kathy officiously. 'Baron MacKinnon has been looking for you everywhere.'

'Tell him I'll be down in a minute.'

'He's waiting now,' said the housekeeper tartly. 'He wants to introduce you to the Lord Lieutenant and his wife.' Narrowing her eyes suspiciously at Iris, she added, 'Is everything OK?'

'Everything's fine,' said Kathy, slipping the note surreptitiously back into Iris's hand before ushering Mrs Gregory back towards the door. She knew that Jock's long-term housekeeper didn't like her, and most of the time she didn't care. But just occasionally the older woman's pursed lips and tutting headshakes got on her nerves. 'Iris and I were just taking a break from the madness.'

'Hmmm. I see,' said Mrs G, who clearly didn't. 'Well, we'd best be going.'

'I'll see you down there,' said Kathy over her shoulder to Iris, rolling her eyes as she followed the housekeeper back to the party. 'Thanks for listening.'

Downstairs, Iris availed herself of two strong whiskies – it had reached that point in the evening – and wandered back into the ballroom, where the dancing was now in full swing. Kilts and costumes swirled through the air in an impressively choreographed display, while a first-class fiddle band played the familiar tunes of the Eightsome Reel, The Duke of Perth and the Dashing White Sergeant. Iris tapped her ruby slippers as she watched the dancers, wildly impressed that they all seemed to know these reels by heart, and slightly drunkenly wishing she could join in, when a male voice behind her made her freeze.

'Well, hello there, Dorothy.'

Jamie Ingall, smouldering as Al Capone in a pinstripe suit and trilby hat and smelling of aftershave and cigars, slipped an arm around Iris's waist.

'Happy Halloween. Very sexy outfit, by the way. I particularly like the socks.'

Iris blushed vermilion. She knew the white schoolgirl ankle socks were too Ann Summers. What had possessed her?

'I didn't see you here earlier,' she mumbled, wishing she weren't already so tipsy.

'No. I just arrived.'

'You never called,' she blurted, the words tumbling out of her mouth before she knew she'd thought them. 'After our dinner.'

'Nor did you,' said Jamie. Looking at her curiously, he asked, 'Are you angry with me?'

'Of course not,' said Iris, hating herself for how pompous she sounded. And also for lying. Because she was angry, whether she had a right to be or not.

'Good.' Jamie smiled broadly. 'Want to dance, then?'

'God, no,' said Iris, wishing that Jamie weren't looking quite so handsome. 'I mean, I can't dance. Not to this stuff. I don't know the steps.'

'Ach, away with you! It's easy as pie,' Jamie insisted. And before Iris knew what had happened he'd hauled her onto the dance floor. They joined a long line of couples, each with clasped hands, forming a tunnel along which pairs of individual dancers each took their turn doing a sort of sideways skip in time to the music.

'Don't look so panicked,' Jamie laughed, clocking Iris's terrified expression as their turn drew nearer. 'Just follow my lead. It's fun.'

To Iris's surprise, it was. Letting herself go, allowing Jamie to lead her through the tunnel to whoops and cheers and whistles of encouragement from the other dancers, she found herself laughing and relaxing properly for the first time all night, the combination of Jamie, the music and Jock's Scotch all working their magic. So what if he hadn't called? It wasn't as if he owed her anything, or she him. He was here now, and suddenly that was all that mattered.

She hadn't realised until that moment quite how suffocating she'd begun to find the various MacKinnon family dramas, the petty rivalries, jealousy and mean-spiritedness that seemed to pervade life at the castle, and how much anxiety they provoked in her. Emma's snobbery, Jock's arrogance, Mrs Gregory's disapproval and Rory's game playing had all combined to bring Iris down, and create a certain unpleasant tightness in her chest. And hanging over it all, of course, was the thought of those two bodies hidden up at the bothy for all those years, and the horrid undercurrent of danger and threat from those sinister notes to Kathy.

Kathy Miller was still a mystery to Iris, despite their many sittings together and burgeoning friendship, if you could call it that.

Why was Kathy marrying Jock? Iris had been asking herself that question since the day she arrived, and she still didn't have a satisfactory answer.

It wasn't just for the money, she felt sure of that, no matter what Rory's views might be on the subject. Kathy had described their relationship in the past as something that made her feel safe. But clearly the events of the last couple of months had eroded those feelings of safety. So what was left? Love? And if so, was that love really strong enough to make it worth living here in Pitfeldy in such a toxic atmosphere and among so many people who hated or, at least, misunderstood her? Not to mention one who, apparently, wanted her dead?

Iris was only an observer, but there were times when being in the castle made *her* feel like a fly caught in a web. It had been like that tonight, until Jamie had arrived and broken all the threads with his big, warm hands and his confidence and his dancing.

He likes my socks . . .

The music stopped and Iris allowed Jamie to lead her to an empty sofa. Dizzy and panting, she sank down into it gratefully.

'You're a pretty good dancer.' He smiled at her. 'How d'you feel?'

'Good,' said Iris. 'I mean, my ruby slippers are killing me, but once you get going, it's actually not as hard as it looks.'

'See? What did I tell you?'

Iris's gaze wandered vaguely over a sea of tartan and masks and glowing skeletons. Without realising it, she'd started to lean into Jamie like a slightly drunken tree in the wind.

'I guess I'm not in Kansas anymore,' she slurred happily, smoothing out her short gingham skirt.

'No indeed,' Jamie whispered in her ear. 'You're in Banffshire. Which is a *lot* better.'

Iris's throat went dry. 'Is that right?'

'It is.' Jamie's handsome face moved dangerously close to hers. At some point his hand had found its way to her bare thigh, and when Iris looked down, *her* hand seemed to be lying on top of his, their fingers lazily interlaced.

'Why didn't you call me?' she asked him, deciding to take the bull by the horns. After . . .'

Leaning forward he kissed her, cutting her off mid-sentence, pressing his lips against hers with the same confident assurance he brought to everything he did. There was nothing tentative about it. But nothing rushed, either. Instead he kissed her as if it were something they did every day. Familiar. Easy.

'Sorry,' he said, looking anything but as, finally, he pulled away. 'I've just been wanting to do that for a really long time.'

'Don't be sorry,' Iris croaked, smiling up at him idiotically.

'Can I get you another drink?'

'Yes. Please.'

A drink was the last thing Iris needed right now. But she seemed to be swept up in a fug of happiness that made the thought of saying 'no' impossible. *I must look like a total moon calf*, she thought despairingly, gazing lustfully at Jamie as he got up and weaved his way to the bar. *Or a moon sheep. Moon mutton, dressed as moon lamb.* At least he was drunk too.

A loud crash interrupted her alcohol-fuelled musings.

The crowd parted like the Red Sea, and Iris had a clear view of Angus Brae, blind drunk and holding the stem of a broken wine glass, waving the jagged edges in front of him like a dagger.

'Don't you fucking touch me,' he slurred. 'I mean it!'

On the floor at his feet, his Batman mask slashed open, lay John Donnelly, Pitfeldy School's headmaster. He was bleeding from his cheek and looked winded, scrambling backwards away from his attacker like a frightened crab, but apparently unable to stand up.

'Angus.' The music stopped as Jock stepped forward, dark and menacing in his Dracula get-up. 'What the hell do you think you're playing at?'

Reaching down, he helped the shaken Donnelly to his feet.

'Are you all right, John?'

The headmaster gave an unconvincing nod. 'I'm fine. It was nothing. Just a . . . misunderstanding.'

'Misunderstanding?' Angus slurred murderously, still clutching the jagged glass.

'Put that *down*,' Jock commanded.

'Angus, please.' Hannah Drummond stepped forward and put a hand on his shoulder, but he barely seemed to register it, his eyes still fixed on Donnelly.

'Put the glass down *now*!' Jock roared.

Momentarily shocked, Angus released the glass, which shattered loudly into a million pieces on the stone floor.

'Take him home.' Jock spoke to Hannah more kindly than he had to Angus, but there was an urgency behind his words that left no doubt this was an order, not a suggestion.

'I'm sorry,' she murmured, leading a bewildered-looking Angus away. 'He's drunk.'

Kathy, who'd been in the library and had missed most of the drama, reappeared at Jock's side just as conversation resumed and the band started playing again.

'What happened?' she asked, seeing the broken glass and the local headmaster with a bloodstained handkerchief pressed to his cheek. 'Does he need a doctor?'

'No, no. I'm fine.' Donnelly approached his hostess, doing his best to put her at ease. 'I'll clean this up at home. It's only a scratch.'

'Are you sure? It looks quite deep to me.'

'Honestly. I'll be fine.'

'I'll see you out,' said Jock.

But the headmaster held up his hand insistently. 'There's no need, baron. Go and dance with your lovely wife-to-be. I'm perfectly all right, I assure you.'

'What happened?' Kathy asked Jock after he'd gone, scurrying away before anyone could stop him. Taking Donnelly's advice, Jock led her onto the dance floor.

'Bloody Angus,' he muttered. 'Glassed the poor man in the face.'

Kathy looked suitably horrified. 'Angus? Surely not. Why?'

'I've no idea,' said Jock.

'But Angus is always so calm.'

'Not always,' Jock observed grimly. 'I mean, I love the boy, but he's got a temper on him, like his father. Especially when he's been drinking.'

Bringing his hand down to the small of Kathy's back, he pulled her closer.

'Let's not talk about it anymore,' he whispered soothingly in her ear. 'I won't have some silly bar brawl ruin your *wonderful* party.'

'It won't,' said Kathy. 'Don't worry.'

If she could put the thought of being 'sliced open like a pumpkin' out of her mind, she could certainly rise above a flash of the gillie's temper.

Back on the sofa, Iris watched the whole scene play out, fascinated.

What was going on with John Donnelly? First, he'd almost come to blows with Angus at the fair. Then there'd been the fracas at Maria's, that was definitely something personal, no matter what Jamie said. And now this.

True, Angus was three sheets to the wind, but Iris felt sure that whisky alone wouldn't be enough to turn the kind and mild-mannered gillie into a glass-wielding maniac. No, there was bad blood between Brae and Donnelly all right. More than that, when Jock stepped in to break it up, Iris had got the distinct impression that he knew what the fight was about. And that he wanted Angus out of there before anything stupid was said.

She was itching to talk to Jamie about it, but he seemed to have vanished during the commotion, heading off to the bar but failing to return with her drink. Perhaps that was just as well, Iris realised, as she scanned the room looking for him and noticed that everything seemed to be swirling around and people's faces were oscillating in and out of focus, like visions in a heat haze.

Suddenly desperate for the loo, she got up and made her way towards the downstairs bathroom. Mercifully, there was no queue, and she was soon alone in a quiet dark stall, a good place for thinking.

The first thing she thought, slightly to her own surprise, was that she wished Stuart Haley had been here tonight. *He*'d have stayed sober, and would have been able to see things clearly, much more clearly than Iris could. Because even in her semi-sozzled state, she couldn't shake the feeling that important things had happened at the castle during tonight's Halloween party.

Despite the fancy dress, certain people's masks were slipping. It was all happening right in front of her and yet, maddeningly, Iris couldn't yet see it.

First there was Rory MacKinnon, and the bizarre overture he'd made towards Iris earlier. He'd hinted that he knew things, things that would make Kathy leave his father if she 'had any sense'. But then he'd suddenly clammed up when he'd spotted Mrs Gregory arguing with his sister Emma.

Was that argument significant? Iris wondered now.

She hadn't seen Emma since. But Mrs Gregory had followed Kathy upstairs later, interrupting her and Iris just as they were dissecting the latest anonymous note.

That's twice tonight Eileen Gregory's shut somebody up when they were trying to confide in me, thought Iris. It was probably a coincidence. After all, the housekeeper couldn't have known that Kathy would be showing Iris a piece of hate mail when she walked in. Could she?

Iris still had the note stuffed in the pocket of her gingham dress. Reaching her hand down she touched it now, running her fingers over the envelope's crisp edges. She would show it to Haley first thing tomorrow. Rightly or wrongly, the language of this last note troubled Iris more deeply than the others. 'Slice' was not a comforting word. There was an element of sadistic pleasure to it that sounded alarm bells, at least in Iris's swirling, uncertain mind.

And then, last but not least, there'd been Angus Brae's apparently unprovoked attack on John Donnelly. Was the gillie's beef with the headmaster a private matter? Some secret resentment from the past, from Angus's childhood, perhaps? And was any of this connected to the bodies in the bothy, as Kathy's threatening note writer had implied?

Whatever the truth, Iris sensed dark forces lurking in the depths of the castle on this supposedly haunted night.

Lots of questions, no answers, thought Iris, emerging from the stall and washing her hands before straightening her hair and wiping off her smudged mascara as best she could in the bathroom mirror. Jamie had kissed off all of her lipstick. Her thoughts returned to him and the giddy feeling of his lips on hers and his warm hand on her thigh.

Heading back towards the sofa where she'd last seen him, she looked to her left and noticed Kathy, backed up against the wall in one of the small, private alcoves near the kitchen. Someone was talking to her, a man, leaning in close, but Iris could only see half of his back view. Hanging back, pressing herself into the shadows of the downstairs corridor as best she could, she strained to make out the male figure. Then suddenly he moved.

It was Rory.

He had one arm out with his hand pressed against the wall, boxing Kathy in. The body language could have been threatening, or intimate, it was impossible to tell from where Iris was standing. In any event, the encounter was over in a few seconds when Rory suddenly turned and walked away, running both hands through his hair in apparent exasperation. Kathy stayed where she was, visibly upset.

Iris began to walk towards her but stopped and doubled back when she saw Jock approach, resuming her hiding place in the shadows.

'What was that about with Rory?' Jock demanded, loudly enough for Iris to hear.

Kathy quivered and said something in reply, but it was too quiet for Iris.

'Like hell it was nothing,' Jock boomed. 'He's obviously upset you. I'll kill him, I swear to God. What did he say?'

'Nothing! He said nothing,' Kathy yelled back, meeting his anger with anger. 'I told you. Why don't you ever listen to me?'

Jock looked wounded.

'He congratulated me on the party. That's all,' Kathy insisted. 'I'm upset, but it has nothing to do with Rory.'

They continued talking, but their voices faded out as they turned away, eventually making up and walking back towards the ballroom together.

Iris never got to hear the rest of the lie Kathy was telling. But she knew it *was* a lie. Because if what Iris had just witnessed was Rory MacKinnon 'congratulating' Kathy on her hostess skills, then Iris was a monkey's uncle.

'Where did you disappear to?' demanded Jamie, pouncing on Iris as soon as she returned to the party.

'Nowhere. Anyway, you disappeared first,' Iris countered, not wanting to say 'the loo' for some reason. 'What happened to my drink?'

'Oh, yeah.' He frowned. 'Sorry about that. I forgot. D'you still want one?'

'Not really,' said Iris, her chocolate-brown eyes locked onto his grey ones. She thought fleetingly about filling him in on Angus's fight with John Donnelly, or asking his opinion about the encounter she'd just witnessed between Kathy and Jock's son. But as he bent down and kissed her again, she changed her mind.

'Let's get out of here,' said Jamie, his fingers now coiled deeply in her hair.

Iris nodded.

This time there would be no misreading of signals. Iris and Jamie understood one another perfectly.

Chapter Sixteen

It wasn't until a few days after the Halloween party that Iris found herself up at the castle again, this time gingerly picking her way along the frosted path to Angus Brae's cottage. It was November now, and properly wintry, and Iris was enjoying the childish game of watching her breath puff out in front of her like dragon's smoke. The reek of a bonfire somewhere up in the woods hung in the still, cold air, mixing with the mulchy tang of rotten leaves underfoot. After a month of near-constant rain, the ground had become a slick swamp of peaty slime, but the drop in temperatures over the last few nights had frozen it solid. Firm ridges of mud cracked under Iris's boots as she walked, their tips snapping like twigs beneath her weight. But the change in weather felt good, crisp. A fresh start.

Had it really been three days since Iris's night of passion with Jamie? The sex had been fantastic, a glorious, if drunken, release, and they'd parted affectionately the next morning. But Iris was nonetheless firmly filing it under 'one-offs'. As lovely as he was, Jamie was much too young for her and their lives were 100 per cent incompatible. His entire world was here in Pitfeldy. Whereas, with a bit of luck, Iris hoped to have finished Kathy's portrait within a month and to be back in London by Christmas – New Year at the very latest. Of course, she'd been invited to the wedding, which was still officially taking place on New Year's Eve, and for which preparations were continuing full steam ahead. Privately, Iris couldn't help but wonder whether Kathy and Jock would make it to the altar. Or whether truths would emerge from beneath the bothy that would make that impossible. Time would tell.

In the meantime, Iris had decided to do everything she could to help Stuart Haley and to try to make progress identifying the Girls in the Wood. Hence this morning's visit to Angus. Haley's hope was that the young gillie might be more forthcoming and less guarded talking to Iris than he would answering questions for the police. Iris was also dying to know what had gone on between Angus and his old headmaster, and how their quarrel fitted into the other mysteries hanging like dark clouds over the Pitfeldy estate. Not just the bodies, but the *real* story behind Alice MacKinnon and Angus's mother Linda Brae running off to Shetland all those years ago, never to return.

'Oh, hello.'

Angus's girlfriend, Hannah, opened the door, smiling broadly at Iris.

'You're the painter, aren't you?'

'That's right,' said Iris.

'Angus has left for work already, I'm afraid, but do come in. I've got the coffee on.'

In thick cotton pyjamas, a fleece dressing gown and Ugg boots, and with her messy hair scraped up in a bun, Hannah looked the picture of cosy domesticity. She was pretty, Iris thought, in a freckled, no make-up, girl-next-door type way. But more than that she seemed happy, radiating the sort of contentment that only the young and in love possessed.

'I should be at work too,' Hannah confided, handing Iris a steaming mug of Colombian dark roast. 'But I'm skiving today. I couldn't face it. Isn't that awful?'

'Where do you work?' asked Iris, wrapping her frozen fingers around the mug for warmth.

'Pitfeldy library,' said Hannah. 'Very high-powered,' she added with a laugh. 'Did you want to see Angus about something specific?'

'Oh no, not really,' Iris fudged. She explained in very vague terms that she was still curious about the bones they'd found up in the woods, and had been hoping to pick Angus's brains on one or two things.

‘I’m curious too,’ said Hannah, dipping a Hobnob into her own coffee before taking a large, satisfying bite. ‘It’s just so sad and awful to think of someone being buried up there, all alone.’

‘Two people,’ Iris reminded her.

‘Right. Which is even more weird, don’t you think?’ said Hannah. ‘That there could be *two* people whom nobody missed, or reported missing?’

‘I suspect it happens more than you might think,’ said Iris, ‘once people drop off the edge of society. Maybe because of drugs, or mental illness, or perhaps if they were here illegally.’

‘I suppose you’re right,’ said Hannah. ‘I had wondered about that. But to be honest, I’m not sure how much you’ll get out of Angus,’ she added thoughtfully.

‘Oh?’ Iris cocked her head curiously to one side.

‘Seeing the bones come out of the ground that day – that skull – after you and Kathy called him to come and pick you up? I think it really affected him.’

‘It affected all of us,’ said Iris, understandingly.

‘Yes, but Angus is unusually sensitive,’ said Hannah. ‘He feels things so deeply. For example, a few weeks ago, I asked him whether he thought maybe the women had been prostitutes. Just because, you know, like you said, they must have fallen out of normal society somehow, for no one to claim them.’

‘Right.’ Iris nodded, waiting for her to go on.

‘Well, Angus was *so* upset when I said that, I can’t tell you,’ said Hannah, looking pained at the memory. ‘Like, “who was I to judge them?” sort of thing. But I wasn’t judging them at all.’ She turned away sadly. ‘Sometimes I forget how differently Angus sees the world.’

‘Why is that, do you think?’ asked Iris.

‘Because his mum left,’ Hannah replied instantly. ‘Simple as that, really. Some scars never heal.’

Her love for her boyfriend was obvious and endearing, and it made Iris warm to this young woman even more. Angus was lucky to have her.

'He's had terrible nightmares since it happened, between you and me,' Hannah went on. 'And Jock – Baron Pitfeldy – being so angry about it all hasn't helped.'

'What's he angry about, specifically?' asked Iris. She'd seen occasional snatches of Jock's temper during her sittings with Kathy. He hated Kathy's dogs, in particular, to a point where Iris almost wondered if he were jealous of Milo and Sam Sam, and the hold they had over their mistress's affections.

'The investigation,' said Hannah, matter-of-factly. 'He loathes the police running roughshod through the estate, and he particularly dislikes the detective in charge. I think part of Angus feels like it's his job to stop them, if that's what Jock wants. But I mean, it's a murder inquiry, isn't it? What's he supposed to do?'

'Yes,' Iris said sympathetically. 'I can see that must be hard. To feel he's letting the baron down. They're quite close, aren't they?'

'Quite?' Hannah laughed. 'Thick as thieves, most of the time.'

Standing up, Iris strolled around the room. She was surprised by how much art was on the walls, and by how good some of it was. For a working man, Angus certainly appeared to have educated tastes.

One piece, a triptych based around Da Vinci's famous *Vitruvian Man*, particularly stood out to her. In this version, Leonardo's figure had been cartoonishly stretched out, with dangling, spaghetti arms and twig-like legs emerging from a swollen, froggish abdomen. The first of the three images had been splattered with dots of vivid green paint, the second with yellow and the third with a rich, reddish ochre. Iris wasn't sure if she loved it or hated it. Was it supposed to be dark, or some sort of comic take on the idea of the perfect human form? Either way it was striking.

'It's good, isn't it?' Hannah said proudly.

'Very,' agreed Iris.

'Angus did that when we were at school together.'

Iris looked suitably amazed.

'He went on a history of art trip to Italy in sixth form and came back all inspired,' Hannah went on. 'Florence and Venice, I think it was. Or it might have been Rome. Anyway, he loved it.'

'I'll bet,' said Iris. She could imagine, growing up as a lonely, only child on a remote Scottish estate, that Florence and Venice must have felt like paradise, or at least a different planet. Especially for a sensitive, artistic boy like Angus.

'You didn't go on the trip?' she asked Hannah.

'Me? No way. For one thing, I was three years below Angus, and for another, I've got no artistic bone in my body. Properly crap at art, I am.'

'That's not true,' said Iris. 'You can appreciate Angus's work, so you have a decent eye.'

'Aye, well, that's true, I suppose,' Hannah admitted. 'But I'd have been bored stupid traipsing around galleries looking at all those Tintins and Cornettos.'

Iris laughed loudly. 'All those Tintorettos, maybe?'

'That's the one.' Hannah grinned. 'All that's right up Angus's alley.' She pointed back to the triptych. 'The teachers took him and the others to see the real one of that,' she told Iris. 'You know, the famous arms and legs man, stuck in the wheel?'

'I know the one,' Iris said kindly. 'Has Angus ever tried to sell any of his work?'

'Sell it? Ach, no.' Hannah batted away the question. 'No, no, nothing like that. It's only a hobby.'

'It could be more, if he wanted it to be,' said Iris, sincerely. Then, suddenly, another thought struck her. 'That history of art trip he went on. Did the headmaster go too? Mr Donnelly?'

Hannah looked at her strangely, setting her coffee mug down on the table. 'He did, as it happens, yes. Why do you ask?'

Iris blushed, blustering something about having met John Donnelly at the St Kenelm's fair. But a subtle shift in Hannah's face and body language suggested she may have already smelled a rat. They'd both been at the Halloween party, after all, and the whole village knew by now that Angus had gone after John Donnelly with a glass.

Before Iris had a chance to steer the conversation back to smoother waters, the kitchen door swung open and Angus walked in.

The surprise on his face when he saw Iris quickly morphed into something else, an emotion that Iris judged to lie somewhere between anger and fear. But he was too polite to confront her directly, instead nodding a brief 'hello', before turning his attention to his girlfriend.

'What are you doing back here?' Hannah asked.

'I forgot the paperwork for the Gordons' new tenancy agreement,' said Angus, rummaging through one of the drawers in the kitchen dresser. 'Shouldn't you be at work?'

Hannah rubbed her throat sheepishly. 'I'm not feeling too good. I thought I might stay home today.'

Angus raised an eyebrow. 'Well, if you're that ill, I suppose you'd best be in bed.'

'You're right,' croaked Hannah. 'I was on my way back up there when Iris dropped by. We were just admiring your artwork.'

'Oh.' Angus blushed, not sure how to take this. 'Well, you should get some rest now,' he told Hannah firmly. 'I can give Iris a lift back to the castle. Or into the village, if you like?' he added, looking at Iris directly for the first time.

It was funny, Iris thought, that despite his good manners and soft, conciliatory tone of voice, Angus's 'offer' of a lift was in fact not an 'offer' at all, but an instruction. It was time for her to leave, and for Hannah to take her imaginary ailment back to bed with her. He wasn't asking them, he was telling them.

'Nice to see you again, Iris,' said Hannah, accepting her fate, which left Iris with no option but to do the same. Not that she minded. The offer of a lift would give her some unexpected one-on-one time with Angus after all, although she suspected his restrained mask might slip a little once Hannah was out of earshot.

She was right. No sooner had the door of his Land Rover closed than he made his disquiet known.

'You were looking for me, I suppose?' he asked Iris bluntly. 'When you dropped by?'

'Yes.'

'Is it about the bodies?'

'Partly,' Iris admitted.

'Look, I don't mean to be rude.' He fixed his gaze on the road ahead. 'But I've really nothing more to say about all that.'

'Fair enough,' said Iris.

'I've already told the police what I know. Which is basically nothing. So if it's all right with you, I'd like Hannah and I to be left in peace.'

It was as close as Angus was going to get to an outright expression of anger. At least when sober, he was a calm and controlled young man. Nevertheless, the tension was palpable. Iris let it sit in the air between them for a moment before she spoke again.

'I'm not trying to harass you. Either of you,' she countered calmly. 'But I would still like to find out who those women were. Wouldn't you?'

Angus exhaled slowly, shifting down into second gear as they reached the main castle driveway.

'May I ask you a question?' he said, echoing Iris's measured, rational tone.

'Of course.'

'Why do you care so much? Is it because you found them?'

Iris thought about it for a moment. 'I suppose so. That's part of it, yes.'

'What's the other part?' asked Angus.

'If I'm honest,' said Iris, 'I disapprove of the baron trying to shut the investigation down. To sweep it all under the carpet, simply because it's inconvenient to him. I saw him at the Halloween party, bending the chief constable's ear.'

'And you think that was about the case?'

'Don't you?' asked Iris. 'Kathy's told me that he wants the police to give the whole thing up. And they might, at some stage, especially if the victims do turn out to have been prostitutes or illegal immigrants. How tragic would that be? I don't think it's right for Jock to try and use his position in that way. To pressure people.'

Angus slowed further as they took another sharp bend onto the village road, listening intently to every word Iris said. She hadn't asked him to take her home, but he seemed to be doing so.

'And what about the police "pressuring"?' he asked her in return. 'What about the way DI Haley drove out to Buckie and bullied my father?'

'Did he, though?' asked Iris, surprised to hear Angus frame it in these terms, in what sounded like Jock's exact words. 'As far as I'm aware, all he did was go to the home to try and ask Edwin some questions.'

'It's the same thing, in my dad's condition,' Angus insisted, somewhat sheepishly. 'Dad had nothing to do with those – with the Girls in the Wood. Neither did Jock.'

How do you know? Thought Iris. *Unless you know something you aren't telling me, or the police?*

Aloud she said, '*You* didn't complain to the police, though, did you? About the interview with your father? You left that to Jock.'

Angus relapsed into silence at this point. It was some minutes before he spoke again, and when he did, he chose his words carefully.

'I don't like conflict,' he told Iris. 'I'm not good at it.'

An image of him brandishing a broken glass in his old headmaster's face instantly popped into Iris's mind, but she decided not to mention it.

'So you leave the battles to Jock,' she replied. 'Is that it?'

Angus looked pained. 'Jock's always been very good to me. I know how he comes off sometimes, and I can understand why you might not like him. But there is another side.'

He sounded just like Kathy, Iris thought. Why was it that so many good, kind people, people she liked, seemed compelled to defend Jock MacKinnon?

'When my mother left . . .'

He cleared his throat and paused for a moment. Iris waited patiently, sensing that they had strayed into important waters.

'Your father blamed her?' She cast out a tentative fly.

'Yes,' said Angus, sucking air through his cheeks and grimacing. The subject was clearly still a painful one, even after all these years. 'He did blame her. And I blamed him, at the time. Although later I found out there were other people – anyway.' He cut himself off, apparently thinking twice about confiding whatever it was he'd been about to say to Iris. 'The point is, Jock sort of bridged the gap between Dad and me.'

'OK.' Iris nodded, willing him to go on.

'They were all close friends,' explained Angus. 'Not just Dad and Jock, but my mother too. I remember them as this trio. When Mum left, it was like she left all of us.'

That's a strange thing to say, thought Iris. She found herself wondering exactly how 'close' Jock MacKinnon and Linda Brae had been, and what the nature of their relationship really was. Whether, perhaps, it had anything to do with the later falling-out between Jock and Edwin, a rift that Angus denied but everybody else in Pitfeldy seemed to confirm.

Is Jock fighting Edwin's corner now because he feels guilty about something? Could he have been part of the reason that Linda Brae fled?

Perhaps sensing her confusion, Angus carried on.

'Jock wasn't happy with Fiona,' he said, choosing his words carefully. 'Something broke in him I think, after his first wife left him. Their baby died, you see.'

'Mary. Yes. So I heard,' said Iris.

'Jock never really bonded with Rory and Emma. I think maybe it was because of that.'

'He bonded with *you* though,' Iris pointed out.

'Aye,' Angus said softly, pulling up outside Murray House.

'Why do you think that was?'

He shrugged, not entirely convincingly. 'No idea.'

Unbuckling her seat belt, Iris opened the door.

'Thanks for the lift.'

'Any time.'

'Your art's very good,' she told him in parting. 'If you ever thought about doing it professionally, I'd be happy to introduce you to some agents or gallerists.'

Angus blushed vermilion. 'Thanks, but you're all right. It's just a hobby.'

'Don't sell yourself short,' said Iris kindly. 'You've got your whole life ahead of you. Your artistic journey doesn't have to stop with one school trip to Italy, you know. I'm curious,' she added, deciding to take a risk before she missed her window completely. 'Did your teachers never encourage you to take your art further? I mean, I know John Donnelly was on that trip. Did he never . . .?'

'I don't want to talk about Donnelly,' Angus snapped, cutting her off. 'Not now, not ever. Please, just leave Hannah and me in peace. OK?'

And with that he drove away, the mud-splattered Land Rover belching diesel as it headed back up the hill towards the castle.

Watching him go, Iris had two thoughts in quick succession.

The first was that Angus Brae knew more about the Girls in the Wood than he was letting on.

And the second was that something had happened on that school trip to Italy. Something connected with the headmaster, John Donnelly. Something that was neither forgotten, nor forgiven, to this day. A secret, buried by the tight-knit community of Pitfeldy.

Just like those bones.

Iris was deep in dolls' house mode a few hours later when Stuart Haley rang. She hoped he might have good news about the latest note to Kathy, from the Halloween party, which she'd dropped off for him at the station yesterday. But as with the others, there were no fingerprints. Whoever was leaving these notes was fastidious enough to wear gloves. The envelope lead, with the distinctive watermark, had also proved to be a dead end so far.

'Either they came from abroad or they were made bespoke by one of those online printing companies where you choose your own design,' Haley told Iris. 'No stationer in Scotland stocks them.'

'What about the ink on the envelopes?' Iris asked. 'Or the typeface on the letters themselves?'

'Needle in a haystack, I'm afraid,' said Haley. 'With the ink we have the opposite problem to the envelopes – you can buy it anywhere. The letters were typed on an old-fashioned typewriter, probably an Olivetti. But again, there are a few of those around. Just go to any local boot fair and you'll see a couple. I do have some good news though,' he said, sensing Iris's deflation. 'The intimidation campaign against Ms Miller is now an official investigation in its own right, separate to the murder inquiry. The chief constable gave the go-ahead this morning.'

'We'll be working together on two cases, then,' said Iris, perking up. 'Not that I've been much help so far with either.'

'Actually, we won't,' said Haley, rather awkwardly.

'Oh. So I'm not on the team?' Iris tried not to sound put out.

'Actually, *I'm* not on the team,' said Haley. 'Apparently, the family don't feel "comfortable with my approach". The chief constable's asked me to hand over the letters to one of my colleagues.'

Iris felt the anger start to bubble up inside her, remembering the way that Jock MacKinnon had pulled Sir William Roebuck aside at the Halloween party and whispered in his ear. It was obvious he was behind this sidelining of Stuart Haley. *What's he so afraid of?* she wondered. *What's he trying to hide?*

They chatted briefly about Iris's visit to Angus and Hannah earlier, but with no solid leads yet from Iris's Facebook page on the beads, there wasn't much else to say.

'Kathy's coming over to my place for a drink later,' Iris told Haley, signing off. 'Should I mention any of this to her?'

'No, I wouldn't,' he said after a brief pause. 'For the time being at least, I'm still in charge of the murder inquiry. I can't afford to do anything to upset the apple cart any further with her and lover boy.'

Iris grimaced. It was difficult to picture Jock MacKinnon as anybody's lover boy. Although over the years, by all accounts, it was a role he'd reprised many times and with an impressive array of women.

'Just let me know if *she* tells *you* anything interesting. See if you can get her chatting.'

Getting Kathy chatting was never a problem during their sittings, and it turned out to be even less of one sitting by the fire after a couple of strong gin and tonics.

'I would *so* love to know what went down between Angus and the headmaster,' Kathy sighed breathlessly, in full gossip mode as she listened to Iris's edited account of her trip to the gillie's cottage today. 'I mean, *something* happened, right?' she asked, helping herself to another giant handful of salted peanuts, her third. It was astonishing to Iris how much crap Kathy could eat and still look the way she did. 'Do you think Donnelly abused him, maybe? I mean, it happens.'

'It does,' Iris agreed. 'But I've no reason to think that. Apparently, Donnelly's a decent guy,' she added, thinking back to what Jamie Ingall had said about him. 'I suspect whatever happened with Angus was specific and personal, and that there's a connection to his mother somewhere in there. But I really don't know yet.'

She told Kathy about Angus's art, how good it was and about the Italian connection. Also about the school trip to Italy that both Angus and his headmaster had been on and that seemed to have marked a turning point in Angus's life.

'That is so weird you should say that,' Kathy breathed, draining the last of her second, strong drink. 'I've been thinking about Italy *all day* today.'

'Oh?' Iris's ears pricked up, hoping for something relevant to Angus or the case. But sadly this was just a segue back to

Kathy's favourite subject of all – her wedding – and, specifically, her wedding dress.

'I've decided to switch designers,' she announced, boldly. 'I know it's late in the day, but this new guy said he's certain he can do it in time, and I just wasn't feeling it with my original dress. It'll be expensive,' she admitted, noticing Iris's eyes widen, 'but I swear this designer is awesome. He's like, this totally awesome genius,' she gushed. 'His bridalwear is super-simple, but it's all cut from this to-die-for Italian silk and anyway, the thing is, he's in Milan. Which means I have to fly there for a fitting. I was kind of hoping Jock would come with me and we could do Rome and Venice.'

'That sounds lovely,' said Iris, amused by the very American idea that one could 'do' Rome, or Venice, the same way one might 'do' the laundry.

'Yeah, it would be,' Kathy pouted, 'except that Jock says he can't leave Pitfeldy while this murder case is still ongoing. Or this 'nonsense up at the bothy', as he calls it. I mean, seriously, I don't see why. We need a break together so badly. DI Haley might not like Jock, but it's not as if he's told him he can't leave town.'

No, it isn't, thought Iris. *It's Jock who wants to stay and keep an eye on Haley, not the other way round.*

'Will you go on your own, then?' she asked, as Kathy got up to leave. It was getting late, and Jock would not appreciate being kept waiting to start his supper, which cook always had ready at eight o'clock sharp.

'I guess so,' said Kathy. 'At least for the fitting in Milan. I might stay longer. Travel a bit, while I'm there. I haven't decided.'

'What about the portrait?' asked Iris, a touch plaintively. The last thing she needed was weeks of delays.

'Oh.' Kathy's face fell. 'I hadn't thought about that.' Then, brightening suddenly, she grabbed Iris's arm. 'Why don't you come with me? We could go together. Make it a girls' road trip!'

'I'm not sure about that,' Iris backtracked, thinking of all the reasons not to go – her involvement in the case; Jamie Ingall;

the likelihood of two weeks cooped up with Kathy driving her bonkers – and then realising that she couldn't tell Kathy any of them. 'We really ought to finish the sittings in the attic room. A sense of place is important,' she finished lamely.

'Well, sure, but I thought you'd finished the background?' said Kathy reasonably.

'Jock might not be comfortable with the two of us going away,' countered Iris.

Kathy's eyes narrowed. 'You're right. He might not be. But Jock doesn't own me.'

It was an unexpected flash of defiance, one that Iris noted without comment.

'Just think about it, anyway,' Kathy finished. 'It might be fun.'

Iris did think about it, late into the night, as she lay in bed, waiting for sleep to claim her. When finally it did, her dreams were wild and vivid, a kaleidoscope of Vitruvian men and Venetian rooftops, and of two shrouded women, their faces hidden, walking barefoot through a Scottish forest, both wearing fairy-tale wedding dresses of 'to-die-for' Italian silk.

Chapter Seventeen

Iris looked on intently as the jeweller rolled the glass beads between his fat fingers, pausing every few seconds to focus on a subtle variation in texture, or the different ways the light played on the bright, kingfisher-blue surface.

'Hmmm,' he said again. It was his third or fourth 'hmm' in as many minutes, and each time Iris waited for him to elaborate, so far in vain.

She'd driven to Edinburgh specifically in order to show the beads from the bothy to some of the specialist jewellers' on George Street. So far, disappointingly, the photographs she'd posted on her Facebook page had drawn a blank. No one remembered the beads, or the necklace, any more than they remembered the two women who had met such tragic and premature ends up in the Pitfeldy woods. But the beads *were* unusual, of that much Iris was sure just by looking at them. Her hope was that someone in Edinburgh's famed jewellery quarter might know more and provide the key that would unlock this clue, this precious, tangible connection to the girls' identities. But the chubby little man standing behind his old-fashioned mahogany counter was the fourth 'expert' she'd seen this morning, all to no avail, and the last on her list of likely suspects.

'Are they ringing any bells, Mr Harris?' she asked eventually, unable to stand one more 'hmmm'. 'Have you seen anything like these before?'

'Well . . .' He spoke slowly, setting the glass orbs down with unhurried precision on the soft cloth he'd laid out on the counter for the purpose. 'I'm not sure.' Everything about the man was deliberate and measured, Iris thought. It was a way of being that seemed to fit perfectly with his surroundings and this exquisitely old-fashioned shop, all polished wood and dark green baize and little antique brass bells to summon the jeweller from his secret back room like a Hobbit. It wouldn't have surprised her to learn that Harris's Gems had been the inspiration for Ollivander's wand emporium in *Harry Potter*. Certainly it was every bit as romantic and atmospheric.

'The glass is hand-blown, not mass-produced. Each bead is just *slightly* different, you see. I would say the necklace is relatively modern, but the technique used to produce it is old.'

'Would it have been expensive?' Iris asked.

'That depends on one's perspective,' the old man replied, with a twinkle in his eye. 'It's glass, at the end of the day, so it isn't precious. But the craftsmanship might have added to the cost, perhaps considerably.'

'Are we talking hundreds or thousands?' asked Iris, not sure that it mattered but curious anyway. She imagined that not many migrant prostitutes wandered around in thousand-pound necklaces.

'High hundreds,' Mr Harris asserted, with unexpected confidence. 'But we don't sell much of this sort of thing in Edinburgh, my dear, so that's an educated guess.'

'Any idea where they were made?'

He shook his head. 'The Czech Republic, possibly? They make beautiful Silesian glass there. Russia has a big industry. Italy, of course, Murano, although that tends to be more chandeliers and what have you. Israel?'

'OK, thank you,' said Iris, re-bagging the beads.

So much for that.

Disheartened, but not defeated, she decided to treat herself to a fish-and-chips lunch. She had one more visit to pay this afternoon, but she wasn't expected till three, so there was plenty of time.

This last appointment wasn't with a jeweller, but with a woman Iris had been curious about for months, ever since she first came to Pitfeldy. Yesterday, at the last minute, this person had finally responded to Iris's email and had agreed to meet. Iris told herself she was going as a public service, in her unofficial capacity as DI Haley's assistant-slash-consultant on the Girls in the Wood case. But the truth was she just really wanted to meet Fiona MacKinnon: Jock's ex-wife, Rory and Emma's mother, and the woman in whose room, whose sanctuary, Iris had spent the last three months, diligently painting her nemesis, Kathy Miller.

If I were her, I'd hate me, thought Iris. And yet Fiona's email reply, albeit late in coming, had been scrupulously polite, leaving Iris more intrigued than ever.

The politeness, it turned out, concealed an anger so white-hot that at times Iris could have sworn she smelled burning. Luckily, it wasn't directed at her, but exclusively at Jock.

'My ex-husband is evil. Pure evil,' Fiona MacKinnon announced bluntly, before proceeding to spout off like an embittered volcano for fifteen straight minutes on the subject of the baron's numerous extra-marital escapades. According to Fiona, Jock had spent every waking moment of their marriage fucking everything with a heartbeat that came within a ten-mile radius of the castle, and as many 'tarts' as he could get his hands on in London as well.

'Black, white, pretty, ugly, younger, older. It really didn't matter as long as they were 'new'. My husband's libido became a sort of monster, Miss Grey,' Fiona explained in her cut-glass voice, a quivering masterclass in barely controlled fury. 'And after our children were born, things got worse. There was no restraint at all. None. He used to go whoring with his aristocrat friends in London – the Eurotrash were the worst, *Comte* this and *Marchese* that. Jock didn't give a hoot who saw them out with call girls, or whether or not rumours got back to me. In fact, there were times when I think he wanted me to find out.'

'Why would he want you to find out?' asked Iris. 'So you'd leave him?'

Fiona laughed bitterly. 'That wasn't an option. Jock made it very clear he'd ruin me if I tried to divorce him. That he'd come after the children, leave me penniless. Purely out of spite, you understand. He threatened to paint me as an unfit mother, as mentally unstable. Oh, he held every card and he knew it. No, he wanted me to know about his mistresses just to humiliate me. He can be an incredibly cruel, vicious man when he sets his mind to it.'

Fiona MacKinnon was a handsome woman, Iris thought, but you could see the toll that years of emotional torment had taken on her, trapped in a miserable marriage. Deep lines etched into her forehead and around the corners of her mouth spoke as much of a face set permanently to 'unhappy' as they did of her age.

'What about up at the castle?' Iris asked, trying with as light a touch as possible to steer the conversation back towards the Girls in the Wood. 'Did any of these other women ever come to Pitfeldy?'

'Not when I was there,' said Fiona, refilling Iris's iced tea and her own from a pretty pewter jug on the side table. 'Although I couldn't tell you what he might have got up to while I was away. I slightly doubt it, though.'

'Oh?' Iris sounded surprised.

'Jock had no respect for me,' said Fiona, 'and no discernible care for Emma or Rory either. But he did respect the estate and the castle as places sacred to the family, to the MacKinnon name. So I'd be surprised if he brought any of his whores up to Pitfeldy. Apart from his latest one, of course.' Her lips curled, visibly disgusted by the very thought of Kathy. 'Although she didn't actually move in until after we'd divorced. That's Jock's warped sense of morality for you.'

'I imagine the engagement must have been hard for you,' said Iris awkwardly.

'Mmmm,' said Fiona with a clipped nod, indicating that as far as she was concerned the subject of Kathy was closed.

Iris sipped her tea and looked around the flat, trying to get a better feel for this unhappy, controlled woman. Everything about the room they were sitting in was tastefully decorated, she noticed, with each object carefully positioned and curated to add either comfort or beauty or both. The vibe in the Edinburgh apartment was different to the one Fiona had created in her attic sanctuary at the castle, now the backdrop for Kathy's portrait. That space was warm and rich, yet still steeped in tradition. Here the atmosphere was much lighter and more feminine. Less cluttered, but with room to breathe. Having recently been through a divorce of her own, Iris was just reflecting on how much she approved of Fiona's choices when something caught her eye. It was a pretty, grey-blue china figurine of a milkmaid, and Iris was certain she recognised it.

'Isn't that . . . Doulton?' she asked.

'How clever of you, yes,' said Fiona. 'I collect them.'

'I know,' said Iris. 'I painted that very milkmaid a few weeks ago. It was in your old room, up in the castle attic, wasn't it?'

The smile melted, and for a moment Fiona seemed to consider denying it. But in the end she said simply, 'Yes, that's right. The Doulton belongs to me, and although I don't have room for all of it here, I always liked this particular figure. So I reclaimed it.'

'Did Rory bring it down when he visited?' Iris asked casually. She couldn't believe that Fiona herself would have made the trek out to the castle, not given the naked hostility between her and Jock. Apart from anything else, Iris would have heard about it if she had.

'Rory? Oh no, I'm afraid my son's useless with things like that,' said Fiona, indulgently. 'Eileen dropped it off.'

Eileen? As in Eileen Gregory? Were the two of them still friends?

'But enough about me,' Fiona went on, all warmth and hospitality once again. 'I'm dying to know more about you. I've read about you on the Internet, you know.'

'Oh dear,' said Iris. 'Good or bad?'

'Good, of course.' Fiona chuckled. 'All good. I read that you're a celebrated portrait artist, and that you cracked the Dom Wetherby murder case.'

'I wouldn't say that exactly,' Iris said awkwardly. 'It was more a case of being in the right place at the right time. Or the wrong place, depending on how you look at it.'

'Ever since Rory told me about you finding those bones up at the bothy, I've been following the Girls in the Wood case closely,' Fiona went on, not interested in any false modesty on Iris's part. 'Naturally, I was shocked. From what I've read, it seems the victims were killed and disposed of there while I lived at the castle.'

'That's the police's best estimate, yes,' said Iris.

'Which is why you wanted to see me?'

'Yes,' said Iris. *Partly*.

'And you're wondering whether the murdered women might have been lovers of Jock's?' asked Fiona.

Wow, thought Iris, *she didn't waste much time before twisting the knife*. Although the truth was, of course, that she *had* been wondering that, and was very curious to hear Fiona's take on things.

'I'd like to know who the bones belonged to,' said Iris cautiously. 'But I'm trying not to make any assumptions.'

'The thought crossed your mind, though?' pressed Fiona.

Iris hesitated before replying. 'Unless we can establish the victims' identities, the police will probably close the case. So at the moment, all sorts of thoughts are crossing my mind. Tell me: was Jock ever violent towards you?'

'No,' Fiona sounded almost disappointed to have to admit it, 'I have to say he wasn't, not physically. Mental torture, absolutely. And verbal abuse. But he never hit me.'

'And you never knew him to be violent with any of his other girlfriends?'

Fiona shook her head. 'I would have heard rumours, if that were the case, I'm sure. Jock was a bastard but he wasn't a wife beater. Not like Edwin.'

Iris sat up eagerly. 'Did Edwin Brae beat his wife?'

Now it was Fiona's turn to look surprised. 'Didn't you know? It's common knowledge in Pitfeldy that Edwin used to knock poor Linda about. He was ludicrously jealous of her, forever accusing her of having affairs.'

'And was she?' Iris asked.

'Not to my knowledge,' said Fiona, 'although, God knows, I wouldn't have blamed her if she were. Edwin was a pig. A *pig*.'

She spoke with such venom, Iris was intrigued.

'It wasn't only Linda,' Fiona went on, setting down her mug of tea beside the old-fashioned typewriter on her writing desk. 'I think Edwin genuinely hated women. He was a very odd man, even before the Alzheimer's kicked in.'

This was interesting, new information.

Leaning forward, Iris told Fiona: 'Angus Brae said that Jock was close to both of his parents, back in those days. Is that what you remember?'

Fiona frowned, casting her mind back to those dark, unhappy times.

'Not exactly, no. But then I never understood my husband's relationship with Edwin. They were always keeping secrets together, like little boys in a private club. They were more like brothers than friends.'

'How so?' asked Iris.

Fiona attempted to explain. 'There was this knee-jerk loyalty between them, almost a blood bond, but they didn't always like one another. Edwin resented Jock for being the baron, and Jock certainly disapproved of Edwin's behaviour towards Linda. Perhaps that was what Angus meant?'

'Perhaps,' said Iris, although she was certain it wasn't.

'They fell out spectacularly over it before Linda ran off,' Fiona continued. 'I remember Jock threatened to fire Edwin unless he left Linda alone, and they came close to physical blows. But then after Linda left, Edwin sort of disintegrated, and Jock forgave him. And then, of course, there was Angus,' she added, injecting the last word with a heavy dose of disdain.

'You don't like Angus?' Iris probed.

'I don't like or dislike him personally,' sighed Fiona. 'Although I gather he's started to take after his father in terms of a tendency to violence, which is a shame. Rory told me he attacked poor Mr Donnelly with a glass at Jock's tacky Halloween party. Were you there?'

'Yes,' admitted Iris, keen to steer clear of recent gossip and to get back to Fiona's fascinating memories of the past. 'It wasn't Angus's finest hour. But he was very drunk.'

'Again, like father, like son,' said Fiona. 'Anyway, as I say, it wasn't that I didn't like the boy. As far as I was concerned, he was the gillie's son and that was that. What I didn't like was Jock's obsession with him. And I use that word advisedly. After Linda left and Edwin unravelled, Jock practically adopted Angus as his own son. You should have seen the way he favoured him over poor Rory.' She shook her head bitterly. 'Jock never showed a shred of affection to our children, Miss Grey. Not a shred. But "poor wee Angus" could do no wrong. That was hard, for the children and for me.'

She swallowed, and seemed almost to be choking back tears. Iris felt a wave of compassion for her, followed by a second, more familiar feeling of dislike for Jock MacKinnon. What *any* of these women had *ever* seen in him was quite beyond Iris's powers of deduction.

'It still is hard,' Fiona continued. 'And now, of course, he's taken up with this gold digger who's young enough to be his daughter, and is lavishing affection on her by all accounts, not to mention money. *My* children's inheritance.'

Sadness was turning to anger now. Iris noticed the clenched fists and tightening jaw, and the narrowing of the eyes into little slits of hatred.

'Jock never stopped punishing me for what Alice did to him. That was the irony of it. And he never stopped punishing Rory and Emma for not being Mary. For being alive, when the daughter he'd loved so much was dead. But what did we ever do wrong? Tell me that. What did any of us *ever* do wrong, to deserve the way he treated us?'

It was a question Iris couldn't answer.

She stayed for a further twenty minutes, asking Fiona for any specific memories she had of strangers being up at the castle, male or female, or any unusual incidents she could remember. Other than the occasional faceless agricultural workers and their families, migrants whose presence on the estate Fiona confirmed, but whom she didn't know, there was nothing.

Iris was about to leave, and was about to thank her, when Fiona suddenly stopped her.

'This probably isn't relevant. But there is one thing I've just remembered – I don't know if you'd call it an "incident" exactly.'

'Go on,' said Iris.

'Well, we had an au pair girl, an exchange student, I suppose you'd call her, who stayed with us one summer when Rory and Emma were teenagers. Isabella, I believe her name was. Pretty little thing, but lazy as hell, and she barely spoke a word of English. She was connected in some way to one of Jock's Italian friends. I can't remember his last name, but he was a nasty piece of work. Pots of money, absolutely no morals. Anyway,' Fiona smoothed down her skirt disapprovingly, 'I think this Isabella was friends with his daughter, which was how we ended up hosting her. I remember she was supposed to live with us for the whole summer and help out with the children and around the house. But then one morning, all of a sudden, poof!' – she made a disappearing gesture with her hands – 'she was gone.'

'Gone?' said Iris.

'Back home. Jock sent her packing without any explanation. Drove her to the airport and that was that. A few days later, I got a telephone call from her father in Rome, screaming blue murder, accusing us of mistreating Isabella, or some such nonsense, threatening to take Jock to court.'

'And did he?'

'No,' said Fiona. 'We never heard another peep out of him after that. But the whole thing was just strange and a bit unpleasant.'

★

After she left Fiona's flat, Iris walked back to her car, her mind racing. She thought it unlikely that the fiasco with the exchange student had anything to do with the bodies in the wood – the girl, Isabella, had arrived safely back with her father in Italy, after all – but the story still bothered her. Something about it, some small detail that she couldn't pinpoint, niggled at the back of her mind, like a loose thread caught on a nail that kept pulling her back to look again.

More immediately relevant – and worth repeating to Stuart Haley – were Fiona's comments about Edwin Brae. About Pitfeldy's former gillie being violent, a wife beater and, according to Fiona at least, a misogynist. Conveniently, Edwin was now too unwell for anything he told the police to be considered admissible as evidence. Even so, the very idea of DI Haley sitting down for a chat with him had been enough to send Jock MacKinnon into a flat-spin panic, and even to begin his campaign to have the Girls in the Wood investigation shut down.

What was it Fiona had said again, about Jock and Edwin? *They were always keeping secrets together, like little boys.*

Were the little boys still keeping secrets? Iris wondered. Or was Jock now keeping Edwin's secrets for him by proxy, the same way that he fought Angus's battles? There was definitely something odd about the close ties between the MacKinnons and the Braes.

Thinking of 'close ties', Iris's thoughts drifted back to the Doulton figurine on Fiona's dresser, and her casual mention of 'Eileen' returning it to her. Something about the castle housekeeper had been troubling Iris ever since the Halloween party, when she'd seemed to materialise magically at various important moments. Perhaps she was imagining it. But Iris left Fiona MacKinnon's flat wondering just how close Eileen Gregory was to her former mistress.

★

By the time Iris got back to Murray House, darkness had fallen and the lights of Pitfeldy harbour twinkled brightly against the cold, black sky. Leaving her bag by the door, Iris changed into tracksuit bottoms and slippers, lit a fire and put the kettle on, before deciding she'd rather have wine instead and opening a bottle of Tesco's Finest Argentine Malbec. Grabbing a tin of shortbread biscuits on her way from the kitchen back into the living room, she curled up on the sofa and flipped open her laptop. She was about to update her Facebook page when she noticed two new voicemails on her phone.

Jamie? she wondered hopefully.

In fact, the first message was from DI Haley 'just checking in'. He knew she'd been to Edinburgh today about the beads. Iris wondered whether he'd be pleased or irritated that she'd decided to go the extra mile and 'drop in' on Fiona MacKinnon as well. Hopefully, it would be the former, especially once she told him all the juicy titbits she'd learned about Edwin Brae.

'Give me a ring when you get a sec,' Haley had signed off. 'This is Stuart, by the way.' As if she didn't know who he was.

Not for the first time, Iris reflected on what a decent man Stuart Haley was. She sensed a loneliness in his message, a need to connect with another human being at the end of a long working day, that she empathised with profoundly. It was why she wanted to hear from Jamie, after all.

She'd heard around the village that Haley had been fairly recently widowed, a terrible thing to happen at his age. People often compared being widowed to being divorced, although in Iris's view, there was no comparison. Not that divorce wasn't God-awful, because it was. But you could still talk to someone after you'd divorced them. Still argue with them or laugh with them or hate them or love them or throw things at their stubborn head. Iris still did all of those things with her ex, Ian, from time to time. Divorced people could do whatever they wanted. They still had choices.

Death took away all those choices. Death was for ever.

Irrationally, Iris felt the backs of her eyes sting with tears. Perhaps these murders were getting to her more than she liked to admit.

She would ring Stuart Haley back in a minute, she decided, after she'd checked the second message. Disappointingly, that wasn't Jamie either. It was a man's voice, deep, foreign and unfamiliar.

'This is a message for Mrs Iris Grey,' the stranger began, slowly and deliberately, in a thick Italian accent. 'My name is Antonio Corromeo. Father Antonio Corromeo. I am calling you from Venezia, Italy.'

There was a long pause at this point, as if he were considering whether or not to continue. Iris could hear the trepidation in his long, low intake of breath, before finally he resumed.

'You are probably wondering why I did not leave a message on your Facebook page,' he went on. 'But what I have to say is too private. It is not . . . for being in public.' His nerves were getting the better of his English, but he certainly had Iris's attention. 'I got this number for you from your agent, Mrs Brun. I am calling you because I recognise the beads from the necklace that you found.'

At last.

Iris held her breath.

'The young woman they belonged to was a friend of mine. I am very certain about this, unfortunately.'

Iris noticed the sadness in his voice, but also his caution and the care with which he was selecting each word. He was frightened of something – or someone. He was taking a risk by ringing her.

'I will like to tell you about my friend,' Father Antonio went on. 'But this is . . . difficult to talk about. And perhaps dangerous.'

Bingo! Thought Iris.

'Mrs Grey, now I am giving you my telephone number. But if it is possible, I am suggesting that we meet. Perhaps' – Father Antonio cleared his throat anxiously – 'perhaps, you will consider taking a trip to Venice?'

PART TWO

Chapter Eighteen

'How perfect is this?' Kathy gushed, gripping Iris's hand excitedly as the pilot began his approach into Milan airport. 'The two of us, getting away together like this? Almost two whole weeks of fashion, food and culture. Don't you feel blessed?'

'Hmmm.' Iris nodded, just about managing a smile. 'Blessed' wasn't the word she would have chosen. Partly because it was just such an awful, saccharine, simpering word, and partly because, for her at least, this Italian trip was about more than wedding-dress fittings and gelato. It was, she hoped, about finally getting justice for the Girls in the Wood, whoever they were, or at the very least providing them with the dignity of a name.

Not that she wasn't pleased to be getting away from Pitfeldy, and the cold and rain and Jamie Ingall's irritatingly distracting radio silence. Three days in Milan for Kathy's wedding-dress fittings and some sketching sessions together (a few small details of the portrait still needed work – for some reason Kathy's chin just wasn't right) were to be followed by a week in Venice. The plan was that while Kathy shopped, flirted up a storm with handsome gondoliers and 'did' St Mark's Cathedral, Iris would meet the enigmatic Father Antonio and follow up on any leads he might give her.

When she took off her cynical, middle-aged hat, Iris had to admit that it was also quite fun to be going with Kathy rather than by herself. They couldn't have been more different, and yet Iris *was* starting to consider her latest subject a friend. She admired Kathy Miller's confidence, her can-do attitude and her relentless positivity, even if she couldn't share in the younger woman's passion for name-brand designers, dogs in baskets, Californian pseudo-spirituality and elderly, cantankerous Scotsmen.

'Milan is going to be awesome!' Kathy squealed as the runway suddenly emerged from beneath the low clouds. 'Wait till you see our hotel. And the place I've booked us for dinner? Oh my God, you're going to *die*.'

Iris very nearly did die when she saw the prices. Forty-two euros for a gussied-up plate of *parmesan chicken*? But after Kathy reassured her that the evening was on her – 'Well, on Jock, actually, God knows he can afford it, and I'd say he owes us both' – she relaxed, and began to enjoy herself.

They were well into their second bottle of Brunello, not to mention the second doorstop-thick edition of *Vogue Italia* bridal, before the subject of the Girls in the Wood came up. Kathy knew about the priest Iris was going to meet in Venice, the one who'd recognised the blue beads, and seemed fascinated by this angle.

'Just amazing that my little Milo could poop out some beads in Scotland, and someone in Italy recognises them. I mean, what are the chances, right?'

'I know,' Iris agreed, savouring her wine in between spoonfuls of ambrosial tiramisu. 'The Internet's a wonderful thing.'

'Milo's a wonderful thing,' Kathy corrected her archly, pushing aside her own dessert. 'It's my first fitting in the morning,' she explained. 'I can't afford to be bloated.'

'As if,' snorted Iris. The very idea of tiny, perfect Kathy being 'bloated' was preposterous. Throughout dinner, every waiter in the place had been hovering around their table like officious black bees around a honeypot, drawn by Kathy's truly extraordinary beauty. Iris had started to grow used to it after all these weeks together, but it was striking how people who hadn't seen her before, men and women, would stop and stare. Kathy's was the sort of beauty men killed for, Iris reflected. Poor Fiona never stood a chance.

'You're still dead set on this wedding, then?' Iris asked, emboldened by the vino and Kathy's companionable mood.

'Of course.' Kathy sounded hurt. 'Why wouldn't I be?'

Iris could think of a few reasons, but took this to be a rhetorical question.

'I love Jock,' said Kathy, fervently. 'And I don't believe he had anything to do with those murders.'

'Even though they were buried on his estate?'

'So what?' Kathy responded. 'The estate's huge and crawling with people. If your priest recognises the necklace, then chances are the dead women were foreigners. Right?'

'Maybe,' said Iris.

'Probably. My guess is they'll turn out to have been migrants, in the UK illegally,' Kathy went on confidently. 'Maybe they were drug addicts, or hookers, I don't know. It would explain why no one reported them missing, like you said. Jock would have no reason to cross paths with someone like that. No reason at all. And whoever's been writing those letters to me knows it.'

'Why do you say that?' asked Iris, surprised to hear Kathy bring up the letters at all. She hadn't mentioned them since the Halloween party, and seemed to have pushed the whole thing to the back of her mind. Iris assumed that as the months rolled by, and the writer failed to make good on any of their threats, Kathy's fear – and vigilance – were both receding.

'I'll tell you why. Because they went out of their way to drop hints about Jock's past, trying to make me believe there was a connection. All that baloney about Mary, as if Jock had something to hide. D'you think I haven't heard the rumours in the village, about his first wife 'disappearing'? About those bodies belonging to Alice and Linda Brae? I've heard them all. Only they didn't belong to Alice and Linda.' She was starting to sound angry now. 'They belonged to some random migrants, and *you*'re going to prove it. This trip to Italy's gonna change everything, you wait and see.'

She raised her glass in a defiant toast. Iris clinked hesitantly. She didn't know what she was going to prove, if anything. It was true that the remains didn't belong to Alice MacKinnon. The dental records had shown that. And as far as anyone knew,

Linda Brae was still alive. But as for the rest, Kathy seemed to be placing a lot of faith in a handful of glass beads and the years-old recollections of one Italian priest.

'I think Rory wrote the letters,' Kathy blurted out of nowhere.

Iris's ears pricked up. 'Rory? When did you come to that conclusion?'

Kathy shrugged. 'I've suspected for a while it was him or Emma. But I don't think Emma has balls, quite frankly. Rory hates me. And he hates his father. Plus, he has access to my dressing room, my car, my private places. He was there at Halloween.'

'So were a lot of people,' Iris pointed out.

'Yes, but Rory . . .' She tailed off, gazing unhappily into the distance.

'I saw him cornering you at the party,' Iris remembered suddenly. 'Right after the business with Angus and John Donnelly. What was that about?'

'I can't remember exactly,' said Kathy, not entirely convincingly.

'He spoke to me too that night and he was – strange,' said Iris. 'I got the feeling he was about to confide in me about something. But then he didn't.'

'Well, he wasn't confiding in me,' Kathy said bitterly. 'Just spouting more of his usual hate-filled stuff, about how Jock and I would never be married; how Jock would "see through me" in the end.'

'Which is funny, don't you think?' said Iris. 'Because the tone of the letters is the exact opposite. They're all about how *you* need to see through *Jock*. "Leave him, before *you*'re sliced open like a pumpkin. Go home now". "Ask Jock what happened to Mary". The writer tries to intimidate you. But it's Jock whose name they want to blacken.'

'Maybe,' Kathy said thoughtfully. 'Anyway, it doesn't matter. Rory can go to hell, they all can. *I* know that Jock had nothing to do with those murders. And I'm going to marry him, and be happy.'

'Well, here's to your happiness,' said Iris, raising her glass with a little more confidence this time. Not confidence in Jock MacKinnon. As far as Iris was concerned, the jury was still very much out on that one. But confidence in Kathy Miller, and her ability to survive and be happy no matter what.

She'd made it through her father's suicide, after all, and two prior divorces. If she'd made up her mind that Jock was what she wanted, then Iris strongly suspected that nothing on earth was going to prevent her marrying him.

One of these days, she thought, as Kathy signalled for the cheque and a flurry of waiters fell over themselves to bring it to her, *I'm going to find out* why *she wants him.*

But for now, Father Antonio beckoned.

One mystery at a time.

Chapter Nineteen

The vaporetto from Venice airport to San Angelo bounced like a skipped stone across the water, making Iris's stomach lurch. She'd taken the short flight from Milan a day before Kathy, who was due to join her in Venice tomorrow after her final dress fitting. Iris was glad to be alone as a wave of nausea rose up inside her, so violent she was convinced she was about to vomit on the woman next to her. But by closing her eyes and twisting so that she could stick her head out of the window, she was able to ride it out, eventually feeling well enough to open her eyes and take in some of the city around her.

She'd been to Venice before, three times in total, but the wonder of it never faded. This magical city-on-stilts, this accidental masterpiece, propped up on thousand-year-old wooden foundations, pillars ossified by centuries of submersion in salt water, remained a thrill like no other. Every neighbourhood, every bridge, every alley, church, canal and park seemed to burst with beauty, with culture and history and art and romance, with *life*. Even the smell, that heavy, fetid reek of fish and too-stagnant water, which could become so cloying and oppressive in the summer months, spoke to Iris somehow of the richness of life here; of layer upon layer of creating, trading, eating, drinking and carousing, unbroken through the millennia. And then there were the sounds, that unique Venetian medley of traders' shouts and church bells during the day, music and the buzz of conversation out in the piazzas at night, and – best of all, from Iris's perspective – the profound silence of the early mornings, with no cars to shatter the peaceful sunrise and nothing but the occasional seagull's call to break the soft, whispered birth of each new day.

No wonder so many masterpieces had been created here, so many geniuses inspired. From an artist's perspective, even a humble portraitist like Iris, coming to Venice was the equivalent of plugging oneself into the mains. The entire city was a jump-start for the soul.

Hopping gratefully off the boat at the San Angelo stop, right on the Grand Canal, Iris walked the few hundred yards to the Airbnb apartment Kathy had rented for them, dragging her carry-on suitcase behind her. For once, everything worked smoothly. The key was in the lock box, the code to open it worked, and no alarm went off as Iris entered a crumbling but delightful former schoolhouse and took an old-fashioned lift with metal pull-doors up to her top-floor rooms.

Inside were two simple, whitewashed bedrooms, each almost completely filled by a vast four-poster bed, and both with views over the Grand Canal. There was a small but comfortable sitting room, overlooking an exquisite medieval church; a rather basic bathroom; and a kitchenette cheerfully decked out in red and chrome, with the sink conveniently placed beneath the only window, so that you looked out across a sea of red-tiled rooftops towards St Mark's when you did your washing-up. Best of all, though, was the tiny sun-trap of a roof terrace, accessed via a spiral staircase in the corner of the living room, which led up to a small study area, a second small bathroom and a door out to the terrace where there was a table and chairs. *I'll have my coffee up there tomorrow morning*, thought Iris excitedly. *Just me and the seagulls.* Who needed extortionate hotels when, for half the price, you could live like a real Venetian?

Tossing her bag onto one of the beds, Iris took a lightning-quick shower and changed out of her travel clothes into jeans and a baggy T-shirt with palm trees printed on it. Tomorrow she would start enjoying the city, exploring some of the churches and galleries while Kathy hit the upscale boutiques on the Calle Larga. This afternoon, though, Iris had only one appointment on her agenda, and that was her meeting with Father Antonio. Washing down the last of the bread rolls she'd bought at the airport with a glass of water from the tap, she grabbed her handbag and headed straight back out of the door.

San Cassiano was one of a handful of really famous Venetian churches that Iris hadn't visited before. By Venice standards, it didn't stand out architecturally, at least not from the outside. Vast, monolithic walls in a warm, honey-coloured stone that reminded Iris of Oxford, supported enormous but simple arched windows, and the main entrance was a relatively plain set of wooden doors, the frames of which were painted in a dark green paint that was peeling at the edges.

Inside, however, faded grandeur soon gave way to the real thing, most notably in the form of the Tintoretto masterpiece behind the altar. The painting depicted the Resurrection in colours so vivid and mesmerising they could have been brushed on yesterday. And the faces. Of the risen Jesus, and the awestruck women; those took Iris's breath away.

She wasn't alone. A group of art students were gathered with a guide in front of the altar, admiring the work, as well as a steady stream of tourists, milling around the church, some of them stopping here and there to refer to their guidebooks or to the 2 euro print-outs being sold at the front desk.

'Entry is free, but if you'd like to make a donation towards the upkeep of the church and our treasures, you can do so in the box to your left,' the woman at the desk informed Iris in perfect English.

'I'm actually here to meet someone,' said Iris. 'Father Corromeo?'

'Ah!' The woman leaped to her feet, shaking Iris's hand enthusiastically and turning her back on the other tourists standing behind her, waiting to come in. 'Yes, yes, of course. I know all about you. Please, follow me.'

Iris did as she was asked, feeling simultaneously embarrassed and self-important as people turned to look while she was led towards the sacristy.

'Father Corromeo will meet with you here,' the front desk woman said, gesturing towards a sitting area that adjoined the priest's robing room. A wine-red velvet sofa was pushed back against the wall and Iris noticed the deep hollows worn into the sofa cushions, no doubt from years of being sat on by parishioners' bottoms. 'Please, take a seat.'

Iris did, and found herself looking around at a room that was an odd mix of grandeur and tatters. The sofa had seen better days and there were chips on all the furniture and ringed watermarks on the coffee table, a testament to decades of carelessly placed, still-damp mugs. Yet on the peeling walls hung sketches of the last supper that Iris would have bet good money were the work of a Renaissance master, perhaps even Tintoretto himself. Or 'Tintin Cornetto', as Angus's girlfriend Hannah would have called him. Iris was still smiling to herself at the memory of this when Father Corromeo walked in.

'Mrs Grey.' Advancing towards her in full-length black cassock, and with his arms spread wide, he was not at *all* what Iris had been expecting. For one thing he was young. Or at least, not old. He had dark, curly hair, a smooth olive complexion, and green eyes that turned down slightly at the corners, lending him a permanently sad look. But despite this he was clearly an attractive man and couldn't have been older than forty, tops. 'I am so happy that you came to Venice. You flew in from Milano, you said?'

'Yes,' said Iris. 'My friend had some appointments there, and she wanted to visit Venice, too, so we flew out from Scotland together.'

'Very good.' The priest nodded. 'Can I offer you any refreshment? Some tea?'

'Tea would be great, actually,' said Iris, suddenly feeling exhausted from the day's travels and in need of a pick-me-up. 'If it's not too much trouble.'

'Not at all.' He picked up a little gold bell from one of the side tables and rang it, prompting the instant arrival of a minuscule woman dressed all in black, whom Iris assumed must be a nun. After a few exchanged words of Italian the woman scuttled off, nodding and bowing in Iris's general direction like an obsequious beetle.

'I love having an excuse to come to Venice,' said Iris, watching him carefully hitch up and smooth out his robe as he took a seat beside her. 'It's one of my favourite cities in the world. But I must say, I was surprised you didn't feel able to talk to me about the beads and what you remembered over the phone.'

'Yes,' he said awkwardly. 'Perhaps you think me overdramatic?'

'It's not that,' Iris assured him. 'It's just, as I said, I was surprised. You didn't even tell me the young woman's name.'

'No,' his face fell, 'perhaps that was an abundance of caution on my part.'

'Are you afraid of someone?' Iris asked.

'Not for myself,' the young priest replied. 'But perhaps for others. Perhaps for you.'

'For *me*?' It didn't seem to have occurred to Iris that she might be the one in danger.

'The girl I gave that necklace to, the necklace in your Facebook photographs' – Father Corromeo explained, 'she was a wonderful girl. But she had enemies. The last time I saw her, here in this church, I could tell she was frightened. And, you know,' he looked away sadly, 'it seems things did not end well for her.'

The tea arrived, in delicate bone china cups with thin gold rims. Iris waited for the tiny woman to leave them again before turning back to Father Corromeo.

'Who was she?' she asked him.

'Her name was Beatrice. Beatrice Contorini.'

As Iris watched, his eyes glazed, caught up in memory. She tried to read his expression but it was difficult.

'Her mother was a parishioner here. She brought Beatrice to Mass from when she was very young. A baby, although that was before my time.'

'And you gave Beatrice these?' Reaching into her string handbag, Iris pulled out the plastic bag of broken beads and passed it to him.

'My goodness, you have them with you?' The priest took the bag with trembling hands, visibly moved. 'Yes. Yes, I gave them to her. It was a necklace.'

'When was that?' asked Iris.

'It was on St Theodore's Day. Two years almost to the day before the last time I saw her. She was fifteen. She used to come and help out in the church, arranging flowers and setting everything up for the festival. St Theodore of Amasea was Venice's original patron saint, you see, before San Marco. St Mark the Evangelist,' he explained to a blank-looking Iris. 'Bea wasn't especially religious but she loved this city, its history and traditions. She belonged here.'

'It sounds as if the two of you were close,' Iris prompted cautiously. This was a priest she was talking to, after all. But to her surprise, he answered honestly.

'I adored her.' He stared down at the bag of broken beads. 'These were from Murano. They weren't expensive, but they were unusual, like her. She loved them.'

'Did she feel the same way about you?' Iris asked.

He shook his head. 'No, no. I don't think she even knew how I felt. I was her family priest, I was ten years older than her. We were friends, though. Beatrice confided in me.' He twisted the bag miserably between his fingers, while Iris waited for him to go on, but he didn't. The silence grew between them, heavier and heavier, until Iris finally broke it.

'You said she had enemies?'

He sighed deeply.

'Yes. Beatrice was brave. Too brave. She confronted some powerful people. Including her father, or at least the man she believed to be her father. It's a long story.'

'It's why I'm here,' said Iris, leaning back against the sofa cushion. 'Please, Father. Tell me what you know.'

Closing his eyes and pinching the bridge of his nose, Father Corromeo began.

'Beatrice's mother Paola was a chambermaid. She was unmarried, uneducated and from a poor, working-class family. Just a stunningly beautiful girl, but – what would you say? – unsophisticated. She had Beatrice when she was very young and their life together was difficult.'

'Difficult how?'

'Well, there was no money, but that was the least of it. Paola drank, and she and Beatrice fell out frequently. And then there was the whole drama about Beatrice's father.'

'What drama?' Iris asked.

'Well.' Father Corromeo spread his fingers wide and looked away, as if embarrassed. 'Paola always maintained that Beatrice's father was Massimo Giannotti.'

He said it as if the name was supposed to mean something.

'I'm sorry,' said Iris. 'Is he . . . well known?'

'In Italy, yes,' said the priest. 'Very. He's a member of the nobility, from Rome. His family is extremely old, extremely wealthy, extremely powerful. Anyway Paola *claimed* that Massimo was staying in Venice at the Danieli, where she was working at the time, and that – well, there's no easy way to say it – that he raped her. She said that Beatrice was the result.'

Iris frowned. 'You sound as if you don't believe her?'

Father Corromeo rubbed his eyes wearily. 'It's so difficult, Mrs Grey. I've always been very fond of Paola. She did her best. But coming from a religious family as she did, falling pregnant, unmarried, at eighteen years old? It was a scandal. Worse than that, it was a sin, a terrible stain.'

'You make it sound like the Middle Ages,' said Iris. 'Surely there are plenty of young single mums in Italy?'

'Of course, yes, but this is not "Italy", Mrs Grey. This is Venice. For Paola Contorini, I can assure you, falling pregnant was a catastrophe. Saying she was raped meant that it was not her fault. It would have given her some room to breathe. With her own parents. With friends.'

Iris digested this. 'So you're saying she made the rape story up?'

'I don't know. I am saying it's a possibility. Certainly she never went to the police at the time. Never reported it to her employers. Nothing.'

Hardly surprising, thought Iris, *if Venetian society is as sexist and moralistic as you make out.* But she waited for him to continue. It was Beatrice she really wanted to hear about, not Paola.

'As I say, all of this happened long before my time here,' he went on. 'But I know from my predecessor, Monsignor Fratelli, that the rape story came first and that Massimo Giannotti's name was only added in years later, as a sort of salacious detail. By then Paola's life was increasingly chaotic. She was drinking heavily and struggling to control Beatrice, who was hitting her own teenage years and starting to push back against her mother. Please, don't misunderstand me, Mrs Grey.' He looked across at Iris urgently. 'Paola was a decent, kind woman. But I do believe that there was at least a chance that she made up the Giannotti story to try to win her daughter back. She wanted Beatrice to believe that she was special. To have, at least, the fantasy that she was a princess, with a noble birthright. Also, you know, that it was a man who had let her down, and had made their lives so hard, and not Paola herself.'

'Well, wasn't it?' said Iris indignantly. 'I mean, whoever Beatrice's father was, he disappeared and left a teenage girl holding the baby. Right?'

The young priest cocked his head to one side, as if this thought had never occurred to him before.

'I suppose that's true,' he said. 'In any event, Beatrice absolutely believed that Massimo Giannotti was her father. And perhaps I should mention here that Bea was considerably sharper and more sophisticated than her mother. She studied at school and she did well. Anyway, she wrote to Giannotti, many times, angry letters demanding to meet and threatening to go to the police – and to his wife – if he refused to see her.'

'And did he? See her, I mean.'

'Of course not.' The very suggestion seemed to make Father Corromeo smile. 'He reported Beatrice to the police and sent an aggressive lawyer's letter to Paola, threatening to sue her for libel if she ever repeated the rape story again. Beatrice wanted to fight back but Paola was in a terrible state, understandably. Families like the Giannottis still wield tremendous power in our society. Massimo could have had both of them on the streets or in jail with a click of his finger.'

'So this Massimo, he was the powerful enemy you were talking about?' Iris clarified.

But to her surprise, Father Corromeo shook his head. 'Unfortunately, no. Or at least, he was not the only one. Beatrice was an irritant to him, but I suspect no more than that. She was not a real threat. But there were other dramas in her life that summer, before she disappeared. I know she had met someone, a tourist, and that she was in love. There were rumours that she had fallen pregnant by this man.'

'I see,' said Iris.

'I don't know whether that was true or not. But I do know she had also fallen in with a really bad crowd here. And I mean, *really* bad.'

'What sort of bad crowd?' Pulling out a small leather-bound pad, Iris began taking notes. The priest's story was far more detailed than she'd expected.

'Romanians and Bulgarians, mostly. Some of the boys came to church, but these people had fingers in every criminal pie in Venice you could imagine, from pickpocketing to drugs, prostitution, even people trafficking. I know that Beatrice became afraid, and I know she wanted to leave. But I don't know the specifics, or where her new boyfriend fit into any of it. By then she had stopped confiding in me or her mother. She was really lost.'

He handed the bag back to Iris.

'After she left Venice, I was afraid for her. But when she didn't come back, and Paola reported her missing, I knew something had happened. Despite all the battles between them, there was no way Bea would have simply abandoned her mother without so much as a phone call or a postcard. No way. She knew Paola needed her. She would not have been that cruel.'

'What happened to Paola?' Iris asked, curious.

Father Corromeo's frown deepened. 'She died. In Rome, I believe. After Beatrice disappeared, everything spiralled away from Paola. She left Venice. It was too painful for her to stay, I think. Supposedly, there was a job in Rome, although I can't imagine who would have employed her then, the state she was in. I heard she had died a few years ago, through another parishioner here. I don't know exactly how, but I assume it was alcohol-related.'

He glanced up at the clock on the sacristy wall. 'I have to prepare for the next Mass in a few minutes. Perhaps you would like to stay for the service?'

'Oh, thank you, but I can't, I'm afraid,' Iris said awkwardly. Going to church always made her feel guilty for no reason, like when you see a police car approaching in your rear-view mirror. 'I'd like to talk more, though, if you have time, while I'm in Venice.' She jotted down the address of her Airbnb along with her mobile number and tore off the sheet, handing it to him.

'Of course.' He stood up, pocketing the paper somewhere deep in the folds of his robes. 'Anything I can do to help. Do you think it really was Beatrice whom you found buried there?' he asked Iris, a painful hope still lingering in his voice.

She shrugged. 'If you're sure about the necklace . . .'

'I'm sure,' he said grimly.

'Well, the timings fit,' said Iris. 'I'd say it was reasonably likely, but the police will have to look into it. Until we have her records and information, we won't know for sure. Can you think of any connection Beatrice might have had with Scotland? Any reason that she would have wound up in a remote, rural spot like Pitfeldy?'

'None.' He shook his head. 'I have thought of little else, since I stumbled upon your Facebook page, believe me. But it makes no sense to me.'

'How *did* you come across my page, if you don't mind me asking?' said Iris.

He blushed sweetly. 'I'm a bit of a true-crime fan. My guilty pleasure. Not that it brought me any pleasure in this case,' he added, sadly.

'There were two bodies buried at Pitfeldy, as you know,' said Iris. 'Do you know if Beatrice left Venice with a friend?'

'I don't think so. But as I say, she left in a hurry and she left in fear. She had crossed the wrong people and she was out of her depth. Someone here was trying to hurt her.'

Looks like they succeeded, thought Iris, shaking his hand and thanking him for his help. 'You've certainly given me plenty to think about.'

'You're very welcome. Please keep in touch, Mrs Grey. And please also . . . be careful.'

Outside San Cassiano, leaning against the wall of a nondescript *tabaccaio*, a man watched Iris emerge from the church, her string bag drawn across her body and flapping at her side.

'She's leaving now,' he whispered into his phone, simultaneously snapping pictures, just as he had when Iris had arrived.

'Is she alone?' the voice on the other end asked.

'Yes.'

'Follow her.'

Wordlessly, the man hung up.

Chapter Twenty

Kathy arrived the next morning in a whirlwind of wedding-dress-related excitement, tossing her Vuitton suitcase onto her four-poster bed and pronouncing herself 'in love' with Venice, the apartment and everything.

'How beautiful is this?' she sighed ecstatically to Iris, throwing her arms and twirling around as if she expected fairy dust to start falling from the ceiling at any moment. 'I literally feel like I'm in a dream.'

'No, you *metaphorically* feel like you're in a dream,' Iris corrected her patiently. 'Haven't we already had this conversation?'

'About a hundred times.' Kathy grinned. It amused her when Iris picked her up on 'Americanisms', as she called them, which, as far as Kathy could tell, just meant 'talking normally', and she never took offence at the impromptu grammar lessons.

'So how was Father Antonio?' she asked, kicking off her shoes. 'Was he like the hot priest from *Fleabag*?'

'Actually, he was a bit,' Iris admitted, hastily whipping out her sketchbook. There was no way she was letting Kathy slip out to Gucci until they'd got in at least an hour-long sitting together. 'He was much younger than I expected, and quite handsome, if you're into –'

'Priests?' Kathy offered, helpfully. 'And are you?'

'Me? God, no,' said Iris. 'Men are complicated enough without throwing God into the mix, don't you think? If I ever marry again, it'll be to a sinner.'

'Bravo,' laughed Kathy. 'I approve.'

Over the course of the next hour, Iris filled Kathy in on Beatrice and her mother, and the long, sad story Father

Corromeo had told her yesterday. At long last, it seemed, they might have an identity for at least one of the Girls in the Wood. Whichever way you cut it, that was a huge step forward.

'So he loved her, this Beatrice?' Kathy asked wistfully, once Iris had finished.

'Clearly,' Iris agreed. 'He remembered that necklace like it was yesterday.'

'But he had no idea who the other girl might have been?' Kathy frowned. 'Or how either of them ended up at our bothy?'

There it was again, that 'we'. '*Our* bothy.' In Kathy's mind, she and Jock were already married and Pitfeldy castle was already hers. Again, Iris's mind drifted to Rory, and the anonymous letters, but only for a moment.

'No,' she told Kathy. 'He had no clue. Other than the general sense that Beatrice was in trouble, that she was afraid of something.'

'Or someone.' Kathy looked thoughtfully out of the window and across the red-tiled rooftops.

'Quite,' said Iris. 'So that's the burning question, really, if one set of remains does turn out to have been Beatrice's: how did a troubled young girl from Venice wind up murdered in Scotland?'

'Well,' said Kathy, hopping to her feet and stretching out her limbs in one long, languid motion, like a cat. 'The burning question for *me* is how do I get from here to the Calle Larga? Murder mysteries are all very well, but Graff are holding a diamond tiara that might be perfect with the MacKinnon family veil, and I promised to be there before three.'

Happy with her work on the portrait, and pleased to have a few hours to herself, Iris ate a simple lunch of salami and cheese up on the roof terrace and then tried again to call Stuart Haley. She'd left him a message last night, as soon as she'd got home from San Cassiano, but he hadn't yet responded. In fairness, the message had only said 'call me', as she'd decided

Father Corromeo's evidence was too complicated to get into on a voicemail, so he may not have realised it was important.

This time, however, he picked up immediately.

'Well, hello there.'

Gratifyingly, he couldn't have sounded happier to hear from her. Unlike Jamie Ingall, who appeared to have forgotten how to use a telephone altogether. Not that his radio silence was any great heartbreak. Iris was filing it firmly under 'live and learn', but still . . .

'How's Venice?' asked Stuart Haley cheerfully.

'Indescribably beautiful,' Iris sighed. 'Enchanting. Not too crowded. How's Pitfeldy?'

'Ach, you know . . . shite,' said Haley, in between mouthfuls of hot, vinegary chips from the bag he'd bought at the van on the harbour. 'It's sleeting just now, as it goes. But you didn'ae call to chat about the weather, so don't keep me in suspense. Tell me about your mysterious priest.'

There was a lot to tell. For almost fifteen minutes straight Iris repeated the story she'd just told Kathy, her words tumbling out one after the other as she filled Haley in on her meeting with Father Antonio and the triumphant unearthing of a name: Beatrice Contorini.

'So the question is,' she paused, finally drawing a long, deep breath, 'are you able to check Beatrice's dental records, from Italian missing persons, or whatever, to see if they match our body?'

'Aye, that shouldn't be a problem,' said Haley. 'I'll make some calls. Give the Italians the name, maybe Interpol too. See what they come up with.'

'Great.' Iris smiled to herself. She liked talking to Stuart Haley. Painting was her life, but it could be a solitary business. And being divorced didn't help. It was gratifying, every once in a while, to feel like part of a team.

'If it is Beatrice, what would be the next step?' she asked, suddenly energised. 'Father Antonio mentioned these Eastern Europeans she'd fallen in with here a number of times. Evidently they were quite violent.'

'Let's just see if one of the bodies *is* this girl first,' said Haley. 'Before we go getting our knickers in a twist.'

He pronounced it 'twest' to rhyme with 'rest'. Hearing his Scottish brogue, Iris imagined him parked in his cramped Ford Fiesta on a dour Pitfeldy side street, sleet pounding his windscreen. It seemed impossible, somehow, that he was there and she was here, basking in the winter sun on her Venice roof terrace. Impossible, not only that those two realities simultaneously coexisted, but that Beatrice Contorini had somehow managed to straddle them. Or rather, she hadn't managed it at all. Instead, somehow, she'd fallen to her death in the chasm that divided these two opposite worlds, breaking her poor mother's heart in the process.

'OK,' she said aloud to Stuart Haley. 'I'm untwisting my knickers for now. But you will keep me posted?'

'Of course,' said Haley. 'And likewise, if you pick up any more titbits over there. Maybe when you're back, we could have dinner and exchange notes?'

Iris's stomach gave a lurch. Was he asking her on a date? Or would this be a 'team' dinner? A 'work' dinner? Oh God. If it *was* a date, was that good or bad? At least with Jamie she'd known where she stood. Then again, she'd fancied Jamie. The bastard. Whereas with Stuart . . .

'Iris? Are you there?'

'Hmm? Oh, yes. Sorry. I'm here.'

'So we're on for dinner, then, when you're back?'

Say something, you idiot!

'Sure. Dinner. Absolutely. Why not?'

'Good,' Haley said briskly. 'And I'll give you a ring if I hear anything before that. Nice work, by the way.'

'Thank you,' said Iris, and she hung up.

What on earth had just happened?

Chapter Twenty-one

Massimo Giannotti tightened the belt on his bespoke silk dressing gown and wandered out to the terrace. He liked to have breakfast here, beside the vast, azure-blue swimming pool he never swam in, in the shadow of the Palatine Hill. Massimo adored Rome. *The eternal city*. He owned grander homes all across Italy: a seventeenth-century palazzo on the shores of Lake Maggiore, a sprawling estate in Tuscany and an opulent town house in Milan. But his apartment in Rome, sandwiched between two embassies on one of the city's most prestigious vias, felt more like home than any of them. Perhaps it was the sense of power that he still felt here, as a member of the aristocracy, the *old guard*? Rome was a city where status and wealth still mattered, and where the ruling class still ruled. A place where there was one law for the ordinary people, and another for the likes of Massimo and his friends. Some people called it corruption. But to Massimo it was simply tradition, the preservation of a natural and divine order that other, lesser countries seemed to have lost sight of.

He felt sorry for his friends in Paris and London, men born to great old families like his who had seen their influence and status eroded, along with their crumbling estates. Some had been bankrupted by draconian inheritance taxes, others by divorce laws that gave preposterous sums to discarded wives, something quite unheard of here in Rome. Massimo's first ex-wife, Julia, had run back to her wealthy father in Capri. His second, Angela, was without connections and had been jettisoned with nothing more than her clothes and jewellery. Out of spite, he had also fought her for custody of their eight-year-old daughter Livia, who now lived with a nanny/housekeeper out in Maggiore and whom Massimo hadn't laid eyes on in over a year. Last he heard, Angela was living in a cheap apartment in Florence, slowly drinking herself to death, but it wasn't a subject that exercised his attention.

Recently, of course, the appalling #MeToo movement had made things even worse, giving a voice and a sense of self-importance to every two-bit whore from New York to Naples. Glancing back over his shoulder, Massimo could just make out the naked, sleeping form of the teenage girl he'd picked up last night at the Moda Models party. No one in Rome cared that, at well over sixty, he was old enough to be her grandfather, or that she may have been trafficked into Italy by some unscrupulous Eastern European pimp, using the model agency as a front. Here, she was a commodity, something that Massimo could enjoy at his leisure, like a glass of fine burgundy or a new Bugatti car.

'Coffee, sir?' Armando, Massimo's excellent butler, appeared silently at the outdoor breakfast table bearing a tray with a silver coffee pot, a bone china cup and saucer, this morning's copy of *Il Corriere della Sera* and his master's iPad.

'*Grazie.*'

Massimo sipped at his espresso, allowing the hot, bitter liquid to help jolt his senses into life as he scrolled through his inbox. A vain man despite his age, he ate and drank sparingly, anxious to maintain his lean physique. Massimo Giannotti pursued his own pleasure vigorously, but he also knew the value of self-discipline. It was what had kept him rich, powerful and on top, what had made him one of life's winners.

The second email he opened, however, soured his good mood like an unwelcome squirt of lemon juice. It was sent from Venice, and consisted of three short lines of text, a link to a UK website and some attached JPEG pictures of a woman by the name of Iris Grey.

Massimo read the information, his quick mind whirring, and clicked open the pictures. His patrician upper lip curled with disdain. She looked like a nobody, this Grey woman. A little, dark-haired, middle-aged mouse. Only her eyes were notable, wide set and too big for her face. Attractive to some, perhaps, but they reminded Massimo of the eyes of a fly. An irritation to be swatted away.

Walking back inside, he picked up the phone on his desk.

'Ugo? It's me.'

'Wha . . .? Massimo?' Venezia's chief of police had clearly just been dragged from his slumbers, but Giannotti didn't care. He explained the reason for his call matter-of-factly, keeping his eyes fixed on the life-sized, solid-gold statue of a horse that dominated the apartment's vaulted sitting room, a present from his erstwhile father-in-law.

'OK,' said the police chief once he'd finished. 'I'll take care of it.'

'By the end of the week,' said Massimo. It was an instruction, not a request.

'Yes, yes.' Ugo sounded irritated. 'I'm on top of it, my friend. Don't worry.'

With a short, mirthless laugh, Massimo Giannotti hung up.

It would take a lot more than an obscure, middle-aged English portrait painter to worry a man like him. On the contrary, it was the snooping busybody Iris Grey who should be worried.

The Gallerie dell'Accademia in Venice was close to deserted when Iris arrived at opening time. Stepping off the vaporetto into the little square in front of the museum, there were no more than a handful of tourists perusing the tatty souvenir stand, and only a few students smoking and sipping coffee around the building's grand front entrance.

At first, she thought she must have made a mistake. Surely, if Da Vinci's iconic *Vitruvian Man* drawing were being displayed to the public this week, the crowds would have been epic? But the girl at the front desk assured her in flawless English that the iconic ink-on-paper sketch was indeed on show upstairs, and that for a modest additional fee Iris could buy a ticket to see it. 'We don't get so many tourists this time of year,' she explained. 'I think the museum prefers to show the important works when it's not, you know, a stampede.'

Incredibly, there were only two other people in line in front of her when Iris approached the roped-off gallery. The room containing Leonardo's masterpiece was in almost total darkness, with only the glass display case illuminated; the temperature was carefully controlled and it was chilly, presumably the better to preserve the fifteenth-century parchment. Visitors were being asked to walk through in single file, approaching the exhibit one by one. As she waited her turn, Iris's mind drifted back to the painting in Angus Brae's cottage back at Pitfeldy, a bold teenage interpretation of the original masterpiece. She wondered whether Angus, too, had had a chance to glimpse the original on his school art trip, or whether he'd simply been inspired by the posters that hung permanently outside the Gallerie dell'Accademia.

She felt her own excitement build as she was waved forward, and soon found herself staring down at perhaps the most recognised and written-about drawing of all time, representing the ideal human body proportions. To be this close to history, to the actual paper touched by Da Vinci's own hands, was a humbling feeling. Embarrassingly, it was soon replaced by another feeling when it suddenly struck Iris how *very* alike Da Vinci's naked man was to Jamie Ingall in the buff. She was still blushing as she exited the exhibition room and headed for the gallery café. She had just sat down when her mobile rang, flashing up Haley's number.

'It's Beatrice,' he announced breathlessly, before Iris had even said hello.

'I'm sorry?'

'Our jawbone. The younger girl? She was definitely Beatrice Contorini.'

'Oh my God,' Iris gasped. 'Are you sure?'

'Positive.' She could hear Haley's grin down the line. 'Italian Missing Persons pulled out her file and matched the dental records. Boom. Nice work, Sherlock Grey.'

Iris couldn't hide her delight, jumping to her feet to the surprise of her fellow café customers and punching the air with her fist.

'That's fantastic!'

'Aye,' said Haley.

'We have a victim.'

'We do.'

'I can't believe they got back to you so quickly.'

'I know. It's a big step forward,' conceded Haley. But something about his subdued tone was beginning to set off alarm bells.

'I'm sensing a "but"?' said Iris.

'Aye.' His heavy sigh confirmed it. 'It's quite a big one, I'm afraid. Chief Constable Roebuck is shutting us down.'

'I don't understand,' said Iris. 'You don't mean he's closing the case?'

'I do, unfortunately.'

'But . . . we have victim,' she stammered. 'Does he *know* about Beatrice?'

'He does.'

'Then how . . .?'

'I know,' said Haley. 'Believe me, I'm disappointed too. Especially as I'm as sure as I can be that this is Jock MacKinnon's doing, putting the hard word on Roebuck. But it is what it is. If the chief constable doesnae want to pursue it, then that's an end of it. At least here in Scotland.'

'Who cares what the chief constable wants to "pursue"? It's not a bloody fox,' Iris retorted angrily. 'Two women have been murdered, and now we know who one of them was.'

'Look, I agree,' said Haley wearily. 'You're preaching to the converted. But it's out of my hands.'

'Yes, but what *reason* has he given?' Iris refused to let it go. 'Surely he has to have a reason?'

'Limited resources,' said Haley.

'*Resources . . .*' muttered Iris disdainfully.

'It's not all doom and gloom,' said Haley more brightly,

trying to lift Iris's spirits. 'Now that we know an Italian national was one of the victims, the Italian police have made noises about opening their own inquiry.'

'What sort of "noises"?' asked Iris, still fuming.

'Loud enough that I expect they're going to do it,' said Stuart. 'I'll know by tomorrow, but they've asked if Banffshire police would cooperate with an Italian-run effort, which, of course, we would.'

'And you're OK with that, are you?' Iris asked Haley indignantly. 'With just handing the case over to the Italians?'

It did not improve her mood when Stuart laughed.

'Iris, it makes no difference whether I'm OK with it or not. This is the police force, not a WI meeting. I follow orders. No one's asking for my opinion.'

'Well, I am,' said Iris stubbornly. '*Are* you happy to have the Italian police running this?'

'Of course I'm not.'

'Because the impression Father Antonio gave me was that no one here is going to give any kind of a shit about what happened to the runaway daughter of a poor, alcoholic, chanbermaid single mother,' Iris ranted on. 'A single mother who's now dead herself. So there's literally nobody left on earth who actually cares about what happened to poor Beatrice.'

'I care,' Stuart Haley said softly.

'I didn't mean you,' said Iris, chastened.

'And you care. Right? We wouldn't be having this conversation if we didn't,' he reminded her.

Iris responded with a grudging 'Hmmmph.'

'I suspect the readers of your Facebook page care, too,' said Haley. 'Don't forget, we wouldn't even have got this far if it weren't for your posts. As for the Italian police, let's not damn them before they've even started, eh?'

'I suppose so.' Iris knew that his calm, patient, rational approach was much more likely to help move things forward than her own, outraged ranting. But still, some things were worth getting outraged about. 'Is the investigation into Kathy's letters still open?'

'Oh yes,' Haley said wryly. 'Jock MacKinnon's perfectly happy for that one to go ahead. Just as long as I'm not involved.'

'I get the strong feeling from Kathy that he'd rather I weren't involved either,' said Iris.

'He can't have everything his own way though, can he?' said Haley smugly.

'No. He can't,' Iris chuckled.

'We'll talk about everything properly when you're back,' said Haley. 'When's your flight?'

'Saturday,' said Iris. 'Unless we extend our trip.'

'Why would you do that?' For the first time, a note of anxiety crept into Haley's voice.

'Well, Kathy still has a *lot* of shopping to do,' said Iris, only half-jokingly. 'And I'd like to talk to Father Antonio again. Maybe try and find some other people who knew Beatrice. Apparently, her biological father was some big-shot nobleman from Rome. Someone-or-other Giannotti, I think the name was. Or at least, he may have been her father . . .'

'Be careful, Iris,' said Haley. 'You and I know each other. But in my experience, foreign police forces don't take kindly to visiting amateurs telling them how to do their job. Or to running around their cities, tampering with potential witnesses.'

'I'm not a visiting amateur,' said Iris. 'I'm a helpful member of the public. Who just happens to be the person who both found Beatrice's body *and* identified it.'

She expected Haley to laugh, but he didn't. 'I mean it, Iris. You should come home. You'll do more harm than good, if you stay out there longer.'

Iris made a crackling sound in the back of her throat. 'Sorry, you're breaking up.'

'I am NOT breaking up,' snapped Haley. 'Don't be an arse.'

But Iris had already hung up.

By the time Iris reached their apartment, she had burned off the worst of her anger. But the simmering stew of emotions that remained stuck to the inside of her ribcage like burned toffee to the base of a saucepan, making it hard to breathe and impossible to relax. And then there were the questions. So many questions.

How had Beatrice Contorini wound up in a Pitfeldy bothy? Who had killed her, and why? If her 'dangerous' Bulgarian associates really had pursued her all the way to Scotland, she must have known something that they considered to be very important indeed. But what could that have been? Was it coincidence that she wound up buried on the MacKinnon estate? Or was Jock, or Edwin Brae, or someone else at the castle involved in what had happened to her? Kathy might be convinced by her fiancé's protestations of innocence, and ignorance, but Iris was by no means so sure.

Finally, there was the question of the other woman, the second victim whose bones were found with Beatrice's and who had suffered the same grisly fate.

Tonight, Iris would fill Kathy in on all today's developments. If nothing else, she might provide a window into Jock's state of mind, and whether it was indeed pressure from him that had prompted the chief constable to close the case, just as they were finally making progress.

And then, tomorrow, she would pay a second visit to Father Antonio Corromeo, despite Haley's objections, confirming the sad news about Beatrice and pressing him for more information about her friends, and enemies, here in Venice. Perhaps, after that, she would go to the police, introduce herself, and put whatever pressure she could on them to take the investigation seriously. Stuart Haley might be right about the risk of putting the Italians' backs up. But if Iris didn't advocate for Beatrice Contorini, she was sure nobody else would.

Sliding her key into the lock, she was surprised to find the front door of the apartment building already open. One of the other residents must have left in a hurry, as there were signs up everywhere reminding people to close the door firmly behind them. Sliding the concertina doors of the elevator open, Iris stepped inside and pressed the button for the top floor.

Stepping out of the elevator, she saw that the door to the apartment was not just unlocked but also wide open, swinging on its hinges in the breeze. Kathy must have returned early from shopping and been too weighed down to shut it.

'Kathy!' Iris called out crossly. 'Listen, love, you *must* be more careful. You left the door wide open. Anyone could walk in here and –'

She stopped, the words catching in her throat. Whoever had broken in had opened every window in the place, sending any loose papers or brochures fluttering around the various rooms. Drawers were open, and clothes from Iris's and Kathy's suitcases were scattered everywhere, across the floor and furniture.

'Kathy?' Iris ran from room to room, her anxiety building. 'Kathy?'

'In here.'

The voice came from the upper-floor study area. Iris bounded up the spiral staircase, past various broken objets d'art, including a lovely, delicate Venetian glass vase that now lay shattered on the Persian carpet below. But all Iris could see was Kathy, slumped down in the corner of the room beside the desk. Blood covered the whole right side of her face and was matted into her long blonde hair. Her face was ashen-white and she was shaking violently.

'Oh my God!' Horrified, Iris crouched beside her. 'Are you OK? I'll call an ambulance.'

'No. Don't.' Kathy's hand shot out and grabbed hers, squeezing Iris's fingers tightly. 'I'm OK.'

'What happened?' Iris asked, gently pushing back the bloodied hair to look at Kathy's face. Apart from a small gash just above her right eyebrow, where most of the blood seemed to have come from, there were no visible injuries beyond some bruising around the cheekbone.

'I honestly don't know.' Kathy shivered. 'It was so quick. I walked in on them up here. Two men, rifling through the desk. I think I screamed, and then one of them hit me across the face and I fell. I must have passed out, because when I came to they were gone.'

'How long ago?' said Iris.

'I don't know,' Kathy trembled. 'An hour maybe?'

'Would you recognise the men, if you saw them again?'

She shook her head. 'I don't think so. It was too quick. I'm sorry.'

'There's nothing for you to be sorry about,' said Iris, attempting to extricate her hand. 'Let me call the police.'

'No!' Kathy said loudly, almost hysterically.

'Why not?' Iris looked puzzled.

'I just – don't want you to.'

Standing up, Iris scanned the desk. Her laptop was gone.

'Are you all right here for a moment?' she asked Kathy. 'While I check downstairs.'

Kathy gave a small, frightened nod. 'Just promise you won't call the police. Or an ambulance.'

'I promise,' said Iris. 'Not if you don't want me to.'

In Kathy's bedroom, the thieves had taken all the diamond jewellery – quite a haul – and designer-label handbags. Iris's room had fared slightly better. Thank God they hadn't destroyed or taken Kathy's portrait, which was still by the window where Iris had left it. The intruders had also left her passport sitting on the nightstand, much to her relief. But they'd taken everything else of value, including the travellers' cheques in her bedside drawer. Worst of all, Iris realised with a heavy heart, her notebook was missing, a battered, leather-bound volume containing everything from personal diary entries, to jottings about the Girls in the Wood, to ideas for sketches.

Iris groaned aloud.

Why? Why would anybody but me want that worthless old book?

Losing the laptop was bad, but at least it was mostly backed up. Losing her notebook was a tragedy. And the irony was it had no value to anybody else. Not like her passport, for example, which a thief could easily have sold.

Unless . . .

Father Corromeo's words drifted back to her, about 'being careful'. Stuart Haley's, too.

What if this was more than just an opportunistic robbery? What if somebody knew Iris was here asking questions about Beatrice Contorini? Somebody who didn't like it one little bit.

'Iris . . .?' Kathy's voice drifted plaintively downstairs.

'I'm coming,' Iris said guiltily. She shouldn't have left her alone for so long.

Upstairs, she helped Kathy to her feet and into the bathroom. 'Let's clean you up,' she said kindly, running a bath. 'And then I really think we need to call a doctor. And the police.'

'I don't want to,' said Kathy stubbornly, allowing Iris to help her out of her bloodied clothes and into the water.

'Why on earth not?'

'Because.' Kathy flinched, dabbing a flannel to the wound above her eye. Once the blood was rinsed away, it didn't look *that* bad. But if she'd been knocked unconscious, then she might have concussion, or, God forbid, a brain bleed. 'Because I want this trip to be a success. I don't want Jock to know. I want things to be happy for us.' She started to cry. 'I *need* that, Iris. Can't you understand?'

Iris couldn't. Not in the least. But she nodded sympathetically anyway, assuming Kathy was still in shock.

'Jock doesn't have to know if you don't want him to,' she reassured her. 'But I have to call the police, Kathy. For one thing, they've taken my laptop. And some other personal things of mine. And it looks like a lot of your jewellery's gone as well.'

Kathy shrugged. 'It's all insured.'

'Maybe, but without a police report, you won't be able to claim,' Iris pointed out. 'And in any case, Kathy, these men attacked you. They're dangerous. We can't just pretend it didn't happen.'

'OK,' Kathy said reluctantly. Clearly pretending it didn't happen was exactly what she wanted to do. 'Call the police, if you must. But I won't see a doctor. And you can tell the police, I don't remember anything.'

*

Much later that night, after the polizia had been and gone and Kathy was sleeping soundly in bed, wiped out from the trauma of the afternoon's events, Iris lay in her own four-poster, thinking.

There was something very odd about Kathy's reactions earlier. Something more than just shock. Not wanting Jock to know about the attack was one thing – a bit weird, perhaps, but then their whole relationship was weird. But not wanting to involve the police, or even to go to a hospital for a check-up? That smacked of something more.

Kathy Miller was hiding something. Or afraid of something. Or both.

Another thought struck Iris then, one that she couldn't back up with any firm evidence, but that, nevertheless, felt disconcertingly possible: what if Kathy was the one the intruders were after – not Iris?

Iris had automatically assumed that *she* was the one who'd put *Kathy* in danger, with all her awkward questions about Beatrice Contorini. But perhaps it was the other way around? After all, from the very beginning, Kathy had sought Iris out because she needed protection. First, from the writer of the anonymous notes. But perhaps now from someone else, too?

Could Kathy have had an ulterior motive for wanting the two of them to come to Italy together? Iris didn't know, and a part of her felt bad about suspecting her friend. But increasingly, she was coming to believe that there had been more to this trip all along than wedding-dress fittings and organza veils.

One thing was for sure. Whatever had happened today while Iris was out had shaken Kathy badly. She'd already come up with a cover story for Jock about her injuries, some nonsense about falling down a flight of steps, which Iris had agreed to back up, somewhat against her better judgment. Kathy told her that she'd decided to leave earlier than originally planned. She was going to take the next available flight to Paris for a short stopover. She would look at some jewellery, perhaps find herself a going-away outfit, recover her nerves before returning home. But Iris wasn't coming. Not yet.

With Stuart Haley officially off the case, and the Italian police still barely on it, it would be up to Iris to keep the flame of truth burning for poor Beatrice Contorini and whoever had died with her. Perhaps she was being superstitious, but she was starting to feel that she'd found those bones for a reason. Almost as if the ghosts of the dead women had come to *her* – to Kathy and her – on purpose, crying out for help, compassion and justice, three things they were not afforded in life.

Here in Italy, the pieces of the puzzle were slowly beginning to come together. *I have promises to keep*, thought Iris, *and miles to go before I sleep*.

She was far from finished in Italy.

Chapter Twenty-two

'It sounds terrifying,' said Father Antonio, his face a picture of concern as Iris told him about the break-in at her apartment and the attack on Kathy. 'Are you sure I can't offer you any tea? Or something stronger. Brandy, maybe?'

Iris shook her head. 'I'm fine. It was a lot more terrifying for my friend than it was for me.'

Father Antonio Corromeo nodded kindly. Iris had stopped by the church that morning to let him know the news about Beatrice. Or rather, to confirm what he'd known in his heart ever since he'd first seen the picture of the beads on Iris's Facebook page. He'd had weeks to grieve since that moment, and a decade or so of loss before it, so it was hard to feel anything now beyond a lingering poignancy, and perhaps a certain sense of closure. To be frank, he was more gripped by Iris's account of intruders at the Airbnb she'd been sharing with Kathy Miller, the subject of her latest portrait.

'I'm glad you reported it to the police,' he told her, 'and I'm relieved that your friend has decided to leave on the next available flight. But you didn't want to go with her?'

'Not really,' said Iris. 'Not yet. I needed to see you.'

'And I appreciate that,' said the priest, spreading his hands wide and bowing his head in a gesture of gratitude.

'But my visit isn't purely altruistic,' Iris clarified. 'There's still so much I don't know about Beatrice, and I want to learn everything I possibly can about her while I'm here.'

She explained about the UK police dropping the case and the Italians taking it over.

'I see,' Father Antonio frowned, 'that's a shame.'

'It means that Italy's at the centre of this mystery now,' said Iris. 'At least until I find out how Beatrice ended up in Scotland and what brought her there.'

'I understand all that. But I'm worried about your safety here in Venice,' the priest said bluntly. 'And I think you should be, too. It doesn't sound to me like this break-in was an opportunistic robbery.'

'I agree,' said Iris.

'They were targeting you specifically.'

'Me or my friend,' corrected Iris. 'Trust me, Kathy Miller has her share of enemies.' She told him about the threatening letters Kathy had been receiving, and how she sensed there might have been more behind this trip to Italy on Kathy's part than she'd been letting on. 'I don't know that, obviously,' she added, noticing his sceptical expression. 'It's just a feeling I get.'

'You said you had some more questions. About Beatrice?' said Father Antonio. He was still far from convinced about the wisdom of Iris staying on in Venice, but he let it go for now.

'Yes.' Iris leaned forward eagerly. 'I wondered if there was anything else you could tell me about these Eastern Europeans Beatrice fell in with before she ran off.'

The priest frowned again. 'I don't think so. It was so long ago. Why, do you think that might be important?'

'I don't know,' said Iris. 'But I do know that plenty of migrants make their way to Scotland every year. Some have come of their own free will, to work the fields or on construction sites. But plenty of young girls also find themselves trafficked. For sex, or domestic slavery, in some cases.'

Father Antonio glanced over at Iris. 'And you think that's what happened to Beatrice?'

'Not necessarily,' said Iris. 'But if these Romanians, or whoever they were, were involved in that sort of thing, then it's not impossible that she might have been caught up in the net. Are there any names you remember?'

He closed his eyes tight and pinched the bridge of his nose, as if physically reaching for a memory.

'Barbu,' he blurted at last. 'Andrei Barbu. He was one of them. There were a lot of Barbu brothers and cousins, a big, feral clan, but Andrei was the one I used to see with Beatrice. I'm ninety-nine per cent sure that was his name.'

'Amazing,' said Iris. 'Any idea what happened to him?'

'None, I'm afraid.'

'With these gangs, the young women are often trafficked in pairs,' said Iris, moving on. 'We still don't know who the second victim was. I wondered if Beatrice had a close friend you can recall? Someone she might have run away with?'

'There were a couple of girls . . .' He cast his mind back, but with less success this time. 'Most of her friends were older, but I can't think of anyone specific, I'm afraid. I'll let you know, if something comes back to me.'

'Thanks,' said Iris. 'And then, finally, I wanted to ask you about the boyfriend, this man you think she was seeing. As often as not in murder cases involving young women, a significant other ends up being involved somewhere.'

'I'm sure that's true,' said Father Antonio. 'But I never met Beatrice's love interest.'

'She talked about him, though?'

'Yes. But not by name. She was cagey about him, at least with me.'

'Is there *anything* she might have said?' Iris pressed. 'Any detail you can remember, however small, might help.'

He opened his mouth to say something, but then seemed to think better of it.

'I'm sorry. I wish I could be of more help.'

'Never mind,' said Iris, hiding her disappointment. 'Believe me, if it weren't for you, we'd be nowhere. And as you say, something might come back to you later.'

'Yes.' He looked away, his expression unreadable.

'In the meantime, I wondered if by any chance you have any photographs of Beatrice?' asked Iris. 'I'd like to post one on my page, just in case it jogs anyone's memory, here or back in Scotland.'

'Ah.' The priest brightened. 'Now there I might be able to help you.'

Standing up, he walked slowly to the back of the sacristy. Opening a drawer in one of the dressers, he pulled a large, brown envelope out from beneath a pile of folded altar cloths.

'I keep a few personal things in here,' he told Iris, stroking the faded paper, smoothing out its creases and folds. 'Pictures, letters, you know.'

He seemed almost embarrassed about it. Iris wondered if it was against the rules for priests to hold onto personal effects, mementos of their private lives?

'This was Beatrice when I first met her.'

He handed Iris a colour photograph showing a young girl, not much more than twelve, laughing on a riverbank, at what looked like some sort of church picnic. She was wearing an old-fashioned, crocheted dress and had her long hair loose in a riot of untameable curls. It was heartbreaking.

'That's her mother behind her,' he added.

Paola Contorini's face was harder to make out than her daughter's, fading somewhat into the background. Iris thought she looked thin and drawn, not unattractive but careworn and with none of the free-spirited joy that Beatrice seemed to radiate like a lit firework.

'And that's you?' She pointed to a handsome young man in a rolled-up white shirt and black trousers, looking sheepishly at the camera.

'That's me.' Father Antonio grinned. 'I'd only just arrived at the parish. Monsignor Fratelli must have taken the picture.'

Iris looked at the shot for a long time, her portrait painter's eye searching unconsciously for what each individual's expression and body language revealed about them. After a few minutes she pulled out her phone and took three separate images, before handing the original back to its owner.

'I don't suppose you have anything more recent, do you? Something of her as she was around the time she disappeared?'

Some more rummaging, and Father Antonio retrieved a second print, smaller this time and visibly peeling at the edges.

'I took this after Beatrice's confirmation.' His awkwardness intensified. 'I shouldn't have kept it, but – anyway. Here you are.'

The laughing girl from the riverbank had lost her puppy fat, but the wild mane of hair was unchanged. Some traces of the mother's seriousness had worked their way into Beatrice's countenance by this time, but Iris was pleased to see that the joy from the childhood picture was still very much alive and present in the teenager's merry, dark brown eyes.

'This is perfect,' she told him, snapping another three shots on her phone.

'She was perfect,' Father Antonio said wistfully, placing both photographs back in the envelope, which he replaced carefully in the drawer.

He really loved her, thought Iris. *Poor man.*

Perhaps reading her thoughts, he added quickly, 'Of course, in God's eyes, we are all perfect.' He was the dutiful priest again. 'Or, at least, we all have the potential to be.'

Snapping his fingers, he suddenly sat bolt upright. 'I do remember someone!' He looked excitedly at Iris.

'Oh?'

'Not a boyfriend, but someone close to Beatrice who may know more than I do. There was a woman named Julia Mantovani, a teacher. Beatrice was very close to her, I believe.'

'That's brilliant. Thank you,' said Iris, making a note of the name.

'She used to teach art at the Istituto Venezia. Perhaps someone at the school has an address? I still think you should leave Venice,' Father Antonio said, as he led Iris back out through the main body of the church. 'At least until the police find out who broke into your apartment and attacked your friend.'

'That might be a long wait,' said Iris wryly. 'Although, as it happens, I am leaving Venice, this afternoon.'

He stopped, perplexed. 'But I thought –'

'I'm not going to England,' she explained. 'I'm catching the three o'clock train to Rome.'

'Rome?' Iris couldn't quite tell if he was surprised, or worried, or disapproving, or some combination of all three. 'Is there anyone in particular you're going to see?'

'A few people,' Iris replied cryptically. 'Although it may well turn out to be a wild goose chase. We'll see. Also, if I can find it, I'd like to stop at Beatrice's mother's grave. Lay some flowers, you know. Pay my respects.'

Father Antonio put a hand on her shoulder, visibly moved. 'God bless you.'

Opening the door, he watched Iris go, then turned and walked back into the dark church, his footsteps echoing off the ancient walls.

The train to Rome was packed. Families shared picnics, the parents reading while the kids played cards or passed around iPads. A few commuters attempted to work, their laptops balanced precariously on the tiny fold-out tables, while all around them tourists chatted loudly, mostly in English, about things they'd seen in Venice and their various plans for Rome. The American voices always carried the furthest, Iris noticed, and somehow managed to be more grating than anybody else's, like a loud carriage full of quacking ducks. But the general vibe on the train was friendly, and it was clean and fast with edible food and properly good coffee, all of which made it a vast improvement from English rail travel. Better yet, it left on time.

Settling into her seat by the window – she was facing backwards, which was annoying, but at least she got the view – Iris pulled out her phone and began uploading the photos of Beatrice onto Facebook. It was much easier to write on the computer, but her replacement laptop wouldn't arrive at her Rome hotel until tomorrow morning. It was bound to take forever to set up and she wanted the images live as soon as possible.

No sooner had she started to type than the texts began rolling in, their irritating *ding, ding*s ruining her concentration.

The first was from Stuart Haley, urging her again to come 'home' and reminding her about their plans for dinner.

I know nothing I can say is going to convince you to stop pissing off the Italian police, he wrote, *but surely you wouldn't be so cruel as to leave a poor widower sitting at Pizza Hut by himself, would you?*

Poor widower, my arse, Iris texted back, wondering what she might be getting herself into.

For the next twenty minutes she edited her Facebook page, posting updates on all the latest developments from Venice and interrupted only occasionally by the intermittent wails of an Italian toddler whose box of apple juice had tragically been finished. After that she caught up on admin. There were five emails from Greta Brun, her agent, reminding Iris in ever more strident terms that she wouldn't be getting Jock MacKinnon's cheque until the Kathy Miller portrait was finished, and wondering whether that was likely to happen in this life or the next.

Your Facebook updates are not encouraging, Greta observed caustically. *Gallivanting around Europe's all very well, but it won't pay your tax bill.*

Unkindly, Greta had then attached a demand from Iris's accountant, the aptly name Mr Grimm. Iris opened it, then immediately closed it again, wishing that she hadn't splurged quite so wantonly on a fancy, five-star hotel room in Rome. After the break in Venice, she decided she was over Airbnbs, but the place she'd booked on the Piazza Navona, overlooking the Fontana dei Quattro Fiumi and Sant'Agnese in Agone was definitely on the pricey side. *My accountant's going to be in agony if I don't bring in a pay cheque soon*, she thought as the train rumbled on, wondering if she still stood a chance of finishing Kathy's portrait by Christmas.

On the plus side, Iris's hotel room turned out to be every bit as stunning as it had been billed, with an enormous bed, Frette linens and a marble en suite bathroom bigger than Iris's old flat in Clapham. She could happily have spent an hour in the shower, lathering herself with fancy Elemis products and allowing the powerful jets of water to massage every knot out of her aching shoulders. But instead she forced herself to get dry and changed into the closest thing she owned to a formal evening dress, a ruinously expensive red shift from Amanda Wakeley that Greta had talked her into buying years ago (presumably when she'd been in a less parsimonious mood).

'You must have at least one outfit you can wear to exhibitions that doesn't look like you bought it at Oxfam, or stole from some child's dressing-up box,' Greta had insisted, with her usual blunt candour. Iris liked to think of her dress sense as eclectic, but others (notably her ex-husband Ian) had been known to favour adjectives such as 'deranged' or the more standard 'appalling'. The red dress was one of the few items in Iris's wardrobe that other people liked and that she felt good in. Not that tonight was about feeling good. Tonight was about one thing and one thing only: getting justice for Beatrice Contorini.

Massimo Giannotti leaned back in his usual seat, not by a flicker betraying his profound irritation. Despite being up on the evening, as the neatly stacked piles of chips in front of him attested, he'd made some foolish mistakes tonight. These slips in strategy and concentration had cost him money, but more importantly, they'd wounded his pride. Being a successful gambler was as important to Massimo's self-image as being a good lover, and despite his advancing years, he still considered himself to be both. Perceived lapses in either area could sour his mood for hours or even days. In Roman high society, a man in Massimo's position and with his lineage could never stoop so low as to work for a living. As a result, he'd had to develop other outlets for his talents, and other means by which to benchmark his success. He was a good shot, well read, a polyglot, a celebrated art collector and a shrewd political operator. But women and gambling were his passions.

With a signal to the dealer, he withdrew from the table, taking his usual seat at the bar, where a whisky and soda appeared in front of him as if by magic. Almost immediately an attractive woman in a red dress sat down on the nearest empty stool, and ordered a gin and tonic in the sort of cut-glass English accent that instantly attracted attention.

'Please add the lady's drink to my tab,' Massimo told the barman, his spirits lifting as he turned to face the woman. 'Good evening, *Signora.* You are on holiday in Rome?'

'Sort of.' The woman smiled. 'A working holiday.'

Slowly, it began to dawn on him that her face was vaguely familiar, although he couldn't place it. He looked at her more closely.

'Forgive me. We haven't met before, have we?'

She shook her head. 'No.'

'Massimo Giannotti.' He extended his hand and she shook it.

'I know who you are, Signor Giannotti. As a matter of fact, I've been trying to get in touch with you all week. Iris Grey.'

It took a second or two for the name to register. When it did, he frowned, first with anger but then with confusion. Iris Grey, the busybody artist who'd been poking her nose into things that did not concern her in Venice? Iris Grey, the frump? *Well, well, well.* Ms Grey was certainly *far* better-looking in person than she was in her photographs. Almost unrecognisable, in fact. The dowdy, middle-aged mouse had somehow transformed into this emboldened, red-sheathed siren.

'You followed me here?' he asked her, no longer sure whether he felt annoyed or intrigued.

'Not followed,' said Iris, taking a sip of her drink which had just arrived and which turned out to be considerably stronger than she'd expected. 'I did a little research on your movements, that's all, hoping to run into you. You're a creature of habit, Signor Giannotti.'

'Massimo, please.' He smiled, deciding to allow intrigue to win out, for now. 'I must say, I'm curious, Ms Grey.'

'Iris.'

'Iris.' He nodded graciously. 'Why on earth would you go to so much trouble simply to try to speak with me?'

'Don't you know?' Iris looked at him archly.

'Well, you mentioned in your emails something about a murder case in the UK,' he replied, a touch defensively. 'And that one of the victims came from Venice.'

'You read my emails, then?' said Iris.

'I did,' he admitted.

'But you didn't reply.'

He shrugged. 'I had nothing to say on the matter. The young lady you mentioned –'

'Beatrice Contorini.'

'If you say so. I didn't know her. Not at all.'

'Perhaps not. But you knew her mother, Paola?' Iris pressed him, scanning his face for any signs of guilt or deception but finding neither. Either Massimo Giannotti was not as black as he'd been painted or he was an excellent poker player. Iris suspected the latter.

'I have no recollection of either of them,' Massimo replied coolly, sipping his own drink.

Iris raised a disbelieving eyebrow. Massimo could have stuck to his guns, but for whatever reason he decided to allow that his bluff had been called.

'All right,' he admitted. 'The daughter did write to me, many years ago now, making wild accusations.'

'Paola Contorini told Beatrice that you were her father,' Iris said bluntly.

'So I was given to understand.'

'Were you?'

Massimo smirked. 'The woman was a chambermaid,' he replied, as if this statement alone answered Iris's question.

'Paola claimed that you raped her,' said Iris, her heart pounding. 'At the Danieli Hotel, about thirty years ago.'

Lifting his glass, Massimo swirled the amber liquid slowly around, gazing into it thoughtfully like a seer staring at a crystal ball. When he spoke he did so slowly, with a measured tone that wasn't threatening, and yet, nonetheless, warned Iris to take care.

'As you continue your research, Iris, and talk to people who know me, as I have no doubt you will, you will soon discover' – he took a long, slow sip of his drink – 'that despite my many faults, I am not the sort of man who has *ever* needed to force himself on a chambermaid.'

'You deny it, then?' said Iris.

Looking up, he smiled at her in an open, utterly disarming manner. 'Naturally, I deny it. It never happened. I have no connection whatsoever with either of these women, and anyone who tells you differently is misleading you. To what end, I can't say.'

He's very convincing, thought Iris, suddenly feeling unsure of her own ground. It was Father Antonio who'd given her Giannotti's name, and told her about the rape, and Massimo's connection to Beatrice. Was it possible that the priest was mistaken? Or that he had lied to her? But if so, as Massimo himself said, to what end? No. It made no sense.

'You're an artist, I understand?' said Massimo, changing the subject.

'That's right.'

'Portraits, isn't it?'

Iris nodded, happy to keep the conversation going until she got a better handle on this arrogant but intriguing man.

'Perhaps I could commission you to paint my portrait? Once you've tired of solving cold cases. Is that how you say it in English? "Cold case"?'

'It is,' said Iris. 'Your English is flawless. Have you spent much time in England?'

'Some.' He finished his drink, gestured for another. 'I enjoyed London as a young man. So what do you say? Would you be interested in painting me?'

I would love to paint you, thought Iris. All that hauteur and intelligence and (perhaps) cruelty; the handsome features betrayed by the papery, ageing skin, each line and liver spot an affront to the vain, arrogant man still inside, his rage burning fire bright behind his ice-blue eyes.

'Perhaps,' she said aloud. 'Once I've finished my current commission.'

'Who is your subject at present, if I might I ask?'

'Her name is Kathy Miller,' said Iris. 'She's a young American woman, planning to marry a wealthy Scottish baron: Jock MacKinnon. I've been painting Kathy up at Pitfeldy Castle in Scotland, which is how I got drawn into this case. Beatrice Contorini's body was found buried in the castle grounds, you see.'

All the colour drained from Massimo's face and he gripped his glass so tightly that the veins on the back of his hand popped up like thick blue cords.

Aha! Thought Iris. *I've struck a nerve. But which one?*

'Do you know Pitfeldy?' she asked, as casually as she could.

'No.'

'Perhaps you've heard of Kathy, then?' Iris tried another tack. 'She was quite a famous socialite, I believe, before she hooked up with Jock. Lived in New York for a while, and London. Very beautiful.'

'Then we may have met,' said Massimo, recovering some of his composure, although the unshakeable confidence of earlier had evaporated, apparently for good. 'Very beautiful socialites are rather my milieu, as you can imagine.'

Draining his drink, he stood up.

'Time for me to call it a night, I think.'

'Are you sure?' Iris's disappointment was genuine. They'd only just begun talking and now already she'd scared him off.

'Quite sure. It was a pleasure to meet you, Iris.'

He kissed her on both cheeks, gallantly but not warmly.

'I hope you find . . . whatever it is you're looking for. Goodbye.'

Damn it, thought Iris, watching him go. *What just happened?*

She woke early the next morning to find a package outside her hotel room door. After a few moments' confusion, she ripped off the paper and realised with joy that it was her replacement laptop. Later she would take it to the Apple Store on Via Alberto Lionello to get help setting it up. Syncing her phone was just about within Iris's technological capabilities, but 'the cloud' and how it worked was still a total mystery. Ian used to do all that stuff when they were married. Now it would have to be Paolo from the Genius Bar.

After another too-short shower, Iris changed and headed down to breakfast. She had a lot to do today, aside from the Apple Store. Number one on the list was tracking down Paola Contorini's grave, which she was determined to visit before she left Rome. Number two involved going to the public records office to see if she could find any old addresses for Paola. Perhaps, by knocking on doors, Iris would stumble across someone who'd known Beatrice's mother during those tragic last years of her life. Surely she would have confided in someone about her daughter's disappearance and what had happened in Venice? Or perhaps shared her claims about Massimo Giannotti and the rape? It was important to get to the bottom of that.

Sitting at a table by the window directly overlooking the famous fountain, Iris ordered coffee and pastries, with fresh orange juice and a mouth-watering assortment of home-made jams. It was all ambrosially delicious, but she'd barely got through a quarter of her first cinnamon twist when three uniformed carabinieri appeared in the doorway and promptly marched over to her table.

'Mrs Grey?'

'Yes?'

'Polizia di stato.' One of the men, presumably the most senior, flashed his ID. 'There's a problem with your tourist visitor status. You need to come with us.'

'A problem with my what?' Iris looked up, baffled. 'Are you sure you've got the right person? I'm here on holiday from –'

'We know why you're here.' The steel in his tone was unmistakable. 'There are problems with your papers, Mrs Grey. We have orders to escort you to Fiumicino.'

'You're deporting me?' Iris pushed her plate aside. 'You can't do that.'

But even as she said it, one look at the men's faces told her that they could. There would be no time for lawyers or phone calls. No time for anything. Someone – Massimo Giannotti? – had stitched her up.

The senior officer smiled thinly. 'We appreciate your cooperation, Mrs Grey. You have ten minutes to pack.'

Iris leaned back in her cramped seat as the easyJet flight juddered up into the blue, still reeling from the events of the last few hours. Without doubt, this had been one of the most surreal mornings of her life. From the immigration police showing up at her hotel, to being bustled into the back of an unmarked car, then whisked through the airport on some sort of supercharged fast track, past every line and desk and checkpoint, handed a ticket and deposited on a plane to Luton, the whole thing was like a bad, chaotic dream. And now here she was, heading home, not even sure whether or not she'd officially been deported, and if so what for.

She couldn't wait to tell Haley about this. So much for giving the Italian police a chance. Whatever their motivation was for kicking her out of the country, it sure as hell wasn't a burning desire to get justice for Beatrice Contorini. Like everyone else, it seemed, the local police wanted the two women buried beneath Jock MacKinnon's bothy to stay buried, metaphorically if not literally.

If it hadn't been for Milo and Sam Sam, they would be, Iris reflected, imagining the two dogs' fluffy faces on an Interpol most-wanted poster and smiling to herself. Thinking about the dogs made her think about Kathy, and the frightening attack in Venice which she'd been so adamant must not be mentioned to Jock. What *was* that about? Who had broken into their apartment, and why?

Despite all the progress she'd made, not least in establishing who Beatrice was, Iris couldn't help but feel that her Italian 'jaunt', as Greta put it, had ended up posing as many questions as it had answered.

Pulling the paper sick-bag out of the seat pocket in front of her, Iris whipped a biro out of her handbag and jotted down some notes on the back of it, while the thoughts were still fresh in her mind.

Julia Mantovani – art teacher. Find address.

Names for Haley: Andrei Barbu. Trafficking.

B's boyfriend?

Massimo Giannotti – Kathy/Pitfeldy connection?

At the bottom of the paper she wrote the name *Paola Contorini*, her pen making little swirls and curlicues in the letters as her mind wandered.

She never did get to visit Paola's grave. But she remained very curious. What had happened to Beatrice's mother after she came to Rome, the city her alleged rapist called home? Had she continued searching for her daughter, believing Beatrice still alive? Or had she merely sunk into a drunken depression and died, broken and defeated, never knowing where it all went wrong, or how her beloved daughter had been torn away from her, and from their home in Venice, and everything she loved?

Ridiculously, Iris felt tears prick the backs of her eyes. It must be the shock of being deported, she told herself firmly. After all, she never knew Paola, or Beatrice, for that matter. It was silly to get so emotionally involved.

A beep from her phone reminded her that she'd forgotten to switch it to flight-safe mode. Picking it up, she accidentally clicked on the new message.

It was from Jamie Ingall.

Hear you're in Italy, he wrote. Casually, as if he hadn't disappeared off the face of the earth for the past couple of weeks. *Call me when you get back. We shld get together.*

'The cheek,' Iris said aloud, to the surprise of the old man sitting next to her. Deleting the text, she switched off the phone and thrust it angrily back into her bag.

She knew she had no right to expect anything from Jamie. Things had never been serious between them. But even so, it rankled that he seemed to feel he could drop her and then pick her up when he felt like it, like some sort of toy. Perhaps she'd been out of the dating game too long, but that simply didn't seem right to Iris.

Feeling unaccountably anxious, and irritated – with herself as much as anything – Iris gazed unhappily out of the window at nothing as the plane flew on.

Chapter Twenty-three

Jock MacKinnon turned up the heat in his Volvo estate and eased into fifth gear as Wagner's *Das Rheingold* blasted through the car speakers. It was odd how music affected one. Wagner simultaneously relaxed him and gave him courage, filling his chest with a surge of energy and optimism. It was masculine music, Jock decided, wondering if, subconsciously, that was why he'd chosen it for this drive to the airport to pick up Kathy. Did he need strength for their reunion? One never knew with women.

He'd missed her while she was away in Italy, although it was a longing tinged with anxiety, thanks to her choice of travelling companion. He'd finally managed to get rid of the loathsome DI Haley, thanks heavens, but Iris Grey was trickier. Kathy liked her, and leaned on her in ways that troubled Jock deeply. But the more he tried to prise the two women apart, the tighter Kathy seemed to cling to Iris, like a barnacle on the keel of a boat. That frightened him. *He* wanted to be Kathy's boat, the one she clung to, trusted, needed. Try as he may, he couldn't help but think of Iris as a threat.

With his first wife, Alice, he'd let himself love in that passionate, thoughtless, needy way that young men did. He'd given himself up completely to the wild, reckless co-dependence of youth, and for a while everything was perfect. But then their daughter Mary had died, and Alice had left him, and every single piece of Jock's heart had been ground to dust, to atoms, to nothing.

The void that was left had lingered for over thirty years, all through his marriage to Fiona and the twins' childhood. He wasn't proud of that. But he wasn't ashamed either, because in Jock's mind these were simply things that had happened. External forces of nature like an earthquake or a flood or a fire. From time to time emotions would roll like tumbleweed through the vacuum that had once been *him*. Anger, most often, in its various forms: rage; bitterness; spite. Lust reared its head from time to time. *Was lust an emotion?* And then, occasionally, softer feelings, like humour, or wonder, or regret. But other than Edwin Brae, and in later years the boy, Angus, Jock had survived the entirety of middle age without forging a single close human relationship. It simply wasn't worth the risk. Especially not with a woman.

Kathy had changed that. Without even trying she had cracked open a shell deep within him, a brittle core that Fiona had been hammering away at uselessly for decades. Perhaps, Jock reflected, it was *because* she hadn't tried that Kathy had succeeded where his second wife had failed. Like Alice, Kathy was independent and strong. Fiona had been soft and weak. She had needed him, and Jock could never quite forgive her for that.

But now here he was, an old man, by society's reckoning, beginning again. How strange life was.

Poor Kathy had hurt herself in Venice, it seemed, fallen down a flight of steps and acquired some bruises. Evidently, the accident had rattled her enough to make her want to leave Venice early. *And come home to me*, Jock reassured himself, pulling into the airport car park.

Perhaps he was worrying too much about Iris Grey. He was the one Kathy loved, and would marry, no matter what anybody tried to do to stop them. The police were already gone from the castle and the murder inquiry was closed. Soon enough the portrait would be finished too, and Iris would leave as well, out of their lives for ever. Then all the bad, sad things would sink back into the past where they belonged, and Jock and Kathy would live happily ever after, in the peace that only Pitfeldy could bring.

*

'Have you seen this?'

Hannah Drummond yawned extravagantly as she held the iPad out to Angus. It was Sunday morning, her favourite time of the week, and the two of them were in their pyjamas at the breakfast table at Keeper's Cottage surrounded by a sea of Sunday supplements and half-eaten rounds of toast.

'If it's got the words "Meghan" or "Markle" in it, I'm not interested,' Angus groaned, not looking up from the *Sunday Times* sports section. Scotland had trounced England in the rugby yesterday, so it made good reading for once, and Hannah's obsession with all things royal was legendary.

'It hasn't,' she said, shoving the tablet under his nose. 'I'm serious, Angus. You should read it. It's Iris Grey's Facebook update, about those bodies. They know who one of them was.'

Angus's hands tensed, the tendons rising like tiny ropes beneath his skin. Slowly, he folded his newspaper and set it down, taking the iPad from his girlfriend.

'Beatrice, her name was,' said Hannah unnecessarily, as Angus read Iris's latest post for himself. 'She was a student in Venice, apparently, went missing over ten years ago. How she ended up in Scotland is anybody's guess, but the Italian police are looking into it. There's a picture – look – if you scroll down. Angus?' A note of concern crept into her voice. Something very odd seemed to have happened to Angus's face all of a sudden.

'Are you OK, love?'

'Migraine,' he whispered through clenched teeth, dropping the iPad and clutching his head in his hands. Moments later he started making a terrible groaning sound.

'I'll call Dr Harris.' Hannah rushed to the phone, looking on in alarm as he slumped forward, pressing his forehead to the table in obvious agony. He'd had migraines before, bad ones, but she'd never seen the symptoms come on like this, from one second to the next.

Perhaps she should have been more sensitive about Iris Grey's news. Ever since they'd found those bloody bones up at the bothy he'd not been himself. Some well of pain deep inside him seemed to have been stirred to life by the tragedy of these unknown women, like a stone dropped into still water, its ripples summoning echoes of Angus's own loss, of emotions long buried.

'Hello, yes –' Hannah could hear the worry in her own voice. 'I'm sorry to bother you on a Sunday, doctor –'

Pressing his temples to the wood, barely breathing in case the tiny movements worsened his pain, Angus was only dimly aware of what Hannah was saying. He was grateful to her for trying to help. But he knew there was nothing Dr Harris could do for him.

He had been here before. His suffering would pass when it passed. Until then he was trapped in this throbbing prison, like a foetus in the dark fluid of the womb.

He must accept it. He deserved it. He had brought himself to this dark place, after all, and not even Hannah, with all her love and light, could save him.

'My poor baby.' Jock reached a hand out tenderly and lightly stroked Kathy's bruised cheek. 'You must have taken quite a tumble.'

'I guess I did,' she sighed, kissing his hand. 'But I'm OK now. It's not as bad as it looks.'

They were on the motorway, heading back to Pitfeldy, and the conversation was still a little stilted between them. Jock put it down to the 'bumpy re-entry' couples often felt after a spell apart, but he still didn't like it. There was definitely something subdued about Kathy, a reticence that he wasn't used to.

'I missed you,' he said gruffly, returning his hand to the wheel. 'So did the dogs. They've been looking awfully down in the mouth without you.'

'They're OK though?' said Kathy, sounding panicked. 'I mean, they're not sick?'

'Not as far as I know,' said Jock, fighting down his irritation that she seemed more anxious about Milo and Sam Sam than she did about him. 'Mrs G's been keeping them to their normal routine. I've just noticed they've not been their usual bouncy selves.'

'Well, I've missed them too,' said Kathy, relaxing a little.

'And me, I hope?' Jock couldn't help himself.

'Of course, honey.'

Reaching out she put a hand on his leg and squeezed. Jock beamed. It was ridiculous how happy she made him.

'So tell me more about Italy,' he said brightly. 'How was Milan? I suppose you've bankrupted me with the dress?'

'Dress*es*,' Kathy corrected him impishly. 'I got three.'

'Three?' Jock spluttered. 'How many weddings are we having?'

'Only the one, dearest,' Kathy cooed, cheering up herself now that the subject had turned to couture. 'But I wanted something traditional for the service, and then maybe something a bit more flirty for the reception. That's very common these days.'

'Is it indeed?' grumbled Jock, only half-jokingly. 'That's still only two dresses. Unless I've lost complete control of my senses. Which, of course, I may have.'

'Not your senses, *mi amore*,' Kathy laughed. 'Only your Amex card. The third dress is for the rehearsal dinner.'

He looked at her blankly.

'Jock!' she admonished. 'Don't tell me you've forgotten?'

'Course not,' said Jock, who clearly had.

'Good,' said Kathy, 'because I was actually thinking we might move that forward, to December. I just figured no one's going to want to get all dolled up for a party between Christmas and New Year. That's, like, everybody's downtime, right? When all you want to do is sleep off your hangover and –'

'Go shooting,' Jock finished the sentence for her, earning himself a slap on the thigh. 'What?' he said indignantly, glad that things between them seemed to be resetting to normal. 'Just because you're all save-the-whale and let's go vegan, doesn't mean all of our guests will be doing the same. Boxing Day shooting parties are a big deal in Scotland. That's a busy time.'

After that, conversation flowed more easily, with Kathy happily chatting away about the wedding, and her dresses, and the stunning antique lace she'd picked up in Venice for a '*very* reasonable' price. Eventually, as naturally as he could, Jock brought the topic around to Iris.

'I was surprised she didn't fly back with you.'

'Me too, a little bit,' admitted Kathy, cagily. 'But, you know, we can't resume work on the portrait until this heals.' She touched her battered cheek and eye. 'So she might as well take the time off, I guess. Plus all artists *love* Italy, right?'

'Hmmm,' said Jock. 'Did she ever meet up with that priest you told me about? The fellow who thought he recognised a necklace or some such nonsense?'

'Uh-huh,' said Kathy excitedly. 'And it's not nonsense. I can't believe you don't know about this, but then you never go on Facebook and you're hardly ever in the village . . .'

'Know about what?' Jock interrupted her.

'The priest was right. The girl he gave the necklace to *was* one of the victims. Her name was Beatrice Contorini. The Italian police have confirmed it.'

'I see,' Jock said stiffly, his eyes glued to the road.

'Apparently, they've taken over the case now,' said Kathy.

With Iris Grey's unwanted assistance, no doubt, Jock brooded bitterly.

Sensing his disquiet, Kathy leaned over and planted a kiss on his cheek. 'You know, honey, I *have* missed you,' she said softly. 'It's good to be home.'

Rory MacKinnon gripped his Hermes overnight bag tightly as he stepped out of the castle into the bitter wind and clicked open the boot of his new silver Range Rover Velar.

Gingerly placing the bag in the car, he heard the familiar rumble of his father's Volvo hurtling up the drive.

Damn it. Rory had hoped to avoid running into Jock and Kathy. The traffic back from the airport must have been better than usual. Half hidden behind the raised door of the open boot, Rory watched as his father got out of the car and walked around to the passenger side to open the door for his soon-to-be stepmother.

How chivalrous, Rory thought bitterly. He couldn't remember a single occasion when Jock had opened a door for his mother, or performed any other act of kindness, for that matter, big or small.

He observed the change in Jock's gait, how he moved now with the jerky stiffness of an old man. The old bastard would not live for ever. Perhaps not even for long. Sadly, barring an unexpected accident, the same could not be said for his gold-digging slut of a girlfriend.

And there she was now, *Kathy*, unfurling her skinny legs from the car like a snake, coiling her viper's arms around Jock's neck and kissing him. Something seemed to have happened to her face. She looked as if she'd been punched, but sadly not by his dad, thought Rory, looking at the two of them pressing their noses together lovingly, Jock sliding a hand around the small of Kathy's back before lowering it to stroke her pert backside. They didn't know they were being watched – neither of them seemed to have noticed his car – so one had to presume that this sickening display of affection was genuine.

'Don't mind me.' Slamming the boot shut, Rory crunched over the gravel to open his driver's door.

Releasing Kathy, Jock glared at his son and heir. 'What are you doing here?'

'Picking up a few things,' Rory said casually. 'Don't worry. I'm not staying. Not now the Wicked Witch of the West is back. Nice shiner, by the way,' he added snidely to Kathy. 'I won't ask.'

'Oh, grow up,' snapped Jock. 'And what "things" were you picking up?'

'Things of Mother's,' Rory snapped back.

Jock opened his mouth to speak again; as far as he was concerned there was nothing left at Pitfeldy Castle over which Fiona had the slightest claim, but Rory had already slammed his car door shut and started the engine, spinning his wheels so as deliberately to spray gravel in his father's direction. Taking off at speed, he swerved dangerously close to Kathy, who had to flatten herself against the side of Jock's car to avoid being hit as he drove away.

'Moron,' Jock muttered furiously, turning back to comfort his shaken fiancée. 'Are you all right, darling?'

'I'm fine,' lied Kathy, smiling bravely. 'Totally fine.'

'My darling.' Fiona MacKinnon's expression lifted as her son walked into the restaurant, an expensive American oyster bar just off Princes Street. Rory had grown into such a handsome man, mixing the best of Jock's features, his height and bearing and his wide, patrician forehead, with traits from Fiona's own family. The thick dark hair, heavy brows and moss-green eyes were all Harris characteristics. On top of his genetic blessings, Rory dressed beautifully, and carried himself like the rich, successful man he had become. People turned and looked when Rory MacKinnon entered a room. The pride Fiona felt in him was a great comfort to her, a glorious, unsullied phoenix risen from the ruined ashes of her marriage. She'd been looking forward to tonight's dinner for a long time.

'Ma.' Striding over to the table, Rory embraced her warmly, enveloping her in a sweet fug of Floris aftershave. 'You look lovely, as always. Shall we have some Pol Roger? I always think champagne goes marvellously with oysters, don't you?'

Mother and son sat and talked, about Rory's latest case in which he'd triumphed at the high court, and about the latest Edinburgh society gossip. He dodged questions about his love life with his usual deft charm, and listened with genuine interest to all Fiona's plans for improvements to her apartment and possibly travelling to Asia next spring with some of her friends from Bridge Club.

Rory could sense his mother's loneliness. Her longing to talk, and to have someone listen. He wasn't a patient man by nature. But Fiona was perhaps the only person on earth whom he loved completely and unconditionally, and he made a point of waiting until she'd exhausted every topic she wanted to share with him before getting down to business.

'So.' He leaned back as another platter of succulent *Ostrea edulis*, the sweet European flat oysters making a comeback in Scottish waters, was set down in front of them. 'I dropped in at the castle earlier. I got everything we needed while Dad was at the airport, picking up you know who.'

'He drove to get her? Himself?' Fiona's brow furrowed.

Rory kicked himself. He shouldn't have added this last detail. It was insensitive.

'Forget about him, Ma. He's bewitched by her, but we knew that already. What matters is it gave me a window to rummage through the house on my own. For us. Which I did. I'll show you everything back at the flat later.'

'Did you go up to my old study?' Fiona asked, toying anxiously with an empty oyster shell.

'Of course,' said Rory. 'Did you know that's where the dreadful Grey woman is having Kathy sit for her portrait?' he added, knocking back a bitter gulp of champagne.

'I like her, actually,' said Fiona, unexpectedly.

'Who? Iris Grey?' Rory looked astonished.

Fiona nodded. 'And I'm sure that the choice of my study for the portrait would have been Kathy's choice, not Iris's.'

'Have you met her, then?' Rory frowned.

'I have,' said Fiona. 'She came here, a couple of weeks ago, asking questions about the "Girls in the Wood". That's what they're calling them, you know.'

'*Iris Grey* came to your flat?'

'There's no need to sound so outraged, Rory. I invited her,' said Fiona, laying a reassuring hand on his.

'Well – what sort of questions?' Rory blustered, thoroughly blindsided.

'Let me think.' Fiona leaned back calmly in her chair. 'She wanted to know about my marriage to your father. About his affairs, and the Braes and, you know, what life was like on the estate at around the time those two women would have been killed.'

'Ma, you never told me this.' Rory put his head in his hands. 'You *must* tell me these things. That woman, Iris – I don't think you can trust her.'

'Why not?' Fiona asked guilelessly.

'Because she's a meddler. A professional meddler,' said Rory. 'She's looking for trouble, always poking her nose in where it's not wanted.'

'You sound like your father,' Fiona laughed.

'And she's thick as bloody thieves with Kathy. They're always together, taking little *walks*,' Rory added angrily, clearly expecting this nugget of information to change his mother's mind.

Instead, Fiona merely looked at him thoughtfully. As a general rule, she trusted Rory's judgment. But on this occasion, she wondered if he were letting his emotions get the better of him.

'Look, I'm sorry I didn't mention it before,' she said soothingly. 'You're right, I probably should have. But I don't think you're right about Iris Grey. She's a portrait painter. Part of her job is getting to know her sitters.'

'Even so . . .' began Rory, but Fiona cut him off.

'The fact that she spends time with Kathy and they take walks together doesn't mean they're close. Iris struck me as rather a serious person. Thoughtful. And, I would say, moral. If she's "meddling", I suspect she's doing it for honourable reasons. She has nothing in common with your father's . . . with that woman. More importantly,' Fiona MacKinnon looked her son right in the eye, 'I think she could be useful to us.'

'Useful? I don't see how,' Rory said bluntly.

Fiona smiled lovingly. Her darling boy was impressive in

so many ways. But at times, though it pained her to say it, he lacked imagination.

'Your father has secrets, Rory. Some of them we know, but can't prove.'

'Can't prove yet,' Rory corrected her.

'But what if Iris Grey *can* prove them?' Fiona's eyes lit up. 'Not for our sakes, but because she's determined to learn the truth. What if Iris were to stumble upon things that even we don't know about? Dark things from before my time, before you and Emma were born? Because there were other secrets, Rory. Other sins your father buried. I know there were.'

Rory paused, surprised and intrigued by his mother's passion.

Was she right? Could Iris Grey end up being an asset rather than a liability, a help rather than a hindrance to their plans?

At the end of the day, all Rory MacKinnon cared about was avenging his mother and destroying his father. It was that simple. Whether or not he liked Iris was irrelevant. Not if she could be manipulated to advance those ends. He would give the matter some thought.

'It will all be OK, you know, Ma,' he told Fiona lovingly, raising his glass to hers. 'In the end. I'll make sure of it.'

'I don't doubt it, my darling,' his mother replied proudly.

He truly was the best son a woman could wish for.

Chapter Twenty-four

Iris sat bolt upright in bed, eyes wide open. Her hands were gripping the bedspread so tightly her palms ached, and her heartbeat raced at a quite nausea-inducing rate.

What a vile dream. She'd been in Venice, on a gondola, sprawled out on one of the tasselled velvet seats on a beautiful, cloudless day when the waters suddenly started to rise. Then one by one, faces, some alive and some dead and rotten, began bobbing up to the surface of the canal, including Dom Wetherby's, decomposed and ghastly. Finally, there was Beatrice Contorini as she was in Father Antonio's photograph, her eyes reproachful, arms stretched out to Iris for help, *Save me, for God's sake!* But she didn't, she couldn't; instead, she watched helplessly as Beatrice sank back into the fetid water. After that she was back in the Venice apartment, and masked men were chasing her, grabbing her by the throat. She struggled, unable to breathe, as Kathy Miller's screams rang in her ears . . . *Iris!*

Even after she woke, it took a few moments for her pulse to calm and the reality of her surroundings to reassert themselves.

I'm at home, in bed. I'm fine. Everything's fine.

To her left, the bedside clock said 6.04 a.m. It was still pitch-dark outside Murray House, but Iris could already hear clattering and the faint call of male voices from the docks. Pitfeldy's fishing fleet set out early, even in the dark, cold depths of winter. She thought briefly about Jamie Ingall, before chasing the image of his handsome face away.

Rolling over, she tried to get back to sleep but it was no use. The dream was still bothering her, its strands of meaning demanding to be untangled. It was the last parts that stuck with her the most: being unable to save Beatrice, or Kathy. Fighting for her own breath. So many threads of connection seemed to emanate from Venice – people, places, motives, coincidences – each one like a shaft of light, enticing yet intangible, impossible to grasp.

Sod it. Heaving herself out of bed and the warm fug beneath the covers, Iris pulled on her sports bra and cold-weather running gear. She wasn't going to get any more sleep now, so she might as well get out there and wake herself up properly.

'Aye, aye. Isn't that your wee girlfriend?' Jamie Ingall's crew-mate, Ross Ables, nudged him in the ribs as the two of them checked their nets. 'I thought you said she was on holiday?'

Jamie looked up. There, indeed, was the diminutive figure of Iris Grey, jogging down the steep cobbled hill towards the harbour, her face scrunched up against the bitter early morning wind.

'She was,' he mumbled, dropping his end of the net and hopping off the boat onto the jetty. 'Just give me a minute, OK?'

He'd been out on the boats almost solidly since their night together at Halloween, and he told himself that was the reason he hadn't responded to Iris's texts. Not that there had been that many of them. After a week of silence, she'd given up. Deep down though, Jamie knew there was more to it than that. The simple truth was he'd been afraid, frightened by how much he liked her.

'Iris,' he called out to her now.

She looked up and stopped. Nervously, Jamie walked over. Behind him, unhelpfully, a few of the fishermen wolf-whistled and clapped, but their noise soon faded into the distance.

'You're back, then.'

He smiled, but Iris's expression remained blank.

'Looks like it.'

He shuffled awkwardly from foot to foot. 'Are you angry?'

Iris shrugged.

'I'll take that as a yes.' He smiled again, but she wasn't letting him off the hook. 'Look,' he cleared his throat, 'I'm sorry I didn't ring you. I should have. I wanted to, but –' He hesitated, unsure how to finish the sentence. 'I've been out on the boats pretty much constantly. It's been exhausting, and –'

Iris held up a hand, cutting him off. 'It's all right. You don't owe me an explanation.'

'Yes, I do,' he said, reaching out and resting a rough, heavy hand on her shoulder. 'Of course I do.'

Iris shook her head. 'I've been very busy myself.'

'So I hear,' said Jamie. 'I gather your Italian trip was eventful.'

'Who told you that?' Iris asked, frowning.

'I might have checked your Facebook page once or twice,' Jamie admitted sheepishly.

'Yes, well.' Iris blushed, perturbed by how much the touch of his hand jolted her, and by how physically attracted she still felt to him. 'It's not as if we were a couple or anything.'

Jamie grimaced. 'No. I know that. But even so, I . . . I'm sorry. That's all. I'm sorry because I like you.'

They stood there for a moment, eyes locked. Every rational bone in Iris's body screamed at her to walk away. She had *far* more in common with Stuart Haley than she ever would with this unpredictable, unreliable boy. And yet perhaps that was *why* she was still so attracted to him. He was her opposite in every way.

'Can I see you again? I'll be back onshore again later in the week. I could buy you an apology dinner?'

Iris bit her lip. 'I'm not sure that's a good idea.'

More shouts from the boat had Jamie looking back over his shoulder.

'I'd better go. They're waiting for me.'

'OK,' said Iris, doing her best to sound nonchalant.

'Just – think about dinner, OK? I have missed you, Iris.'

Walking back to his boat, Jamie felt a little lighter. That hadn't gone perfectly. But he'd broken the ice at least. It was a start.

★

'Same again, headmaster?'

John Donnelly nodded gratefully as the new, young barman at the Fisherman's Arms drew him a fresh pint of bitter. He didn't often stop by the pub on a Sunday lunchtime. Half the children from Pitfeldy School and their parents were usually crammed into the snug bar, and very few felt any compunction about collaring him to express their concerns or complaints during his precious hours off. Not that he minded, really. John Donnelly loved teaching, and he loved being part of the Pitfeldy community even more. Not married and with no children of his own, Donnelly's vocation had become his life, and the modest local school he'd run for the past thirty or more years was, in effect, his world.

It was a safe world, on the whole, wholesome and good. Within the four walls of the school, John Donnelly was, in his own humble way, a king. He liked to think of himself as a benign leader. Certainly, he believed, he had done more good than bad during his years at the helm of Pitfeldy School. But, of course, none of us are perfect. We all have our secrets. Our regrets. Our sources of shame. Headmaster Donnelly had done his best to move on from his own 'mistakes', as he liked to think of them.

If only others could do the same, he thought now, feeling the pleasant smoothness of his beer being soured by a dirty look from across the bar. It was Hannah Drummond, a nice girl, generally, and one of his brightest former pupils, although, sadly, her erstwhile good opinion of him had been poisoned by her relationship with Angus Brae. The Brae family had long been a thorn in John Donnelly's side, but since Angus's attack at the Halloween party, the rift had become both more public and more serious. Perhaps coming to the pub had been a mistake after all?

'Oh, hello, headmaster. I'm surprised to see you in here.'

Charlotte Tillings, the local vet's wife and a stalwart of Pitfeldy School's PTA, appeared at Donnelly's elbow like a friendly ghost.

‘Enjoying a quiet pint?’

I was, thought Donnelly. But he put on his game face, as usual.

‘Hello, Charlotte. Yes, the weather’s so grim; I thought I’d treat myself to one of Brenda’s first-rate haggises. Are the children with you?’

‘No, thank God,’ Charlotte replied. ‘It’s just me and Harry today. The boys are both at rugby practice and Kira’s at a birthday party in Buckie.’

She ordered some drinks and handed over a twenty to the barman, before carrying on.

‘Terrible about this girl, isn’t it? Have you seen the pictures?’

‘I’m sorry?’ The headmaster frowned, momentarily thrown by the woman’s non sequitur. ‘What girl?’

‘The dead girl,’ explained Charlotte. ‘The one they dug up, up at the castle. Couple of months ago?’

‘Oh. Yes,’ said Donnelly, distractedly. ‘Awful business.’

‘Yeah, well, now they reckon they know who it was, don’t they?’ said Charlotte excitedly. ‘One of the bodies, anyway. That nice artist lady’s been all over the village this morning, handing out fliers, asking if anybody remembers seeing her. I don’t, personally. Mind you, it was over ten years ago, so you can hardly blame folk for forgetting a face.’

Reaching into her coat pocket, oblivious to the headmaster’s ashen face, Charlotte Tillings pulled out a badly folded piece of paper, with a colour photograph above a printed question: *Do you recognise this girl?*

‘Here she is, look. Pretty, wasn’t she? And so young.’ She shook her head sadly.

Silently, John Donnelly stared at the paper in his hand. The young, dark-haired girl, standing by the riverbank, her merry eyes almost dancing for the camera.

‘You didn’t know her, did you?’

Donnelly shook his grey head slowly. ‘Me? No. I don’t think so.’

‘Nobody seems to, so far,’ said Charlotte, reaching over the bar for her tray of drinks and crisps, and pocketing her change.

'But this artist is convinced she must have come to Pitfeldy before she died. Must have had some connection here. Anyway, I'd better go. Harry'll be dying of thirst by now. Nice to see you. You can keep that, if you like.'

'Oh, no – thank you. It's fine,' said Donnelly, holding out the paper, but the Tillings woman was already halfway across the snug and surrounded by a noisy sea of people. Scrunching up Iris Grey's flier with an anger he didn't know he was feeling, he tossed it into the wastepaper basket behind the bar.

Iris had seemed nice enough when John had met her. But what on earth had persuaded her to take up this macabre crusade? Why couldn't she leave people alone? Leave the dead buried and the past in the past?

'A lemonade, please.'

It was Hannah Drummond, standing at the bar not three feet away from him. Not to acknowledge her would be churlish, so John Donnelly raised a tentative hand in greeting.

'Hello, Hannah.'

She blanked him, staring straight ahead.

Sod this, thought Donnelly, deciding to take the bull by the horns. He had nothing to be ashamed of; or at least, he refused to be broken by shame, just to make Angus bloody Brae feel better.

'How's Angus?'

'He's at home in bed with a crippling migraine,' Hannah said stiffly, still not looking at him. 'Not that you care.'

'On the contrary,' said Donnelly, sipping his beer. 'I'm sorry to hear it.'

'Doctor says it's PTSD,' hissed Hannah. 'That's what brings on the attacks. Traumatic events from his past.'

'Again,' muttered Donnelly. 'I'm sorry.'

Taking her drink, his former pupil turned and looked right at him. To his dismay, John Donnelly saw there were tears in the girl's eyes.

'Not sorry enough,' she said bitterly.

*

Two days later, Iris was at home, engrossed in her dolls' house, when her phone rang. She was meeting Stuart Haley for dinner in a couple of hours, which she was really looking forward to, so when she saw the caller ID, she almost didn't pick up. But then she decided that was cowardly and pathetic, and that two wrongs didn't make a right.

'Jamie?'

'Hi.'

Even in that single syllable she could tell he sounded nervous. *Good. As well he should be.*

'I was going to come round, but then I thought it might be better if I rang.'

'Right,' said Iris. She was determined not to give any ground. If they were going to be friends again – on any level – then it was up to him to make all the running. 'So what is it?'

He cleared his throat. 'I saw your flier, when I got back last night. You know, with the picture of the girl?'

It was the last thing Iris had been expecting him to say. For a moment she felt on the back foot.

'Oh?'

'I recognised her.'

The silence went on for so long that Jamie thought the line must have gone dead. 'Iris? Are you there?'

'Yes, yes, I'm here,' Iris croaked. 'Are you sure?'

'I'm sure I've seen her before, aye,' said Jamie.

'Because it's very important.'

'I know that. I wouldn't have called if I wasn't certain. The only thing is,' he hesitated, 'I cannae remember exactly where it was, or when.'

'It was in Pitfeldy, though?' Iris pressed him, her heart in her mouth.

'I suppose it must have been,' said Jamie. 'I mean, if I'm not out at sea, then I'm basically here, aren't I? And I don't think I met her fishing for herring.'

'No,' Iris agreed.

'Anyway, if anything more comes back to me, I'll let you know.'

'OK,' said Iris.

'But I thought I should tell you . . . what I just told you.'

'Thank you.'

Neither of them hung up as a second excruciating silence ensued.

'I hope you catch the guy who did it,' Jamie said eventually.

'Me too,' said Iris.

'I miss you.'

Me too, said Iris – but only to herself.

'Take care, Jamie.'

She hung up.

DI Stuart Haley dashed into the restaurant shaking the rain off his coat and unleashing a volley of apologies.

'Sorry, sorry, sorry! Have you been here ages? I hope you've ordered a drink at least. I just couldn'ae get away.' He sat down, shaking his hair like a wet dog, while Iris offered reassurances. It did feel a little strange, sitting here at the same restaurant she'd been to with Jamie. But Pitfeldy wasn't exactly awash with fine-dining options, and Maria's felt slightly more private than the pub.

They ordered pasta and two glasses of Maria's rather disgusting Lambrusco, which was the closest they could get to champagne, 'to celebrate your safe return', as well as a decent bottle of Chianti. Still unsure whether this was a 'date' or a sort of unofficial business meeting, Iris waited for Haley to open the conversation. She wasn't sure whether she was relieved or disappointed when he jumped straight to Beatrice Contorini.

'The progress you've made has been fantastic,' he told Iris. 'But it still bothers me to think that whoever killed her is still out there.'

'True.' Iris looked into her wine glass thoughtfully.

'Probably enjoying a nice glass of red as we speak,' said Haley bitterly. 'Just like us.'

'Oh, I don't know about that,' said Iris. 'Imagine if you'd buried those girls under a remote bothy, more than a decade ago. You'd be certain you'd got away with it, wouldn't you, by now? And then all of a sudden, boom. There are skeletons and dental records and a *name*; police forces in two countries raking over what's left of the evidence.'

'Not to mention a nosy-parker portrait painter with a stubborn streak,' Haley said wryly, raising his glass.

'Well, quite,' said Iris. Was he being flirtatious? It was hard to tell. Hard, also, to tell if she felt any sort of attraction towards him, other than on a personality level. He wasn't *un*attractive. A little pale, maybe, but he had pleasant features and really quite striking pale blue eyes, now that Iris stopped to look at them. Then again, if you had to ask yourself whether or not you fancied someone, didn't it automatically mean that you didn't? That you were just divorced and lonely and clutching at straws, trying not to think about unreliable trawlermen who . . .

'So, any more leads to tell me about?' Stuart broke her self-indulgent reverie with his usual down-to-earth bonhomie. Which, ironically, was exactly what Iris liked about him. 'I've seen your fliers, with Beatrice's picture. Have you had any bites?'

'Funny you should ask that, actually. I had my first one right before I came here.' She told him about Jamie Ingall's phone call. 'He was convinced he knew her. Which, I think, means she must have spent time in Pitfeldy before she died.'

'I agree,' said Haley.

'The problem is, no one else remembers her,' said Iris. 'Not so far, anyway. So maybe Jamie's mistaken?'

Haley rubbed his jaw thoughtfully. 'Maybe. We need to figure out the Scotland connection. Because there is one.'

'I agree,' said Iris. 'But at the same time, I can't stop thinking that there's something I missed back in Italy. Something important enough for Massimo Giannotti to have me literally thrown out of the –'

She stopped, dead, pressing both hands against her temples.

Haley looked concerned. 'What? What's the matter?'

'I just remembered something,' said Iris excitedly. 'Fiona MacKinnon. Jock's ex-wife.'

'What about her?'

'You remember I went to visit her in Edinburgh?'

'Aye.'

'Before Father Antonio contacted me, before I went to Italy?'

He nodded again. 'I remember.'

'Well, when I was there – *how did I forget this?* – she told me about a young Italian au pair girl who'd worked for her and Jock up at the castle when Rory and Emma were teenagers,' said Iris. 'Some "Eurotrash aristocrat" friend of Jock's introduced her. That was what Fiona said.'

'OK,' said Haley patiently, still waiting for the punchline.

'Isabella!' Iris snapped her fingers, delighted that the name had come back to her. 'That was the name. Anyway, according to Fiona, there was some unpleasantness, some sort of row with Jock, and he shipped this girl back to her father – in *Rome*. The father was furious about the whole thing, threatening to take Jock to court and whatnot, although he never did.'

'So, you're thinking . . .'

'Rome?' said Iris, as if it were obvious. Which to her, apparently, it was. 'The "Eurotrash aristo" friend could be Massimo. I *knew* he had a connection to Pitfeldy,' she added excitedly. 'When we spoke and I mentioned it, he went as white as a sheet. I thought it was something to do with Kathy, but perhaps it was this Isabella? What do you think?'

'I don't know,' said Haley.

It was hardly the ringing endorsement Iris had been hoping for. 'Come on. It can't be a coincidence,' she cajoled him.

'Why not?' asked Haley, playing devil's advocate. 'Rome's a big city, and Massimo Giannotti's not the only aristocrat playboy who lives there.'

'He's the only one accused of being our victim's father,' Iris pointed out, reasonably. 'I met him, Stuart, and I'm telling you, when I told him I was painting Kathy Miller's portrait – Jock MacKinnon's fiancée – alarm bells went off. He knew something. I don't know what, or who, but he *knew* something. This girl Isabella was from Rome and *she* knew one of Jock's aristocrat friends. Meanwhile, Beatrice Contorini, potentially Massimo's illegitimate daughter, just *happens* to turn up dead in Jock MacKinnon's back garden?'

Haley rubbed his brow, confused. Iris was talking at nineteen to the dozen, and it was no mean feat to keep up.

'OK, OK, slow down. So Beatrice believed this Massimo was her father.'

'Yes.'

Haley raised a hand patiently. 'Talk to me about that. What did Father Antonio have to say about the whole paternity thing?'

Reluctantly, Iris took a deep breath and explained again, slowly, the story of Paola Contorini's rape accusation against Massimo, as relayed by Father Antonio.

'And you believe this story, I take it?' asked Haley.

'I believe Paola was raped,' said Iris. 'She may have been unstable, and an addict, but you don't make up something like that. And you don't forget it either.'

'Well,' Haley cautioned. 'People *do* make these things up. I mean, not often. But it happens, especially when there's money involved. Women aren't all saints, you know, Iris.'

'Yes, yes,' Iris said crossly, irritated because she agreed. But she just felt in her bones that Paola Contorini had not been that kind of woman.

'Let's forget about this Isabella for now,' said Haley. 'And let's just say Massimo *did* rape Paola, and he *was* Beatrice's father.'

'OK,' said Iris.

'Well . . . so what?'

'I don't follow.' Iris frowned.

'It's hardly a motive for murder, is it? If what you say about Italian society is true, and I've no reason to think it isn't, then a man like Massimo Giannotti was never in any danger of being done for rape. It would have been his word against a chambermaid's, and we all know how that goes.'

'True,' admitted Iris.

'So then think it through. What would have happened next? The rape case is a non-starter. So let's say there was a blackmail attempt. Beatrice asks him for money, Massimo says no. What was the worst she could do to him? Accuse him of being a philanderer? A dead-beat dad? What does he care? People already knew those things about him, and his high-society mates obviously don't care. Nah,' Haley shook his head. 'I'm not buying it. Giannotti may be an arsehole, but I don't think he's our man. He had no need to kill Beatrice, whether he knew this mysterious au pair girl or not.'

Iris digested this for a minute. She didn't disagree, but at the same time there was something there, something she didn't want to let go.

'If Massimo's one hundred per cent innocent in all this, why go to all the trouble of getting rid of me?' she asked. 'Of having me deported, bundled onto a plane back to the UK, like I'm some sort of terrorist?'

'You don't know that was him,' Haley pointed out.

'Who else?' Iris shrugged.

'Well, I'm not sure,' Haley admitted. 'Someone who didn't want you sniffing around the Contorini women.'

'OK, but who?'

'Whoever broke into your apartment in Venice, maybe?' said Haley, thinking aloud. 'The really interesting question is *why* were they so threatened. I've a feeling this may go deeper than Beatrice's murder. That there's more to it than that.'

'Such as?'

'Maybe her death was incidental.'

'Incidental to what?' asked Iris.

'Well, that's just it, I don't know,' said Haley, muttering to himself between forkfuls of pasta. 'Perhaps this Romanian gang connection . . .? What was the name of the fella? Barbu?'

'Andrei Barbu,' Iris confirmed. 'His whole family were dodgy, according to Father Antonio. I wondered if he might have been Beatrice's boyfriend. Apparently, she'd fallen in love with some foreigner.'

'Who else knew you were in Italy, asking questions?' Haley asked Iris, having apparently lost interest in the Barbu thread already.

'Well, Father Antonio,' she replied. 'But he invited me, so I highly doubt he was the one behind getting me deported, or ransacking my apartment and attacking poor Kathy. He told me about an art teacher, Julia Mantovani, who was close to Beatrice. I need to ask the school for her address.'

'OK. And who else? Other than Massimo?'

Iris thought about it. 'The Italian police.'

'And?'

'That's it.'

'It's like everything fits, but nothing fits.' Iris sighed, exasperated. 'Like two hands reaching across a river, and the fingertips touch but you can never quite get a grip.'

'Welcome to my world,' said Haley.

For a while they ate and drank and discussed other things. Iris's plans once she was finished with Kathy's portrait. The upcoming MacKinnon wedding. Eventually, the conversation turned to Haley's thoughts about his own future.

'I have thought about moving,' he told Iris. 'You know, now that Jean's gone. Making a fresh start. But then I think, where would I go? You can't outrun grief, or memories, and I wouldn't want to, even if I could.'

'Of course not,' said Iris, sympathetically.

This isn't a date, she realised. Maybe he'd wanted it to be, when he first asked her to dinner. But the truth was the poor man was clearly not ready to move on. *He's still in love with his wife.*

'Plus, truth be told, I do still really enjoy my job,' Stuart went on.

'That's because you're good at it,' said Iris, truthfully.

'Look,' he said, pushing his empty plate to one side. 'I'm due some leave. Maybe, if I keep my head down, we could work on this together?'

'That would be great,' said Iris, 'if you're sure it won't get you into trouble with the chief constable?'

'It won't if he doesn't hear about it.' Haley grinned. 'Maybe, for now at least, *you* should keep looking into all the local leads here in Pitfeldy. In the village and up at the castle. Keep pushing on Beatrice; maybe see if you can find out any more about this Isabella girl. And meanwhile, I'll get in touch with our Italian friends. Go softly-softly, see what I can dig up at that end. The polizia will respond better to a fellow copper asking for favours off the record, than they will to . . .'

'A nosy-parker portrait painter with a stubborn streak?' Iris offered, wryly.

'I was going to say a woman,' said Haley, teasingly. 'But I suppose that would offend your feminist sensibilities? Always the victim, you lot.'

'Kiss my arse, Braveheart,' Iris shot back, smiling broadly. 'You SNP whingers have "poor me" down to a fine art.'

God, it was nice to feel relaxed with a man. To be able to banter and joke around without feeling anxious or fearful or embarrassed about what might come next. Tonight's dinner had been easy. Ian, Iris's husband, had always been an interesting conversationalist, at least when he was sober. But dinners with Ian, even the good ones, had never been 'easy'.

And more recently, with Jamie Ingall, everything had seemed easy, until suddenly it wasn't. What she'd thought of as his triple-F agenda – Food, Fucking and Fishing, which seemed to be the only three things he cared about – had made a refreshing change, until she realised they actually came with a fourth 'F' – Fear of commitment. That was the zinger, the sting in the tail, and it had hurt her more than she cared to admit.

'Penny for 'em?' Haley looked at her curiously.

Blushing, Iris realised she'd been lost in thought for some minutes.

'I think your plan's a good one,' she said, coming back to the present. 'You do Italy and I'll focus on things here. I can't promise not to get Jock MacKinnon's back up, though.'

'Fine by me,' said Haley, studying the menu intently. Lava cake or sticky toffee pudding. That was the big question.

'I'm already firmly on his shit list,' said Iris. 'And I've a feeling that might be about to get worse.'

'Oh?' Haley looked up at her. 'How so?'

'Because unless Beatrice's photo suddenly prompts a flood of jogged memories down in the village,' said Iris, 'I'm afraid I'm going to have to pay a visit to his old friend Edwin Brae.'

Chapter Twenty-five

Aileen Chapman smiled brightly as she cleared away Edwin Brae's morning tea tray. Aileen enjoyed working at the nursing home. She hadn't been at all sure about taking her SVQ in Elderly Care after she left school in Buckie. It was her mam who'd pushed her to do it, but four years into her job at Passages, Aileen was so glad that she had. It was hard to describe exactly what she loved about her work. It certainly wasn't glamorous, or well paid, and the residents could be difficult at times and sometimes downright rude – old Mr Brae one of the rudest of them all. Although, of course, that was the Alzheimer's, not him. But there were also all the other times, when something as simple as bringing someone a cup of tea and a biscuit or stopping to chat about their families made a visible difference to the old people's lives. The smiles and the thank yous and the tightly squeezed hands all lifted Aileen more than she could express. And they meant even more when they came from a tricky old bugger like Edwin.

'You remember you've a visitor coming this morning, Mr B?' said Aileen, setting down the tray to plump up the old man's pillows. 'Miss Grey?'

'The artist,' Edwin muttered contentedly. 'My son's an artist.'

Aileen nodded, delighted he'd remembered. His illness was pronounced. He'd had it since his fifties, the poor devil; so much of his brain was damaged beyond repair, a jumble of plaque and tangles that could make even the smallest act of recall a challenge. But it was also bizarrely intermittent. On the times he *did* remember things, he could be sharp as a razor, blurting out incredibly vivid details.

'And that's still all right with you, is it?' Aileen asked. 'You're not too tired?'

'Tired? Och, no. I slept like a baby.' Looking up at Aileen through watery grey eyes, the corners of his thin mouth twitched upwards in what might have been a smile.

'I'm glad to hear it,' said Aileen. He certainly seemed to be in an awfully good mood today.

'Those shortbreads you brought me before were delicious.'

'A compliment?' The nurse's eyes widened. 'Well, I never. Someone's woken up on the right side of the bed.'

'It's all these young women, coming to see me,' Edwin Brae chuckled naughtily. 'Makes a change.'

'I'm sure it does. Well, I'll bring some fresh flowers in a bit,' said Aileen happily. 'For your guest. Do our best to make her feel welcome.'

The old man was still alert and smiling fifteen minutes later, when Aileen returned with a vase of chrysanthemums and Iris.

'This is Miss Grey.' She spoke loudly and slowly, well aware that in the last quarter of an hour Edwin might have forgotten everything. 'I found her in the lobby.'

'Yes, yes, I know who it is,' he grumbled, shooing the nurse away good-naturedly. Once she'd gone, he turned to Iris.

'Have a seat, Miss Grey. You're an artist, they tell me?'

'That's right,' said Iris, pleased to find the old man so amenable. He'd refused even to speak to DI Haley, and lots of people had told her that Edwin Brae could be prickly and difficult, including his own son.

'And you're working up at the castle?'

'Yes.'

'My boy paints.'

'I know,' said Iris. 'I've seen some of his work. He's good.'

'On the side, mind you,' muttered Edwin. 'He has a real job.'

Iris laughed. 'Art can be a real job, Mr Brae. It is for me.'

'Aye, but you're a woman,' said the old gillie bluntly. 'Messing about with paint's no job for a man.'

Deciding for expediency's sake to let this go, Iris looked around the room, searching for an angle with which to begin the conversation; a subject that wouldn't threaten the old man, but would hopefully put him at ease before she took the plunge and showed him Beatrice Contorini's photograph.

'Is that one of Angus's?'

She pointed to one of the landscapes beside the wardrobe, a pretty watercolour rendition of a winter moorland, presumably somewhere on the MacKinnon estate.

Edwin nodded. 'He painted everything in here. Makes me feel close to him,' he added, with a wistfulness Iris hadn't expected.

'Does he come to visit you?'

'Sometimes.' The old man looked away. 'I don't know. They tell me he comes sometimes, but I don't remember.'

Walking over to the side table by the window, Iris picked up one of the framed photographs standing beside the vase of flowers. There were five or six in all, mostly of Angus in various stages of childhood and adolescence. But the one that caught Iris's eye looked like it had been taken in the early fifties. It showed two teenage boys, one tall and skinny, the other shorter and more solidly built, standing arm-in-arm beside a lake.

'That's not *Jock*, is it?' asked Iris, squinting at the familiar features of the taller boy. He was young, of course, and happy, both of which differences made him harder to recognise from the dour old curmudgeon that she knew. But the aquiline nose and patrician curl of the lip gave it away.

'Certainly is, bless him,' said Edwin, a big, genuine smile spreading across his sunken face. 'That's the two of us at Loch Lomond. What a summer that was.'

'You remember it?'

'Oh yes. Jock's father, the auld baron, took the pair of us up there fishing for a fortnight. I was thrilled to be included. Happiest two weeks of my life.'

He means it, thought Iris, although it felt like an odd thing for a grown man to say, especially one with a child.

'As boys, you know, we were like brothers,' said Edwin, warming to his theme. 'People find it surprising, given our different stations in life. But I tell you, Miss Grey, we roamed that estate like two wee kings. In and out of the woods we were, thick as thieves, hunting and making camps and I don't know what.'

'And when you grew up?' asked Iris. 'Did you stay close?'

'Aye,' said Edwin. But he'd looked off to the side again, the joy of his boyhood reminiscences slowly draining out of his frail body like air being wheezed from a lung. 'Jock will always be a brother to me. But you know, when you get older, things change. She ruined everything.'

The old man's expression darkened almost comically.

'Who ruined everything?' asked Iris, although she already had a good idea from what Angus and Haley had told her.

'Linda. That bitch,' Edwin muttered, his mouth shrinking and puckering into a tightly pursed 'o' of hatred. 'Folks blamed me, but it was her. With her lies and her sneaking around behind my back. She poisoned him against me.' He jabbed a liver-spotted finger at Iris, as if she were the long-absent Linda Brae, a woman who, by all accounts, had been treated dreadfully by her then husband. And was so afraid, in fact, that she'd run off into the night, leaving her young son behind.

'What did people blame you for?' Iris asked. But Edwin didn't register the question, so lost was he in his old resentments.

'She made him hate me,' he ranted on. 'Encouraged him to disrespect me. To think that taking over as gillie one day was beneath him. All that bloody art nonsense, that was all her. The bitch. She did it to spite me. No respect, I tell ye, in my own house. What was I supposed to do?'

It dawned on Iris that he was talking about Angus now, not Jock. That somewhere along the line he'd lost the thread of their earlier conversation. Or perhaps, in his confusion and agitation, he'd simply conflated Angus and Jock into one person.

'That must have made you angry,' she said, feigning sympathy. 'Not being respected.'

'Angry? I could've fucking killed her.'

Balling his hand into a fist, he brought it down as hard as he could on the side table. It was an impotent, pathetic echo of the violent man he had clearly once been. The rage was still there, and the self-pity, and the entitlement. That deep-rooted belief that as a man he had a right to treat his wife as he pleased and still demand her loyalty. But Edwin Brae's physical strength had long since left him. Just like Linda.

'How did Jock get along with her?' Iris fished, trying to keep her tone casual in the face of Edwin's increasingly splenetic outbursts.

He peered at her, confused. 'Jock? Get along with who?'

'With Linda,' said Iris. 'With your wife.'

'My wife . . .' His confusion seemed to deepen, and his anger to collapse completely and instantly, like sails after a storm. As if something in Iris's question had inadvertently flipped a hidden 'off' switch. 'No, no,' he muttered. 'No, no, no. Jock and I go way back. He's a good man, MacKinnon. Always been there for the boy and that's all I'll say aboot that. What did you say your name was again?'

It was one of the strangest things Iris had ever witnessed, this Jekyll-and-Hyde transition from embittered ex-husband to sweet, rambling old man. Almost as if Edwin's Alzheimer's had made him a more decent person, even as it robbed him of his faculties. Deciding that she'd better show him Beatrice's picture now, while he was calm again and before he grew too confused, she pulled it out of her handbag.

'Iris,' she told him gently. 'My name is Iris, Mr Brae. I came to ask you if you recognise the young woman in this photograph?'

She pressed the picture into his hands and watched him look at it, intently, for quite a few seconds.

'Pretty girl,' he said softly.

'Her name was Beatrice.'

'Beatrice. I see.'

'Do you think you might have seen her before, Mr Brae?'

He frowned, handing the picture back. 'No, miss. I've not seen that young lady.'

Disappointed, Iris slipped the photograph back into her bag. She didn't like Edwin Brae, not the original version anyway, and she certainly didn't trust him. But there was no doubt in her mind that he was telling the truth about this. He didn't know who Beatrice was.

'OK. Well, thank you for your time. Enjoy the rest of your day.' Standing up to go, she turned and looked again at the framed photographs clustered together by the chrysanthemums. One, of Angus in Edinburgh, caught her eye. He was in his late teens or early twenties in the picture and standing alone, leaning back against a wall. It was an innocuous enough snap, but something about it was bothering her, and she couldn't put her finger on why. Some detail she was looking at and yet, somehow, not seeing. Something that wasn't quite right.

'Will you bring my biscuits next time, Aileen?' Edwin called after her, mistaking Iris for his nurse.

'Of course,' said Iris, tearing herself away from the picture. It was probably nothing anyway.

Chapter Twenty-six

'Doesn't it feel strange to you?' Kathy asked Iris. 'Being back here again?'

Lying back against the cushions in Fiona's old study with her precious dogs at her feet, lithe and lovely in tropical-print leggings and a huge, vibrant yellow Brora wrap, Kathy looked more exotic and out of place than usual in the cold, grey environs of the castle, like a bird of paradise trapped in a rusty cage. Even the attic room's cosy interiors couldn't totally dispel the encroaching chill of winter, creeping through the thick stone walls. Frosted, mullioned windows revealed a crisp blue winter sky, flooding the room with the sort of unforgiving light that would have shown every flaw in the face of a less ravishing sitter. But Kathy Miller only seemed all the more glowing and youthful, with her white teeth and glossy hair and with her legs pulled up beneath her like a teenager. All the bruising from the attack in Venice had healed, and Kathy looked for all the world like a bride-to-be without a care in the world.

'It does feel odd,' Iris agreed, one brush clamped between her teeth as she reached for a smaller one to finish the detailing on Kathy's hands. 'Jarring. Especially after Venice and – everything that happened.'

Kathy stiffened. 'Yes, well,' she said briskly. 'Let's not go back over all that. It's in the past.'

Iris raised an eyebrow, surprised by the firmness with which Kathy declared the conversation closed. She wondered how the cover story about falling down the steps had gone down with Jock, and how things had been between them generally since Kathy had got back, but she sensed that it would be a mistake to ask too many questions too soon.

'I was deported from Rome, you know,' she said, conversationally.

'I heard!' Kathy relaxed, excited by the prospect of some juicy gossip. 'You should totally sue them.'

'Sue who? The Italian police?'

'Sure,' said Kathy indignantly.

Iris grinned. 'That's a very American solution.'

'Maybe so, but sometimes we Yanks have a point,' Kathy insisted. 'And what's the alternative? You can't let people just get away with treating you like shit.' Iris was struck again by Kathy's gutsiness, that potent mix of resilience and determination that, like her intelligence, ran contrary to the bimbo, gold-digger stereotype that most people in Pitfeldy seemed intent on labelling her with.

'Like you said, it's in the past,' said Iris, with only the slightest hint of irony. 'And to be honest, I'm more interested in finding out who killed Beatrice, and whoever was buried with her, than I am in long and expensive legal battles.'

'Any progress on that?' asked Kathy, reaching down to pet a rather limp-looking Milo.

'Nothing concrete,' said Iris evasively.

'Did you ever track down that guy in Rome, the one that the priest said might have been Beatrice's father?'

'Massimo Giannotti,' said Iris. 'Yes, I did. He denied paternity. And Paola Contorini's rape.'

'Well, *duh*,' said Kathy. 'Not too many guys are gonna cop to an unproven rape charge.'

'True,' agreed Iris. 'I don't know, though. I didn't like him, or trust him, but I'm not certain he was lying, at least not about that. The strangest thing was that I happened to mention to him when we met that I was working in Pitfeldy at the moment, and that I'd been commissioned to paint *you*. And it was weird. Something seemed to click with him.'

'Click?' Kathy raised an eyebrow.

'Yeah. It was almost as if he knew you, or Jock, or he had some connection here. Might you have met him in New York?'

'I don't know. I mean, I guess.' Kathy frowned. 'The name doesn't ring any bells, but maybe if I saw him. Do you have a picture?'

'I don't,' said Iris, pulling out her iPhone. 'He put an end to our little chat before we got to the cosy selfie phase, unfortunately. But I suspect we could dig one up on Google Images. He's fairly well known in Italy. Let's have a look.'

As she scrolled through pictures, one of Kathy's dogs made a disconcerting gurgling sound and abruptly vomited all over the end of the couch.

'Oh my God! Sam Sam.' Scooping the tiny creature up into her arms, Kathy held him as his small body buckled and retched violently. When finally he finished, the little dog gave a series of hacking coughs, before slumping miserably back into his mistress's lap.

'Poor thing,' said Iris. 'How long has he been ill? I was actually thinking earlier that Milo looked a bit peaky.'

'It's more than "a bit peaky",' said Kathy with a worried shake of the head. 'They've both been so unwell. I saw something was wrong as soon as I got home. Jock took us to see the vet in Buckie.'

'And what did they say?'

Kathy bit her lip, tearing up. 'He said he couldn't find anything wrong with either dog. Nothing specific, anyway. He gave me some vitamin and iron supplements, but I mean, you saw that, right? It's bullshit. That is not normal.'

'No,' agreed Iris, wrinkling her nose as the smell of canine vomit wafted over to her side of the room. 'No, it's not.'

'Is that him?' Kathy asked suddenly, glancing across at Iris's phone.

'Oh – yes,' said Iris, who'd momentarily forgotten about Massimo. 'That's an old picture. It must have been taken ten years ago, I'd say. But this is him.'

Kathy studied the image closely and for a long time before

shaking her head. 'Nope. Sorry. I wish I could say I knew him, but I don't think we've ever met.'

'Oh well,' said Iris. 'Never mind. It was just a thought.'

She was about to head downstairs when the study door flew open with a bang and Jock burst in, red-faced and panting.

'I thought I'd find you here,' he said, glaring at Iris, his body taut with tension.

'Is something wrong?' Iris asked coolly.

'Yes, something bloody well is wrong!' Jock fumed. 'And you know *exactly* what it is. Did Haley put you up to it? Hmm?'

'Jock?' Kathy looked at him with dismay. 'What's wrong with you?'

He'd been in such a warm, conciliatory and lovely mood ever since she'd got back from Venice, even helping her with the plans for their wedding rehearsal dinner, which heaven knew wasn't his thing. But around Iris he seemed to become a different person, angry, unreasonable, his entire body wound tight, like a spring.

'Nothing's wrong with me,' he turned to Kathy, making an effort to soften his tone for her benefit, 'but your "friend" Iris here has been – good God.' Belatedly, his eyes fell on the pool of dog sick, dripping from the couch onto the carpet. 'When did that happen?'

'Just now,' said Kathy.

'Christ,' murmured Jock.

'I'm really worried about them.' Kathy's eyes welled up with tears, and for a moment Jock forgot all about Iris and his anger and hugged her.

'They'll be all right, my love,' he whispered soothingly. 'The vet said it was nothing serious, and he knows his stuff.'

'I know, but –'

'Why don't you nip downstairs and ask Mrs Gregory to come and clean up the mess? Take the dogs with you. They look like they could use a bit of fresh air. That way Iris and I can have a word in private.'

'What sort of a "word"?' Kathy asked warily. 'I won't have you being rude, Jock.'

'Really, it's fine,' Iris interjected. 'I'm sure whatever it is Jock and I can work it out between the two of us. You go and take care of Milo and Sam Sam.'

Reluctantly, Kathy left. Jock waited till she was out of earshot before turning back to Iris. 'I'd like to know what the hell you think you're playing at,' he hissed, more quietly but every bit as venomously as before.

'In what regard?' Iris asked levelly.

'I'm talking about your little visit to my old friend Edwin Brae,' Jock seethed. 'I already made it clear to DI Haley and his superiors that I won't stand for this sort of harassment.'

'I'm sure you did,' said Iris.

'Edwin's old, and ill. He has the right to be left in peace,' Jock ranted.

'With respect,' Iris defended herself, 'Mr Brae knew in advance what it was I wanted to ask him about, and he was perfectly happy to talk to me.'

'*Mr Brae* doesn't know his own name half the time,' Jock snapped. 'He's in no mental state to make those decisions.'

'What decisions?' asked Iris. 'It was a friendly chat, not a police interview. I was curious about what he remembered, that's all, and I can assure you, there was no harassment on my part,' Iris insisted. 'In fact, we had a very pleasant exchange.'

'Is that so?' Jock's colour and voice were both rising, like a slowly boiling kettle.

'Yes,' Iris said steadily, her nerves receding in the face of Jock's boorish entitlement. 'It is.' He was clearly used to getting his way, especially with women, and while Iris didn't enjoy confrontation, after years of bullying behaviour from her ex-husband she had learned how to stand up for herself when she needed to. 'He certainly had a lot of nice things to say about you.'

'About me? And what *business* do you think you have to be gossiping about me, Miss Grey?' Jock exploded, the last remnants of his self-control cracking like a dropped egg.

'Baron Pitfeldy, two women were brutally murdered and buried here on your estate, during the time that Edwin Brae managed it,' Iris shot back. 'You've succeeded, shamefully, in my view, in having the police investigation into those murders shut down. But you can't stop ordinary people like me continuing to seek the truth. Until whoever murdered those women is brought to justice, their deaths are everyone's business, mine included. Two women are *dead*, for God's sake.'

'I daresay they are,' said Jock, his voice cracking with emotion. 'But Edwin doesn't know anything. Why can't you all just leave him alone?'

Wow, thought Iris. *He really cares*. It hadn't occurred to her that Jock's concern for Edwin might be genuine. She'd assumed he was simply trying to cover his own tracks, afraid that the confused old man might blurt out something embarrassing or incriminating. But now she saw that at least part of his anger did seem to stem from a brotherly protectiveness towards Edwin that she couldn't totally condemn.

'The man's brain's a damned cabbage,' he continued his impassioned plea. 'It has been for years. Whatever he might have known once, Miss Grey, I can assure you he doesn't know it now.'

'All right,' said Iris. 'I won't bother him again.'

Jock gave her a disbelieving look, followed by a stiff 'Thank you'.

'But I assume you won't mind answering a few questions?' Iris continued. 'After all, there's nothing wrong with *your* brain, is there?'

'My brain? Of course not,' Jock grumbled.

'Good.' Whipping Beatrice's photo out of her shoulder bag before he could protest, Iris thrust it under Jock's nose. 'This is one of the victims. Her name is B—'

'I know her name,' said Jock, turning away. 'Kathy told me.'

'So do you recognise her?' said Iris.

'No.'

Kathy returned from downstairs and reappeared in the doorway just in time to witness the exchange.

'The least you can do is look, honey,' she chided Jock. 'That girl *died* here.'

Grudgingly, Jock examined the picture before turning back to Iris. 'No,' he said calmly. 'I don't recognise her. Satisfied?'

'You're sure you've never seen her before?' Iris pressed.

'Positive. And now if that's all . . .'

'Actually, it isn't,' said Iris, determined to grill him as hard as she possibly could while she had the chance, and with Kathy as a witness. 'Do you remember an au pair girl named Isabella?'

Jock's frown deepened. 'What the devil does that have to do with anything?'

'Who's Isabella?' asked Kathy.

'She was a young Italian woman, like Beatrice,' Iris explained. 'She worked here at the castle one summer, when Rory and Emma were teenagers.'

'I remember her vaguely,' said Jock, his irritation building. 'I remember she was lazy and we had to send her home. But I fail to see what on God's green earth she has to do with any of this.'

'Have you ever been to Venice, baron?' Iris asked, shifting gear. She hoped that if she fired questions quickly enough, and if Jock got angry enough, he might inadvertently let something slip.

The anger part, at least, seemed to be working. A muscle on Jock's temple began to twitch, and his face contorted, as if resisting the urge to punch Iris was causing him physical pain. But he wasn't a stupid man. When he spoke, it was slowly and deliberately.

'No,' he told Iris. 'Never. Tell me, was it Rory who brought up Isabella? Or have you, by chance, been talking to my ex-wife?'

Kathy gave Iris a wounded look. 'Have you? Spoken to Fiona?' she asked.

Iris nodded.

'Why didn't you tell me?' Kathy asked.

'Yes,' Jock piled in, 'why *didn't* you tell Kathy? Seeing as the two of you are such close friends. Or do the confidences only work one way, Miss Grey? Hmmm?'

'What about this man?' Iris held out her phone and the image of Massimo Giannotti that she'd googled for Kathy earlier. 'Do you know him?'

'That's enough,' Jock said firmly. Walking over to Kathy, he put an arm around her. 'I want you to leave now, Miss Grey. I understand that you see yourself as some sort of warrior for justice. But these questions are ludicrous, and I won't consent to being interrogated like a bloody criminal in my own home.'

'Fine by me,' said Iris, calmly starting to gather up her things.

'What? No!' said Kathy, sounding increasingly distressed. 'There's no need for this to get so hostile. We're on the same side.'

'With respect, I don't think we are,' said Iris.

'Something we agree on at last,' Jock chimed in snidely. Turning to face Kathy, he added: 'I know it's hard for you to hear, darling. But the fact is, Iris has been using you to try to get at *me*. Running off to see Fiona behind your back? Behind both *our* backs? Falling for whatever spiteful nonsense the silly cow has been spewing about me? About both of us, I daresay. Just you wait. It wouldn't surprise me if in a few weeks' time she starts trying to accuse *you* of these damned murders. She can't be trusted.'

Iris and Kathy exchanged glances, but for once Iris couldn't read the younger woman's expression. She saw the anxiety, and the pain. But whether Kathy agreed with Jock or not about her and her motives, she couldn't tell. Shaken but dignified, she left the room.

For almost a full minute after she'd gone, Kathy and Jock remained in silence, frozen in their places like two actors in a scene who'd both forgotten their lines. In the end, it was Kathy who spoke first.

'Why did you lie to Iris just now?' She laid the accusation softly, like a gift set down on a pillow.

Jock walked over to the far window, the one that looked out towards the moor. Opening it to clear the noxious smell of Sam Sam's vomit, he took a deep breath of crisp, cold air before replying.

'I didn't lie.'

'Yes, you did, darling,' Kathy replied patiently. 'You said you'd never been to Venice.'

'Ah.' Jock rubbed his forehead exhaustedly. 'That.'

'Yes. That. I know you've been to Venice. That's where you bought the mask in the study. That hideous, beaked plague-doctor thing you wanted to wear at Halloween.'

She waited for him to explain, to say something. But instead he simply sighed deeply and turned away, looking back out over the moor.

'In fact, I think you must have been there several times,' she went on, piecing things together as she went. 'That lovely painting of the saint you have hanging in baby Mary's old room? Didn't you tell me once that that came from Venice? St Theodore, that was it. It was special to you for some reason. I distinctly remember you saying so.'

He held up a hand in a 'stop' motion. 'You're right,' he said wearily. 'I did lie about Venice.'

'Why?'

'I told you already,' he snapped. 'Because I don't trust Iris as far as I can spit. And it's not as if I owe her an explanation.'

'Nuh-uh.' Kathy shook her head. 'I'm not buying it. There's more to it than that, I know there is. What else did you lie about?'

'Nothing. I swear to you . . .'

'*Don't* swear when it isn't true!' Kathy lashed out, turning on him angrily. 'Don't you dare. You knew her, didn't you? You knew Beatrice.'

'Kathy, please.' He pressed his hands to his temples, a look of desperation in his eyes.

'No. Don't "Kathy, please" me, Jock.' Her heart was pounding, but she had to keep going. She had to know. 'I understand if you don't trust Iris. But if you don't trust *me*, then I can't marry you.'

'I DO trust you,' he insisted, close to tears. 'I trust you with my life. My God, if you only knew, Kathy. You're the first person I've trusted since the day Mary died.' Shaking, he sat back down on the sofa.

Taking a deep breath, Kathy sat beside him.

'Then tell me the truth,' she said simply. 'The whole truth. I think I have a right to know.'

'You do,' he said quietly, clasping her hand. 'You do have a right to know. And you also have every right to leave me, if you choose to. Because I know I'm putting you in an impossible situation. But the fact is, my darling, *I* don't have the right to tell you the whole truth. Even if I want to, and I do, more than you know. But there are some secrets that are not mine to tell. Promises I made, long, long before we met, that I can't break.'

'Can't or won't?' asked Kathy. Although to Jock's surprise, she didn't sound angry.

'Won't, I suppose,' he admitted.

A knock on the door made both of them jump. 'Only me. I'm here to clean up.' Mrs Gregory stood in the doorway with a mop in one hand and a bucket in the other, like a creature from another world. 'I gather one of the dogs has been sick again.'

'Not now, Mrs G,' Kathy said politely.

'But you *asked* me to come up,' the housekeeper said sourly. 'Do you know how many stairs . . .'

'Are you deaf?' Jock roared, turning on her furiously. 'She said not now.'

Mrs Gregory turned white before beating a flapping retreat, like a frightened bat.

'I don't want to lose you,' said Jock once she'd gone, turning back to Kathy.

'I don't want you to lose me either,' said Kathy, laying her hand over his. 'And I understand if you can't tell me everything. I can't tell you everything either. But this is murder, Jock. It doesn't get any bigger than that.'

'I know that.' He swallowed hard.

'So what *can* you tell me?' Kathy pressed. 'Why don't we start with that?'

Jock paused, choosing his words carefully. 'I can tell you that Venice was a part of my life a very long time ago. Before Mary was born. And that after she died, I – we – Alice and I – tried to find solace there again. But it wasn't to be.'

'OK,' said Kathy, stroking the back of his hand. 'But what about later? During your marriage to Fiona. You went back?'

'Not with Fiona. By myself.'

'Why?'

'I had friends there,' he mumbled awkwardly. 'One friend in particular.'

'A woman?'

'No, actually.' He looked up at her and she could tell at once he was telling the truth. 'There was never anyone – not there . . .' His voice trailed off.

'Did you know Beatrice Contorini?' Kathy asked him bluntly.

'No. I didn't know her.'

'But you recognised her picture?'

A look of anguish flashed across his face. 'Yes. I recognised her picture. But that's all I can say.'

'OK,' said Kathy after a pause.

'Really?' Jock's eyes widened in delighted surprise.

'Yes.' She respected his loyalty to whomever it was he was protecting. Past secrets were something that she understood all too well, nor did she subscribe to the notion that marriage necessitated sharing everything with one's spouse. New vows did not negate all the old ones, after all, and friendships could be as sacred as any other bond of love. But there were still some things she did need to know. If she were going to stay, and still be able to look at herself in the mirror. 'But Jock, I need you to tell me the truth about something. About a few things, in fact.'

'All right,' he said cautiously. 'What?'

Kathy took a deep breath. 'Did you ever – hurt your first wife, Alice?'

'No.' He looked astonished by the question. 'Absolutely not. Never.'

'OK,' said Kathy. 'Next question. Did you kill Beatrice? Or the other woman we found up at the bothy?'

He clasped both her hands tightly, his eyes welling with tears, willing her to believe him. 'No. I didn't.'

'But you know who did?'

'I never said that,' he replied with a sharp intake of breath. 'What I do know is that what Iris Grey is doing, raking up the past, will bring nothing but sorrow to people who don't deserve it. And I'm not speaking about myself here.' He cleared his throat. 'Iris may believe that justice for the dead justifies destroying the lives of the living. For all I know, you may believe it too. But I don't. So I'm asking you – begging you – not to tell her what I've told you today.'

Kathy took his hand in hers. 'I won't tell her.'

Jock started to tremble, overwhelmed with emotion.

'You've told me you didn't kill Beatrice, and I believe you. I'm on your side, Jock. I won't share anything with Iris.'

'Thank you,' he gasped, clutching her hand like a life raft. 'Oh, my darling, thank you.'

'But I am going to see her again,' said Kathy.

'What? Why?' Jock asked, pained.

'For one thing, because she's my friend and I can't simply cut her off. And, for another, because I want her to finish the portrait. It's only a few weeks till the wedding rehearsal dinner. I'd like it to be done by then.'

Jock was about to protest again – he couldn't understand why a painting should be so important to Kathy, and he desperately wanted the Grey woman gone – but then thought better of it. Whatever her reasons, Kathy clearly felt strongly about both the portrait and her friendship with Iris. And at the end of the day, what did it matter if she did a couple more sittings? She'd already more than proven her loyalty to him; offered him her trust when he'd done nothing at all to deserve it. Stayed with him, when any other woman would have left. If Kathy stood by him, Jock felt, he was untouchable, invincible.

Asking her to marry him truly had been the single best decision of his life. Once she was Lady Pitfeldy, once the portrait was completed and Iris was gone, all his troubles would be over. It wasn't long now.

Later that night, while Kathy sat fussing over the dogs by the parlour fire – neither had vomited again, but even Jock had to admit they didn't look right, and had booked a follow-up appointment at the vet's tomorrow – Jock slipped out for a walk. He often took a quick turn outside before bed, after supper and before his Drambuie nightcap, even in winter. The crisp night air and starry skies helped to clear his head of the day's stresses. And today had been more stressful than most.

He'd apologised to Eileen Gregory for his loss of temper earlier, and had promised Kathy that she and Iris could finish the portrait together. No more had been said about Venice, or Alice, or the bodies buried in the bothy, and he trusted that it wouldn't be. Kathy believed him. She was on his side. In the end that was all that mattered.

Even so, as he crunched over the frosty gravel in front of the castle, Jock found himself inexorably drawn in the direction of the woods. He wouldn't go as far as the bothy itself. Not in this cold. But he wanted to be closer to it, and to the lonely pines, to the silent corners of this ancient estate where he'd been born and his father had been born, and that was as much a part of him as his own bones and blood.

He felt sad in so many ways that Kathy's dogs had found those remains. Part of his sadness was for himself. But another part was for the dead women; for the shattering of their peace, and of what should have been eternal rest in what Jock considered to be one of the most beautiful spots on earth.

Passing the stable yard and the last of the castle's lights, he turned on his torch to light the way, when he felt his phone buzzing in the pocket of his Barbour jacket.

A text. No one ever sent him texts.

Intrigued, he clicked it open.

We need to talk. You know why. Call me tomorrow on this number. Massimo.

Jock clamped his hand over his mouth, waiting for the wave of nausea to pass. Then, with a shaking hand, he deleted the message.

He would not call Massimo Giannotti tomorrow, or ever. The man was dead to him. Dead. But dead was no longer enough, it appeared. Thanks to that cursed Iris Grey, the past was coming to get him in his old age, insidious and fatal, like tendrils of ivy around a withered elm. First it was bones, rising up out of the earth. And now ghosts, long dormant, were shaking off their chains and marching on him, like Macbeth's Birnam Wood marching to the hill of Dunsinane.

But Jock MacKinnon wouldn't crumble. Wouldn't weaken. After a lifetime of broken promises, he was going to keep this one. He would fight back, fight them all, to his dying breath. He would protect the ones he loved. And he would win, too. Safe in his fortress. Safe with his beautiful, loving, loyal fiancée.

His Kathy. His treasure. His *reward*, God damn it, for all that had happened, all that he'd lost.

Turning on his heel, he walked back to the castle and to the one woman he hoped could still save him.

Chapter Twenty-seven

'Morning, gorgeous.' A calloused hand snaked around a sleeping Iris's belly, then upwards to cup her right breast. 'Happy Birthday.'

''S not the morning,' Iris mumbled groggily. Reluctantly opening one eye, she was able to confirm this from the fact that it was still pitch-dark and her bedside clock said 4.45 a.m.

'It is for me.'

Iris sighed contentedly as Jamie Ingall nuzzled her neck, hopefully pressing his impressive erection into the small of her back. She waited to feel regretful about last night. About going to the Fisherman's Arms after her run-in with Jock MacKinnon, having far too much to drink, running into Jamie and pretty much hitting him over the head and dragging him back home for sex like a horny cavewoman. Not that he'd needed any persuading. But the guilty feelings refused to come.

God, she reflected now, half-heartedly pushing him away as he tried to slip back inside her. *I must have been very drunk if I told him today was my birthday*. That probably meant she'd also divulged exactly how ancient she was. *What was I thinking?*

'You're so fucking sexy,' Jamie whispered, sighing as she turned around to face him. 'But I have to go.' Reluctantly throwing back the duvet, he crawled out of bed and started pulling on his clothes. 'We said we'd put out by six. I'll ring you later, OK?'

Will you? Iris thought, mumbling something incoherent as he pulled on his boots and clumped down the stairs, closing her front door with a thud behind him. *We'll see.*

Fishermen kept ridiculous hours, she reflected, staring at the clock again. Another reason to add to the hundred and fifty or more that meant she and Jamie were a bad idea. A ridiculous idea, really, even though the sex was great and sort of hard to argue with at the moment. *Happy Birthday to me.*

A hot shower helped to wake her up, and three slices of toast and Marmite washed down with strong Italian coffee made a modest but noticeable impact on her hangover. By nine o'clock, Iris felt strong enough to turn on her phone and check her birthday messages. She'd never been big on birthdays, her own or anybody else's. They were fine for children, of course, but the idea of grown adults insisting on fuss and cake and presents had always seemed a bit pathetic, especially after forty, and very few people knew that today was Iris's special day. Even so, she couldn't help but feel a tad disheartened to see that almost all her 'birthday wishes' seemed to be junk mail – Starbucks offering her a free latte, Space NK plugging the latest hope-in-a-jar face cream on her 'special day'. The only actual human being who'd remembered her was Greta Brun, her agent, which somehow felt like a rather damning reflection on her life generally.

Kathy Miller had also left a voice message, but only to follow up on her apology for Jock's 'temper' yesterday and to try to arrange a date for their next sitting.

'Maybe we could do it at your place next time,' she suggested. 'I know it's not an excuse for how he spoke to you. But he truly has been under a lot of pressure recently. I think it might be better if you steer clear of the castle, just until the dust settles.'

Iris was pleased Kathy wanted to finish the portrait. She hated leaving work half done, and the commission gave her a reason to stay on in Pitfeldy. A real, professional reason, besides the murder case, and a certain trawlerman whom she could not allow to become her motivation for staying.

After the way Jock had thrown her out of the castle yesterday, Iris had half expected Kathy to pull the plug completely. Understandably, Kathy's feelings were torn between her friendship with Iris and loyalty towards the man she was about to marry.

Iris sensed it was the latter that was gaining the upper hand. But perhaps that was as it should be. In any event, finishing the portrait bought her some time to work on the myriad unanswered questions still haunting her about the Girls in the Wood.

On that subject she had a late lunch arranged with Stuart Haley today. Apparently, there'd been some 'developments' in Italy he wanted to fill her in on, although Iris suspected he might also just want to have lunch with her, given how maddeningly cryptic he'd been over the phone. She hadn't told Haley it was her birthday, but the thought occurred to her that somehow he might have found out – he was a detective, after all – and be planning some sort of surprise, an idea that filled her with dread. She and Stuart were firmly back in the friend zone since their dinner the other night. But even so, Iris was not a person who liked surprises, even platonic ones.

Just then her phone buzzed loudly to life in her hand. It was Kathy's number.

'Good morning,' said Iris brightly. 'I just got your message. I was going to –'

'Oh, Iris!' Kathy sobbed, her usual zen, Californian drawl replaced by raspy, gulping tears. 'I didn't know who else to call.'

'What's happened?' Iris stiffened. Despite her penchant for drama, Kathy wasn't given to hysterics, or tears. Had the vile Jock done something? Finally snapped and hit her, or worse?

'It's Sam Sam,' Kathy gasped.

'Oh,' Iris said lamely, too surprised to think of anything more constructive to say.

'He's dead!' Kathy wailed.

'What?'

'He's dead,' Kathy repeated, between shuddering breaths. 'The vet thinks both dogs have been poisoned. Milo might not make it either, apparently.'

'Oh, Kathy. I'm so sorry,' said Iris, painfully aware of how inadequate the words sounded. She knew how much those animals meant to Kathy.

'They've given him some shots, but – we're waiting to see.'

'When you say poisoned,' Iris asked, 'do you mean accidentally?'

'We don't know yet,' Kathy sniffed. 'They're still doing blood tests. But it looks like it might have been Bromadiolone. It's an anticoagulant people use to control rats and mice. You can buy it over the counter, apparently.'

'So, ordinary rat poison?'

'Basically, yeah,' Kathy sniffed.

So it was probably an accident, thought Iris.

'But the thing is, according to the vet, for it to have this sort of effect on dogs Milo and Sam Sam's size, and with so many weeks of symptoms, they would have to have been exposed to multiple small doses, increasing over time,' said Kathy, reading her mind. 'So it wasn't something they randomly found one day and ate. I think it *was* deliberate,' she said after a pause. 'But I mean, who would do such a thing?'

'I don't know,' said Iris. 'Whoever wrote you the letters, perhaps?'

'Right,' said Kathy bitterly. 'That was my first thought too. But who would hate me enough to – to –' She started crying again.

Iris's mind raced. Despite their best efforts, neither she nor the police had been able to find the author of the threatening letters. And now it had come to this. Kathy had plenty of enemies, of course, both in Pitfeldy and up at the castle. And perhaps elsewhere, too. But poisoning her dogs obviously went way beyond writing a few notes designed to scare her off from marrying Jock MacKinnon. It spoke of a deeper, more dangerous hatred.

'Are you going to report it to the police?' Iris asked.

'That was partly why I called you,' Kathy sniffed. 'I can't prove it was deliberate. Jock's convinced it wasn't, and he's just so edgy about the police at the moment generally, as you know.'

'Hmmm,' said Iris, biting back her anger for Kathy's sake.

'I don't think I can report it. But you could. I wondered if you might "unofficially" mention it to DI Haley? With the two of you being friends and all.'

'I'd be happy to,' said Iris.

'I did wonder,' Kathy swallowed hard, 'if maybe someone was trying to punish me, or the poor dogs, for finding those bodies? For finding Beatrice and – whoever it was with her?'

Iris hadn't considered this. But in an awful, cruel, psychopathic way, it did sort of make sense.

'Let me talk to Haley first,' she said soothingly. 'I'll let you know if anything comes of it. And maybe give me the name and number of the vet?'

Kathy did.

'You just try to focus on Milo and stay calm,' said Iris. 'I really am very sorry, Kathy.'

She hung up, feeling troubled.

Poisoning those dogs was a wicked thing to do, an act of malice that smacked of a vendetta more personal and private than the unearthing of a decade-old murder. Who hated Kathy enough to risk doing something so spiteful, and why? She was curious as to what Stuart Haley would make of it.

'Gamekeepers use rat poison all the time up on these big estates. It might have been an accident.'

Haley talked rapidly between mouthfuls of fish and chips, shovelling down his battered haddock like a man who hadn't eaten in days.

'Dogs sniffing around in a shed or stable or whatnot, swallowing something they shouldn't have.'

'Yes, but on top of the letters, and everything else that's happened?' said Iris, dipping warm bread into her bowl of broccoli-and-stilton soup. 'I don't think this was an accident. Besides, the vet told Kathy that the massive amount they ingested meant it probably happened over several days. It smells fishy to me.'

'I'll look into it,' Haley promised, through a mouthful of mushy peas. 'How did your chat go with old Edwin Brae?'

Iris sighed. 'Frustratingly. I mean, we talked. He was open with me – or, at least, I felt he was. But he didn't recognise

Beatrice, and Jock MacKinnon threw his toys out of the cot big time that I'd gone to see him.'

Haley raised an eyebrow. 'Did he now?'

Iris filled him in on what happened yesterday at her sitting with Kathy. 'I'm going to finish the portrait, but our next session will be at my place, as I'm definitely persona non grata up at the castle. Jock made that crystal clear.'

'D'you think he's hiding something?' Haley asked, finishing the last of his chips and pushing his plate aside.

'He's certainly very defensive,' said Iris. 'But I also sort of got the feeling that a part of that was for Edwin, rather than himself. I mean, he's an arsehole. But I think his concern for Brae is genuine.'

Haley nodded, taking this in.

'You know it's odd,' Iris went on. 'While I was talking to Edwin, something kept bothering me. But I can't seem to put my finger on what it was. He talked about his ex-wife, and Jock and his son. Sometimes he was lucid, sometimes less so, but' – she shook her head, frustrated – 'have you ever had that feeling, when you interview a witness, that you're missing something? That they're giving you the answer, that it's right in front of you, but you aren't putting the pieces together correctly?'

Haley smiled. 'Frequently.'

'I mean, I know it sounds nonsensical,' said Iris, 'but I keep dreaming about Edwin and that afternoon. His room, his nurse. It's like there's something there that I'm not seeing. Anyway.' She changed the subject. 'Tell me about Italy. You said you had news?'

'I do. Quite a bit, actually.' Rolling up his sleeves, he leaned forward eagerly, grabbing one of Iris's bread rolls without asking and starting to eat it as he spoke. 'I've been speaking with Vice Questore Mancini of the Polizia di Stato in Venice.'

'You do know your Italian accent's awful,' said Iris.

'No it's not.'

'It is. And you don't need to wave your arms around all the time either, like you're in a Cornetto advert.'

'Shut up and listen.' Haley grinned. 'I've been talking to my counterpart in Venice, OK? And doing a wee bit of my own research as well. Turns out the Romanian Beatrice used to knock about with, Andrei Barbu, is in prison in Milan. He was done for armed robbery in Genoa less than a month after Beatrice went missing. Barring a few months of freedom about seven years ago – so long after our girls were killed – he's been inside pretty much constantly for most of his adult life. And he hasn't left Italy since he arrived with his family from Romania as a child. He's never been to Scotland, and was almost certainly inside when the murders took place.'

'So he's not our man,' said Iris.

'He's not our man. And I actually don't think his relationship with Beatrice Contorini was a big deal either, at least not from his side. According to the Italians, Barbu doesn't even remember who she was. I've no reason to think that's not true.'

'OK,' said Iris. 'So what else?'

'That art teacher your priest fella mentioned, Julia Mantovani.'

'Oh, yes,' Iris perked up. 'Beatrice's friend. The one who worked at the Istituto Venezia?'

'Yes. But I'm not so sure they *were* friends. I know Father what's-his-name told you they were close, but no one else I've talked to seems able to confirm that.'

'All right, well, anyway, what did Julia have to say?' asked Iris.

'Nothing.'

'Nothing?'

'She's dead, unfortunately,' said Haley, finishing off the last of the bread roll and eyeing what was left of Iris's half-eaten one. 'Pancreatic cancer. She passed away a few months ago.'

'Damn it,' muttered Iris. These weren't 'developments'. These were yet more closed doors.

'But I've spoken to her husband and numerous friends and no one remembers ever hearing the name Beatrice Contorini,' said Haley. 'So I'm wondering a little bit about this priest of yours. Could he be sending us down some dead ends?'

'He *could* be,' Iris sounded sceptical. 'But why would he? Given that he was the one who gave me Beatrice's name in the first place. *He* contacted *me*, remember? And don't forget, if there was a friendship between Julia and Beatrice, it would have been ten to fifteen years ago. That's a long time. People forget.'

'True,' Haley conceded. 'But I still have my doubts about this priest. I've found nothing more to corroborate his story about Massimo Giannotti raping Beatrice's mother either, and believe me, I've been digging. Although I will admit I agree with you about the Italian police being in the guy's pocket. Are you going to eat that?' He nodded towards Iris's last remaining bread roll.

'When was the last time you ate?' Iris asked, handing it to him while she spooned up the dregs of her soup.

'Yesterday some time,' Haley said vaguely, between mouthfuls of bread. 'I forget sometimes, since Jean died, especially when I'm busy.'

'You should eat,' said Iris, frowning. 'You need to take care of yourself.'

'Yes, Mum,' said Haley, and Iris thought simultaneously how much she liked him and how completely she didn't fancy him. 'Anyway, I do have some good news, which is that Massimo *did* know Jock MacKinnon back in the day. They were both members of the same wanky gentlemen's club in London in the eighties and nineties, and they frequently gambled together at Aspinalls.'

Iris's eyes lit up. 'But that's brilliant. That connects both of them to Pitfeldy, and to Beatrice.'

'Sort of. It's pretty tangential,' cautioned Haley.

'Oh, come *on*,' said Iris. 'That's a link.'

'It's a start,' said Stuart. 'I'm still working on it. One other thing I wanted to mention to you in the meantime, though. I've been making a few calls in Rome, about Paola Contorini, Beatrice's mum. But apart from that one old address that you gave me, I can't seem find a single thing about her. Not even where she's buried.'

'Hmmm,' Iris mused. 'Are there no public records on that sort of thing?'

'Aye, there are, and I'm still making calls on that,' said Haley. 'The Italians don't make things easy, mind you. There's a lot of city and state bureaucracy to get through. But in the meantime, I've contacted neighbours, Catholic charities, even rehabs, anything I can think of. I've found no trace of her.'

'That's weird,' Iris admitted. 'And she was never reported missing?'

'Nope. I mean, after her daughter took off, she had no one to report her, did she? People do drop off the grid, especially if they become homeless or what have you. But even so, if your priest knew that Paola had died in Rome – if that news made it back to Venice – then surely it stands to reason someone in Rome must have told *him*.'

'Another priest, probably,' suggested Iris.

'Right. And if *they* knew, then there should be a grave in one of the Catholic parishes. But if there is, I cannae find it. Which leads *me* back to good old Father – what was his name again?'

'Antonio.'

'Right, Father Antonio. I'd like to talk to him myself. Ask him who told him Paola was dead. How that even came up, you know?'

'What are you thinking?' asked Iris. 'Do you suspect Father Antonio of something?'

'I don't know.' Haley sounded uncomfortable. 'Something doesn't sit right, that's all. All I know is I'm banging my head against a brick wall, and I think maybe Father Antonio knows more than he's –'

He stopped in his tracks, eyeing Iris curiously. She was sitting stock-still, barely breathing, and staring past him at a painting on the pub wall. She looked as if she'd seen a ghost.

'Are you all right?'

'That's it,' Iris mumbled to herself, still fixed on the painting. Haley turned to look at it. As far as he could tell, it was a rather poorly executed watercolour of Edinburgh University's Old College.

'Hello? Mystic Meg?' He waved a hand slowly across Iris's line of vision. 'What is it?'

'Brick walls,' muttered Iris, still in a world of her own.

'OK, so I'm gonna have tae ask you to explain that.'

'Edwin Brae. His room,' Iris said excitedly, pulling on her coat. 'I know what it is. What I was missing.'

'Hold on a minute,' Haley protested. 'Slow down, would you?'

'I can't. I have to go. There's someone I need to see.'

'Iris,' Haley called after her as she headed for the door. 'For God's sake –'

'I'll ring you tonight,' said Iris. And with a blast of cold air, she was gone.

Angus Brae was outside his cottage, loading logs into a wheelbarrow when he saw Iris approaching. In a bright red puffa coat and clashing orange woolly hat, with her skinny legs tucked into big, fluffy white boots, she looked like a particularly determined Christmas elf, power-walking her way towards him.

'Hello!' He waved cheerfully. He was surprised to see her on the estate, given her blow-up with the baron yesterday. Everyone up at the castle was talking about it. Gossip was thin on the ground in Pitfeldy and as a result tended to go from nought to sixty in a matter of seconds. 'What can I do for you?'

'You lied to me.' She said it so matter-of-factly, and without anger, that at first he thought he'd misheard her.

'I'm sorry?'

'You lied to me. You said you'd never been to university. That you never went away to study. But you did. There's a picture of you in your dad's room at the home, at Edinburgh. You're leaning against a wall outside Old College. You were a student there, weren't you?'

She watched his expression change from shock, to denial, to a sort of grim acquiescence. 'You'd better come in.'

The gamekeeper's cottage was messier than the last time Iris had visited, with dirty washing-up in the sink and the remnants of last night's takeaway strewn around the living room.

'Hannah's away at her mam's,' Angus offered by way of explanation, taking Iris's coat and clearing aside a pile of newspapers so that she could sit down on the couch.

'Why did you lie to me about Edinburgh?' Iris asked, in the same gentle, probing tone as before.

'Because I felt guilty, I suppose,' said Angus, looking guilty as he sat down opposite her, picking at his frayed shirt cuffs with bitten-down fingernails.

'I don't understand,' said Iris. 'Why would you feel guilty about having gone to university? That's an achievement.'

'Not for me it wasn't.' He looked away miserably. 'It was a really bad time. My dad – wasn't well. I should never have left him. But I was young, you know? I felt trapped.'

'I can imagine,' said Iris, looking around her. 'You're artistic, creative. I daresay you had dreams of your own, beyond spending the rest of your life fixing the baron's fences.'

Angus looked wounded. 'I'm proud to work for the baron,' he insisted. 'I was then, too, I just . . . I don't know. I was restless. I got offered a place at the art school and my teachers thought I should go. I really wanted to, but dad wouldn't even discuss it. He just said "no, no way". I felt he shut me down without even really listening. And I think mebbe, you know, that was the last straw. So I took the place. I went off to uni. And then everything unravelled.'

'Unravelled?'

'Dad got worse,' Angus said bluntly.

'His illness, you mean?' asked Iris.

'Aye. Me leaving, I think it pushed him over an edge.'

Even now, clearly, it was hard for him to talk about. The disjointed rhythm of his sentences spoke of the pain these memories still caused.

'Anyway, he drove to the city. Came to my halls. That would have been the day he took the picture you saw, in his room.

I've no idea why he kept it.' Angus pressed his fingertips against the bridge of his nose. *He's trying not to cry*, thought Iris. 'Dad begged me to come home.' Angus went on, his voice dropping almost to a whisper. 'My father's a proud man, Miss Grey. He doesn't beg.'

'So you decided to drop out?'

Angus nodded. 'I came back to Pitfeldy. We never really spoke about it afterwards, but I think, you know,' he cleared his throat. 'The damage was done.'

'Angus.' Iris leaned forward, looking at him kindly. 'You do realise that your father's illness isn't your fault? By your own account, he'd already begun to deteriorate long before you left for college.'

'I know that.' Angus smiled weakly. 'But it wasn't his illness that broke him. Not alone, anyway. It was the abandonment. First my mother and then me.'

'Going away to university isn't abandonment,' Iris said gently.

'It was to my dad,' said Angus.

'I'm not sure that leaving an abusive marriage is abandonment either, other than in the most technical sense,' she added. She knew the comment about Angus's mother was a risk and his reaction was instant. He sat back, shoulders stiffening, his features resetting themselves into a cold, emotionally closed mask.

'Is that all you wanted?' He got to his feet. 'Because I need to get back to work. And no offence, but the baron wouldn't be happy if he knew you were here.'

'Yes.' Iris took the hint and reached for her coat. 'That was all. So you came back to Pitfeldy out of concern for Edwin's welfare. There was no other reason?'

'No.' Angus's jaw seemed to have locked so tight, he could barely force the word out.

Hurrying back to the warmth of her car, Iris's mind raced, the cogs of her consciousness clicking almost audibly as she processed everything she'd just witnessed.

There was still so much that confused her about the weird emotional triangle that bound Angus Brae, his father and Jock

MacKinnon. But there was now one thing she knew for sure.

Angus was lying. Lying through his clenched, frightened teeth.

'Where have you been all afternoon? Did you no get my messages?'

Haley's voice was half irritated, half concerned. Iris made an effort to placate him as she pulled two burned crumpets out of the toaster and started scraping off the black bits, pushing aside her own disappointment that it was Stuart and not Jamie who'd rung her four times.

'I went to see Angus Brae,' she told him, taking her first, hot bite. 'He lied to me about going away to university and I wanted to know why. It would have been right around the time that the two girls were killed.'

Haley fell silent for a moment. 'What did he say?'

'That he lied because he felt guilty about leaving his dad. But I know there's more to it than that. He's hiding something, I'd bet my life on it.'

'OK, well, *I* got a call after you left the pub today, for what it's worth. Massimo Giannotti wasn't Beatrice Contorini's father.'

Iris put down her crumpet. 'How do you know?'

'He took a paternity test at the time, after Paola first started making accusations against him.'

'But . . .' Iris frowned. 'That makes no sense. Why wouldn't he have told me that when I met him?'

'No idea,' said Haley. 'But the Venice police have a copy of the test. I've seen it. It's legit. Oh and by the way, I'd prefer it if you stayed away from the castle for the next few days, including the gamekeeper's house. I'll be going up there myself at some point to look into this business with the dogs. I'd rather not have to arrest you for trespassing.'

'Don't worry,' said Iris. 'I'll either be here or in Edinburgh. I thought I might ask around at the university, see if anybody remembers Angus Brae being there.'

She hung up feeling dispirited, and more confused than ever. Settling down in front of the fire she'd lit earlier, that for once was blazing successfully in the grate instead of spluttering away into nothing the moment she turned her back, she attempted to get her thoughts into some sort of order.

Where did Massimo Giannotti fit into this?

Massimo knew Jock. They were members of the same London club, back in the days of his marriage to Fiona, and Iris mentioning Pitfeldy Castle had scared the living shit out of him when they spoke. He *might* have raped Paola Contorini decades ago in Venice; but he wasn't Beatrice's father. And yet, somehow, Beatrice had ended up murdered and buried under the ruined bothy in Jock MacKinnon's woods.

Right now, as far as Iris could work out, Massimo remained the only link they had between Venice and Pitfeldy. And yet there was nothing actually to connect him with Beatrice's death.

Then there was Paola Contorini, Paola whose grave nobody seemed able to find and whose neighbours in Rome apparently barely remembered her. What exactly had happened to her after she'd dared to challenge the powerful Massimo and lost? How had she died, and what secrets had she taken with her to her lonely resting place?

Finally, Iris's thoughts turned to Angus and Edwin Brae, and to Jock MacKinnon himself. All three protested their complete innocence, and ignorance, about the women buried up on the estate. But all three were lying, or at best revealing only half-truths about what they knew, Iris felt sure of it. And through it all, the dark cloud of the two abandoning wives, Linda and Alice, and the dead baby Mary, hung over this unholy triumvirate.

What were the common threads?

Silent, missing women, thought Iris. *Alice and Linda. Paola and Beatrice.*

And frightened, lying men. Edwin and Angus. Massimo and Jock.

Perhaps Jock's adult children, the prickly Rory and the vacuous Emma, had more to tell than they had thus far? Apart from Haley's initial interview when the bodies were found, no one had questioned the younger MacKinnons again. Iris had spoken to their mother, Fiona – which reminded her that the au pair lead was still out there, this mysterious 'Isabella', also from Rome – but Iris had rather let the ball drop on Rory and Emma.

Maybe now was the time to pick it up again?

Chapter Twenty-eight

It was a bright, clear morning when Iris drove into Edinburgh, and the city seemed positively to sparkle with life and cheer. Coloured lights and gaudy decorations lifted the famous grey stone streets, and the blue sky above and white-frosted ground below gave everything a Christmas card feel that seemed to raise everybody's spirits. Iris had counted several cheerful 'good mornings' before she'd even arrived at Pollock Halls of Residence on Holyrood Park Road, which was pretty much unheard of in Scotland as far as Iris could tell. In Pitfeldy it was a red-letter day if the lady at the village stores made eye contact and gave you a grunt when you came in for your milk and paper. But at the Starbucks near Old College it was smiles all round. Iris had even been offered one of yesterday's mince pies for free ('we have to chuck them out, otherwise, so you may as well.') She hoped this boded well for her interview with the Pollock Halls warden.

It didn't.

Sour-faced, underpaid and miserable, Mrs Claire McCready was a pinched, grey-haired harridan who made it clear from the beginning that she had little time for Iris, and zero interest in answering her questions about Angus Brae.

'I've only been working here seven years,' she told Iris tersely, handing back the copy of the photograph of Angus as a student that Edwin's nurse had kindly copied for Iris. 'This young man would ha' been well before my time.'

'I understand,' said Iris. 'But I wondered if perhaps your predecessor . . .?'

'My predecessor died of a heart attack on the job,' Mrs McCready snapped, glaring at Iris through thick, bottle-lensed glasses as if this untimely death were somehow her fault. 'Forty-five he was, poor man.'

'I'm so sorry to hear that.'

'Even if he hadn't died, he couldn't tell you about a specific student.'

'Couldn't he?'

The old woman shook her head. 'Data protection. We can't even talk to the police,' she added, folding her arms self-importantly across her drooping chest. 'Not without a court order.'

'I see. Well, thank you,' Iris said politely. Clearly there was no point flogging a dead horse. She would have to ask around informally, see what she could find out at the art school, or maybe even at the local pubs. Angus hadn't been at Edinburgh long, but he was a handsome lad and a talented one. She only needed one person to remember him.

'Oh, yes.' Laila Davenport held the photograph of Angus between her charcoal-stained thumb and forefinger. The life-drawing teacher had a mane of long grey hair that cascaded down her crooked back like mist down a mountainside, and the sort of craggy, characterful face that Iris instantly wanted to paint. 'Yes, I do remember him. Shy boy. He had a gift for landscapes.'

Laila, it turned out, had been teaching at Edinburgh for over thirty years and was a living legend within the art department. Helpfully, she had also heard of Iris, and was only too happy to offer what help she could to a fellow artist.

'I've seen a number of your portraits,' she told Iris eagerly, as the two of them took a seat in Laila's studio. 'You're terribly good. I'm afraid I first came across you during the Wetherby murder case,' she confided guiltily, 'you know, when there was so much media coverage. I'm not normally one for gossip, but it was rather *gripping*.'

'Oh, that's all right,' said Iris, instantly warming to this woman. 'Dom Wetherby loved a gripping story. He wouldn't have minded the attention, or the fact that all the coverage ended up helping my career. He was nothing if not an opportunist.'

'And you solved his murder.' Laila wagged a finger admiringly at Iris. 'Well done you.'

'Oh, no,' said Iris modestly. 'I turned over a few stones, that's all.'

'And is that what you're doing now? Stone turning?' the older woman asked.

'In a way, I suppose,' said Iris. She explained her interest in Angus, and her connection to the bodies found up at Pitfeldy. 'Angus's father, Edwin, managed the castle estate during the period when those girls were murdered and their bodies were buried up there. We can't be certain of exact dates, but there's at least a chance that it happened around the time when Angus was up at Edinburgh.'

'And you think that's significant?' Laila asked, pushing a stray strand of silver hair out of her eyes.

'Honestly, I've no idea,' admitted Iris. 'That's why I'm here, trying to glean whatever information I can.' She explained that Edwin's Alzheimer's and Baron Pitfeldy's reluctance to cooperate with either her or the police made reliable evidence hard to come by. 'Angus has given me his own version of events. But I'm not convinced I got the full story.'

'Well, I'm not sure how much I can add,' said Laila apologetically. 'I recognised him from your photograph, but I wouldn't even have remembered his name if you hadn't told me.'

'You remembered his work, though?'

'Oh yes. Vividly.' She leaned forward, eager to help where she could. 'As I said, he had real promise. And I remember he was very eager, you know. Serious, not like most of the freshers.'

'Serious in what way?' Iris asked, interested. 'About his work?'

'Well, yes, that. But he was also just much more mature than most of my students. He had a job, I believe, at one of the restaurants they all went to. What was it called, now?' She rolled her eyes up, searching her memory, then looked back at Iris, delighted. 'Oh yes, I've got it! The Rib Shack. He worked at the Rib Shack to support himself.'

Iris made a note.

'There was no "Mummy and Daddy's money" involved, as I recall,' Laila went on. 'He paid his own bills. And he was in a serious relationship, I believe. Not married but, you know, living with someone. He was just a lot more grown-up than the others.'

'Did you ever meet his girlfriend?' Iris asked, intrigued. Angus hadn't mentioned any sort of partner, although, to be fair, she hadn't asked.

'Or boyfriend,' Laila said archly. 'It could be either nowadays.'

Hadn't Jamie mentioned something once, ages ago, about people at school thinking Angus was gay? thought Iris. The art teacher had only meant it as a throwaway comment, but something about it resonated.

'I'd try the restaurant he used to work at, if I were you,' Laila suggested helpfully. 'There might still be staff there who remember him. I'm sure they could tell you more.'

'Thank you,' said Iris, looking at her watch before shaking the woman's hand. 'I will. And thank you so much for your help. You've an extraordinary memory.'

'Not at all,' said Laila. 'Good luck. I hope you find whoever did it.'

So do I, thought Iris. Although it struck her at that moment just how far-off a prospect that seemed. They didn't even know who the second victim *was* yet. And apart from herself and Stuart Haley, nobody seemed to care.

'Sorry, love. We don't have anybody here who's worked for that long. Hospitality tends to have a lot of turnover.'

The manager of the Rib Shack restaurant on Morrison Street was a friendly, whip-thin Danish girl with heavily dyed black hair and an impressive set of tattoos running up both her arms. Either she was remarkably young to have reached a managerial position, or Iris was getting old. Sadly, Iris suspected the latter.

'Oh! You know what?' the girl corrected herself suddenly, grabbing Iris's wrist. 'There is one person you could talk to. Steve. One of our bouncers.'

'You have bouncers at a restaurant?' Iris looked surprised.

'You should see this place on a Saturday night.' The Danish girl rolled her eyes. 'Drunks as far as the eye can see. I'm not knocking students, they're our bread and butter, but the state some of them are in by the time they roll up at our door – staggering around, puking. Steve stops the worst of them from getting in. He works at a few places, and I don't know exactly how long he's been here. But I know it's a long time.'

'Brilliant,' said Iris. 'I don't suppose he's here now by any chance?'

'Sorry. His first shift's not till Wednesday night,' said the manager. 'I can give you his number, though, if you like,' she added cheerfully.

'Yes, please,' said Iris, thinking back to the dour old witch she'd met at Pollock Halls this morning, and giving silent thanks for the younger generation's cavalier attitude towards data protection laws.

Steve was more than happy to meet with Iris at a pub round the corner, particularly when she made it clear that the drinks would be on her. A short but stocky Glaswegian around Iris's age, he remembered Angus instantly.

'Sure I knew him,' he told her, between velvety slurps of Guinness. 'Pretty well, actually. Lovely guy. We started at the Shack around the same time.'

'Did you ever meet his partner?' Iris asked, choosing her words carefully.

'I saw her now and then, aye.' *Her.* 'I didn'ae know her well or anything, but she came in sometimes to see her man. Walk home together at the end of his shift, you know.'

'Do you remember her name?'

Steve thought about it, but shook his head. 'Like I said, I never really knew the lass. All I remember was that she was pretty, she didn't speak much English and Angus was deadly serious about her. Wanted to marry her, you know. Even before the baby.'

'Baby?' Iris's eyes widened.

'Oh, aye,' said Steve, taking another deep gulp of his pint. 'Did you not know? That was why he left uni in the end. Why he quit his job at the Shack. His missus was expecting.'

Iris's heart started racing. 'Can you describe this girl?'

Steve looked worried. 'Er . . . dark hair? Pretty, like I said. She was foreign. Spanish or Italian or something.'

'Would you recognise her if I showed you a picture?' asked Iris, struggling to contain her excitement.

'Ach, I don't know,' Steve shook his head doubtfully. 'Mebbe, I suppose. It was a long time ago, and I only saw her now and again.'

Pulling out her phone, Iris showed him the photographs of Beatrice Contorini from her blog.

'Was this her?'

He looked at the pictures in silence, scrolling back and forth.

'It *could* be,' he said hesitantly. 'She looks a bit like her – a bit like what I remember. But I cannae say for sure, I'm sorry.'

'Don't be sorry,' said Iris, hugging him, to his simultaneous surprise and delight. It wasn't often he found himself spontaneously embraced by a beautiful woman, certainly not a sober one. 'You've just helped me more than you know.'

Chapter Twenty-nine

The following morning, DI Stuart Haley hung up the phone and leaned back contentedly in his desk chair. Since Jean's death, he'd been trying consciously to savour moments like this; small flashes of happiness in an otherwise mundane day. A rather good bereavement therapist that his GP had put him on to, back when he struggled to get out of bed in the mornings, had given Haley two excellent pieces of advice. 'A packet of crisps is not a meal,' was the first. Hard to argue with that. But it was her second nugget of wisdom that Stuart had really taken to heart. 'Think of each second of pleasure as a tiny wee flame. Cup your hands around it. Guard it. Maybe blow on it gently. But never ignore it. Because, one day, that light will lead you out of the cave.'

Back then, when everything seemed so bleak and pointless, pleasure had meant things that seemed silly now. Like giving himself permission to enjoy a hot bath, or the taste of chocolate on his tongue. Jean was dead, but Cadbury's Dairy Milk still tasted great, and that was OK.

Now, months later, the 'cherishing the moment' thing had become more of a habit. Something he did because it made life that little bit better, not because he needed it to survive. Today's good news from his counterpart in Italy was a welcome chink of light in the gloom of the Girls in the Wood case. Small, perhaps. But DI Haley knew better than anyone that these tiny wee flames, in the end, really *could* lead one out of the cave. So he allowed himself a moment to be happy before picking up the phone to Iris.

'Guess what?'

'I can't. You're going to have to tell me.' Iris's voice sounded groggy on the other end of the line.

'You OK?' Haley asked.

'I'm fine. I got back late from Edinburgh last night,' said Iris. 'But don't keep me in suspense. What's happened?'

'OK, so I just got off the phone from the desk in Venice,' Haley said excitedly, frowning at one of the new PCs who'd just walked into the station wearing felt reindeer antlers and a red nose that flashed on and off and played a tinny version of 'Jingle Bells' whenever you pressed it. *Idiot*. 'Apparently, no death certificate has *ever* been issued for Paola Contorini. Not in Rome, not in Venice, not anywhere in Italy. There's a centralised national database and she's not on it.'

'You mean she's alive?' Iris asked, baffled.

'Looks like it,' said Haley. 'There are relatively few Jane Does on their system – unclaimed female bodies, homeless, addicts, you know – and none matching Paola's description. Anyway, the Italians have officially listed her as missing, which is a big step forward, and they've put out an alert to forces in the Rome and Venice areas. They've also given me a picture of Paola. I'll send it through to you now so you can post it on your Facebook page alongside her daughter's. See if we can't jog someone's memory.'

'Will do,' said Iris. 'That's great, Stuart.'

'Isn't it?'

'I take it you got my messages last night, about Angus?'

'Oh, aye,' said Haley. 'I should have said. The pregnant girlfriend he never mentioned, back at the university he claimed he never went to? Fantastic.'

'We're finally making progress,' said Iris, happily.

'Let's hope so,' said Haley. 'Do you really think the girlfriend might have been Beatrice?'

'I do,' said Iris. 'I mean, I'm not certain. But Beatrice ended up buried at the castle. So she must have had some connection there. Why *not* Angus?'

'Why not indeed,' said Haley.

'And, you know, he lied about it,' Iris went on. 'Plus, according to the bouncer I spoke to from his old work, this girlfriend was foreign and definitely looked *somewhat* like Beatrice's picture. Are you going to question him?'

'I think I am, yeah,' said Haley.

'What about the chief constable?' asked Iris. 'Won't he come down on you like a ton of bricks, with the case officially closed?'

'I've been thinking about that,' said Haley. 'I think the fact that the Italians have asked for Banffshire's support gives me some degree of cover. But I'll need to tread carefully, that's for sure, with the baron still on the warpath. I'm hoping to use this business with Kathy's poisoned dogs as an excuse to show my face up at the castle, to see if I can corner our boy while I'm up there. If Jock complains to Roebuck again, then I'll just have to handle it. Hopefully, I'll have what I need from Angus by then.'

'Well, good luck,' said Iris. 'Let me know how it goes. And I'll post Paola's picture in the meantime. We're getting closer, Stuart. I can feel it.'

Hanging up, Haley felt the same, a swelling optimism that, at long last, momentum seemed to be on their side with the Girls in the Wood case. He wanted to get up to the castle now, while he still felt energised and on form.

'Take that off, you prat,' he said briskly, pinging the young constable's reindeer antlers as he headed for the door.

'But it's the Christmas spirit, sir,' the young man responded.

'Bah, humbug,' Haley growled back, before relenting. 'Oh all right. You can wear it in here, just don't take it out on the streets. And try to at least pretend you're doing some work while I'm gone, would you?'

'Sir.'

Everyone at the station liked DI Haley. He was one of the good ones.

*

Mrs Gregory looked astonished to see DI Haley at the front door of the castle, but she showed him inside with her usual frosty professionalism.

'You may have a bit of a wait, I'm afraid,' she said, offering him a seat in the drawing room. 'I'm not sure where the baron is just now, and I know Miss Miller went out for a walk earlier by herself. She was rather upset.'

'Hardly surprising, under the circumstances,' said Haley.

'Circumstances?' The housekeeper cocked her head to one side, a touch defensively in Haley's opinion.

'The dogs?' he said.

'Oh, yes, well,' Mrs Gregory mumbled awkwardly. 'That was . . . unfortunate. But not a matter for the police, surely?'

'That depends,' said Haley. 'While I'm waiting for Ms Miller, I'd like to talk to any domestic staff who work at the castle regularly. Including you, Mrs Gregory, when you have a moment.'

'Me?' The housekeeper sounded flustered.

'We're not sure yet,' Haley went on, 'but we understand from the local vet that the dogs may have been deliberately poisoned over a period of weeks or even months.'

'Surely not.'

'If that *is* the case, we suspect it probably began during the period when Kathy was away for her wedding-dress fittings in Italy. I gather that the animals were showing signs of being unwell the day she returned?'

'Well, they were a touch off colour, yes,' Eileen Gregory stammered. 'But – *I* took care of Milo and Sam Sam while she was gone.'

'You did?'

'Yes. I fed them myself, every day, and I can assure you there was nothing wrong with the meals I prepared for them.'

'No one's accusing you of anything, Mrs Gregory,' Haley assured her, 'but I will need to talk to anyone who may have had access to the animals during that period. Cooks, cleaners, groundskeepers. Family members. Guests.'

'Very well,' Mrs Gregory said stiffly. 'I'll get you a list and see who's around today.'

She left the room, and a few moments later, to Haley's surprise, Jock's daughter Emma Twomey walked in. Iris mentioned that Emma had been at the Halloween party, but Haley himself hadn't seen her since the day the bones in the bothy were found, four long months ago now. His memories of her then were hazy. The heavyset woman he saw now in a tweed shooting skirt and cashmere sweater projected a jarring combination of entitlement and nervousness, simultaneously managing to project an air of superiority and the sort of panicked guilt of a schoolgirl who'd just been caught out doing something illicit by a teacher.

'Detective!' she squealed, her large bosom heaving uncomfortably beneath the too-tight cashmere. 'This is a surprise.'

'Mrs Twomey.' Haley nodded a greeting. 'Here for a wee visit, are you?'

'That's right. They moved the wedding rehearsal dinner for-ward to next week for some unearthly reason. Some nonsense about people not wanting social engagements between Christmas and New Year, I don't know. We were coming for that anyway, so we thought . . . but what brings *you* here?' she asked, frowning, suddenly changing tack. 'Surely not this business with the bodies, still? Isn't the case closed?'

'Not entirely,' said Haley. 'My Italian colleagues are still actively investigating. But that's not why I'm here.'

'Oh?' said Emma, the blood rushing to her face and then draining from it again before she sat down on the sofa, wildly flustered.

'I daresay you heard about your stepmother's dog passing away last week?'

'Oh. That.' Emma seemed relieved. 'Yes, of course. Poor thing. I'm not a big fan of my father's – of Kathy – as I'm sure you can imagine, detective inspector,' she added honestly. 'But losing a pet is not something one would wish on anyone.'

'Well, quite.' Haley nodded. 'Although it looks as if someone may have wished it on Ms Miller.'

'I'm sorry to have to tell you that the other little fellow died last night, too,' Emma went on, failing at first to register the significance of Haley's comment. 'Pa found him in his basket first thing this morning.'

Haley stiffened.

'So of course, he had to tell Kathy,' said Emma, shaking her head. 'You could hear the screams all the way down the East Wing. That was what woke us up, before six o'clock this morning. Not that I'm complaining, you understand. I mean, obviously, she must have been devastated. But my husband, Fergus, well, between you and me he's not what one would call a morning person. Forgive me, detective inspector, but I'm wondering what all of this has to do with the police?'

'There's a possibility that the animals were deliberately poisoned,' Haley replied bluntly, turning around as two young kitchen staff appeared at the door.

'No!' Emma gasped.

'I'm only making preliminary inquiries at this stage. But I'll be needing a statement from everyone.'

The staff arrived quickly, one by one – two maids, a cook, the full-time gardener and his part-time assistant. Mrs G, unable for the moment to locate either of her employers, returned to give a detailed statement about Milo and Sam Sam's mealtimes and exercise schedule, and the onset of the animals' symptoms. From what Haley could tell, she seemed to be genuinely distraught over what had happened. It was obvious that there was no love lost between the housekeeper and her soon-to-be mistress, but she did appear to have applied the same professionalism and thoroughness in caring for those dogs as she did to all her other duties.

Having only arrived yesterday, Emma and Fergus Twomey had little to add. Although Emma did mention that her brother Rory had visited their mother in Edinburgh and 'stopped by' Pitfeldy while Kathy was away in Italy. Haley had just finished making a note of it when Jock MacKinnon burst in. Back from a visit to one of his farms, he was his usual explosive self.

'You again,' he boomed, glaring at Haley and dismissing everybody else from the room with an imperious sweep of his tweed-jacketed arm. 'You're like a bad bloody penny, DI Haley, do you know that? But you won't stop, will you? I can see that now. Not till I have you actually fired.'

'We have reason to believe that your fiancée may have been the victim of a hate crime, baron,' he explained coolly, pointedly not getting up.

'Hate crime?' Jock snapped. 'What on earth are you talking about, man?'

'I'm talking about the poisoning of Ms Miller's wee dogs.'

'For pity's sake. That is not a "hate crime"!' Jock sighed heavily. 'They swallowed something they shouldn't have, that's all.'

'Aye, but how?' Haley asked. 'That's the question.'

'They're *dogs*.' Jock could barely contain his frustration. 'Dogs come across all sorts of things, and they'll eat ninety per cent of them, given half a chance. This is a vast estate, DI Haley, in case you hadn't noticed. *Hate crime* indeed,' he muttered furiously. 'Did Kathy contact you about this?'

Haley shifted uncomfortably. 'Not directly, no.'

'What do you mean "not directly"? Did she or didn't she?' Jock demanded.

'I'm under no obligation to give you the source of our information, baron,' Haley said primly. 'But I will say that a concerned member of the public –'

'It was Iris bloody Grey, wasn't it?' Jock fumed. 'I've had just about enough of that woman's meddling. *And* yours. The chief constable will be hearing about this.'

'Oh, I'm sure he will,' said Haley getting to his feet in as leisurely a way as he could manage.

'You're finished this time, Haley,' Jock hissed spitefully as Haley walked to the door. 'You picked the wrong man to cross.'

'As did you, baron,' Haley replied, looking his adversary square in the eye. 'I'll see myself out.'

*

Angus Brae saw the familiar figure of the diminutive detective from three hundred yards away. He'd already had a call on his mobile from one of the estate gardeners, so he knew this was about Kathy's dogs. Milo had died this morning, apparently, and poor Kathy was in pieces about it, out roaming the estate somewhere in a terrible fit of grief. With the rehearsal dinner only a week away, it was hard not to feel that her wedding to Jock was somehow being cursed.

Angus felt for her. Those dogs had been like family to her, and he knew what losing your family felt like. Turning off the engine of his tractor, he climbed down from the cab and trudged across the frozen field to meet Haley.

'I heard about the dogs,' he said, offering Stuart his gloved hand in greeting. 'Do you really think someone did it on purpose?'

'It's a possibility,' said Haley. 'Won't be easy to prove, mind you, and it's not a theory your boss the baron subscribes to. But I think we owe it to Ms Miller at least to look into it.'

'I agree,' said Angus.

'And there is at least the chance that what happened could be connected to our Girls in the Wood,' Haley went on, casually. 'Those dogs dug up the remains, after all. Maybe that made somebody angry.'

'With a dog?' Angus frowned. 'That'd be pretty irrational, don't you think? Pretty screwed up?'

Haley shrugged. 'No more screwed up than murdering two innocent young women and burying them under a load of rubble.'

Both men slowed their paces and eventually stopped. The ploughed field was exposed, open to the elements, and a cold wind like a razor whistled past them, cutting painfully against both of their faces.

'This isn't about the dogs, is it?' Angus asked, staring down at his heavy work boots.

'No,' said Haley. 'It's about the girl we found up there. Beatrice.'

'I see.'

'She was your girlfriend, wasn't she, Angus?'

Angus shook his head, eyes still glued to the ground. 'No.'

'I think she was,' Haley said softly. 'She lived with you in Edinburgh while you were a student. Didn't she?'

'No.' It was almost a whisper.

'And she was pregnant, wasn't she?' Haley pressed on. 'Beatrice was pregnant with your child. What did your dad have to say about that, Angus? I'll bet he wasn't too pleased.'

Angus pressed both hands to the sides of his head, trying to block out Haley's words.

'Is that why you dropped out? Why Edwin made you come back here?'

The wind blew harder, carrying Angus's mumbled reply with it. None of this would be admissible, if, by some miracle, Haley and Iris ever managed to get this case to court. But Stuart Haley felt in his bones that if he could just get Angus to open up, then the dam would break and the truth would come gushing out. There'd be time enough for formal statements later. Today was about breaking that dam.

'Did you kill her, Angus?' He pushed harder. 'Did you murder Beatrice Contorini?'

'*No!*' With a wild, animal roar Angus turned around, raising his hands and looking for all the world like he was about to attack Haley. But then at the last moment he stopped, like a clockwork toy suddenly running out of time, stuck in suspended animation.

'Then who did?' Haley challenged him. 'Who are you protecting?'

'No one,' Angus said quietly, slowly lowering his arms. Haley could see in his eyes that he'd missed his chance. The dam had held. 'None of what you said is true. I never knew this girl. I told you.'

'Aye, you did. You told me. But I don't believe you,' Haley replied slowly.

'That's your problem.' Angus shrugged. He was doing his best to sound like Jock, arrogant and disdainful, but it wasn't working. Heartless nonchalance was not an easy look to pull off when one actually had a heart.

'We know you had a girlfriend in Edinburgh,' Haley continued, not ready to give up, even now. Once Jock got on the blower to the chief constable, he might not get another chance to speak to Angus.

'Not true.'

'We also know she was pregnant.'

'You're mistaken,' said Angus.

'Our witnesses say otherwise,' said Haley.

'Well, then, they're mistaken.' Another shrug. 'I have to get back to work, detective inspector. I hope you get to the bottom of things. With the dogs.'

'They also say that this girl you lived with was a foreigner. Probably Italian,' Haley called after him as Angus started to walk away, back to his tractor. 'You know it's only a matter of time before we get someone to positively ID Beatrice,' he shouted into the wind. 'You lie about this now, that's obstruction of justice. That's jail, Angus, whether you hurt anybody or not. Talk to me.'

But the tall, upright figure kept walking.

'Damn it,' Haley muttered under his breath. He'd blown it, scared the boy off *and* put Jock MacKinnon back on the warpath, just when they were making some headway.

He needed to talk to Iris. And Kathy Miller. And he needed to come up with something to mollify the chief inspector, sharpish. That last part, he suspected, was not going to be easy.

Father Antonio Corromeo was at home in his apartment behind San Cassiano, watching reruns of *Vivere* when Iris Grey called.

'Who told you Paola was dead?'

'I'm sorry?' Switching off the television, it took him a few moments to register who she was, never mind what she was talking about.

'Paola Contorini. Beatrice's mother.'

'Yes, I know who she is,' said the priest.

'You told me she had died in Rome.'

'That's right.'

'No, it isn't.' Iris filled him in on Haley's conversations with the Italian police. The lack of a death certificate, or any matches on the Jane Does. 'We don't know where she is, but the police are now working under the assumption that Paola's still alive.'

'That's – wow. I'm astonished,' Father Antonio stammered.

'Who told you she'd died?' Iris asked again, a note of impatience creeping into her voice.

'I – *perbacco* – I'm not sure. I feel like I heard that from many people. Parishioners, here in Venice. Maybe one of my brothers in Rome, but it was a long time ago. I can't really remember.'

'Hmmm.' Iris sounded unimpressed. Father Antonio couldn't tell if she was disbelieving or just disappointed. Either way, her reaction made his stomach churn unpleasantly.

'If anything comes back to me, I'll let you know.'

'Please do,' said Iris. 'And in the meantime, I've posted some new pictures of Paola up on my Facebook page. As I said, she's officially been listed as a missing person by the Italian authorities, but maybe you could circulate those photographs to anyone you know who might be able to help us? Other priests or whoever?'

'I will. Of course.'

After he hung up, Father Antonio sat for a long time, thinking. About right and wrong, truth and lies. And about consequences. Keeping secrets – confidences – was part of a priest's job. More than that, it was part of his vocation, ordained and sanctified by God. *It's not wrong*, he told himself. *You've done nothing wrong.*

A part of him still believed it. But another part, the part of him that wasn't a priest, but a man; the part of him that had loved Beatrice Contorini with all his heart, body and soul; that part twisted and turned painfully inside him, its stifled voice screaming from within.

Oh God. He put his head in his hands. *What have I done?*

Back at Buckie station, the festive mood of the morning had evaporated, and apparently been replaced by a palpable sense of foreboding.

'The chief's called for you, sir. Twice,' said the constable on the desk. 'He didn't sound too happy.'

'No, I imagine he didn't,' Haley sighed.

'He wants you to call him back right away.'

'OK,' Haley said grimly, heading into the private, Perspex-walled 'office' in the corner of the room, really more of a see-through cubicle, and closing the soundproofed door behind him. He may as well get it over with.

By the time he emerged, a full fifteen minutes later, Haley looked like he'd just run up Ben Nevis. Red-faced and sweating, and with his hair sticking up at all angles from having run his hands through it so many times, he nevertheless managed to crack a smile.

'He's giving us a week to conduct inquiries on the dog poisoning,' he announced to the five-strong team of men and women huddled over their desks, furiously pretending to work, 'and an unofficial green light to pursue any *genuinely active* leads on the Girls in the Wood.'

'That's amazing, sir,' Karen Downey, one of the newly minted sergeants, piped up. 'I thought he was going to sack you.'

'So did I, Karen.' Haley chuckled. 'So did I. But it turns out even Sir William has his limits when it comes to being pushed around by Jock MacKinnon. Who knew, eh? Just goes to show you never can tell.'

'Sir.'

'There are some conditions, though, and it's vital that we all work within them,' Haley went on. 'Number one, we turn over anything and everything we may find to the Italians. This is still their investigation.'

The group nodded.

'And I've promised, personally, to steer clear of the castle and the baron. Turns out I'm not top of his Christmas card list. Although I *may* need one of you to go up there eventually, depending on how things progress. So,' he clapped his hands together eagerly, 'does anyone have any good news for me? Any *actual* good news?'

At the back of the room, a slow hand made its way into the air, its owner still glued to his computer screen as he spoke.

'Andy?' Haley looked over at PC Brookes, the youngest member of the team and Banffshire police's resident IT wizard.

'Immigration, sir,' the pale, spotty young man answered cryptically. 'I've been trying a new cross-referencing software. By matching data inputs from the BIA and ECO, and scanning for overlap between HSMP and ISG entrants between 2000 and 2010.'

'OK,' Haley interrupted, 'and in English now, if you don't mind, son.'

'Sorry.' PC Brookes blushed. 'I've got a hit for Beatrice Contorini. Look here, she entered the UK at Stansted Airport on a student visa. She'd taken a direct flight from Venice Marco Polo. easyJet, flight EZY182.'

Haley raced over to look at the boy's screen for himself. Then he laughed out loud, clapping Andy on the back.

'You little genius. You little bloody genius. Right, boys and girls.' Rolling up his sleeves, he clapped his hands and addressed the rest of the team. 'It's action stations. Everybody listen up and I'll tell you what you're going to be doing. And if any of you had social plans for the next few nights, you'd better cancel 'em. Things are moving fast here, but we need to move faster.'

'I need to talk to you.'

Eileen Gregory stood on Iris's doorstep casting anxious glances over her shoulder, as if she were afraid she was being followed. Her voice trembled and her face looked pale and drawn. She sounded nothing like her usual, capable self.

'Can I come in?'

'Of course,' said Iris, bundling the jumpy housekeeper into Murray House's living room and offering her a seat on one of the tartan sofas. 'Can I get you a cup of tea? Or a hot chocolate?' she offered kindly. 'You look frozen.'

'No. Thank you.' Mrs G sat with her hands in her lap, wringing the hem of her cardigan in a manic, miserable manner. 'Would you mind closing the curtains, though? We're awfully visible here.'

Iris did as she asked. It was obvious this wasn't a social call, but Iris didn't push, sitting down and waiting patiently for Mrs G to explain.

Eventually, after much heavy sighing, she did. 'I've wrestled and wrestled with my conscience about coming to see you,' she began. 'The baron's always been a fair and generous employer to me, and I hate to do anything to betray his trust.'

'I understand,' said Iris.

'If he knew I was here –' She twisted the hem again. 'But I felt I had to say something. Because the thing is, well, this is murder, isn't it?'

Iris cleared her throat. 'Do you have some information, Mrs Gregory?' she prodded gently. 'About the bodies?'

'Not about the bodies, exactly,' the housekeeper explained, looking more pained with each word. 'I don't even know if it's relevant. But I do look at your Facebook page from time to time. And the photograph you posted yesterday – the mother of the dead girl – I recognised her.'

'You recognised Paola Contorini?' Iris tried not to show her excitement.

'Yes,' Mrs Gregory said firmly. 'She came to the castle on a few occasions. Once just for dinner, but usually she stayed the night. Her visits were always very secretive. All of the staff but me would be dismissed when she came. I don't even think that Edwin knew about her.'

'When was this?' Iris leaned forward.

'Oh, a good number of years back,' said Mrs Gregory.

'Rory and Emma were away at boarding school. The baron would pack Lady Pitfeldy off for a few nights, usually to her parents' estate in Fife. And then she, that woman, would show up.'

'So, you're saying Paola Contorini was Jock's mistress?' Iris sounded suitably stunned.

'I assume she was. One of them.' Mrs Gregory rolled her eyes heavenward. 'There were a lot of girls in those days, but this one was different. Important in some way. He was discreet about her.' She bit down on her lower lip nervously. 'Almost as if he felt *guilty*. Like I say, I would never normally discuss the baron's private life. I never have before.'

'Not even with Fiona?' Iris ventured. 'I know the two of you have remained friends.'

Mrs G looked astonished that Iris would know this – astonished and annoyed – but she didn't deny the relationship, although she did qualify Iris's description.

'I wouldn't describe us as friends, exactly. Lady Pitfeldy was my employer for many years and I felt sorry for her. We all did. But in answer to your question, no, I never spoke to her about the baron's behaviour. That wasn't my place.'

God, she's stiff, thought Iris. *Even now.*

'I'm only here now because two women are dead,' Eileen Gregory insisted. 'And when I saw that picture . . .'

'I understand,' said Iris, whose mind was still racing. *Jock and Paola? How? When?* 'You've done the right thing, Mrs Gregory.'

'I hope so,' said the housekeeper, getting to her feet. 'Will you tell the police what I've told you?'

'Yes,' said Iris, trying to imagine what Stuart Haley was going to say to *this* little bombshell. 'But they're going to want to talk to you directly eventually.'

'He mustn't know it was me,' Mrs G blurted out, grabbing Iris's hand. 'The baron. Please. You mustn't tell him.'

'*I* won't tell Jock anything,' Iris assured her. 'And I'm sure the police will handle things sensitively. Try not to worry.'

She was afraid of him, she thought, showing Eileen Gregory out and watching her scurry off into the darkness. Not just of losing her job. Of *him*.

The net was tightening; more, it seemed, with every hour. But what, exactly, they were about to catch, Iris still didn't know.

Chapter Thirty

Jamie Ingall peeled back the wet tea towel from over Iris's frying pan to reveal the charred remnants of her breakfast. 'I don't think your Michelin star's in the post for this one,' he said, waving his arms to waft more of the acrid smoke out of the kitchen window. 'Maybe stick to cereal in future?'

Iris nodded glumly. Jamie had stayed over last night, and the sex had been as good as ever. But something had shifted between them, something intangible but very real. And, Iris suspected, mutual. They'd both woken up this morning realising that whatever there was between them couldn't last. That it had been a bright and lovely flame, but one which was burning out – just like Iris's bacon and eggs.

'Sorry,' she said, watching him toss he contents of the frying pan into her bin and starting to wash it up on autopilot. 'I was distracted.'

'That's OK,' he said, keeping his eyes fixed on the sink. 'This isn't going to work, is it?'

'No,' Iris said quietly. 'I don't think it is.'

'It's been nice, though,' said Jamie, turning off the water and methodically drying the pan.

'It has,' agreed Iris. 'Very. But we're too different. Our lives are too different.'

'Aye.'

'And we can't survive on sex and . . . burned bacon for ever.'

'No, we can't,' Jamie agreed, finally putting the pan down and turning to look at her. 'You don't need to explain. I'm the one who fucked things up in the beginning. I should ha' been more –'

'Don't,' said Iris. 'It wouldn't have mattered, in the end. We wouldn't have worked anyway.'

Jamie smiled ruefully. 'You're probably right. Listen, there's something I wanted to tell you. It's not about us. I meant to tell you last night, actually, but then things sort of – took another turn, you know.'

'Yes,' said Iris, blushing. 'I know.' God, she would miss having sex with him.

'It's about the dead girl, Beatrice,' said Jamie. 'I remembered where I saw her before. And it wasn't in Pitfeldy.'

'What?' said Iris, all memories of last night's lovemaking flying out of her head in an instant in her excitement. 'Where was it?'

'In Italy,' said Jamie. 'Venice. When we were at school. There was a trip,' said Jamie.

'The art history trip, that Angus Brae went on,' said Iris. 'You were on that too?'

'How d'you know about that?' asked Jamie, surprised.

'Hannah Drummond told me. Angus's girlfriend.'

'Aye, well, that's where I saw the girl. She was working as a helper to one of the Italian art teachers who was showing our group around.'

Julia Mantovani? Iris wondered. 'Was the teacher a woman?'

Jamie nodded.

'And you're sure about this? Sure that the girl helping her was Beatrice?'

'One hundred per cent,' said Jamie. 'I also remember that Angus liked her. I didn't actually notice anything at the time. Angus and I weren't friends, particularly, so I didn't hang out with him. But after we got back to school, some of the kids used to rag him about fancying the helper.'

'Didn't you say kids at school used to think he was gay?' queried Iris.

'Aye, they did, but you know what teenagers are like. They'll tease you for being a poof one week and for liking a girl the next. I mean, I don't think it was anything serious, you know.

Just a bit of a laugh at Brae's expense. Anyway, that's where I saw her. So I thought I should tell you. In case it's important.'

'Thank you,' said Iris, still reeling. 'It is important.'

'All right, then.' Walking over to her, Jamie planted a kiss on her cheek. 'I'll say Happy Christmas.'

'Happy Christmas,' said Iris, kissing him back.

'And I'll see you around.'

'Yes,' she nodded, smiling, 'I hope so.'

After he'd gone, she sat down at the smoky kitchen table, shivering in the cold draught from the open window. It was the wedding rehearsal dinner tonight up at the castle, an event that Iris was already nervous about, given Jock's current feelings towards her. But Kathy had insisted on inviting her, and now she was glad she'd accepted. Angus would be there too, and Iris might get a chance to speak to him.

She needed to talk to Stuart Haley first, though. Let him know what Jamie had told her. Because they now knew for sure what Iris had long suspected. That sweet, shy, kind Angus had been lying through his Mr Nice Guy teeth. He *did* know Beatrice. They'd met on the fateful school trip. More than that, he'd been in love with her. *Angus* must have been the foreign 'boyfriend' Father Antonio had hinted at. And Beatrice *was* the girlfriend who had lived with him in Edinburgh, and been pregnant with his baby when his father Edwin turned up and demanded that he return to Pitfeldy.

Iris didn't want to believe it. But it was hard to come to any other conclusion than that the Pitfeldy Estate gillie was in this up to his pasty white neck.

'Thank you for coming. Really. It means a lot.'

Kathy greeted Iris in the grand hallway of the castle, clasping both of Iris's cold hands in her own warm ones.

'Of course,' said Iris. 'I wouldn't have missed it. You look fabulous, by the way, as ever. Is that the dress you got in Milan?'

Kathy nodded, smiling, smoothing down her scarlet taffeta bodice. The dress was indeed spectacular, a strapless, couture vision of red ruffles and feathers that came right to the floor, revealing just a hint of sky-high gold stiletto.

'I know the red's a bit of a statement. I'm just waiting for Rory to say something about "scarlet women". But I don't care.'

'Nor should you,' said Iris.

'I'm happy,' Kathy added defiantly, as if daring Iris to contradict her. 'Jock and I are happy and excited about our wedding, and I want tonight to be about that. About us, for once.'

'Well, I'm sure it will be,' said Iris, trying to find a way to hug Kathy that didn't involve getting a mouthful of feathers. Iris herself had opted for a slightly more low-key look for tonight's wedding rehearsal dinner, a wine-red jumpsuit with a matching velvet wrap for her bare shoulders. She felt good in it, confident, which was just as well, given that she was about to have to face Jock MacKinnon and the rest of his hostile family. Worse, she'd as good as promised Stuart Haley that she would act as his unofficial spy this evening.

'Don't say anything to Angus,' Haley had instructed her, after Iris filled him in about Jamie's latest revelation. 'I don't want him spooked, not yet anyway. But watch him. His reactions, his mood, who he's talking to. Or not talking to. And if you have a chance to talk to Eileen Gregory privately, let her know I'll be wanting to take an official statement from her about Paola Contorini in the next couple of days.'

'Can't you tell her yourself?' asked Iris. 'She was jittery enough when she came to see me, about Jock finding out. I expect she'll be avoiding me like the plague this evening.'

'I would, but I'm up to my eyes here,' said Haley. 'We're close to cracking this thing, Iris. I can feel it.'

Taking Kathy's arm now, Iris allowed herself to be led through the hallway, past the fire crackling impressively in the vast baronial hearth. Scented candles made everything smell of myrrh and cinnamon, like a Christmassy church, and sprigs of holly and berries added to the festive atmosphere.

'So how was the actual rehearsal?' Iris asked. 'It was this afternoon, wasn't it?'

'Yes, and believe it or not, it was pretty smooth,' said Kathy, with a sigh of relief. 'Jock's best man's been laid up with flu, but Rory stood in for him and actually managed to get through the entire thing without being a douche.'

'Imagine that,' said Iris.

'I know, right?' said Kathy, but the brief flicker of happiness quickly faded into a more solemn look. 'It felt really strange not having Milo and Sam Sam there. You know I'd planned for the two of them to be part of the ceremony? I had these super-cute outfits made, and they were going to have our rings in little velvet pouches on their collars . . .'

'I know. It must be hard.' Iris gave her a supportive squeeze, and tried not to think unworthy thoughts about silver linings. Although, on the other hand, it *would* have been fun to watch Emma's and Rory's faces at the sight of two furry little ring bearers. Whatever happened with the case, or the finishing touches to the portrait, she'd promised Kathy she would be there for the wedding. Even without Milo and Sam Sam, she was expecting some 'Californian' surprises. 'So who's here tonight?' she asked, changing the subject.

'Only family, really,' said Kathy. 'Apart from the Reverend Michaela and you. We were going to do something bigger and splashier, but after my babies – I couldn't face it.'

'Isn't Angus coming?' Iris tried to keep the note of alarm out of her voice.

'Oh yes, he and Hannah are here,' Kathy said airily. 'I was counting them as family. Or at least as part of the furniture.'

They'd reached the door to the drawing room, where a low hubbub of voices suggested that the other guests were already assembled for a pre-dinner drink.

'You go on in,' said Iris. 'I need to pop to the loo.'

Slipping away, she made her way along the empty corridor towards the kitchen and staff offices. This would be her best chance to catch Eileen Gregory privately and pass on Haley's message. A quick poke of her head into the kitchen revealed that the housekeeper wasn't there, so Iris tried her office, a tiny little room next to the laundry with a desk and an armchair and a few of Mrs G's personal things. There were no photographs, Iris noticed, other than a formal MacKinnon family portrait taken in front of the castle when Rory and Emma were teenagers, with Jock and Fiona standing stiffly on either side of them and the castle staff, including Mrs Gregory, lined up behind. But a few knick-knacks and postcards provided a modest sense that this was Eileen's private space. She wasn't here either, though, and Iris would have to get back to the drawing room in a minute.

Grabbing a pen and a sheet of notepaper from the immaculately organised desk, Iris began writing a quick message:

Tried to find you. Police will need a statement in coming days. Happy to help if you need me.
Iris.

Folding it over and writing *PRIVATE*, she placed it on the top of the neatly stacked in-tray before something caught her eye.

It was a little pile of small white envelopes, right beside the in-tray. The one on the top was at an angle, its corner jutting out, breaking the otherwise perfect symmetry of the housekeeper's desk. Slowly, Iris pulled it from the stack, rubbing the familiar stiff paper between her thumb and forefinger before she turned it over.

There it was. Faint. Almost invisible to the naked eye, unless you were looking for it:

A round imprint of a thistle.

'There you are! I was about to send out a search party.' Kathy, all smiles and red ruffles, advanced warmly on Iris as she walked into the drawing room. 'Darling, get Iris a drink, would you?'

Jock, looking as stiff as ever and a little tired in his formal jacket and tie, handed Iris a flute of champagne from a silver tray of pre-poured glasses, avoiding eye contact.

'Thank you,' said Iris. The envelope was burning a hole in her pocket. She still found it hard to believe that Mrs G could have written all those horrid, spiteful letters to poor Kathy. Clearly, she'd misjudged the housekeeper's character badly. Iris had always thought of Eileen Gregory as rather cold and brittle, but never as actively malicious. But now she questioned everything. Could Mrs G also have poisoned the dogs? Her distress about Milo and Sam Sam had seemed genuine, as had her frightened confession about Paola Contorini having been Jock's mistress. But what if both of those things had been a front? What if Jock had never known Paola? What if, somehow, Eileen Gregory was trying to frame him, and was using Iris to help do her dirty work?

Evidently, tonight wasn't the time to act on any of this. At some point she would have to let Kathy know about the envelope, if nothing else. But first she would need to talk to Haley, and make a plan. Tomorrow.

Meanwhile, she took a look around the room. Angus and Hannah were sitting together on the sofa nearest the door, looking faintly awkward, Iris thought, and not quite part of the group. Eliza was flitting around, collecting empty glasses and canapé plates. And at the other end of the room, standing around the fireplace, Rory, Emma and Emma's husband Fergus formed a separate group, deep in conversation with the vicar.

'Iris, you know the Reverend Michaela, don't you?' said Kathy, beckoning the vicar over.

'Of course,' said Iris, forcing a smile. 'Nice to see you again, Reverend.'

'Michaela, please,' said the vicar. 'I first met Iris at the church fair back in August,' she told Kathy. 'She and Jamie Ingall trounced headmaster Donnelly and I at the coconut shy. Poor John's pride was terribly hurt.'

Iris snuck a glance at Angus, who stiffened visibly at the mention of 'poor John'.

'It feels like a very long time ago now,' the vicar went on.

'Doesn't it?' agreed Kathy.

'I suppose because such an awful lot has happened since then. You've certainly seen Pitfeldy at its most eventful, Iris. Autumns up here are usually very sleepy affairs.'

A slightly awkward silence fell at this veiled reference to the Girls in the Wood. To everyone's surprise, it was Hannah who broke it, getting up from the sofa and joining the group.

'How's the portrait going?' she asked Iris. 'Have you finished it yet?'

'Not quite,' said Iris. 'I'm still tinkering.'

'*I* think we've finished it,' said Kathy. 'It looks awesome. But artists are all perfectionists.'

'Tell me about it,' said Hannah, smiling down at Angus.

'I'm not an artist,' he muttered, not smiling back, but Hannah seemed not to notice his bad mood.

'Iris is going to give it to us formally on our wedding day,' said Kathy, turning to look lovingly at Jock, who was sitting by himself in one of the brocade armchairs, staring off into space. 'Are you tired, darling?'

'Hmmm?' He looked up, distracted. 'No, no. Not tired. I am hungry, though. Now that Iris is here, I think we should sit down and eat. Where's Mrs G disappeared to?'

'I'll go and find her,' said Rory.

He looked well, Iris thought, handsome as ever in a dark suit and light blue shirt, and less brooding and bitter than usual. There was a confidence about him, she decided, that she hadn't seen before. As if whatever private battle he was fighting with his father had either been won, or called off. Even the smile he gave her as he left the room was relaxed and easy.

Iris was still wondering what might have brought about this change of heart in Rory when he returned with a distinctly unrelaxed-looking Eileen Gregory, ushering her into the room with his hand resting reassuringly on the small of her back. Not for the first time it struck Iris that Jock MacKinnon's housekeeper and his eldest son seemed to have an unusually close relationship. *They're allies*, she realised now, although Mrs G looked nothing like a woman whose private battles had been won. Quite the contrary.

'You wanted to eat, baron?' she asked Jock nervously, at pains to avoid looking at Iris or acknowledging her presence in any way.

Has she read my note? Iris wondered, watching her. *Or realised one of her envelopes is missing?*

'Yes,' said Jock tersely. 'Is cook ready?'

'Almost,' said Mrs G. 'But I can seat you all now while she plates the starters?'

'That sounds great,' said Kathy. 'Should we bring our drinks through or leave them here?'

Before Mrs G could answer, there was a loud rap on the drawing room door and two uniformed policemen walked in, a gangly young man whom Iris vaguely recognised as one of Stuart Haley's underlings and a shorter, fatter colleague she hadn't seen before.

'Sorry to disturb you all,' the first man began sombrely, pulling out his ID card. 'Sergeant Danny Spencer, Banffshire Police. This is PC Gordon.'

Iris watched as the blood drained from Jock's face and his fists clenched together in rage. 'You have *got* to be joking,' he muttered venomously. 'Dear God. This is our wedding rehearsal dinner.' He wrapped a protective arm around Kathy's shoulder. 'It's a private family celebration. What the *hell* do you bastards want this time?'

'I'm looking for Mr MacKinnon. Mr Rory MacKinnon,' said the sergeant, ignoring Jock's rant.

'I'm Rory MacKinnon.' Rory stepped forward, looking puzzled and only slightly less confident than before. 'How can I help?'

'Rory MacKinnon, I'm arresting you on suspicion of animal cruelty and criminal damage.'

'Don't be ridiculous.' Rory let out a short, mirthless laugh. 'There's obviously been a mistake.'

'No mistake, sir. You have the right to remain silent. If you do . . .'

'Animal cruelty?' Kathy cut him off, her eyes widening. Disengaging herself from Jock, she looked from Rory, to the policemen, to Iris, and then back to the sergeant. 'Is this about my dogs?' she asked, both hands fluttering agonisingly over her heart.

'Yes, ma'am,' the sergeant replied bluntly. 'We have reason to believe that Mr MacKinnon is responsible for the poisoning of the animals.'

'What reason?' Jock demanded, looking ashen.

'We have CCTV evidence of Rory MacKinnon buying rat poison at McGinty's Hardware in Buckie the week before Ms Miller left for Italy,' the sergeant explained.

All eyes turned to Rory, who stood in shocked silence, shaking his head.

'We've also had a signed confession from one of the kitchen staff here at the castle that Mr MacKinnon paid her to slip small amounts of white powder into the dogs' food, on five separate occasions.'

'That's a lie!' Rory exploded.

'Which part?' Kathy shot back tearfully. 'You buying the poison or you bribing the maid?'

'All of it,' said Rory. 'This entire story is a revolting fabrication from start to finish.'

'Who? Who made this "confession"?' Jock asked.

'I can't release any further information at the moment, baron, I'm sorry.'

'Haley put you up to this, didn't he?' Jock shouted, his voice breaking.

Ignoring him, the sergeant put an arm on Rory's shoulder. 'If you'd like to come with us, Mr MacKinnon.'

'I wouldn't *like* to,' snapped Rory, shrugging him off. 'This whole thing is a hideous mistake. But I will come with you, sergeant, for my family's sake. Enjoy your dinner, everyone,' he said shakily to the room at large. Turning to Eileen Gregory directly, he added, 'Call my solicitor, please, Mrs G. Dad has the number.'

And without another word, flanked by the two policemen, he left the room.

Chapter Thirty-one

Stuart Haley watched on his monitor as Rory MacKinnon was read his rights for a second time, relieved of his watch and wallet and escorted cordially to an interview room. Stuart reckoned his expression was angry but controlled, a potentially dangerous combination, particularly in a highly educated and cunning barrister with an axe to grind.

On the one hand, Stuart had solid evidence that Rory had poisoned Kathy Miller's dogs. More than enough to arrest him, and hopefully enough to charge the bastard in due course. The fact remained, however that, evidence or not, and sticking to procedure or not, if he'd got this one wrong – if it somehow turned out MacKinnon was innocent – then his career was over. To put it mildly, that was not a comfortable feeling.

A few minutes later, Sergeant Spencer appeared at Haley's office door.

'He's in Room Five, sir.'

'Well done, Danny.' Haley offered his sergeant a seat. 'How did it go?'

The young man exhaled deeply, the stress of the evening beginning to show. 'Not too bad, in the end,' he replied. 'The baron was not happy to see us, and Ms Miller was upset, you know. Obviously. But MacKinnon came without too much trouble.'

'He denied it, I take it?'

'Oh, aye. He denied it all right.'

'And he asked for his brief, I assume?'

'He instructed the housekeeper to call his solicitor before we left,' said Sergeant Spencer.

Haley nodded. 'Well, he won't talk till his lawyer gets here, which won't be till the morning. So you'd better settle him in for the night.'

'You're not going to question him now, sir?' the sergeant sounded surprised.

'No,' said Haley. 'There's no point. He's too smart to say anything to me on the record. Besides, it'll do him good to have a night in the cells,' he added, the faintest hint of a smile playing at the corners of his lips. 'Did you see Iris Grey up there when you arrested him?'

'She was there, yes, sir.'

'And who else?'

Sergeant Spencer reeled off the list of names. 'It wasn't a big party.'

'OK,' said Haley. 'You let MacKinnon know what's happening and then get off home and get some sleep. Nice work, sergeant.'

Rubbing his eyes, he glanced up at the clock on his office wall. It was only eight o'clock but it felt like midnight. He ought to get home and try to sleep himself, but he wanted to get the download from Iris once she got back from the castle. With any luck that would be sooner rather than later. After Rory's arrest, they might just call the whole thing off and not even have the dinner. Then again, if they did, he'd be curious to know how Angus Brae had reacted to everything. Curious about a lot of things, in fact.

The ringing desk phone made him jump.

He picked it up at once. 'Haley?'

'Detective! I didn't know if you'd still be at work this late.' Martha Lane's soft, southern American tones dripped down the line like warm honey. Haley had contacted the pathologist at her Edinburgh lab yesterday, after Iris's tip-off from Mrs Gregory, but he hadn't really expected anything to come from it.

'Oh, I'm still here, professor,' he said wryly. 'I've got nowhere else to go.'

'Well, I'm happy I caught you,' said Martha.

Haley perked up. 'Dare I hope it's good news?'

Martha chuckled. 'Well, it's certainly news. Whether it's good or not rather depends on who you are . . .'

The rehearsal dinner was an extraordinary affair, and perhaps the most absurd example of the English 'keep calm and carry on' spirit that Iris had ever witnessed. All of the guests took their assigned seats at Mrs Gregory's beautifully laid table, studiously ignoring Rory's empty place. The entire baronial dining room, in fact, looked like a scene from *Beauty and the Beast*, all gleaming silverware, sparkling crystal and candelabra, with vases overflowing with winter greenery and berries set against a backdrop of medieval tapestries that wouldn't have looked out of place in a museum. And at the head of the table Kathy, an exquisite, scarlet Belle, held court and made conversation with the numbed, dead eyes of a woman forced to pretend that this was still a happy occasion. And that her soon-to-be son-in-law hadn't just been arrested for fatally poisoning her beloved pets.

Iris herself was seated between Rory's empty chair and Fergus Twomey, which instantly brought back memories of her first-ever dinner at the castle.

'Can you believe that was four months ago?' said Fergus, noisily slurping his lobster bisque before launching into yet another story about hunting. 'It's been a terrible season for the Dumfriesshires and Stewartry. That's my local pack,' he complained to Iris. 'Of course, now we've the shooting to look forward to. Although a certain wedding's put a spanner in the works here at Pitfeldy. Between you and me,' he added in a stage whisper, 'I suspect the new Lady P might put the kibosh on the whole thing permanently. Bit of an animal rights nutter. All these Yanks are.'

Iris nodded politely, interjecting the bare minimum of 'hmmms' and 'yes, I sees' needed to keep Fergus oblivious while she observed the other guests. And Mrs Gregory, who flitted in and out of the room between courses looking shell-shocked and close to tears. Iris assumed this must be about Rory and 'the thing no one was talking about', but the strength of the housekeeper's reaction was interesting. Angus Brae looked subdued, sitting between Kathy and the Reverend Michaela, but that wasn't out of the ordinary. His girlfriend, Hannah, was on Jock's right, and too busy making polite conversation about the wedding and honeymoon plans to be able to rescue her boyfriend socially, as she so often did when the two of them were out together.

'Yes, where *are* you going on honeymoon?' the vicar asked, tuning in to Jock and Hannah's conversation while the maids finished clearing the beef Wellington and Mrs Gregory carried in the pudding, a towering raspberry pavlova that looked as much like a work of art as a dessert. 'Or is it a secret?'

'Not a secret,' said Jock, reaching across the table for Kathy's hand and squeezing it lovingly. 'A surprise.'

'He's promised me it's somewhere hot,' said Kathy, returning his loving look, to Emma Twomey's ill-concealed disgust. 'As much as I adore him, if he takes us on a camping trip to Ben Nevis or to some dreary fishing holiday in Canada, it'll be the shortest marriage in history.'

Iris, Hannah and the vicar laughed politely, and Fergus guffawed, earning himself a sharp look from Emma.

'I must say,' said Jock, wearily, 'as much as I love Pitfeldy, it will be nice to get away. The last few months have been a strain on all of us.'

It was the closest anyone had come to acknowledging what had happened tonight, and all the suppressed tension in the room. Iris was as surprised as everybody else that Jock had been the person to do it, and even more surprised when Angus spoke up after him.

'You deserve a break, baron,' he murmured, tearing his eyes up from the bowl of meringue in front of him to look directly at Jock and Kathy. 'Both of you do.'

'Hear, hear!' said the vicar, raising her glass. 'I propose a toast. To a new year, and new beginnings.'

Eight glasses were lifted, some freely, some, Iris felt, more reluctantly.

'To new beginnings.'

Just then a bright light arced into the room through the sash windows. It was a car headlight, and it was rapidly followed by two more and the spraying of gravel as a trio of cars pulled up in front of the castle. The whole room sat in silence as engines were switched off and doors opened and closed. Iris scanned the sea of faces for their different reactions. Emma, Hannah and the Reverend Michaela looked worried. Kathy, Jock and Angus all looked strangely blank. Fergus kept attacking his pavlova, oblivious, and Eileen Gregory froze like an escaping prisoner of war caught in a machine-gunner's searchlight.

No one spoke as the front door was opened and the sound of footsteps on the ancient stone floors grew louder and louder.

By the time DI Haley actually walked into the room, the second police appearance of the evening, the mood around the table was more expectant than surprised. But that changed as soon as Haley opened his mouth.

'We've identified the second victim,' he announced bluntly, and more than a touch triumphantly, his eyes boring into Jock's. 'Jock MacKinnon, I'm arresting you on suspicion of murder.'

Chapter Thirty-two

Back at the station, Stuart Haley looked soberly across the interview desk at Jock MacKinnon, who met the DI's gaze with an impressively blank stare. He'd been unusually calm up at the castle when Haley arrested him and read him his rights. Unlike Eileen Gregory, the housekeeper, who'd fainted dead away on the spot and had to be revived by the Reverend Michaela, and Kathy Miller, who'd let out a sort of animal howl that rang through the vast dining room for what felt like an hour. She was still going, slumped in Iris's arms, as Jock was led away.

'Interview commenced at ten p.m.,' said Haley gruffly for the benefit of the tape. 'So.'

'So,' said Jock.

'Tell me about Paola Contorini.'

Haley had had a hunch about Beatrice's mother, Paola, ever since it emerged that the stories of her untimely death in Rome were untrue. Eileen Gregory's testimony to Iris deepened his suspicions, but it was tonight's hard evidence from Professor Martha Lane that clinched it. It was a phone call Haley would never forget.

'You're absolutely sure, Martha?' he'd asked, with his heart in his mouth. 'I can't stress enough how much rides on this.'

'I'm positive,' said Professor Lane firmly. 'The X-ray results you sent me showed fractures in the left calcaneus and talus identical to those on our second set of remains. That would have made it ninety-nine per cent sure, but a few minutes ago my colleague at Sapienza University in Rome rang me with the DNA results from our bone marrow. Those were a match, too.'

It was a rare moment of unadulterated triumph for Stuart Haley, although he owed at least part of it to Iris Grey. He'd learned more than a week ago that Paola Contorini wasn't on any of Italy's criminal DNA databases. But Iris was the one who'd suggested that she might have provided a private DNA sample when she was chasing Massimo Giannotti for a paternity test. That had led Haley to the Contorinis' GP in Venice, who had no genetic samples but who had helpfully provided Paola's old X-ray results, and, eventually, to a private clinic in Rome, for whom she had, indeed, provide a sample.

Jock breathed in and out slowly, allowing Haley's question to hang in the air.

'Is Rory here?' he asked eventually, sounding oddly detached.

'Yes. He's spending the night in one of our cells,' said Haley. 'Is that important, baron?'

'Not especially,' said Jock. 'He's waiting for his solicitor, I suppose?'

'Paola Contorini,' Haley leaned forward over the desk, bringing his face close to Jock's. 'Why did you do it, baron? Why did you kill her?'

Leaning back, Jock sighed heavily. 'I think I'll wait for my lawyer, too, if it's all the same to you, detective,' he announced, after a long pause. 'I'm happy to cooperate. But it doesn't make sense for me to answer the same questions twice. And John's going to want to hear everything for himself when he gets here.'

'OK,' Haley said briskly, matching the baron's relaxed tone, albeit with an effort. Two could play at that game. 'Well, he's on his way, I understand.'

'Yes.'

Unlike Rory's solicitor, John Mills, Jock MacKinnon's brief, had picked up his phone at nine-thirty at night and was already on his way to Pitfeldy. Haley knew him by reputation. The man was as slippery as a snake dipped in olive oil and had a hawk-like eye for irregularities of procedure. Haley would have to be on top of his own game to stand a chance of outwitting him.

'We'll take a break, in that case, and resume once your man arrives. Interview suspended.'

It was almost midnight by the time John Mills sauntered into the station looking worryingly rested and efficient in an immaculately cut suit and smelling of expensive aftershave.

'We obviously want to help, detective inspector,' Jock's lawyer said obligingly after almost an hour of 'no comment's, partial answers and evasions from Jock that made it quite clear that was the last thing they wanted. 'But I'm not sure how much more information my client can give you.'

'Nor am I,' said Haley doggedly, undeterred. 'That's why we're still sitting here, Mr Mills. And we will be for the next,' he looked at his watch, 'seven and a half hours. After which, unless he stops lying to me, I fully intend to charge your client with obstruction, and very possibly with murder. Why did you lie about knowing Paola Contorini, Jock?'

'I didn't lie,' Jock sighed. 'I just didn't remember her.'

'We have witnesses who've testified Paola visited you at the castle, more than once.'

'Forgive me, detective, but weren't these visits more than a decade ago?' John Mills piped up. 'My client can't be expected to remember every house guest he's ever had on the estate.'

'No indeed,' said Haley, archly. 'And I'm not interested in all of them. Only the ones who ended up murdered and buried under his bothy.'

For a blissful moment, that shut John Mills up.

'Were you and Paola Contorini lovers?' Haley demanded, turning back to Jock.

'No,' Jock drawled.

'OK,' said Haley. 'So how did you know her?'

'I told you. I don't remember.'

'Did you meet her in Venice?'

'I don't remember.'

'Did you rape her, baron? When you and your friend Massimo Giannotti were staying at the Danieli Hotel together?'

'Don't answer that,' John Mills instructed his client, before turning on Haley. 'That's an outrageous accusation, detective inspector. I trust you have the evidence to back it up?'

'It's not an accusation, it's a question,' Haley shot back. 'We know that Paola Contorini claimed she was raped while she worked at the hotel. And according to my Italian colleagues, the attack took place during the period that your client was staying *in* Venice, a city he previously claimed never to have visited, *at* the Danieli. So here's another question.' He turned his attention furiously back to Jock. 'Are you Beatrice Contorini's father?'

Just for a second, a flash of panic registered in Jock's eyes. It was gone as soon as it arrived, but not quick enough for Haley, who pounced like a cat, steamrollering over the lawyer's 'no comment'.

'I'll tell you what I think, shall I?' Haley leaned over the table, as close to Jock's face as the space allowed. 'I think you remember Paola Contorini very well indeed. She *wasn't* your mistress.'

'I believe I already told you that,' said Jock, in a rare flash of temper that earned him a warning look from his lawyer.

'She was the chambermaid who wouldn't shut up, wasn't she?' Haley continued. 'That rape happened late at night and in pitch-darkness, when Paola was drunk. She always believed it was your friend Massimo Giannotti who attacked her. She believed that till she died, didn't she? But it wasn't Massimo. It was you. *You* were Paola's attacker.'

'No.' Jock shook his head repeatedly. 'That's not right.'

'I think it is,' Haley persisted softly. 'I think you raped Paola in Venice, and then you went home to Scotland and forgot all about her, letting your so-called buddy Massimo take the heat for what *you* did. Until, as awful fate would have it, eighteen years later, young Angus Brae went to Italy on a school trip. And who should he meet there, in Venice, and fall head over heels in love with, but *Beatrice* Contorini, Paola's daughter. The product, according to Paola, of that rape. In other words, your daughter.'

Jock's head shaking became more frenzied, but his former sangfroid seemed to have deserted him and he said nothing.

'My client utterly refutes these outrageous allegations,' Mills piped up, filling the silence.

'Good for him,' said Haley. 'But I'm not finished. Angus fell in love with Beatrice on that school trip, and she with him. So much so that when he won a place at Edinburgh to study art, she ran away from home in Venice and followed him here, to Scotland. To be with him. Isn't that right?'

'No,' Jock said, quietly but firmly.

'Yes,' Haley countered. 'And it got worse, didn't it, baron? Because by the time Edwin Brae went to Edinburgh to beg his son to come back home, Beatrice was already pregnant. But you couldn't have that, could you? Because you knew something Edwin didn't know, something he must never know. That Angus was your son. That you'd betrayed Edwin, your oldest and closest friend, by having an affair with his wife, Linda. Am I getting close, baron?'

John Mills looked utterly panicked, watching his client slump forward with his head in his hands in what looked very much like a tacit gesture of admission; to this last accusation at least.

'Baron Pitfeldy, can you confirm that you are, in fact, the biological father of Angus Brae?' Haley asked.

John Mills opened his mouth to speak but Jock held up a hand.

'It's all right,' he said quietly. 'I never knew for sure. But I always believed Angus was my son, yes.'

Haley leaned back, exhaling deeply. At last. At *last* the bastard was opening up and the pieces of the puzzle were beginning to fit.

'Is that why you've always been so involved in his life?'

'Yes.'

'But he never knew?'

'No. Neither he nor Edwin –' Jock's voice wavered. 'Whatever you may think of me, detective inspector, I have always loved Edwin like a brother. I deeply regretted my affair with Linda. But you can't turn back the clock.'

'No,' Haley agreed. 'Although you can hide the evidence, can't you?'

'What do you mean?'

'I mean I think you panicked, baron. When Angus, probably your son, shows up living with a girl who you know is probably your daughter? Well, you can't have that, can you? You have to put a stop to it. So you get Edwin to do his part, packing him off to Edinburgh to emotionally blackmail Angus into dropping out and coming home. Using his Alzheimer's to pressure the poor boy into returning to the estate.'

'It wasn't like that,' Jock insisted hotly.

'But Beatrice wasn't prepared to just sit back and lose him, was she? She came to Pitfeldy. Maybe she was still pregnant, or maybe she'd lost the baby by then, I don't know. But I think you confronted her, threatened her, told her she had to leave and forget about Angus. You just didn't tell her why.'

'No,' said Jock. 'That didn't happen.'

'And when she wouldn't leave? I think you killed her,' said Haley.

'That is not true.' Jock looked over at John Mills, apparently remembering his solicitor's presence for the first time. 'Yes, Angus had a girlfriend and yes, Edwin and I disapproved. But not for the reasons you think. And I certainly didn't kill her.'

'All right, that's enough,' said John Mills forcefully. 'This is conjecture on top of conjecture. You've asked a question, detective inspector, and my client has answered it.'

Haley shrugged, keeping his eyes on Jock. 'OK. Let's agree you didn't kill Beatrice Contorini. Then who did? Maybe it was Angus, hmm? Maybe he killed the girl?'

'Don't be ridiculous,' Jock snapped.

'I agree,' John Mills piped up. 'This isn't a game of Cluedo, detective inspector.'

'You're right, it's not,' said Haley grimly. 'It's a double murder. But I don't see anything ridiculous about what I just said. If your client is innocent, as he claims. Because, I mean let's face it, guys, someone killed Beatrice Contorini, her *and* her mother, and buried them on your estate.' He glared at Jock openly. 'That much we know. Now, of course, Angus Brae would have no reason to kill Paola Contorini. *You* had a motive there, baron, but he didn't.'

Jock closed his eyes and pinched the bridge of his nose. He looked exhausted.

'So let's leave Paola for later,' Haley pressed on. 'Let's stick with poor Beatrice for now, shall we? If you didn't kill her, then I'm thinking Angus might have lashed out at her in an argument or whatnot? Maybe things got out of hand. He was under a lot of pressure, after all. From his dad, from you. From Beatrice herself, presumably, with a baby on the way. So I'm thinking, what if *Angus* killed her, and *you* helped him dispose of the body?'

Like a lit firework, or boiling water erupting from a geyser, Jock literally exploded up out of his seat.

'That's a LIE!' he roared. 'You're a bloody liar, Haley. Angus had nothing to do with this. NOTHING!'

'Sit down, Jock,' his solicitor said sternly, as two uniformed officers stepped forward to restrain him.

'I won't sit down. You leave the boy out of this!' he bellowed at Haley.

'Sit down now,' Mills repeated, 'and stop talking.'

Still shaking, but sensing the gravity of the situation, Jock did as he was asked.

'You're not helping anyone by losing your temper,' Mills went on. 'Detective Haley has spent the last three hours trying to provoke you with these deeply hurtful and untrue allegations. But that doesn't mean you have to let him succeed. Let me respond from now on. That's my job.'

Jock nodded, sinking back into his chair. Haley sat back too, taking a moment to compose himself. That had been his game, and set, but if John Mills was allowed to take over, he knew he could still easily lose the match.

On an instinct, he decided to make an abrupt change in tactics.

'That won't be necessary,' he said, getting to his feet and looking at the tape recorder. 'Interview terminated. Baron Pitfeldy, you're free to go.'

'What?' Jock and his solicitor asked in unison. Both were equally astonished. John Mills looked suspicious, while Jock still seemed vulnerable and close to tears.

'I said you're free to go,' said Haley lightly, gathering up his things and leaving the room. 'I'm not charging you. Thank you for your help. Goodnight.'

After he'd gone, Jock sat for a moment alone with his lawyer, too surprised and emotionally drained to move.

'Well,' he said eventually, getting creakily to his feet. 'I didn't expect that.'

'No,' said John Mills. 'Nor did I.'

And I don't like it. Not one little bit. What the hell are the police playing at?

It was almost dawn when Jock walked into the castle, but winter darkness still clung stubbornly to the low Scottish sky, the night's blanket unwilling to be peeled back by a pale, useless December sun that would bring no warmth, no comfort.

Inside, the house itself was just as cold, dark and empty, a sad shadow of the warm, welcoming home it had been yesterday evening, just a few short hours ago. Walking stiffly across the stone floors towards the stairs, Jock was surprised to see Eileen Gregory emerge to greet him. Still in last night's clothes and with her mascara streaked in ugly black lines beneath exhausted eyes, she looked ill and broken.

'They released you, then?'

He nodded. 'Yes.'

'So it was all a misunderstanding? You're not being charged?'

He looked at her curiously, too tired to ask any of the myriad questions flying through his brain, as to where his housekeeper fitted into all of this. All he wanted right now was to collapse into Kathy's arms. To be with the one person who understood, who loved him unconditionally.

'No.' He kept walking. 'Not being charged. But I'm tired, Mrs G. I'm going to bed.'

'Of course, baron. Goodnight.'

As an afterthought, Jock asked, 'How was Kathy after I left, by the way?'

Mrs G looked awkward. 'She was very upset.'

'Poor thing,' he sighed. 'I take it she's asleep now?'

'Actually, baron, she – she's not here,' the housekeeper stammered nervously.

Jock froze. 'Not here? Well, where is she?'

Mrs Gregory winced, as if it caused her physical pain to break the news.

'She's with Iris Grey.'

Jock gripped the bannister for support.

'She packed a bag and left soon after the police – soon after you did. I believe she left a note for you, baron. It's on your bed.'

'I see,' said Jock, in a small, strangled voice, staring straight ahead. 'Thank you, Mrs Gregory. Goodnight.'

At Murray House, in bed beside Iris and wearing a spare pair of Iris's pyjamas, Kathy sat up suddenly, waking them both.

'No,' she panted, sweat coursing down her face and chest.

'It's OK,' said Iris, sitting up groggily and wrapping an arm around her. 'It was just a dream.'

The poor girl had been too traumatised last night to sleep by herself, even in Iris's spare room, so Iris had given her a sleeping pill and had lain down beside her until, finally, she fell asleep.

As soon as Haley said the name 'Paola Contorini' out loud last night, and started reading Jock his rights, something had snapped inside Kathy. The tenuous string holding together the fragile pieces of her mental health and her frayed hopes of a normal, happy married life up at the castle broke in spectacular style. The death of her dogs, Rory's arrest and now this, all on the night of her wedding rehearsal dinner, had combined to catapult her over an edge. Iris had done what she could to break the fall.

'No,' Kathy said again. 'It's not a dream. It's true. It's all true!'

'What's true, love?' Iris asked gently.

'Jock. He did it, didn't he? I asked him, asked him to his face, if he'd hurt those women, and he swore he didn't. But he lied, Iris. He *lied*.'

'We don't know what happened yet,' said Iris, still reeling herself from the news about Paola and desperate for a chance to talk to Haley. All of a sudden Mrs Gregory's envelopes didn't seem remotely important, but at least they gave Iris an excuse to report back to him, and hopefully find out what had happened in the last twenty-four hours. It wasn't a stretch to imagine that Jock was guilty of killing one of his mistresses. But at the same time, she suspected there was more to the story than that. Not least the fact that it could hardly be a coincidence that Jock MacKinnon's erstwhile 'girlfriend' was the mother of Angus Brae's. 'Try and get some more sleep. We'll find out in the morning if he was charged, but until then –'

'It doesn't matter.' Kathy cut her off, her face a picture of anguish. 'Don't you see? It doesn't matter anymore. The trust is gone, Iris. It's gone and I can't get it back. I *loved* him!' she ended passionately, willing Iris to believe her.

'I know that,' said Iris, easing her back down onto the pillow. 'I know you loved him. I think he loved you, too.'

She lay back herself, thinking and stroking Kathy's head until she slipped back asleep.

Why am I defending Jock MacKinnon? Iris asked herself. *Was* that what she was doing? Or was she merely comforting a friend? She wasn't sure herself anymore. But she did know that something felt wrong. Missing. And that 'something' made her deeply uneasy.

Chapter Thirty-three

'I can't stay long,' Stuart Haley told Iris, before ordering a full English breakfast and a large coffee. 'I'm up to my eyes, as you can imagine.'

'I can, and I appreciate you seeing me.'

'Ach, get on with you.' He waved a hand dismissively. 'I wanted to see you. Needed to, in fact. What a bloody night, eh?'

They were in Mel's, a greasy spoon café down by the harbour popular with the trawlermen. Iris usually avoided the place, partly because she didn't want to run into Jamie Ingall – there were no hard feelings, but it was still awkward – and partly because the coffee famously tasted like mud, the breakfasts were deep-fried, and she strongly suspected that Mel's fryer contained rodent remains. But it was close to the station, Haley had suggested it, and beggars couldn't be choosers.

'Before I forget,' said Iris, reaching into the pocket of her puffa coat with mismatched fingerless gloves, and pulling out the envelope from Eileen Gregory's office. It was snowing outside, the air so cold it hurt your face, and she'd dressed accordingly. 'Not a priority now, I know. But I found this on Mrs G's desk yesterday. It looks like she was our threatening letter writer. Check out the thistle seal on the back.'

'Hmmm,' Haley said contemplatively, turning the envelope over in his hands. 'That woman's an enigma. I'm still not sure what game she's playing.'

'What do you mean?' said Iris.

'Well, for one thing, I'm starting to wonder whether she lied to you about Jock and Paola.'

'What?' Iris's eyes widened. 'Why?'

Haley filled her in on the salient points of Jock's confession. His vehement denials of any sort of a relationship with Paola Contorini, 'which, apart from the housekeeper's "confession" to you, we have bugger all evidence for, by the way', and, more importantly, Jock's admission that Angus Brae was in all likelihood his son.

'That explains a lot,' said Iris.

'Aye. It does,' agreed Haley.

'But do you really believe Mrs G made up the affair with Paola?' Iris asked.

Haley frowned. 'I'm not sure.' He told Iris his theory about the rape. How Jock knew Massimo Giannotti, and how the two of them had been in Venice, staying together at the Danieli Hotel where Paola worked at around the time she claimed the attack happened. 'If she was drunk and it was late, she could have confused Massimo for Jock.'

'You mean . . . *Jock* could have been Beatrice's father?' asked Iris, putting the pieces together.

'Or not,' said Haley. 'But Paola might have believed he was, the same way she did with Massimo. Maybe, when Massimo's paternity test came back negative . . . I don't know. Thanks for your suggestion about the paternity test, by the way,' he added, smiling. 'That was how we identified Paola, you know.'

'I'm glad,' said Iris. 'So what's happening with Jock?'

Haley took a big slug of truly rancid coffee before answering. 'We released him a few hours ago.'

Iris looked astonished. 'You're not charging him?'

'Not yet,' said Haley. He explained about John Mills's intervention, and how he'd decided to cut the interview short and quit while he was ahead. 'Bottom line, I could charge him with obstruction for all the lies he's told, about Venice and where he was, when. But I don't have enough for a murder charge yet. Not without a confession. Plus, I don't see any harm in letting him sweat it out over Christmas, and I know where to find him if I need him. At his age I can hardly see him legging it to Brazil.'

'Do you still think he did it, though? Do you think he killed them?'

Haley pulled a face. 'Probably. Maybe. Ach, Iris, I don't know. I think he's involved. But I also think he's covering for someone, and I'm not sure who or why.'

'I had exactly the same feeling this morning,' said Iris. 'Not about Jock specifically, but just about the case in general, those two poor women and all the ways this ties together.' She told him that Kathy Miller had come home with her last night, and spent a fitful night's sleep in Iris's bed.

'I take it the wedding's off?' Haley mused.

Iris nodded. 'I think she still loves him. But I wouldn't run out and buy a morning suit, no.'

'Somehow I don't think I'd have made the guest list anyway.' Haley grinned. 'All right,' he said, wolfing down the last morsel of fried bread and looking at his watch. 'I'd better go. We're releasing Rory MacKinnon on bail and I want to be there when he leaves.'

'You've charged him, then.'

Haley nodded. 'We had a formal interview with his solicitor present a couple of hours ago. Lots of 'no comments' and a denial, but nothing to actually counter our evidence, which is strong. We've got a signed statement from the maid that he paid her to poison the animals, plus CCTV of him buying the rat poison. What does a London barrister need with two kilograms of rat poison?'

'Rats in his garden?' Iris played devil's advocate.

'He lives in a fourth-floor flat.'

Pulling on his coat, Haley left a ten-pound note on the table and kissed Iris on the cheek. 'Take care. And keep an eye on Kathy Miller, would you? If MacKinnon's told her anything, you're the one she'll confide in.'

'Are you sure I can't get you anything, love? A cup of tea?'

The WPC on the front desk looked anxiously at the young man in the waiting room. Something about the way he stared blankly ahead, and the stillness of his body, gave her chills. She wasn't sure what a suicidal person might look like, but the young man gave her the distinct impression of a person teetering on the brink. He'd sat there almost two hours now, waiting for DI Haley – he wouldn't speak to anyone but Haley, not even to give his name – and in all that time he had barely moved a muscle.

He didn't respond now, either. Not a 'yes' or a 'no' or even an acknowledgement that he'd heard her question. So it was a huge relief when the double doors opened, letting in a blast of arctic air, and DI Haley came barrelling back into the station.

'Where's MacKinnon?' he asked the WPC, without stopping to draw breath or even take his coat off. 'Is he still in Room Three?'

'Yes, sir, but there's someone here waiting to see you,' the girl blurted, nodding towards the desolate young man. 'I think it's urgent.'

Haley turned around. 'Angus?'

The young man jumped to his feet.

'Are you going to charge him?' he demanded.

'Am I going to charge who?' Haley's eyes narrowed.

'You know who.' The young gillie's voice cracked. 'The baron. I know he came home this morning. But are you going to charge him with murder?'

'Angus, you know I can't talk about that,' Haley said, his voice softening. 'The case is still ongoing and we –'

'I did it,' Angus cut him off.

The WPC froze.

'I beg your pardon?' Haley said quietly.

'I did it. I killed them,' said Angus. 'I buried them. It was me.'

Haley looked at him intently, cocking his head to one side.

'Angus.' He cleared his throat. 'I know Jock MacKinnon means a lot to you. But do you not think there's a point where loyalty ends? And where the truth has to begin? I don't need to remind you that two innocent women are dead.'

'This is the truth,' Angus insisted, holding DI Haley's gaze. 'I did it. I want to make a statement. I want to confess.'

Chapter Thirty-four

'What d'you reckon?' the girl from BBC Scotland news leaned over to Gavin Douglas, her opposite number at STV, offering him a piece of gum. 'D'you think they're gonna give us a name?'

'They won't name the suspect, if they've got one,' said Gavin, fiddling with his earpiece. 'But mebbe the victims? I tell you what, they'd better give us something after dragging us all the way up here at five minutes' bloody notice.'

Like most of the journalists in attendance at today's press conference in Pitfeldy Village Hall, Gavin Douglas had been taken by surprise when the head of the STV news desk told him that 'major developments' were to be announced imminently on the Girls in the Wood case.

'Those old skeletons they found up at the castle?' Gavin scratched his head. 'Wasn't that case closed?'

'Aye, well, now it's open, and the chief constable's holding a press conference in' – Gavin's boss looked at his watch – 'two hours' time.'

'*Two hours?*'

'That's what I said. So you'd better get your arse up there.'

'OK,' Gavin sighed, grabbing his car keys and phone. 'Up where, exactly?'

'Pitfeldy.'

'Pitfeldy? But that's the arse end of nowhere.'

'Then I suggest you stop farting about here and get bloody going,' the head of the news desk observed robustly.

Gavin had made it on time, just, but he was relieved to see stragglers from the BBC and ITN also puffing and panting their way into the hall. All of the good seats had already been taken by the local radio and newspaper guys who hadn't had to belt up the A90 to get here.

'Aye, aye, here we go,' said the BBC girl, as the immense figure of Chief Constable Sir William Roebuck stomped and creaked his way across the stage in full uniform like a pantomime giant. In his wake came Detective Inspector Stuart Haley, as small and physically unassuming as his boss was larger than life.

'Roebuck looks pleased with himself,' said the BBC girl, as the big man eased his vast frame into the first of two chairs on the dais.

He does, thought Gavin. *But the other bloke doesn't.* DI Haley had entered the room with the look of a man about to undergo root canal surgery, and his pained expression only worsened as the chief constable began to speak.

'Thank you all for coming,' Sir William boomed. 'I'm going to read a prepared statement, after which Detective Inspector Stuart Haley will take some of your questions.' Having heavily emphasised the 'some', he cleared his throat. 'Last night, as a direct result of diligent policing by DI Haley and his team, a thirty-year-old man came forward to police and confessed to the murders of two women whose remains were found buried beneath a ruined bothy on the Pitfeldy Castle estate last August. These were the victims commonly referred to online and in the wider media as the 'Girls in the Wood'.

A low buzz of excitement reverberated around the room.

'As you know,' Sir William went on, 'when the bodies were first found, despite exhaustive inquiries, we were unable initially to establish the identity of either of the victims. A few weeks later, thanks to new information from a member of the public, we confirmed that one of the bodies belonged to a young Italian woman who went missing from her home in Venice over a decade ago. At that point the Italian authorities assumed the lead role in the investigation and they have remained in close contact with DI Haley and his team throughout. However, neither they, nor we, were aware of the identity of the second victim. Until now.

'Today, I am able to announce that the two murdered women were Paola and Beatrice Contorini, and that they were mother and daughter.'

He paused to allow the import of this to sink in.

'Earlier today, the individual who made himself known to us yesterday as the killer was formally charged by my colleague, DI Haley with two counts of murder and one count of the illegal disposal of human remains. The suspect has been remanded in custody and cannot be named at this time. That is all the information we're able to share with you at the moment, but DI Haley will be happy to answer select questions in regards to the above statement.'

Haley, who'd sat uncomfortably throughout his boss's triumphant speech, now looked as if someone had squirted lemon juice in his eyes as the big man sat down and let him do the spadework.

'Yes. Lisa.' Haley pointed to one of the many raised arms. It belonged to a journalist he knew and liked from one of the local papers. The BBC and STV rabble could wait their turn.

'Can you tell us, detective inspector, why Jock MacKinnon, Baron Pitfeldy, was arrested less than forty-eight hours ago and then released? Did you suspect him of involvement in these murders?'

'I can't comment in any detail on that, I'm afraid,' Haley said cautiously, aware of Roebuck's eyes boring into him. 'However, I can confirm that Baron Pitfeldy has been questioned under caution on matters related to this inquiry. Yes –' He pointed to another hand.

'Gavin Douglas, STV. Can you tell us any more about the two Italian women? What were they doing in Scotland? And did they have any connection to the estate, or to the MacKinnon family?'

Haley glanced at Roebuck, who gave an imperceptible shake of his jowly cheeks.

'I'm afraid I can't expand on that at the moment.'

'You can't expand on much, can you, detective?' a female reporter from Radio 4 shouted out from the back of the hall. 'Isn't it true that it was actually a private Facebook page belonging to the portrait painter Iris Grey which led to these women being identified and, ultimately, to this morning's arrest? And that it was nothing to do with 'diligent police work' at all? Should we be going to Ms Grey for information, the same way we had to after Dom Wetherby's murder last year?'

A ripple of agreement spread audibly around the room. Haley could practically hear the chief constable sweating.

'It's certainly true that we owe Iris Grey, and other members of the public, a huge debt of gratitude for keeping interest in this case alive,' replied Haley, with the straightest face he could muster. He knew that Iris would be as unhappy about having her name dragged into this on television as Roebuck was, and he wanted to do his best to shield her from the inevitable press intrusion.

'I'd say it was more than that,' the Radio 4 woman scoffed. 'Isn't it also true that Banffshire police completely abandoned this investigation, shutting it down when it had barely begun, under pressure from the MacKinnon family?'

'That is categorically *un*true,' boomed the chief constable, looking as if he'd swallowed something large and unpleasant. Not for the first time, Haley wondered what hold Jock MacKinnon had had over Roebuck. He'd come through in the end, to everyone's surprise, and allowed them to effectively reopen the case at the eleventh hour. But up till that point, getting him to cooperate had been like pulling teeth. Haley strongly suspected it was only the advances that Iris and the Italians were making that had forced his hand, and helped him find the balls to stand up to the baron.

'Deciding which investigations to devote resources to at any given time is a complicated process,' Roebuck went on pompously, 'one that takes into account a wide variety of factors.'

'Including the patronage of wealthy members of the establishment?' the journalist pushed him. 'Even ones who may well be implicated themselves?'

'In this case, we were lucky enough to have the support of our Italian colleagues,' Roebuck ploughed on, ignoring her. 'Together, we have succeeded in bringing a very difficult investigation to a satisfactory conclusion. That's what we're here to focus on today.'

Haley raised his arm to single out another journalist, but Sir William shook his head with vehement finality.

'No more questions,' he announced to the packed hall below, to loud protestations as he clattered to his feet. 'Thank you all for coming.'

Afterwards, in a private anteroom, he turned furiously on Stuart Haley, as if the difficult questions had been his fault.

'What the fuck was that?'

'I did try to warn you, sir.'

'Jesus Christ! We solved the case, we got our man and *still* they're not happy? What do they want, blood?'

'I believe they want details, sir. A story. They're journalists. That's their job.'

'Well, it's not our damned job. This isn't bloody entertainment. It's a murder inquiry. And I tell you this,' Sir William jabbed a fat finger in Stuart Haley's direction, 'I've had it just about up to here with that bloody painter friend of yours. If she goes shooting her mouth off to the press, giving interviews . . .'

'She won't, sir. Iris enjoys the challenge but she hates the attention.'

The chief constable shot Haley a look that would have melted the skin off a lesser man.

'Hates the attention? Are you blind? Dear God, she's got you where she wants you, hasn't she, Haley?'

'Sir?'

'Make a fool of yourself, if you want to, Stuart,' the finger jabbed again, 'but make a fool of this force and I'll see you finished in Scotland. Finished.'

*

Up at Pitfeldy Castle, Jock, Emma and Fergus all sat huddled around the ancient television set in the small sitting room off the kitchen, glued to the screen.

'They must be very sure of themselves, if Bill Roebuck's making the statement in person,' Emma observed smugly, unable to conceal her relief at the morning's developments. Not only had her father been released without charge, but Angus Brae – the perfect, do-no-wrong gillie whom her father had always inexplicably favoured over her and Rory, had turned out to be a murderer. Apparently, he'd turned himself in at the police station and confessed.

Emma didn't know the details. None of them did. But she didn't really care. What mattered was that Angus was guilty of something awful and that he'd be carted off to prison, disgraced and forgotten about, and that Jock would finally be forced to transfer his affection to his own children. Or at least to Emma. It might be a while before he forgave Rory for killing Kathy's dogs, and finally (it seemed) driving her away.

That was the other good news. Vile Kathy had moved out of the castle and was apparently staying with Iris while she decided what to do next. Fingers crossed that would be flying back to America, never to return. But either way, judging from her father's depressed mood, Emma assumed the wedding was off.

'Of course they're sure,' Fergus added, pushing a greasy strand of reddish hair back from his pale forehead before clasping his wife's hand. 'When a chap confesses, that's all there is to it.'

'Well, I know,' said Emma. 'But then why won't they mention Angus by name? I mean, it's not as if it can compromise his trial. There won't *be* a trial if he's pleading guilty, will there?'

'Quite,' said Fergus. 'And everyone in Pitfeldy knows who it is by now anyway.'

While the Twomeys continued their commentary, Jock sat stock-still and poker-faced, too gripped by what he was watching even to register what they were saying. Once it was over, and Emma turned the TV off, he continued to stare into space, lost in thought.

'Are you all right, Daddy?' Emma asked, belatedly noticing his stunned reactions, and putting her hand over his. 'I couldn't believe the things that ghastly woman from the BBC was saying about you, implying that you'd somehow pressured the police. I mean, the nerve.' She squeezed Jock's hand supportively. 'We should speak to John Mills right away. Don't you agree, Fergus? After all, how can it be all right for them to protect the identity of a *known murderer*, but to smear Daddy's good name? I think we should –'

'Be quiet, Emma.'

They were the first words Jock had spoken, the first sound he'd uttered, in fact, in over an hour. Despite them being delivered with uncharacteristic quietness and calm, they had an immediate effect. Emma's mouth slammed shut like a trap door and she sat there looking hurt and awkward.

'Come along, darling,' said Fergus, for once accurately reading the signals that his wife had missed. 'Let's leave your father in peace. It's a lot to take in, for all of us. We should pack.'

'Pack?' Emma shot him a confused expression. 'Don't be silly, Fergus. We can hardly abandon poor Daddy now that Kathy –'

'Really, Emma,' said Fergus, with rarely shown firmness. 'No one's abandoning anyone. But Jock needs some space.'

It was the first time Jock could ever remember respecting his son-in-law.

After Fergus and Emma left the room, he sat for a long time, alone at last, staring at the now-blank television screen. The longing for Kathy was dreadful, like a gunshot wound to his chest. But that wasn't the worst pain he suffered.

Angus had confessed to the murders.

Angus – his Angus, the one wholly good thing he'd ever done in his life – would go to prison. *Prison!*

Tears welled in his eyes and he felt every one of his seventy years.

How on God's green earth had things come to this?

*

Iris stood on Stuart Haley's doorstep in the same full-length puffa coat she'd been wearing yesterday, hopping from foot to foot with cold like a penguin.

'Can I come in?'

'Of course.' Haley stood back from the door, allowing Iris and a blast of Siberian air into his narrow hallway. 'How's Kathy?'

'Still in shock, I think,' said Iris, following him into the living room, her words muffled by the various layers of coat, scarf and sweater she was pulling in turn over her head and dumping unceremoniously on Stuart's sofa. 'It doesn't help having half the Scottish press loitering outside my place, begging me for an interview as soon as I show my face at a window.'

'Aye. I'm sorry about that.' Haley grimaced. 'But I didn't have much choice. I take it you saw the press conference?'

'Kathy and I watched it together,' said Iris. 'I assume the chief constable forced you into it?'

'He did, as it goes, but what makes you say that?'

Iris smiled. 'No offence, Stuart, but your poker face could use some work. You looked like you'd been marched in there at gunpoint.'

Haley shrugged. 'Yeah, well, that's because I had. You know, one minute Roebuck's shutting us down and insisting I walk away from the case. And the next, I've got Angus Brae turning up at the station and confessing, and all of a sudden the fat bastard wants to shout about our "successes" from the rooftops and take the credit for a job well done.'

'And I take it you don't, because you aren't sure about Angus's confession?' Iris surmised.

'That's the problem,' Haley said wryly. 'I *am* sure about it. I'm sure it's complete bullshit.'

'Thank God you said that,' Iris exhaled. 'Angus didn't kill the Contorinis. He loved Beatrice.'

'I agree,' said Haley. 'His statement's got more holes in it than my nan's crocheted blanket. I warned Roebuck, told him straight he was going to end up with egg on his face if he went public with Angus as our man,' said Haley, 'but he didn't want to know. He didn't actually name him, which is something, I suppose.'

'Someone's going to, though,' said Iris. 'One of the papers. The whole village already knows, and the Fisherman's Arms is heaving with reporters as we speak. I'm sure his name's already out there online.'

'Course it is.' Getting up, Haley walked into the kitchen and returned with two small cut-glass tumblers of whisky. 'The whole thing's a mess, to be honest with you,' he told Iris, handing one glass to her.

'What was it about Angus's confession that troubled you?' she asked him.

'All of it.' He sank back down into his chair with the drink in his hand, looking more exhausted than ever. 'The timing: right after Jock MacKinnon's arrest.'

'You think he's protecting Jock?'

'He's protecting someone,' said Haley. 'Either that or he's afraid of someone. Plus, you know, just his entire personality. You and I have talked about this before. I've been a policeman for a long time, Iris, and I've met many different kinds of killer. The evil, sadistic ones; the softly spoken "driven to it" ones; some are violent by nature, others crack under pressure and lash out just the once. But none of them, not one, was even remotely like Angus Brae.'

'All right,' said Iris, who didn't disagree with this assessment, but felt that at this point they needed more than just a hunch about Angus's character. 'But what did he actually *say* that sounded off?'

'Well, he didn't say that much. Which is another red flag, by the way. By the time killers are ready to confess, they're usually keen to get everything off their chests. Either out of guilt or because they want to boast about what they've done. So they tend to share a lot of detail. Angus gave me almost none. But his basic story was that he killed Beatrice by accident after an argument.'

'He admits she was his girlfriend, then?'

'Yes, he does admit that,' conceded Haley. 'He confirmed that he met her on the school trip, like we thought, and that they fell head over heels in love. He said she followed him to Edinburgh a few months later.'

'Did he admit he'd got her pregnant?'

Haley nodded. 'According to him, things went wrong after she lost the baby. They'd been fighting a good bit due to her grief. Then when his dad came up to Edinburgh to have it out with him, and Angus agreed to go back to Pitfeldy, he says he broke things off with Beatrice of his own free will.'

'OK,' said Iris, listening.

'But Beatrice wouldn't accept him leaving her, so she followed him to the castle. They got into an argument, and he pushed her. According to him, she fell and hit her head and never got up.'

Iris was silent for a moment.

'Where did he say this happened?'

'At his cottage.'

'Hmmm.' Iris mulled this over. 'So he continued living in the house where he killed her? The first true love of his life? He has breakfast with Hannah every day, feet away from where Beatrice died?'

'That's what he says,' said Haley. 'I'm not buying it either. He'd move, wouldn't he? There must be half a dozen cottages at least on that estate. He wouldn't stay there.'

'Does his story about Beatrice hitting her head fit with what the forensic pathologist told you? About the injuries to the skeleton?'

'It doesn't *not* fit,' said Haley. 'Blunt-force trauma to the skull was the likely cause of Beatrice's death, if you remember. But that could mean anything from a hard fall to a whack with a hammer. Anyway, it's the next bit that I really can't swallow.'

'Go on,' said Iris.

'So his version is, he's killed Beatrice accidentally. He panics, and buries her up at the bothy in the woods, by himself.

But then about six months later, her mother turns up at Pitfeldy Castle, asking questions. Paola knows about Angus and Beatrice's relationship by this point.'

'How?'

'Don't know.' Haley sipped his drink. 'Angus just said she knew her daughter left Venice to be with him, and that she followed him from Edinburgh to Pitfeldy when he dropped out. And that no one's seen Beatrice since.

According to Angus, Paola tells all this to Jock MacKinnon, who refuses to believe Angus would have harmed her daughter, but nonetheless allows Paola to *stay* up at the castle while she tries to trace her.'

'So Mrs Gregory *was* telling the truth?' Iris asked.

'According to Angus's version, yes,' said Haley. 'Meanwhile, Angus, terrified that Paola will eventually learn the truth, and/or turn the baron against him, jumps her one night when she's walking back to the castle from town. Kills her.'

'Kills her how?'

'He says he dragged her into the undergrowth and strangled her.'

'And then buried her too?'

'Uh-huh.'

'On his own?'

'That's what he said.' Haley took another long sip of whisky. 'I mean, even if he's telling the truth and he *did* kill Beatrice, like he said. Which I don't believe for a second, by the way, but let's just say that's what happened. That's an accident. He pushed her, she died, he panicked. But what he says happened with Paola, ambushing her, strangling the woman in cold blood?' he shook his head. 'No way. He doesn't have it in him. He's protecting someone. Presumably the baron.'

'I assume you pushed back?' said Iris. 'Cross-examined him?'

'Well, sure, I tried,' Haley said ruefully. 'I dropped every bomb on the kid I could think of to get him to rethink his loyalty to MacKinnon. I told him that Jock might be his father.'

'You didn't!' Iris gasped.

'Aye, I did. Told him that Jock had had an affair with his mum. Betrayed Edwin, his oldest friend. Wrecked his marriage, then let Edwin believe *he* was to blame when Linda ran off.'

'How did he react?'

'He didn't,' said Haley, exasperated. 'Blank bloody face the whole time. I don't know whether he simply didn't believe me, or he already knew so he wasn't bothered by it. I told him there was a chance Jock was Beatrice's father, too – that he and Beatrice might have been brother and sister. But even *that* didn't get a rise. He didn't even flicker, Iris. Just kept looking at me. Looking through me. It was almost like he was brainwashed. Like he was part of a cult or something.'

Iris finished her drink, her mind whirring. If Angus Brae stuck to his confession and pleaded guilty to the charges against him, he would spend the rest of his life behind bars. What hold did Jock MacKinnon have on the boy that would make him do that? Make him give up his life, his freedom, make him walk away from Hannah, whom he clearly loved, and their future together?

'He's guilty,' she said aloud, as much to herself as to Haley.

'I beg your pardon?'

'He's guilty. Maybe not of killing the Contorinis. But he's guilty of something, Stuart, at least in his own mind,' said Iris. 'He *wants* to be punished. To atone.'

'Yeah, well, he can atone all he likes,' Haley muttered bitterly. 'But those poor women, Beatrice and Paola? They deserve justice. We can't just let Brae take the fall for two murders he didn't commit.'

No, thought Iris, *we can't*.

Somewhere, in the back of her mind, she was beginning to formulate a plan.

Chapter Thirty-five

Jock MacKinnon gripped the head of his walking stick tightly as he trudged through the snow, his breathing tight and shallow in the bitter air. It was three o'clock in the afternoon on Christmas Eve, and for the first time he could remember he was alone at the castle. Completely alone. Mrs Gregory had gone to her sister's in Elgin for Christmas and the rest of the staff had also been given the week off. Emma and Fergus had mercifully returned home, and Rory had disappeared without a word since his release on bail. Scuttled back to London, Jock presumed, or to his mother in Edinburgh. Fiona never could see any faults in the boy and would no doubt welcome him with open arms.

As for Kathy, his angel, his saviour, his hope through despair – she was gone. Gone for good. It wasn't that he didn't deserve the pain. He did, and in a way, he almost welcomed it. It was more that he didn't yet know whether he had the strength to bear it. Each day, each hour, seemed harder than the last. Like a death.

As far as Jock knew, Kathy was still only down in the village, staying with Iris Grey. She hadn't returned to America yet, so theoretically he could still have driven to see her. Pleaded with her. Tried to explain. But he knew it would be futile. Her letter to him on the night she left had said as much. The love was still there. But without trust, there could be no future for the two of them. Nothing Jock could do would restore Kathy's trust now. Because the truth wasn't his to tell.

The slope leading up to the bothy was steep, and the snow deeper and more uneven through the pines, but Jock didn't mind the effort. Stopping frequently to catch his breath, sweat pouring down his shoulder blades and chest beneath his fleece-lined Barbour jacket, he picked his way gingerly over roots and animal burrows towards the crest of the rise. There, in the gathering gloom, the first of the grey stones loomed out of the darkness, a random scattering of rubble lining the way to what was left of the building.

Sweeping aside the settled snow with a gloved hand, Jock eased himself down onto one of the larger slabs, leaning on his walking stick for support. The stick had been his father's, and perhaps his grandfather's too. He felt comforted by the connection, rubbing his thumb up and down the grain. The bothy would still have been standing in his grandfather's day. He wondered if old Rufus MacKinnon had ever stood where he was sitting now, perhaps holding this same stick? Back before everything happened. Before tragedy struck, and then struck again, the blows falling continuously one after another, like a boulder gaining momentum as it crashed its way down a hill.

Closing his eyes, Jock tried to feel something, but nothing came. He laughed at himself. What had he expected? To encounter the spirits of the dead? The ghosts of Christmas past? To find forgiveness? Redemption?

You don't deserve it, he reminded himself. Besides, there were no spirits here. Perhaps they were in Venice, beautiful, light-filled Venice? Perhaps they had escaped this dark place.

Jock hoped so. He knew that he never would.

'May I sit with you?'

He turned around slowly, surprised but not startled.

'Of course.'

Iris Grey was standing at the top of the rise, just a few feet away. In an ugly grey puffa coat and scarf, she looked faintly ridiculous, like a human larva, or a bizarrely shaped balloon. But her expression was open and her voice kind. And Jock was ready to talk. More than ready.

'How did you know I'd be here?' he asked, clearing a space for her beside him in the snow.

'I didn't,' said Iris. 'But you weren't at the castle, and I saw that your coat and stick were gone. And then what was left of your footprints in the snow seemed to be heading towards the woods . . .'

'Quite the detective,' he said sadly.

'Oh, I don't know,' said Iris. 'There's still so much I don't know. So much in the shadows.'

Jock leaned back, closing his eyes. He looked ineffably tired.

'Shall I tell you what I wish, Iris?' he sighed. 'I wish to God that you and Kathy and those dogs of hers had never found those bodies.'

'Do you? Really?' asked Iris.

'I do.' He looked at her steadily. 'I wish I'd never invited you here. Never given you that commission. Because without you, Kathy would have let it go. The police, too, in the end. The dead could have remained buried, resting in peace.'

It wasn't said angrily, but rather matter-of-factly. Somehow, that puzzled Iris more.

'What on earth makes you think they were in peace?' she asked him. 'Dumped in an unmarked grave, unmourned, with their killer still at large?'

'They weren't unmourned,' Jock corrected her. 'I can promise you that. In any case, it doesn't matter now. The dead are dead and what's done is done. What *matters* is that Angus has been charged. And I know he'll go through with it and plead guilty, because he's a good boy, an honourable boy. But I can't sit by and let that happen.'

'You can't let him keep lying to protect *you*, you mean,' said Iris, suddenly finding herself angrier than she'd meant to be, despite Jock's honesty.

'That, certainly,' said Jock, accepting her censure without complaint. 'But that's the easy part. You see the problem is, Iris, it isn't only *me* that he's protecting.'

Stuart Haley drove around the side of the castle to the stable block, parking his car out of sight of the main house. Then, grabbing his coat, gloves, torch and phone from the passenger seat, he stepped out into the snow.

It would be dark in less than hour. Pitch-black, in fact. No moon tonight, and too much low cloud even for stars. He prayed that Iris was inside, talking to Jock somewhere in the castle. But all the lights seemed to be off and as far as Haley could tell, the house looked deserted. Not a good sign.

How the hell had he let Iris talk him into this hare-brained scheme? If anything happened to her . . . but it wouldn't. It mustn't.

Quickening his pace, he approached the castle doors.

'Tell me about Venice,' said Iris.

'All right.' Jock exhaled, his breath visible as dragon's smoke in the cold air.

Even in the fading light, Iris could clearly see how the strain of the last few months had aged him. His thin face sagged noticeably at the jowls, and for the first time Iris was aware of a slight tremor in his right hand as it rested, knotted and veiny, on his knee as he began slowly to recount his long association with Venice, the city where this all began.

'My first wife, Alice, and I first went to Venice together the spring after we married.' His rheumy eyes glistened with nostalgia as he cast his mind back. 'It was a magical place for us both. We didn't have a lot of ready cash in those days. My father had left the estate with a good deal of debt, so we were working hard to get things back on track. Alice was always good about that sort of thing. She grew up on Shetland, so she was used to making do and mucking in. Anyway, we stayed at some cheap little pensione near St Mark's Square. Alice loved all the art and the history. I was more interested in the pasta.' He smiled weakly and it struck Iris that this was a side to Jock she had never seen before. Warm. Funny. Engaged. Was this what he'd been like as a young man, she wondered? If so, something very fundamental had changed.

'I remember I got Alice a framed print of a medieval painting of St Theodore that she'd been mad about, for some reason,' he went on. 'Later, when our daughter Mary was born, she hung it over the baby's crib. I think the saint was supposed to protect her. He did a fairly shitty job, unfortunately.'

A short laugh indicated that this was meant as a joke, but the pain and bitterness in Jock's eyes voided it of any humour. Iris sat patiently, waiting for him to continue. Expressing these underlying emotions was evidently important to him, a necessary precursor for whatever confession might be to come.

'After Mary's death, Alice changed. I suppose we both did. You expect the sadness, you see, but nobody warns you about the anger. The rage that comes with losing a child. I took Alice back to Venice a few months afterwards, to get away. I thought it might help bridge the distance between us, to return to a place where once we'd been so happy. But it was a huge mistake. The beginning of the end.' He looked away sadly. 'She left me soon after that. I didn't handle it well.'

In the ensuing silence, Iris cleared her throat, deciding to risk a question. 'Is that when you began your affair with Linda Brae?'

Jock flinched, then nodded. 'Yes. I slept with a vast number of women in the months after Alice left,' he explained bluntly. 'I wasn't in my right mind. But Linda was the only constant. I cared about her, actually, although of course I knew it was wrong.'

'Because of Edwin?'

'He was my oldest friend. My brother, really. But I justified it at the time because I was so angry at the world and I felt I deserved whatever shreds of happiness I could find. Also because Edwin was drinking heavily then and knocking Linda around. So I told myself she needed me.'

'Perhaps she did,' Iris heard herself saying, moved by Jock's honesty.

'No.' He shook his head sadly. 'She needed a better man than me. Someone prepared to help her, to rescue her. I couldn't do that, not without destroying Edwin completely. So like a fool I went and got engaged to Fiona.'

'Why?' Iris asked. 'I mean, why the need to marry again at all, but especially so soon?'

Jock looked at her uncomprehendingly.

'I needed an heir for Pitfeldy, of course,' he said, as if this explained everything. 'A legitimate heir. Alice was gone, Mary was dead, Linda could never be mine in *that* way and Fiona was available. Pretty enough, good family. So I married her, and we had the children, and that was that. I built my own prison, you see?' He looked up at Iris. 'I became as trapped as Linda in my own way, and every bit as miserable. Our affair limped on, but it became more sporadic.'

'And at some point during this period, Linda got pregnant with Angus?' Iris prompted.

'Yes. The year after the twins were born.'

'Was he yours?'

'Yes.'

'How can you be sure?' asked Iris. 'Presumably Linda and Edwin still had relations?'

'I assume they did, although we never discussed it. But it didn't matter because Edwin wasn't fertile. The doctors had told him as much years earlier. When Linda conceived he just assumed they must have been wrong, or that the baby was a freak occurrence. It never occurred to him that she would dare to have an affair. Least of all with me. Anyway, I knew Angus was mine but I could never confess to it, obviously.' He rubbed his eyes, frowning. 'I think, honestly, I'd become quite mentally unwell by that stage. I don't offer that as an excuse for my behaviour, only as an explanation of sorts. In any event, I abandoned poor Linda completely after the baby was born, I just couldn't cope with the guilt. Meanwhile, Edwin's drinking was getting worse and worse. Linda was in an appalling situation. So one day, she left. She wrote me a letter, asking me to take care of Angus. And she just left.'

'Why didn't she take Angus with her?' Iris asked the obvious question. 'Why leave him behind with two men, both patently unfit to care for him?'

'That's a good question,' said Jock. 'And I don't know the answer.' When he looked up, there were tears in his eyes. 'She loved him, I know that. I can only conclude that my behaviour had pushed her – between us, Edwin and I had pushed her to the brink. I suppose she simply couldn't cope, in the end. So.' With an effort he pulled himself together, sitting up taller on the stone slab. 'Life went on at the castle. Edwin sobered up after Linda left. Not perfectly, but he was a lot better for the first few years at least. He tried. He brought up Angus alone, but I stepped in as much as I could and always tried to ensure the boy was safe and happy and well cared for, especially when his father relapsed. Edwin loved Angus. We both did.'

'And you had your own family to care for, of course,' observed Haley. 'Rory and Emma.'

Jock's expression darkened. 'Fiona raised our children. It's no secret that my second marriage was an unhappy one, and the simple truth is I have never been close to my children with Fiona. Love can't be forced, Iris. After my daughter Mary died, something shifted in me. I loved *her* more than I can express. And later, to my surprise, I have to say, I came to love Angus. But I never felt that way for Rory or Emma.'

He looked away again, his thoughts drifting to some far-off region where Iris couldn't follow him. Eventually, he resumed his story.

'I didn't return to Venice for many years after Alice left me. But at some point, as you and DI Haley managed to work out, I *did* go back. I stayed at the Danieli with a group of gambling friends from London.'

'Including Massimo Giannotti?' Iris asked.

'That's right. Yes.'

Silence fell, and Iris hesitated before filling it. She knew from Haley that Jock had denied raping Paola Contorini on this trip, but neither of them was sure whether that was the truth. Pressing the point and asking him again risked alienating him, just as he was starting to open up. On the other hand, this was in many ways the million-dollar question.

In the end, to Iris's surprise, Jock took the matter out of her hands.

'Paola Contorini was working as a chambermaid at the hotel,' he said, rubbing his forehead with a gloved hand. 'I know that now, although naturally none of us knew any of the maids' names at the time. Nor did I remember any one of them more than another. I do remember several of the maids being very eager to offer wealthy guests 'extras' if the price was right.'

'And did you avail yourself of any of those "extras"?' Iris asked, fighting down her distaste at Jock's shameless description of the sexual exploitation of impoverished young women by rich, entitled tourists; as if there were nothing wrong with him and his friends treating hotel maids like objects to be bought.

'Yes.' He looked away.

'Did you rape any of the maids, Jock?'

'I might have.' His voice was so quiet it was almost a whisper. Slowly, imperceptibly at first, his shoulders began to shake. The tears that had been threatening to come ever since they began talking finally started to roll down his cheeks. 'The police, Haley, asked me the same thing and I denied it. And the truth, the absolute truth on my little Mary's *soul*, is that I don't remember. If I did, I blocked it out. That's all I can tell you. We were drunk. The girls all merged into one. When Paola turned up at Pitfeldy all those years later, I didn't even recognise her.'

'But she recognised you?' said Iris.

'Not at first. But eventually, yes.' He nodded miserably and took a deep gulp of air, wheezing audibly as it filled his ageing lungs and coughing as he expelled it. Instinctively, Iris rested a hand on his back, rubbing and patting until the fit had passed. Perhaps she shouldn't, but she felt sorry for him. It was impossible not to in that moment.

'The whole business with Paola was one of those dreadful, freak coincidences,' he explained, running a hand through his thinning hair. 'A real black swan event. One in a million. She didn't come here because of the rape, you see. Not at all. She came here looking for her daughter.'

'Go on,' said Iris. 'I'm listening.'

'What happened was this,' said Jock shakily. 'Years after my stay at the Danieli, Angus went to Italy for a school art trip. They visited Florence first, I believe, and then went on to Venice. While he was there – only for a few days, mind you – he met a girl, Beatrice, as we now know, and fell in love. An eighteen-year-old's version of love, anyway. He was obsessed. The first I heard about it was months after the fact, from Edwin, who by this time was beside himself with worry. More than worry. Panic. Encouraged by Beatrice, it seemed Angus had secretly applied to study art at Edinburgh University behind his father's back and been accepted. Edwin found out and hit the roof. Forbade him to go. But for once Angus stood up to him. He took the place, left Pitfeldy for the city, and had Beatrice fly over from Italy and move in with him. Five minutes later, she's pregnant and they're getting married. It was all a bit of a mess, to say the least.'

'So it was Edwin Brae who told you all this?' Iris asked. 'You didn't hear it from Angus?'

'No,' said Jock. 'Angus was quite secretive about the whole thing, at least at first. It was Edwin who told me. He came to see me up at the castle and asked my advice.'

'And what advice did you give him?' asked Haley.

'Not to lose his temper,' said Jock. 'Which, I daresay, he felt was rich coming from me. But it was good advice, and it seems he took it at first. He went to the university to try and reason with Angus. He was already quite unwell by then, remember, and I didn't have high hopes for this mission, but miraculously it seemed to work. Edwin kept a level head, and somehow convinced Angus to come home.'

'How do you think he managed that?' Iris interjected. 'If Angus had ambitions of being an artist, which he obviously did, *and* he was in love, why would he agree to go back?'

'You'd have to ask him,' said Jock. 'Beatrice had lost the baby, and I think they were struggling. But I suspect that was only part of the reason. Angus always had a pronounced sense of duty,' he observed, a note of pride creeping into his voice. 'That was one of his strengths.'

'Duty to whom? His father?' Iris asked.

'Yes, to Edwin. And to the estate. And to me. To his role at Pitfeldy,' Jock mused.

My God, thought Iris, *he really does live in another world. What about Angus's duty to poor Beatrice? Or to himself? To his own hopes and dreams and wishes?*

'In any event, Angus came back to the castle and at first all seemed well enough. But then a few weeks later, Beatrice showed up on the castle doorstep.' His eyes darkened suddenly, like a gathering storm. 'That's when everything began to spiral . . .'

Stretching out his arms, he intertwined his bony fingers and bent back both sets of knuckles with an audible crack.

'Beatrice came to try to convince Angus they should get back together?' Iris prompted.

'Yes. It was Mrs Gregory who let her in, not me. But my understanding is that she wanted Angus to come back to the city with her, to resume his degree,' said Jock. 'He was out working on the estate when she turned up, so she wandered out to find him. She must have come up here.' He looked around at the desolate ruins of the bothy.

'And she found Angus?'

Jock shook his head. 'No. If only she had.' He looked Iris straight in the eye. 'She found Edwin.'

A heavy silence fell. After what felt like an age, Jock said quietly, 'I don't think he meant to kill her. I think it was an accident.'

'What happened?' asked Iris.

'Well, I wasn't there,' said Jock. 'All of this is what Edwin told me later. But according to him they argued about Angus. Edwin was already drunk when Beatrice showed up, which didn't help matters. Anyway, at some point things got physical between them and he pushed her. She fell backwards, hitting her head on one of these stones.' He touched the palm of his hand to his own skull to mark the spot where Beatrice Contorini had suffered her fatal injury. 'Edwin said she died instantly.'

Iris's mind raced. She could picture the scene: Edwin, drunk, shocked and panicked, already mentally confused. The girl, lying dead in the open.

'When did you first hear about this?' she asked Jock.

'About two hours after it happened.' He screwed up his face, as if willing the awful memories to go away. 'I'd just got back from Edinburgh and Angus came running into the castle. I'll never forget it. He was as white as a sheet, crying uncontrollably. We were in my study.'

'It was *Angus* who told you?' Iris asked. 'Not Edwin?'

'No.' Jock shook his head slowly. 'Angus said nothing, and I mean *nothing*. Not a damned word. The poor boy was mute with shock. But it was obvious something pretty serious must have happened, so I put him in my car and we drove up to the woods.' Jock took two deep breaths to steady himself. 'Evidently, he'd heard a scream and had headed to the bothy. I think he thought Edwin might have been injured, caught in a badger trap or something. In any case, he arrived here and found – he found –' Jock started shaking. 'By the time he brought me back here, Edwin was already trying to cover the body with rocks. He was babbling about Linda, hateful things. He was out of his mind.'

'So what did you do?' asked Iris.

'I slapped him,' said Jock. 'To stop the hysteria.'

'And then?'

'Then we buried her.'

'All three of you?'

'No. Just Edwin and me. Angus couldn't. I told him to go home.'

'And did he?'

'No. He wouldn't touch her, but he insisted on staying. He didn't want to leave her. It was awful.' Jock's voice broke. 'I remember him lying down on the ground sobbing, with his face literally pressed into the stones we'd used to cover the grave site. I had to physically drag him away in the end. Edwin couldn't do it. Couldn't even speak.'

'Tell me about what happened in the days that followed?' Iris asked eventually, once Jock had regained his composure.

'What do you mean? Nothing happened.'

'Well, did Angus not blame his father for what had happened?'

'No, I don't think so,' said Jock. 'It was an accident.'

'According to Edwin.'

'According to Edwin, yes. But Angus believed him, and so did I. His grief, Edwin's grief and guilt over what had happened – that was real. You couldn't fake that.'

'He wasn't guilty enough to go to the police though, was he?' Iris observed. 'To face justice for what he'd done, even if it was an accident? To put that poor girl's mother out of her misery?'

'No,' Jock admitted. 'He was afraid of being sent to prison. So was I. Angus, I think, would have gladly gone to the police. It would have given him some relief, poor boy. But he'd already lost his mother, and now this girl who'd been his first real love. He couldn't lose Edwin and me too.'

'So, you all just lived with it?'

Jock stared ahead blankly. It was dark now, and his expression was hard to make out, even from so close.

'We all just lived with it,' he repeated. 'For weeks we waited for the police to turn up at the castle. For someone to come looking for Beatrice. But no one did.'

'Until Paola.'

'Until Paola,' Jock sighed. 'That was the first time I learned –' His voice broke again and Iris finished the sentence for him.

'That Beatrice may have been your biological daughter?'

He nodded. 'And Angus's sister. Yes. But as I say, that wasn't what brought Paola here the first time. She was simply a mother, searching for her missing daughter. She'd retraced Beatrice's steps as far as Edinburgh by that time, and she already knew about Angus and the miscarriage. The first time she came to the castle I was here on my own, thank God. Fiona was off on some months-long course in Surrey – we were spending a lot of time apart by then – and Angus was away, too. He and Edwin were in London, visiting an early-onset Alzheimer's specialist that I'd found for them.'

'And Paola had never been to Pitfeldy before?' Iris asked, thinking of Eileen Gregory's testimony. 'Years before, I mean, when Emma and Rory were still at boarding school.'

'No. Never.' He seemed surprised by the question, and Iris had no doubt that his answer was genuine. Which meant that the housekeeper had either lied, or that she'd got confused, muddling up Paola Contorini with one of Jock's myriad earlier mistresses. That was certainly possible.

'So she met with you alone?'

'Yes. She showed me pictures of Beatrice and I did my best to put her off. I told her that her daughter had never been to the estate; that Angus hadn't seen or heard from her since they broke up.'

'Did she believe you?'

'At first I think she did, yes. But once she started to recognise me, things got tricky. She was certain we'd met before, but she wasn't sure when or where. Then, about two weeks after that first visit she came to the castle again, very distressed and clearly the worse for drink. She'd made the connection between me and Massimo Giannotti, and she started accusing me of having attacked her, and of being Beatrice's father.'

'What did you do?' asked Iris. 'I'm assuming Angus and Edwin had returned by then?'

'Yes. But I lied and told her Angus was travelling in Europe. I knew that if she met him in person and started asking questions there was a good chance he would break down and admit the truth. So I tried to calm Paola down. I admitted I'd been at the Danieli. I denied attacking her, but I offered to take a paternity test and I think that mollified her quite a bit.'

'*Did* you take one?'

'Not in the end, no. The fact is, Paola wasn't sure herself what had happened that night. And the main thing she wanted by this point, of course, was simply to find her child. So I talked her round, with the help of a lot of whisky. I offered to help her search for Beatrice, and suggested she stay at the castle for a few days, while we looked into things together. She agreed. Once she was safely asleep in one of the guest rooms I rang Edwin and told him to go away for a while, taking Angus with him.'

'And he did?'

'Yes,' said Jock. 'I can't remember where they went. It's all a bit of blur now. But they both left and I had a few days to try to talk Paola down from the edge and convince her that her daughter had never been here. At one point I think I nearly managed it. She was close to giving up and going back to Italy.'

'But she didn't, obviously?'

'No.' Jock rubbed his eyes wearily. 'She didn't. One day she walked into the village and ran into John Donnelly at the Fisherman's Arms. Donnelly told her that he thought he recognised Beatrice – which he did, of course, from the school trip to Venice. Not from here. That was the irony. But Paola didn't want to hear it. She came back to the castle screaming blue murder at me, insisting that we call the police and tell them what we knew. I knew then that there was no way around it.'

'You killed her?' Iris kept her voice low and even, as unthreatening as she could make it despite her pounding heart.

'Yes,' said Jock. 'I strangled her with my dressing gown cord, in Mary's old bedroom. It was extremely quick. Then I took her out to the bothy and buried her beside her daughter.'

'Your daughter too,' Iris reminded him.

Jock looked at her, stricken. 'Yes, I think so. My daughter too. Poor girl! I've buried both my daughters, Iris. Can you imagine what that feels like?'

'You still have Emma,' Iris reminded him.

Jock nodded and looked away sadly. *He'd like to love her, but he can't*, thought Iris. She wondered if that might change now, now that the truth was finally coming out. Stranger things had happened.

'When Edwin and Angus came home the next morning, I told them what had happened,' Jock continued, resuming his confession. 'That I'd *had* to kill Beatrice's mother, to protect them both, myself and the estate.' He looked at Iris pleadingly, willing her to accept this rationalisation.

'How did they react?' she asked.

'Edwin went into shock, I think. He was already mentally so fragile. I think Paola was the last straw.'

'And Angus?'

Jock bit his lip, fighting to contain his emotions.

'He cried. He cried and cried. Then he hit me.' He raised a gnarled hand to his cheek, remembering the blow. 'Which I deserved, of course. After that we never spoke of it again. Not until you and Kathy took that walk and the dogs found . . . what they found.'

'So he forgave you?'

Jock frowned. 'I don't know if he forgave me. I hope so. But I don't know. What I do know, now more than ever, is that the poor boy never forgave himself.'

'And you?'

'I blocked it out over the years, I suppose. Tried to move on. But it was always there. If I'd never slept with Linda, never betrayed Edwin in the first place, perhaps I wouldn't have done it. If I hadn't owed him so much, and loved Angus so much – I don't know. But the guilt ate away at me and I took it out on Fiona and the children and myself. I was lost until I met Kathy. She made me feel alive again, happy again, things I'd thought weren't possible. But now she's gone too, and I've no one to blame but myself.'

A stirring in the woodland behind them made both Iris and Jock turn around. Haley, looking smaller than ever beneath the towering pines, took a few steps towards them, the torch in his hands making dancing patterns of light on the bothy's broken stones.

'Ah.' Jock nodded, looking from Iris to Haley and back again, resigned rather than reproachful. 'I see.'

He's relieved, thought Iris. *He wants this to be over.*

'Jock MacKinnon.' Haley's voice rang out like a clarion in the still night air. 'I'm arresting you for the murder of Paola Contorini . . .'

Chapter Thirty-six

Iris pressed her face against the train window, watching the wild Scottish landscape as it shot by like a roll of speeded-up film. Every few seconds the sea would come into view, great grey-white waves frothing madly as they crashed against the shingled shore, before the track looped around another headland and it was snatched from sight. From the comfort of her empty first-class compartment, Iris took it all in: the high, scrubby moors, dotted here and there with pine forests in dark green and brown. The fresh snow of the last few days had all but melted, but there was still an almost visible chill in the crisp, blue-skied January air, a brittle frosting that made the blades of grass on the verges shimmer stiffly and gave a silvery, metallic sheen to the rivers and lochs.

It was a landscape Iris had come to love, and a part of her was sad to be saying goodbye to Pitfeldy. But at the same time, she was ready to leave Scotland. She would miss her cosy little haven at Murray House and Stuart Haley's easy companionship. She would miss sex with Jamie Ingall, and the way he managed to bring her out of herself and forced her to notice and take pleasure in the simple things in life. But she wouldn't miss the morbid gloom of the castle, or the pervasive sense of sadness that still hung over Pitfeldy woods, even now that the truth had been brought to light and justice, of a sort, had been done.

'You look like you're miles away.'

Kathy Miller, sitting beside her looking as preposterously beautiful as ever in a pair of black cigarette pants and a bottle-green cashmere polo neck that brought out her eyes, rested a hand on Iris's shoulder.

'It's not too late to change your mind, you know. Come with me to Tahiti!'

'I can't,' said Iris. 'I appreciate the offer, but I really, truly can't.'

A few days after a very difficult Christmas, Kathy had suddenly decided that she would be going on what would have been her and Jock's honeymoon by herself, and had invited Iris to join her. 'I need a break – we both do. And the hotel is supposed to be totally amazing. It has these cool little huts with floors made of glass, and you can see all the fish and coral and everything.'

It pleased Iris to see Kathy coming back to life, even if she was surprised it had happened so soon after Jock's confession and arrest. But perhaps she shouldn't be surprised. Her latest sitter was nothing if not a survivor. And where better than an idyllic island to begin the next chapter of the wild ride that was Kathy Miller's life?

'You will let me know, won't you, when they set a date for Rory's trial?'

'Of course,' said Iris. 'Stuart Haley's promised to keep me up to date with any news.'

It was ironic to think that, after everything that had happened, Rory would be the only member of the MacKinnon family actually to go on trial. Inexplicably, he had continued to plead innocent of both the poisoning of Milo and Sam Sam and the campaign of poison-pen letters to Kathy, which Haley had finally charged him with on New Year's Day. There would be no trial for the Contorini murders, as Jock had pleaded guilty to killing Paola, and Edwin had been deemed mentally unfit to face court proceedings for what likely would have been a manslaughter charge for Beatrice's death. Angus had also admitted his own part in helping dispose of the bodies. Jock was right; he had never forgiven himself, and almost seemed disappointed when the lawyers told him he would spend no more than a year in prison. But Hannah had stuck by him, and he appeared to be slowly coming to terms with the new realities, not only that Jock was his real father but that Beatrice may have been his biological sister.

'Do you think Rory will change his plea?' Kathy asked.

'I don't know,' said Iris. 'I doubt it. I think he's too entitled to admit his own guilt, even when the evidence is overwhelming.'

After a lengthy second interview with Eileen Gregory, Haley surmised that she had not written the notes, but that someone had been swiping the envelopes from her office at the castle. Now that they had Rory's fingerprints on file, from his dog-poisoning arrest, they were able to prove conclusively that that someone had been him. Iris had filled in the last piece of the puzzle, remembering the old-fashioned typewriter in Fiona MacKinnon's Edinburgh flat. It seemed that Rory had typed the letters during visits to his mother, who may or may not have known about them, and then had found opportunities to leave them, once or twice persuading one of the maids to leave them for him, where Kathy would find them during his many visits to the castle.

'I always meant to ask you' – Iris thought suddenly – 'at the Halloween party, I saw Rory pull you aside – it looked very heated. What were the two of you talking about?'

Kathy bit her lower lip awkwardly. 'I suppose I may as well tell you. At the time I didn't want Jock to know. But Rory had tried it on with me, several times, in fact, when I first moved into the castle.'

'No!' Iris was genuinely shocked.

Kathy nodded. 'He acted like he hated me for pushing out his mom. And I think he did, to some degree. But he also felt humiliated that I wasn't interested in him sexually. That I chose his father over him.'

'Wow. I can imagine,' Iris murmured.

'I never thought he'd go as far as he did, though,' said Kathy, swallowing hard. 'When I think about poor Milo and Sam Sam. I just hope they lock him up and throw away the key.'

It was striking, Iris thought, how much more emotional she felt about her dogs' deaths than she did about her fiancé turning out to have been a murderer who would spend the remaining years of his life in prison. Indeed, Kathy's relationship with Jock continued to be an enigma to Iris. Many times, over Christmas at Murray House, Kathy had expressed ongoing love and sympathy for him. 'We weren't meant to be,' she told Iris, almost whimsically. 'But I know how much he loved me. I'll always hold him in my heart.'

What a strange thing love is, Iris thought. Kathy's for Jock. Jock's for Edwin. Beatrice's for Angus. Paola's for Beatrice. What strange and terrible things it drives us to.

'You know what really gets me,' said Kathy, warming her anger towards Rory like a flame between cupped hands. 'Now that Jock's in prison, the castle and estate will automatically pass to Rory. I mean, how unfair is that?'

'Very,' Iris agreed. 'Does poor Emma not get anything, then?'

'Oh, I wouldn't worry about Emma,' Kathy scoffed. 'She may be many things, but she's certainly not poor. Fergus's dad's sitting on an estate the size of Balmoral, and there's a private income to go with it. Emma's attachment to Pitfeldy is purely sentimental, believe me. No, that's not what bugs me. It's the thought of Rory living there, lording it over everyone. I actually heard a rumour that he's moving his mother back in. Can you believe that?'

'Well, it was Fiona's home for thirty years,' Iris reminded Kathy gently.

'I guess so,' said Kathy. Shrugging, she turned her attention back to her phone, her bad mood dissipating easily and instantly, like dandelion seeds in the wind. 'How long till we're in London, exactly?'

About three hours later with a slow creaking of brakes, the train finally pulled into the platform at King's Cross.

'I guess this is goodbye?' Kathy pouted, once they'd pulled their respective suitcases through the barrier. 'Are you *sure* you won't change your mind? Bora Bora's a whole lot warmer than London in January, you know.'

'I know,' said Iris, hugging her. 'And I hope you have a wonderful time and meet some gorgeous, bare-chested, shark-spearing local and live happily ever after on the white sand. But I have a dreary flat in Clapham calling my name.'

'Thank you, Iris,' Kathy said sincerely.

'For what?'

'For everything. Nailing Rory. Taking me in when it all fell apart. My portrait, which I totally *love*. You sent it on to the States, right?'

Iris nodded. 'To the address in California you gave me. It's on a ship as we speak.'

'Great,' said Kathy. 'Once I get my new place I'll send you a picture. It'll be the first thing to go on my wall.'

Iris waved her off towards the street, where a chauffeured car was waiting to take her to Heathrow. Only once Kathy Miller's blonde head had disappeared completely from view did she head for the taxi rank and home.

It would be strange, returning to her flat after so many months away. Strange, but good. Iris had no hankering to return to Scotland any time soon. Not that she regretted her time at the castle, or any of the strange things that had happened there. In fact, in a funny way, she almost felt as if she'd been *meant* to go to Pitfeldy. As if fate, or something, had predestined her to accept the commission from Jock MacKinnon, and to find those girls, buried in their lonely unmarked graves. Maybe the online trolls were right, and Iris really was a 'weirdo' who 'attracted death'. *I can live with that*, she thought, climbing into the back of a black cab. Artists were supposed to be weirdos, after all, and Iris was finally coming truly to believe in herself as an artist, not just a random woman who dabbled about with paint. If she did say so herself, her portrait of Kathy Miller was really bloody good, in the end.

Perhaps, when all was said and done, that was enough.

Epilogue

Ten months later . . .

Iris closed her eyes and lost herself in the sounds and smells of the church. Father Antonio's voice, as mellow as the stone walls of San Cassiano, echoed off the frescoed magnificence, a soothing burble of Italian that prompted louder, familiar responses from the congregation. Scents of incense and candle wax, of ancient stone and newly polished wood, and of the lilies, massed in vast bunches on either side of the altar, assailed Iris's nostrils. To open one's eyes, and be faced with the unspeakable, timeless beauty of Tintoretto's brush strokes would surely be to risk sensory overload. Only in Venice, Iris reflected, could so much wonder and magnificence be experienced in a single building, and all of it for the glory of a God who, in other, more mundane settings, one might easily choose not to believe in. Venice made believers out of everyone, if only temporarily. It felt fitting that, at long last, the ancient city was welcoming home its two lost daughters.

The memorial service for Paola and Beatrice Contorini had taken many months to organise, a combination of Italian red tape and archaic British regulations about the repatriation of remains after criminal cases. Finally, however, common sense and Father Antonio's persistence had prevailed, and on this chilly November morning, Beatrice's and Paola's bones were being interred at San Cassiano, the church where, for a fleeting few years, both women had felt safe and loved.

'Tremendous turnout,' Stuart Haley, looking even smaller and paler than Iris remembered him in a cheap grey suit and tie, whispered in her ear. Perhaps it was being surrounded by so many tall, olive-skinned Italian men that accentuated his anaemic complexion, but Iris couldn't have been more delighted to see her old friend again. Not only was he intelligent and engaging company, but he was one of the kindest and most generous men she had ever met. Haley had spent his own money flying out to Venice to attend today's memorial, an expense Iris knew he could ill afford. But the Girls in the Wood had always been more than just a case to him. He wanted to pay his respects, and to say goodbye.

'I know,' Iris whispered back, surveying the packed church. 'I'm really pleased.'

At the end of the service the congregation began filing out, friends and neighbours chatting to one another and, Iris assumed, sharing memories of Beatrice and Paola. Other than Father Antonio, there were few faces she recognised. To her astonishment, Massimo Giannotti had turned up, stiffly elegant in an immaculately tailored dark wool suit. Iris had meant to speak to him after the service, although she wasn't sure exactly what she wanted to say. He hadn't raped Paola after all, but Iris couldn't shake the feeling that he had still played some role in the hardships of that poor woman's troubled life. On the other hand, it spoke to some sense of responsibility, and perhaps even remorse, that he'd chosen to attend today's memorial. But by the time Iris reached the peeling green front doors of the church, Massimo had gone, whisked away by private water-taxi. Perhaps it was for the best.

Outside the sky was grey and heavy with threatened rain. A blustery, boisterous wind brought an added bite of chill to the air, and played havoc with the coiffed hair and lace mantilla veils of the women. Iris's own long woollen skirt and fringed sweater shook and shivered, giving her the look of a particularly cold bird as the priest approached her, his cassock billowing in the wind like the sail of a pirate's ship.

'Thank you for coming.' Taking both her hands in his, Father Antonio looked deep into Iris's eyes, and she was struck again by how young he looked for his age, and how unusually attractive for a priest. 'I think it would have meant a lot to Bea.'

'It means a lot to me,' Iris said truthfully. 'The service was beautiful.'

'The man talking to you earlier,' Father Antonio asked. 'The small man. Was he the British policeman in charge of the case?'

Iris confirmed it, looking around for Stuart, who seemed to have beaten a hasty retreat to his hotel already. He never was much of a mingler. 'His name's Stuart Haley. I'm not sure where he's got to, but I know he'd love to meet you, if you have time. He's a very good man.'

'I'm sure he is.' Father Antonio lowered his voice to a conspiratorial whisper. 'Although I think at one time he may have suspected me of being involved in some way. No?'

'It's his job to suspect people,' Iris said simply. 'The same way it's your job to forgive them.'

'That's one way of putting it, I suppose,' the priest laughed, kissing Iris on the cheek goodbye before a stream of chatty parishioners pulled him away.

She was about to leave herself, to head back to the hotel for a warmer coat and some gloves before braving the boat out to Torcello to see the Byzantine mosaics at Santa Maria Dell'Assunta, but decided to find somewhere for lunch. She stumbled upon a blink-and-you'll-miss-it pasta place tucked behind the Grand Canal, not far from Palazzo Grassi, where she enjoyed a delicious meal washed down with some Chianti – rather more than she had intended.

Later, back at her hotel, Iris flopped down onto her to-die-for Frette bed sheets and gazed mindlessly out of the window across the rooftops of Venice. *A right turn here, a wrong one there.* Poor Beatrice Contorini and her mother had been dealt poor cards to begin with. But they'd each tried their best to play their hands to their advantage, to take risks and reach out for something better. For happiness. Neither had achieved it in this world. Closing her eyes, Iris found herself praying that they would find it in the next.

By the time her ringing phone jolted Iris awake, it was dark outside and dark in the room. Fumbling blindly on her bedside table like a hungover mole, she picked up.

'Hello?' she croaked.

'Iris? Good God, you sound like you've been gargling with gravel. Are you all right?' Greta Brun's voice sparkled blithely down the line like cut crystal. 'I didn't wake you, surely? It's only seven o'clock.'

'I'm fine,' rasped Iris. 'Long afternoon, late lunch.'

'Ah,' chirped Greta, 'I see. And there I was thinking you were being terribly worthy going to funerals. Anyway, never mind,' she went on, not waiting for Iris to respond. 'I'm calling because I've got a potential new commission for you. Very prestigious, painting the new Master of St Michael's College in Cambridge. That's *St Michael's*, as in the richest college in the university, and supposedly they have a budget of up to seven figures for this portrait. It's between you, some French artist I've never even heard of, and bloody Martin Sneed.'

'Sir Martin,' Iris corrected. England's most famous, and famously pompous, living portrait artist had been knighted last year, the result of a decades-long campaign of brown-nosing and donations to the Tory party. Greta and Sneed had fallen out years ago over something or other and positively loathed one another. Iris's own feelings were less charged. As far as she was concerned, Martin was a bit of a dick, and certainly self-important. But there could be no denying his talent. For a traditional, high-profile commission like this one, he seemed the obvious candidate. Iris made the mistake of saying as much to Greta.

'Nonsense!' the agent trilled. 'The fact that they're considering three of you proves there must be someone on the college art committee who doesn't want to go with a crusty old fart. You've as good a chance as anyone, Iris, and you need to be in Cambridge on Monday to interview. You did *hear* the part about it being a million quid?'

Iris hung up feeling shell-shocked, then happy. The job wasn't hers. But Greta was right. The chance of it was exciting. To be considered was exciting. Once again, it felt as if a new door was opening, and a new chapter about to begin. She'd been too long with the dead recently, too preoccupied with the lives and loves of others. It was time to focus on herself again.

St Michael's College Cambridge.

Why not?

Acknowledgements

Thank you once again to the amazing team at Trapeze and Orion for all their help and hard work. You are all brilliant, but special thanks to Sam Eades, Rosie Pearce, Marian Reid and Jo Whitford. Finishing and publishing a book during COVID, with all our respective kids at home hogging the WiFi (or being born, as the case may be) has been quite an adventure. But I can't think of better people I would rather have with me for the ride.

Thanks also to my agent, Hellie Ogden, and to everyone at Janklow & Nesbit, as well as to my family, especially my husband Robin and our children, Sefi, Zac, Theo and Summer.

Murder at the Castle is dedicated to my lifelong friend Sarah Glynn, whose courage, positivity and unchanging sense of humour through the last three painful years have blown both me, and everybody else who knows her, away. Sarah, and Kris, thank you for loving my Sefi, for being there for her through thick and thin and welcoming her into your wonderful family. I could not have chosen a better godmother, or friend. You are a complete legend, and I hope you like the book.

Credits

Trapeze would like to thank everyone at Orion who worked on the publication of *Murder at the Castle*.

Agent
Hellie Ogden

Editor
Sam Eades

Copy-editor
Marian Reid

Proofreader
Jenny Page

Editorial Management
Rosie Pearce
Charlie Panayiotou
Jane Hughes
Claire Boyle

Audio
Paul Stark
Amber Bates

Contracts
Anne Goddard
Paul Bulos
Jake Alderson

Design
Lucie Stericker
Joanna Ridley
Debbie Holmes
Nick May
Clare Sivell
Helen Ewing

Finance
Jennifer Muchan
Jasdip Nandra
Rabale Mustafa
Elizabeth Beaumont
Sue Baker
Tom Costello

Marketing
Brittany Sankey

Production
Claire Keep
Fiona McIntosh

Publicity
Alainna Hadjigeorgiou

Sales
Jen Wilson
Victoria Laws
Esther Waters
Lucy Brem
Frances Doyle
Ben Goddard
Georgina Cutler
Jack Hallam
Ellie Kyrke-Smith
Inês Figuiera
Barbara Ronan
Andrew Hally
Dominic Smith
Deborah Deyong
Lauren Buck
Maggy Park
Linda McGregor
Sinead White
Jemimah James
Rachel Jones
Jack Dennison
Nigel Andrews
Ian Williamson
Julia Benson
Declan Kyle
Robert Mackenzie
Imogen Clarke
Megan Smith
Charlotte Clay
Rebecca Cobbold

Operations
Jo Jacobs
Sharon Willis
Lisa Pryde

Rights
Susan Howe
Richard King
Krystyna Kujawinska
Jessica Purdue
Louise Henderson

Help us make the next generation of readers

We – both author and publisher – hope you enjoyed this book. We believe that you can become a reader at any time in your life, but we'd love your help to give the next generation a head start.

Did you know that 9 per cent of children don't have a book of their own in their home, rising to 13 per cent in disadvantaged families*? We'd like to try to change that by asking you to consider the role you could play in helping to build readers of the future.

We'd love you to think of sharing, borrowing, reading, buying or talking about a book with a child in your life and spreading the love of reading. We want to make sure the next generation continue to have access to books, wherever they come from.

And if you would like to consider donating to charities that help fund literacy projects, find out more at **www.literacytrust.org.uk** and **www.booktrust.org.uk**.

THANK YOU

*As reported by the National Literacy Trust